PRAISE FOR ROBERT GODDARD

"A superb storyteller."
—*Sunday Independent*

AND HIS SPELLBINDING NOVELS

"A masterly piece of storytelling . . . combines the expert suspense
manipulation of a Daphne du Maurier romance with those of a
John le Carré thriller."
—Michiko Kakutani, *New York Times*

"Cliff-hanging entertainment."
—*Guardian*

"Reminiscent of Dickens in its scope, huge cast of characters and
evocative descriptions, and of Conan Doyle in its richly layered
plot . . . Goddard's elegant prose and intelligence propel this
novel beyond mere entertainment and place him in the
company of such masters of historical suspense as
John Fowles and Daphne du Maurier."
—*San Francisco Chronicle*

"An engaging mystery novel with a literary angle that will make
comparisons to A. S. Byatt and P. D. James inevitable. The twistings
and turnings of the plot are cleverly executed and entirely satisfying,
right up to the last line."
—*Washington Post Book World*

"Takes the reader on a journey from which he knows he will not
deviate until the final destination is reached."
—*Evening Standard*

"In the best tradition of British storytelling, here murder, deceit, family honor, and intrigue are intricately woven into a compelling drama."
—*Library Journal*

"When it comes to duplicity and intrigue, Goddard is second to none. He is a master of manipulation . . . a hypnotic, unputdownable thriller."
—*Daily Mail*

"The suspense mounts to a fine crescendo. A superior example of Goddard's velvet-cloaked menace."
—*Kirkus Reviews*

"Impossible to put down . . . totally compels you from the first page to the last. . . . Goddard is a wonderful storyteller."
—*Yorkshire Post*

"Cracking good literate entertainment . . . had me utterly spellbound."
—*Washington Post Book World*

"Superbly plotted . . . The novel's movement through time, using additional narrators, adds layers of depth to its mysteries, which fit together as intricately as the pieces of a Chinese puzzle. . . . The author's manipulation of suspense and surprise rarely fails to dazzle."
—*New York Times Book Review*

"Combines the steely edge of a thriller with the suspense of a whodunit, all interlaced with subtle romantic overtones."
—*Time Out*

SIGHT

UNSEEN

ROBERT GODDARD

DELTA TRADE PAPERBACKS

SIGHT UNSEEN
A Delta Book

PUBLISHING HISTORY
Bantam UK hardcover edition published June 2005
Delta Trade Paperback edition / January 2007

Published by Bantam Dell
A Division of Random House, Inc.
New York, New York

Book design by Carol Malcolm Russo

Library of Congress Cataloging-in-Publication data

Goddard, Robert.
Sight unseen / Robert Goddard.
p. cm.
ISBN: 978-0-440-24280-2 (trade pbk.)
1. Kidnapping—Fiction. 2. Murder—Fiction. 3. Criminal investigation—Fiction.
4. Avebury (England) I. Title.
PR6057.O33S57 2007
823'.914—dc22
2006021891

www.bantamdell.com

BVG   10 9 8 7 6 5 4 3 2 1

For the real
Claire Wheatley

PROLOGUE

It begins at Avebury, in the late July of a cool, wet summer turned suddenly warm and dry. The Marlborough Downs shimmer in a haze of unfamiliar heat. Skylarks sing in the breezeless air above the sheep-cropped turf. The sun burns high and brazen. And the stones stand, lichened and eroded, sentinels over nearly five thousand years of history.

It begins, then, in a place whose origins and purposes are obscured by antiquity. Why Neolithic henge-builders should have devoted so much time and effort to constructing a great ramparted stone circle at Avebury, as well as a huge artificial hill less than a mile away, at Silbury, is as unknown as it is unknowable.

It begins, therefore, in a landscape where the unexplained and the inexplicable lie still and close, where man-made markers of a remote past mock the set and ordered world that is merely the flickering, fast-fleeing present.

Saxon settlers gave Avebury its modern name a millennium and a half ago. They founded a village within its protective ditch and bank. Over the centuries, as the village grew, many of the stones were moved or buried. Later, they were used as building material, the ditch as a rubbish-dump. The henge withered.

Then, in the 1930s, came Alexander Keiller, the marmalade millionaire and amateur archaeologist He bought up and demolished half the village, raised the stones, cleared the ditch, restored the circle. The clock was turned back. The National Trust moved in. The henge flourished anew—a monument *and* a mystery.

Nearly forty years have passed since the Trust's purchase of Keiller's land holdings at Avebury. The renovated circle basks unmolested in the heat of a summer's day. A kestrel, soaring high above on a thermal, has a perfect view of the banked circumference of the henge, quartered by builders of later generations. The High Street of the surviving village runs west–east along one diameter, crossing the north–south route of the Swindon to Devizes road close to the centre of the circle. East of this junction, the buildings peter out as the effects of Keiller's demolition work become more apparent. Green Street, the lane is aptly called, dwindling as it leaves the circle and winds on towards the downs.

As it passes through the village, the main road performs a zigzag, the north-western angle of which is occupied by the thatched and limewashed Red Lion Inn. East of the inn, on the other side of the road, are the fenced-off remains of an inner circle known as the Cove—two stones, one tall and slender, the other squat and rounded, referred to locally as Adam and Eve. There is a gate in the fence, opposite the pub car park, and another gate in Green Street, on the other side of Silbury House, a four-square corner property that formerly served as the residence of Avebury's Nonconformist minister.

It is a little after noon on this last Monday of July, 1981. Custom is sparse at the Red Lion and visitors to the henge are few. When the traffic noise ebbs, as it periodically does, somnolence prevails. There is a stillness in the air and in the scene. But it is not the stillness of expectancy. There is no hint, no harbinger, of what is about to occur.

At one of the outdoor tables in front of the Red Lion, a solitary drinker sits cradling a beer glass. He is a slim, dark-haired man in his mid-twenties, dressed in blue jeans and a pale, open-necked shirt rolled up at the elbows. Beside him, on the table, lie a spiral-bound notebook and a ballpoint pen. He is gazing vacantly ahead of him, across the road, towards the remaining stones of the southern inner circle. They do not command his attention, however, as a glance at his wristwatch reveals. He is waiting for something, or someone. He takes a slurp of beer and sets the glass down on the table. It is nearly empty. Sunlight glistens on the swirling residue.

A child's voice catches his ear, drifting across from the Cove. There is, at this moment, no traffic to mask the sound. The man turns and looks. He sees a woman and three children approaching the Cove from the direction of the perimeter bank. Two of the children are running ahead, racing, perhaps, to be first to the stones: a boy and a girl. The boy is nine or ten, dressed in baseball boots, blue jeans and a red T-shirt. The girl is a couple of years younger. She is wearing sandals, white socks and a blue and white polka-dot dress. Both have fair hair that appears blond in the sunshine, cut short on the boy but worn long, in a ponytail, by the girl. The woman is lagging well behind, her pace set by the youngest child, toddling at her side. This child, a girl, is wearing grey dungarees over a striped T-shirt. There can hardly be any doubt, given the colour of her hair, tied in bunches with pink ribbon, that she is the sister of the other two children.

It is much less likely that the woman escorting her is their mother. She appears too young for the role, slim, fine-featured and dark-haired, surely not beyond her early twenties. She is dressed in cream linen trousers and a pink blouse and is carrying a straw hat. Her attention is fixed largely on the little girl beside her. The other two children are dashing ahead.

As they approach the stones, a figure steps out from the gap between Adam and Eve, hidden till then from view. He is a short, tubby man in hiking boots, brown shorts, check shirt and some kind of multi-pocketed fisherman's waistcoat. He is round-faced, balding and bespectacled, aged anything between thirty-five and fifty. The two children stop and stare at him. He says something. The boy replies and moves forward.

The man outside the Red Lion watches for lack of anything more interesting to watch. He sees nothing sinister or threatening. What he does see is a flash of sunlight on glass as the man by the stones takes something out of one of his numerous pockets. The boy steps closer.

The woman is hurrying to join them now, not running, nor even necessarily alarmed, but cautious perhaps, her attention suddenly diverted from the slow-moving infant who follows at her own dawdling pace, before abruptly sitting down on the grass to inspect a patch of buttercups.

The man outside the Red Lion sees all of this and makes

nothing of it. Even when another figure enters his field of vision from behind Silbury House, he does not react. The figure is male, short-haired and stockily built. He is wearing Army surplus clothes and is moving fast, at a loping run, across the stretch of grass beyond the stones. The woman, who cannot see him moving behind her, is smiling now and talking to the man in the fisherman's waistcoat.

And then it happens. The running man stops and bends over, grasps the seated child beneath her arms, lifts her up as if she weighs little more than the buttercup in her left hand and races back with her the way he came.

The man in the fisherman's waistcoat is first to respond. He says something to the woman, raising his voice and pointing. She turns and looks. She puts her hand to her mouth. She drops her hat and begins running after the man who has grabbed the child. Screened as he is by Silbury House, he can no longer be seen by the man outside the Red Lion. The roaring passage of a southbound lorry further confuses the senses. Everything is happening very quickly and very slowly. The beer-drinker does no more than rise from his seat and gape as the next minute's events spray their poison over all who witness them.

A white Transit van bursts into view round the corner from Green Street, its engine racing, its rear door slamming shut. The child and her abductor are inside. That is understood by all, or intuited, for only the woman has seen them scramble aboard. A second man is driving the van. That is also understood, though no-one catches so much as a glimpse of him amidst what follows.

The man in the fisherman's waistcoat has taken a few ineffectual strides after the woman, but has now turned back. The boy is standing stock-still between Adam and Eve, paralysed by an inability to decide what to do or who to follow.

No such indecision grips his sister, though. She is running, ponytail flying, towards the gate onto the main road. What is in her mind is uncertain. From where she was standing, she will have seen the van pull away. She knows her sister is being stolen from her. She is not equipped to prevent the theft, yet she seems determined to try. She flicks up the latch on the gate and darts through.

The van turns right onto the main road. A northbound car, slowing for the bend, brakes sharply to avoid a collision and blares its horn. The driver of the van pays this no heed as he accelerates through a skid, narrowly avoiding the boundary wall of the pub car park.

The girl does not pause at the edge of the road. She runs forward, into the path of the van. She turns towards it and raises her hands, as if commanding it to stop. There is probably just enough time for the driver to respond. But he does not. The van surges on. The girl holds her ground. In a breathless fraction of a second, the gap between them closes.

There is a loud thump as hard steel hits soft flesh. There is a blurred parabola through the air of the girl's frail, flying body. There is the speeding white flank of the van and the slower-moving dark green roofline of the following car. Neither vehicle stops. The car driver proceeds as if he has seen nothing. And maybe he has somehow failed to register what has occurred. He does not have to swerve to avoid the crumpled shape at the side of the road. He simply carries on.

The van and the car vanish round the next bend in the road. All movement ceases. All sound dies.

It is only for a second. Soon everyone will be running. The boy will be crying. The woman will be screaming. The man who was drinking outside the Red Lion will be hopping over the wall of the car park, his eyes fixed on the place at the foot of the opposite verge where the girl lies, her blue and white dress stained bright red, the tarmac beneath her darkening as a pool of blood spreads across the road. And her eyes will seem to meet his. And to hold them in her sightless gaze.

But that is not yet. That is not this second. That is the future, a future forged in the stillness and the silence of this frozen moment.

It begins at Avebury. But it does not end there.

CHAPTER

ONE

It had been a fickle winter in Prague. Yet another mild spell had been cut short by a plunge back into snow and ice. When David Umber had agreed to stand in as a Jolly Brolly tour guide for the following Friday, he had not reckoned on wind chill of well below zero, slippery pavements and slush-filled gutters. But those were the conditions. And Jolly Brolly never cancelled.

Umber's exit from the apartment block on Sokolovská that morning was accordingly far from eager. A lean, melancholy man in his late forties, his dark hair shot with grey, his eyes downcast, his brow furrowed with unconsoling thoughts, he turned up the collar of his coat and headed for the tram stop, glancing along the street to see if he needed to hurry.

He did not. There was no tram in sight, giving him a chance to examine the letter he had found in his mailbox on the way out. Deducing from the typeface visible through the envelope window that it was in fact a bank statement, he thrust it back into his pocket unopened and pressed on to the tram stop.

God, it was cold. Not for the first time when such weather prevailed, he silently asked himself, "What am I doing here?"

The answer, he knew, was best not dwelt upon. He had stayed on after the end of his teaching contract last summer because of Milena. But Milena had gone. And so had the temporary post he had found for the autumn term. He had a small circle of friends and acquaintances in Prague, happily including Ivana, Jolly Brolly coordinator and *entrepreneuse manquée*. But he also had plenty of evidence to strengthen his sense of drift and purposelessness.

He stood at the stop, shifting from foot to foot in an effort to keep warm, or at least to avoid getting any colder. The heating in his apartment block was in dire need of an overhaul. That could in fact be said of pretty much everything in the block. He had moved there as a stopgap measure when his much more salubrious and ironically cheaper flat near Grand Priory Square had vanished under the waters of the Vltava during the cataclysmic flood of August 2002. He had been in England at the time, but virtually all his possessions had been in the flat. The flood had claimed those tangible reminders of his past, leaving a void in his sense of himself that the sixteen months since had failed to fill.

The red and white nose of a tram appeared through the murk. Those waiting at the stop shuffled forward, some of them taking last drags on their cigarettes before flicking the butts into the slush. Umber squinted towards the tram, struggling to read its route number. It was a 24. Well, that was something. If it had been an 8, he would have had to stand there for another bone-chilling few minutes.

The number 24 pulled up and the passengers piled aboard, Umber hopping onto the second car, where there were more vacant seats. He slumped down in one and closed his eyes for a restful few moments as the tram started away. As a result, he did not notice the short, barrel-chested man muffled up in parka, gloves, scarf and woolly hat who jumped on just as the doors were closing. He had no cause to be on his guard, after all. A Prague tram at the back end of winter was hardly where he would have expected the past to creep up on him. He was not thinking about any of that.

But then he did not need to. David Umber's past was of an order that did not allow for genuine forgetting. It was not necessary to apply his mind to it consciously. It was simply there, always, pulling him back, dragging him down. It would never leave him. All he could do was refine his tactics of evasion. And this, he knew but did not care to admit, was why he had stayed on in Prague. It was a refuge, a hiding-place. It was far from anywhere tainted by all that he did not wish to recall. But it was not, he was to discover before the day was out, far enough.

———

The tram trundled on through the streets, picking up more passengers than it shed, so that by the time it reached Wenceslas Square it was crammed. Umber got off with a mob of others and headed for the Wenceslas Monument in front of the National Museum. That was the appointed meeting-place for those hapless tourists who had decided to spend a thousand koruna on a six-hour walking tour of the city's principal attractions, with lunch thrown in, in the care of an old Prague hand replete with local lore. (Jolly Brolly never knowingly undersold itself.)

About a dozen tourists were waiting by the statue of Bohemia's patron saint. The cold weather had taken its toll on numbers, for which Umber was grateful. He would not have to shout to make himself heard by such a small group. They were the usual mix of ages and nationalities, clutching their polyglot of guidebooks. Ivana was in the process of unburdening them of their cash. She acknowledged Umber's arrival with a relieved smile.

"You're late," she whispered as she handed him his staff of office—a rainbow-patterned umbrella.

"*Je mi líto,*" he replied, apologizing being one of the few aspects of Czech he had mastered. "I overslept."

Ivana's smile stiffened only slightly as she set about introducing him to his charges. A doctor of history, she called him, in order to forestall any complaints about his clearly not having been born and bred in Prague. It was not a technically valid description. Umber had never finished his doctorate. But, in another sense, which afforded him some wry amusement, it *was* true. There would be a little doctoring of history before the tour was over. He could guarantee that.

There was one latecomer who settled up with Ivana after she had said her preliminary piece. Having failed to register the man's presence on the tram, Umber naturally made nothing of his last-minute arrival. Ivana wished them a good day and bustled off to the bank with the takings. She would soon be back in the warmth and relative comfort of the Jolly Brolly office. A phone call to Janoušek, proprietor of U Modré Merunky, where they were scheduled to stop for a "typical delicious Czech lunch," and her duties would be concluded.

Lucky her, thought Umber, as he took a deep breath of cold Czech air and launched his commentary with some loosely framed thoughts on the Prague Spring of 1968 and the Velvet Revolution of 1989. It was a well-worn theme. He *was* a historian, after all, albeit not as well qualified as Ivana had implied. He was on autopilot before they had even reached the Monument to the Victims of Communism.

And on autopilot he remained as the tour proceeded. They reached Old Town Square in good time to see the Astronomical Clock's march-past of apostles when it struck the hour, crossed Charles Bridge, popped into and out of the Church of St. Nicholas, then took the funicular railway (fare included in the price) up to Petrín Park. The snow was ankle-deep in the park, which slowed their progress, those inadequately clad and shod only now realizing what they had signed up for. Umber had allowed for this, however. Some deft abridgements during their visits to the Strahov Monastery and the Loreto had them at U Modré Merunky, halfway back down the hill to Prague Castle, more or less when Janoušek was expecting them.

The exact nature of the deal between Ivana and this less than glorious example of Czech innkeeping had never been disclosed to Umber. It was certainly not predicated on the quality of the food. The roast pork was gristly, the red cabbage vinegary and the dumplings unyielding. But no-one complained. Those at Umber's table even praised the food. Perhaps they did not wish to hurt their host's feelings. Umber could have told them, but did not, that Janoušek did not actually have any feelings on the subject that *could* be hurt.

The latecomer to the tour, Umber's fellow-passenger from the number 24 tram, sat at a different table and said little to his companions. Removal of his woolly-hat revealed a bald head with a dusting of shaven white hair above his deeply lined brow, piercing blue eyes and hollow cheeks. He was a short, broad, bony man of sixty or seventy, whom nobody seemed eager to engage in small talk and who looked as if that suited him fine: he was nobody's fool, his bearing proclaimed, and nobody's favourite uncle either. His gaze appeared to be fixed throughout the meal on the back of David Umber's head. But of that David Umber was unaware.

———

Lunch over, but already repeating on some of them, the group slithered down to the Castle in time for the two o'clock Changing of the Guard. This was followed by a circuit of St. Vitus's Cathedral before they made their way to the Royal Palace for Umber's account of the famous Defenestration of 1618 that sparked off the Thirty Years' War. He was mildly worried at this stage by the chance that someone might ask him to explain the whys and wherefores of that long-ago conflict. But the moment passed with questionless ease. They made a gingerly descent of Old Castle Steps, crossed back over the river and entered the Jewish Quarter.

Three synagogues and one cemetery later, they returned to Old Town Square, where the tour ended at the birthplace of Franz Kafka. Umber cracked his customary joke about hoping nobody had found the day too much of a trial. There were more smiles than laughs and a few expressions of thanks, extending in one case to a (very) modest tip. Then the group dispersed.

It was late afternoon now and growing colder. Umber hurried round to the Jolly Brolly nerve centre, two second-floor rooms about halfway between Old Town Square and the Prague branch of Tesco, where he planned to buy his dinner.

There was no sign of Ivana in the office. She had left it in the languid care of Marek, her youthful and, in Umber's view, useless assistant. Marek was sitting with his feet on the desk, smoking a Camel cigarette and texting a friend when Umber walked in. Marek nodded a greeting and slid a small, square manilla envelope across the desk. Umber pocketed the envelope, returned his umbrella to the stack in the corner and made to leave.

At which point he noticed that morning's edition of *Annonce*—the classifieds paper with the most comprehensive accommodation listings in Prague—lying discarded in the waste bin. He fished it out and glanced enquiringly at Marek.

"*Prosím,*" said Marek, with a sarcastic smirk.

Umber exited, checking the contents of the envelope as he descended the rickety stairs. All the money was there. But all, in this case, was not a lot.

Back on the street, solvent if scarcely flush, Umber decided that Tesco could wait. Jolly Brolly HQ's proximity to U Zlatého Tygra, the Old Town's most famous drinking establishment, verged on the unreasonable. At this hour he could be sure of a seat, which, after foot-slogging round the city all day, he needed almost as much as a beer.

U Zlatého Tygra—the Golden Tiger—was its normal soothing, smoky self. Umber settled himself at the table screened by the pub's trophy cabinet, next to the window on which the eponymous tiger frolicked in stained-glass abandon. Half a litre of cellar-cooled Pilsner was swiftly delivered to him and his tab initiated with a slash of the server's pen. Umber took a deep gulp of beer, then unfolded *Annonce* and commenced a less than hopeful search for attractive and affordable alternatives to his present abode.

But his search never even reached the APARTMENTS TO RENT page. A bulky figure rounded the trophy cabinet at that moment and assumed a looming stance above him. Umber looked up and, to his surprise, recognized the newcomer, or at any rate recognized his outfit of maroon parka and matching woolly-hat. He was one of the tour party.

"Hello," said Umber. "What brings you here?"

"You do." The man pulled off his hat and unwound his scarf, fixing Umber with a steely blue gaze.

It might have been the quality of the gaze that clinched it. Or it might have been the flat, faintly menacing tone of voice. Either way, recognition—*true* recognition—dawned now on Umber.

"I don't believe it," he murmured. Which was true. He did not believe it.

"You'll have to," the other man said. Which was also true. It was not a matter of choice. It never had been.

It had begun at Avebury. But it had not ended there.

C H A P T E R

TWO

"Chief Inspector Sharp." Even as he spoke the words, Umber realized that the man he knew as Detective Chief Inspector George Sharp of the Wiltshire Constabulary could by no stretch of the imagination still be a serving police officer, even though his appearance had not been much altered by the passage of years. He must have retired long since. "Here on holiday?"

"Let's get one thing straight from the off." Sharp discarded his parka and sat down. "This isn't a chance meeting. I didn't sign up for that tour today and suddenly think, swipe me, isn't our guide that David Umber I remember from the Avebury case?"

"No?"

"I followed you from your flat this morning. I just didn't know I was going to have to wait this long for a word in private."

"You call this private?"

Sharp glanced around. "It'll do." Then his gaze returned to Umber. "And you can drop the "Chief Inspector." I was put out to grass years ago."

"I suppose you must have been."

At that moment Sharp's beer arrived. He eyed it suspiciously. "Don't they ask what you want here?"

"It's taken for granted. Beer or nothing."

Sharp took a gulp and grimaced. "Not a patch on Bass."

"What do you want . . . Mr. Sharp?" Umber tried to drain the snappishness out of his voice as he finished the question.

"What do you think I want?"

"After more than twenty years? Search me."

"It's not that hard to work out."

They looked at each other for several seconds in uncongenial silence. Then Umber said, "I thought your people reckoned they had the truth when they put Brian Radd away."

"My people? I'll give you that. But *not* me. I never swallowed Radd's story. Not for a second."

"Didn't you?"

"Did you?"

More silence, blanking out for the pair the burble and bustle of the pub. Then Umber shook his head. "Of course not."

"There you are, then."

"You still haven't told me why you're here. Or why you've been tailing me. There was no need for the gumshoe routine, anyway. You could just have called round. Or phoned me without leaving England."

"I like to know what I'm dealing with."

"And what are you dealing with?"

"Unfinished business."

"For Christ's sake." Umber was beginning to feel angry, now the shock of Sharp's appearance had faded. "You're not serious, are you?"

"Why do you think I'm here?"

"Bored by retirement. Writing your memoirs. God knows."

Sharp smiled. "Memoirs. That's a good idea. One I've thought about, matter of fact."

"Really?"

"I handled quite a few big cases over the years. Mostly with the Met, before I transferred to Wiltshire. I thought it'd be a quieter life down there. Didn't turn out to be, though."

"Bad luck."

"Wrong place, wrong time. Like you, I suppose."

"Not *quite* like me."

"No. Maybe not. But you know what I mean."

"I still don't, actually."

"I put a lot of evil people behind bars. There were a good few more I couldn't pin anything on, but *I* knew what they were guilty of. As far as murder goes, there wasn't one I didn't crack. Not one. Except . . ."

"Avebury."

"You said it."

"Well, you'll just have to live with that, won't you? Like the rest of us."

"Will I?"

Umber sat back as his by now empty glass was collected, letting slip the chance to decline a refill and take his leave. He looked at Sharp, steadily and disbelievingly. "What are you on—a conscience trip?"

"Sort of. I should have got to the bottom of it. And I didn't. It may not be as hard to bear as the what-ifs and why-didn't-I's of those who were there at the time, of course, but—"

"What the hell do you mean by that?"

"Well, you must have said to yourself often enough over the years, 'If I'd reacted faster, if I'd moved more quickly . . . I might have saved the girl.'" Sharp broke off as Umber's second beer arrived, then went on: "Don't tell me you never have."

"All right. I won't tell you."

"She'd be thirty this year. If she'd lived."

Umber raised a hand to his brow and closed his eyes for a second. "Oh, Christ."

"What's the matter?"

"Nothing." Umber opened his eyes. "Nothing at all."

"Is that the sort of thing Sally used to say?"

There was another wordless interval. Umber swallowed some beer and looked towards the window. "I don't have to listen to this."

"I only realized you'd married her when I heard about her suicide. The change of surname. It was a surprise, I don't mind admitting. How did that happen—you and her getting together?"

"None of your business."

"Orphans of the storm, I suppose. But maybe the storm never quite blew itself out."

Umber looked back at him. "You don't know what you're talking about."

"Put me right, then."

"It wasn't—"

"Suicide? Not according to the coroner, no. But that's what it sounded like to me. And to you, I'll bet."

This was too close to the bone—and to the truth. Umber stood up and grabbed his tab. He would pay at the bar and go. He would leave and have done with it. "I've had enough," he declared.

"I can make trouble for you, Mr. Umber."

That stopped Umber in his tracks. He looked down at Sharp. "What did you say?"

"I can call in a few favours if I need to and have your affairs given close attention. Uncomfortably close. Your tax status springs to mind. Always a promising place to start where expats are concerned. Catch my drift?"

"You're bluffing."

"Maybe. Maybe not. Why take the risk? All I'm asking you to do is to sit down and answer a few questions." Sharp smiled thinly. "Help me with my enquiries. As the saying goes."

Umber hesitated. Why was Sharp so determined to put him through this? It was all so pointless, so pitifully late in the day. He remembered Sharp as a bluff, no-nonsense policeman. There had been no hint of obsession. What *was* he trying to achieve?

"Sit down."

With a sigh, Umber obeyed. "I could do without going over it all again," he said, almost to himself. "I really could."

"So could I."

"Then spare us both."

"Not in a position to, I'm afraid."

"Why not?"

"All in good time. Besides, I'm not convinced you don't know why."

"You're making no sense . . . Mr. Sharp."

"All right. Let's stick for the moment to the facts. Those we can agree on. Let's just . . . run through a few of them."

"Must we?"

It was unclear if Sharp had even heard the question. "Avebury: Monday, twenty-seventh July, 1981," he said, Umber's heart sinking at the implacable declaration of place and date. "Two days before the Royal Wedding, incidentally, which denied us a lot of valuable publicity in the early stages of the inquiry. Anyway, that's the where and when. Sally Wilkinson, nanny to the Hall family, takes the Halls' three children—Jeremy, aged ten, Miranda, seven, and Tamsin, two—to Avebury for fresh air and exercise. Also because Jeremy's been badgering her to go on account of a school project that sparked his interest in stone circles. They walk around. They look at the stones. Everything's very normal, very peaceful. But there's a white van parked in Green Street. A man gets out of the van, grabs little Tamsin while Sally's back is turned and drives off with her. Or is driven. We'll come back to that point later."

"You're not telling me anything I don't already know," Umber pointed out wearily.

"Tamsin's sister runs into the road, presumably to try and stop the van," Sharp pressed on. "She is struck. And killed. Outright." He paused, as if encouraging Umber to interrupt again. But there was no interruption. "Witnesses," he continued. "Other than Sally and Jeremy, we have three. Percy Nevinson, a local man with a comprehensive knowledge of the circle. Not exactly level-headed, though. Tells me he's working on a theory that Martians built Avebury—and Silbury Hill. That puts him in the nutter category in my book. Then there's Donald Collingwood, who drives through the village as all this is happening, but doesn't stop and only comes forward three weeks later. Explains he was afraid of losing his licence on account of his dodgy eyesight. As a result of said eyesight, he isn't too sure what he saw or where the van went. Finally, there's—"

"Me."

"That's right. David Umber. Sitting outside the Red Lion. With a ringside view of the whole thing."

"I told you everything I knew at the time. Every single thing I could remember."

"Which didn't amount to much. And the same goes for the rest. Confusion is the top and tail of it. No registration number for the van. No decent description of the abductor. No nothing. Result: one dead girl; one missing girl; one traumatized boy; one guilt-ridden nanny; a devastated family; a hamstrung inquiry; an unsolved murder. Maybe two unsolved murders. What happened to Tamsin . . . we have no idea."

"*You* have no idea. Officially, it's down to Radd. That's still so, isn't it?"

"It's a grey area. He was never formally charged. But he did confess. The whole thing had a . . . desk-clearing feel about it to me."

"What do you mean?"

"Nine years after the event, and only a few months after I've taken early retirement, Brian Radd, child murderer, suddenly adds Tamsin

Hall to his admitted list of victims just before he goes into court certain of a life sentence. Says he drove her off, did God knows what to
her, then strangled her and buried the body in Savernake Forest. Can't
remember, even vaguely, which part of the forest, so a search is out of
the question. They'd have found bugger all after nine years anyway.
Radd's from Reading, so it's a Thames Valley case, but Hollins, my successor in Wiltshire—a by-the-book timeserver if ever there was one—
goes with the flow and puts out a statement saying they're not looking
for anyone else in connection with the crime. I smell a rat. Radd's confession gets the murder *and* the abduction off the books. Nobody cares
whether it would stand up in court—whether it's *true*."

"Sally cared."

"Were you married by then?"

"No. Together. But not married. That came later." Later as in
too late, Umber thought but did not say. The marriage had been an
attempt to deny that their relationship was falling apart. Its disinte-
gration would have been easier to accept if the reason had been
something banal like infidelity or incompatibility. But no. The reason was Avebury, 27 July 1981. That was always the reason. "The
police signing up to Radd's version of events really got to her, you
know. She saw the bloke who grabbed Tamsin bundle her into the
back of the van and climb in after her. Then the van took off. But
Radd claimed to have been alone. No accomplice. Therefore Sally
must have been mistaken. She'd been blamed for not taking better
care of Tamsin. Now she was being told her account of what happened wasn't credible. She never got over that."

"It would have been different if I'd still been on the Force."

"Pity you didn't tell her so."

Sharp scowled into his beer. "My old Chief Super asked me not
to rock the boat."

"And you were a loyal cop, even in retirement."

"I should have contacted Sally and assured her I still believed her."

"Yes. You should."

"Is that what made you do it?"

Umber was wrong-footed by the question. He had seemed to
have Sharp on the defensive. It had not lasted long. "Do what?"

Sharp stared at him long and hard. The server replaced their
empty glasses with full ones. Sharp held the stare.

"What are you talking about?" pressed Umber.

"Remind me why you were at Avebury that day."

"For God's sake."

"Remind me."

Umber sighed. "All right. Here we go again. I was one year into a Ph.D. at Oxford, studying the letters of Junius. I was spending the summer with my parents in Yeovil. I got a call from a man called Griffin, who said he was up in Oxford, had heard about my research and had something to show me which he thought would be helpful. We agreed to meet in the pub at Avebury that lunchtime. It's as simple as that. Though, as I recall, you never accepted the explanation at face value."

"I kept my notebooks from the investigation. Took a look through them before I came out here. You're right. There were a lot of question marks in the sections relating to you. And question marks mean doubts."

"Because Griffin never showed up? Well, you had road blocks up within half an hour. He must have got caught up in the traffic jam and . . . decided to turn round and go back to Oxford."

"Plausible enough. But then why didn't he contact you again?"

Umber shrugged. "I haven't a clue."

"You had no phone number for him? No address?"

"He was . . . cagey. I assumed I'd get the details when we met."

"How had he heard about your research?"

"He didn't say."

"And you didn't ask?"

"I was more interested in what he was offering to show me."

"Which was?"

"You already know. It's in your notebook, isn't it? All this stuff must be."

"Junius was the pen name of the author of a series of anonymous letters to the press in the mid-eighteenth century blowing the lid on the politics of the day. A mole, I guess we'd call him now. Correct?"

"Yes. More or less."

"What made him such a big deal?"

"For three years, from 1769 to 1772, he savaged the conduct of government ministers in the letters page of the *Public Advertiser* and succeeded in hounding the Duke of Grafton into resigning the premiership. The reading public lapped it up. Especially since he was clearly either a government insider or someone with access to extremely accurate inside information. But he was never unmasked. The mystery of his identity added to his appeal. And he quit while he was ahead. So, a fascinating figure."

"What exactly were you researching about him?"

"His identity. The classic unanswered question. Recent historical opinion favours Philip Francis, a senior clerk in the War Office, as the culprit. I was aiming to put that theory to the test."

"And did you?"

"I never finished."

"Why not?"

Umber stared Sharp down. "Something else cropped up."

"Was it you or the mysterious Mr. Griffin who suggested meeting at Avebury?"

"Griffin. But, Avebury being about halfway between Yeovil and Oxford—"

"It's a good bit closer to Oxford."

"Is it? Well, he was the one doing me the favour. I wasn't going to quibble."

"And the favour was?"

"After Junius gave up his letter-writing campaign, Henry Sampson Woodfall, the proprietor of the *Public Advertiser*, published a two-volume collected edition of the letters. He and Junius were in secret communication and Junius asked for a special vellum-bound, gilt-edged copy to be sent to him, which Woodfall duly arranged. It's never been seen since. If found, its provenance would obviously be a pointer to Junius's identity. Well, that's what Griffin claimed he had and was willing to show me: the specially bound copy, with, he said, a revealing inscription inside. It sounded too good to be true, but I wasn't about to pass up the chance, was I?"

"If Griffin had this . . . unique copy, why didn't he . . . put it up for auction or something?"

"He didn't say."

"Why involve you, a . . ."

"Piddling research student?"

"You said it."

"I don't know. He promised all would become clear when we met. But we never did."

"Could it have been a hoax? Some fellow student of yours pulling your leg?"

"I don't think so."

"Then what *do* you think it was all about?"

"I don't know."

"Did you try to track Griffin down when you went back to Oxford?"

"I asked around, but nobody had heard of him. After what had happened at Avebury, though, it seemed so . . . trivial. I mean, Junius, who really gives a damn? I suppose that was one of the reasons why I gave up on the Ph.D."

"And the other reasons?"

"They were mostly to do with Sally."

"I was told she went abroad after the inquest."

"So she did."

"You went with her?"

"Yes."

"I'm sorry . . . about her death."

"Me too."

"Was it suicide?"

"How would I know? We'd separated by then."

"But what do you think?"

Umber took a deep swallow of beer and stared at Sharp. "Same as you."

Sharp cleared his throat. "According to my notes, I considered the possibility that you'd made the Griffin story up to explain your presence at Avebury."

"And did you consider *why* I'd have wanted to be there?"

"Of course."

"With what result?"

"I never figured it out."

"That's because there was nothing to figure out."

"It seems not."

"Is that definite, then? You no longer think I might have been lying?"

"I'll go one better. I don't think you're lying now either. I just can't decide whether that's good news or bad."

"What the hell does that mean?"

"It means you're wrong about Junius, Mr. Umber. Somebody does give a damn."

Umber grimaced in bewilderment. Perhaps he had drunk too much. Perhaps Sharp had. What in God's name was the man driving at?

"I had a letter a few weeks ago, basically telling me I cocked up the Avebury inquiry and should do something about it. Anonymous, naturally."

"Did you think I sent it? Is that why you came all this way to see me?"

"Yes."

"Well, you've had a wasted journey, then, haven't you?"

"I don't see it that way. You have to understand. You were the obvious suspect."

"Why?"

"Because of the source of the letter."

"You just said you didn't know who it was from."

"I said it was anonymous. Maybe I should have said . . . pseudonymous. That's the really strange thing, you see. The letter . . . was from Junius."

C H A P T E R

THREE

21. *January*

SIR,

IT is the misfortune of your life, that you should never have been acquainted with the truth WITH respect to the Marlborough murderers

It is not, however, too late to correct the error I am unable to correct it. It is time for those, who have no view to private advantage, it is time for such men to interpose.

You have already much to answer for. The subject comes home to us all.

JUNIUS.

David Umber had read the letter several times and he was still unable to offer an intelligent response. Someone had cut various words and/or phrases out of an edition of the Junius letters and stuck them onto a sheet of paper to form this strangest of messages. It was a photocopy, of course. The letters themselves need not have been mutilated. But that was a small point. The overriding issue was: *why?*

"Aren't you going to say something?" Sharp prompted.

They were in the blandly decorated bar of Sharp's no-frills

hotel near Charles Square. Umber had gone there in a mood of some scepticism, expecting to see something spectacularly un-Junian. But what Sharp had brought down from his room-safe was in fact eerily authentic.

"For God's sake, man, tell me what you make of it."

"I don't know," Umber said at last. "I really don't know."

"Are those Junius's words on the page or aren't they?"

"The words? Oh yes. I recognize some of the phrases. The start's from his famous letter to the King. The rest? I couldn't say exactly which letters they come from, but it's all Junius. The use of the long S confirms it as eighteenth-century type. The splitting up of the word 'acquainted' is obviously an original line break. And the date's authentic too. Junius's first letter was dated the twenty-first of January, 1769. These must be extracts from one of the early collected editions."

"Like the one Griffin was offering to show you?"

"Like it, yes. But—"

"It's tied up with that, isn't it?"

"How can it be?"

"Your guess is as good as mine. Or better. You are the Junius expert."

"*Was*. A long time ago."

"That still makes you one of the few people who could have put this letter together. I'll bet you've got a first-edition Junius tucked away somewhere."

"Not so, actually." It was true, thanks only to the flood, a detail Umber decided not to mention. "Besides, I thought you accepted that I *didn't* put it together."

"I do." Sharp sounded as if he almost resented his own exclusion of Umber as a suspect.

"How was it addressed to you?"

"See for yourself." Sharp slid the envelope across the table.

It was white A5, bearing a first-class stamp with a smudged postmark and what looked like a computer-generated address label. *George Sharp, 12 Bilston Court, Nunswood Road, Buxton, Derbyshire SK17 6AQ*. The word-processed characters held no clue. The clues, such as they were, had all been in the letter.

"London postmark," said Sharp. "Date barely legible. But probably the twenty-first of January. I received it on the twenty-second."

"I was here at the time," said Umber.

"That wouldn't clear you in my eyes."

"Derbyshire, Mr. Sharp. What took you there?"

"A return to my roots. And you can call me George, since we're in this together."

Umber could not decide which was more ominous: the invitation to use Sharp's Christian name—or the hint of an alliance between them. He tried to ignore the point. "My guess would be that whoever sent this chose Junius as the source in order to throw suspicion onto me."

"If you're right, that means they know everything there is to know about the Avebury case. Your reason for being there didn't exactly make the newspaper front pages."

"The implication is that they know the whole truth of it, surely."

"Maybe. But the other implication is that I can find out what the truth is. If I set my mind to it. 'It is not too late to correct the error.' Notice he says 'the Marlborough murderers.'"

"I can't imagine Junius ever mentioned Avebury. But he would have mentioned the Duke of Marlborough. The town's only a few miles from Avebury, so—"

"That's not what I mean. Murderers plural. It rams the point home, doesn't it? It rules out Radd's confession."

"We've already ruled that out, haven't we?"

Sharp sipped his whisky and offered no reply. But the deep furrows in his brow gave a kind of answer. The letter was a reproach as well as a challenge. And he was vulnerable to both.

"What do you mean to do about this?"

Still Sharp said nothing.

"George?"

Now, at last, there was a response. Sharp set down his tumbler with a clunk on the table. "Exactly what it dares me to do."

"'Correct the error'?"

"Dig out the truth. If it's there to be dug."

"What can you hope to learn now that you failed to learn twenty-three years ago?"

"I'm not a policeman any more. I don't have to go by the book."

"Have you reported receiving this letter?"

"Of course not. Wiltshire CID wouldn't want to know. *And*

they'd try to spike my guns. The only advantage I have is that no-body will be expecting me to go down this road again."

"Other than . . . what shall we call your correspondent? . . . Junius?"

"It's what he calls himself."

"Or what *she* calls *herself.*"

"I suppose it could be a woman." Sharp ground his teeth. "'I am unable to correct the error.' 'It is time for *men* to interpose.' I see what you mean."

"You're jumping to conclusions, George. The mid-eighteenth century's a tad early for gender equality. Junius—the real Junius—wouldn't have envisaged women interposing in anything. All I'm saying is that you don't know who you're dealing with."

"Except that he or she is an expert on the Junius letters."

"Not so very expert, actually."

"What do you mean?"

"Well, I said Junius's first letter was dated the twenty-first of January 1769, and that's true—as far as the collected edition is concerned. But his first letter to the *Public Advertiser* appeared in November 1768. For some reason, he decided not to include it in the collected edition. Of course, that makes an original copy hard to come by, but the correct date could be concocted by . . ." Umber broke off and grabbed the letter. A door had opened in his mind. The writer could reasonably have hoped that Sharp would bring this letter to him. It could therefore be a message to both of them. Indeed, the sentiments were in many ways more applicable to him than to Sharp. *"The misfortune of your life."* Yes, what had happened at Avebury on 27 July 1981 was that all right. And the subject came home to him. Only too well. "Bloody hell."

"What is it?"

"Griffin must have sent this."

"Aren't you the one who's jumping to conclusions now?"

"Maybe. But he didn't turn up that day, did he? Either because of road blocks . . . or because he never intended to."

"Meaning?"

"Meaning he wanted *me* there. As a witness."

"That makes no sense, Umber. No-one could have known Sally would take the Hall children to Avebury that particular morning."

"God, no." Umber put his hand to his brow and dropped the

letter. "They couldn't, could they?" He fell back in his chair. "I swore I was finished with this when Sally died. The wondering. The theorizing. Constructing one house of cards after another out of frail suppositions. And then watching them collapse. She never stopped doing that. But I did. In the end, I was just so . . . weary of it . . . that I felt . . . weary of her."

"You're not going to go maudlin on me, are you?"

Umber's answer was a long time coming. "I'll do my best not to."

"I need your help."

"*My* help?"

"To crack this."

"It can't be done, George."

"Which—the cracking or the helping?"

"Both. Contrary to what Junius says, it *is* too late."

"We won't know that till we try."

"*We?*"

"I could have gone on drawing my pension and tending my allotment happily enough, you know. But not now. Not now I've been reminded of what I did wrong all those years ago."

"And what was that?"

"I gave up. I stopped looking. I wrote the little girl off."

"You didn't have much option."

"We'll see about that."

"I can't get involved, George. Not now. Not after . . . putting it all behind me."

"What exactly have you done with the past twenty-three years, Umber?"

"This and that."

"I came here expecting to find you'd sent me this letter because you blamed me for Sally's death."

"Sorry to disappoint you."

"You disappoint yourself. You know you do. You live in a dingy apartment scraping by on odds and sods of casual tour-guiding. Is that how you plan to go on for the *next* twenty-three years?"

"Something will turn up."

"It just has. Your big chance—and mine—to set things right."

"You're kidding yourself, George. It's a fool's errand. Besides, you're the detective. What do you need me for?"

"Younger pair of legs. Keener pair of eyes. And the last word on

Junius. *That's* what I need you for." Sharp drained his glass. "I'll cover your travelling expenses if that's what you're worried about."

"Police pensions must be more generous than I thought."

"I just don't want you to have any excuse for turning me down."

"I don't need an excuse."

"That a fact? Then, tell me, why are you trying so hard to find one?"

"I'm not going back with you, George."

"I'll give you twenty-four hours to think it over."

"It won't make any difference."

"No. It won't." Sharp slid the letter back into its envelope. "Because you already know what you're going to do." He smiled at Umber. "You just can't bring yourself to admit it."

Half an hour later, Umber was on the number 24 tram, trundling north through the darkened streets of Prague—streets Sally had never trodden. Their wanderings had taken them to most of the capital cities of Europe, but never this one. That, he knew, was one of the reasons he had come to Prague—and had stayed. He opened his wallet and took out the snapshot of her he always carried with him. It was the only picture he had of her. The flood had claimed the others. All that was left to him was this spare passport photograph from nearly twenty years ago.

Her dark, shoulder-length hair cast part of her face in shadow, accentuating her high cheekbones and making her look gaunt and troubled, whereas in his mind's eye she appeared neither. He remembered her smile so very clearly. But she had seldom smiled for the camera. Somehow, she had never quite trusted herself to.

He put the picture away again and looked at his own, ghostly reflection in the window. "What do you want me to do, Sal?" he asked her under his breath, watching his lips shape the words. "Just tell me. That's all you need to do. That's all you ever needed to do."

There was no answer. There could never be. It was too late for that.

He dreamt of Sally that night, for the first time in a year or more. They were in the tiny flat in Barcelona that had been their first home together. But he could not understand why she was there. "They told me you were dead," he said, over and over again. She wrapped her arms around him and kissed him on the neck. "Me, dead?" she whispered into his ear. "That's such a silly idea."

He was woken by the telephone. Opening his eyes, he saw that it was light outside. According to his bedside clock, it was nearly ten. He had lain awake for what felt like hours before falling asleep, but sleeping this late in the morning was nonetheless a surprise.

He grabbed the telephone, wondering if it would be Sharp badgering for an answer, then realized it could not be because he had not given him this number.

"*Haló?*"

"*Dobré ráno.*"

"What can I do for you, Marek?"

"Not for me, brother. For Ivana. She needs you to cover Tuesday."

"Ah . . . Tuesday?"

"*Jo.* Day after Monday. Day before Wednesday. I can put you down for it?"

"I'm not, er . . . too sure I . . ."

"I need a decision, like, right now."

"Then it's no." Sharp was right, of course, damn him. There never had been any doubt about what Umber was going to do. "Not Tuesday. Not any other day. For the foreseeable future."

C H A P T E R

FOUR

Travelling light and at short notice was one luxury David Umber could well afford to indulge. When Sharp proposed a Sunday morning departure, he did not demur. Nor did he try to hold Sharp to his whisky-fuelled offer of paying for the journey. But the retired policeman seemed oddly determined to put his pension money where his mouth had been.

"I'll make all the arrangements."

"There's no need. I can——"

"Leave it to me."

"All right. I will."

"I'll pick you up at eleven."

"What time's the flight?"

"Just be ready at eleven."

"I can make my own way to the airport. If you're worried I'll change my mind, I can——"

"Be ready at eleven."

And so the telephone conversation had ended. It was a long way from being the last telephone conversation Umber had that day, however. When Ivana heard he was quitting Jolly Brolly, she rang to congratulate him on landing a full-time job, the only possible explanation for his conduct that had occurred to her. From her the news spread to his other friends that he was in fact going away for a while, prompting various farewell calls and good-luck messages. He assured one and all that he would be back before long. But nobody seemed quite to believe him.

"You think because things have gone bad for you here they will go good for you in England?" Ivana asked in her second call of the day. She had persuaded herself that the parting from Milena was what was driving him away and assurances from Umber to the contrary were futile.

"I don't think that."

"You remember. *Dostat se z bláta do louže.*" It was an old Czech saying. *Out of the mud into the puddle.*

"I'll remember," said Umber.

And so he would.

Several loud blasts on a horn announced Sharp's arrival at dead on eleven o'clock the following morning. Umber looked out the window of his flat expecting to see a taxi waiting for him below and hoping for Sharp's sake that he had agreed to the fare beforehand.

But the vehicle that had pulled up just past the tram stop was not a taxi.

Sharp was waiting outside the entrance to the block when Umber emerged a couple of minutes later, bags in hand, and caught at once his wary glance towards the blue and white camper van.

"Something wrong?"

"Is this our transport?"

Sharp nodded. "A 1977 Volkswagen T2 in tip-top running order. I bought her second-hand when I retired and did her up proud. Lovely, isn't she?"

"You *drove* to Prague?"

"I did. And we're driving back. I've booked us on the midnight ferry from Dunkirk to Dover."

"I thought we'd be flying."

"Wait till we hit the autobahn." Sharp winked. "It'll feel as if we are."

"Tell me, George," said Umber, once they were clear of the city and heading west on the main road towards the German border, "what exactly are we going to do when we get to England?" The van, which Sharp quite unselfconsciously addressed as Molly, had yet to show her alleged turn of speed, but Umber's thoughts were already directed to journey's end. It was one thing to talk about going after the truth, quite another to devise a way of doing so.

"You mean do I have a plan?" growled Sharp.

"Well, do you?"

"Oh yes. But that can wait. First I'd like a little background on you and the last twenty-three years."

"I'm not going to talk to you about me and Sally, if that's what you're getting at."

"Force yourself. We need to know as much as each other in case there are gaps to fill in. I'm an open book. Policing in Wiltshire. Then retirement to Derbyshire. No family. No friends to speak of. What you see is what you get."

"Same here."

"Oh, I doubt that. I'll hazard a guess about you and Sally and you can tell me whether I'm wide of the mark. The relationship began straight after the inquest."

Umber was glad Sharp had to concentrate on driving. Otherwise he would have been sure to notice Umber's wince of dismay. The inquest *was* where it had begun for them. Devizes Magistrates' Court, October 1981. The coroner's summing-up had loaded an unfair amount of blame on Sally's shoulders. She had looked so young and alone, so helpless in the face of criticism. The Hall family had made no move towards her. The press had been lying in wait outside. On impulse, Umber had said to her, "Come out the back way with me. We'll drive somewhere." She had looked at him, her eyes full of gratitude. And she had simply nodded her acceptance. It was all she had been able to do.

"The coroner was out of line," said Sharp. "I was going to tell Sally that, you know. But you whisked her away before I had the chance. Where did you go?"

"The Kennet and Avon Canal. We walked along the towpath."

"Nice choice. And what about the decision to go abroad? Christmas, maybe? New Year?"

"You're not going to give up, are you?"

"Not for the next few hundred miles or so."

"All right. I'll tell you." Umber knew then that he would have to give Sharp some sort of account of his life with Sally. Better, he decided, an edited one of his own shaping than whatever result Sharp's guessing game produced. "Sally needed to get away. So did I. She rapidly became more important to me than a Ph.D of questionable relevance to anything. She'd abandoned a teaching degree before working as a nanny, so teaching English abroad seemed the obvious answer for both of us. We took the qualifying course in Barcelona in the spring and summer of 'eighty-two. We worked in Lisbon after that, then Athens, then . . . all over. The farther from home the better."

"Good idea, I imagine."

"It seemed to be. We had a few happy years."

"Only a few?"

"We were in Turkey—Izmir—when we heard about Radd. Sally was pregnant at the time. Miscarried shortly afterwards. I blamed her Turkish doctor. She blamed . . ." Umber chuckled bitterly. "Herself."

"Come again?"

"She got it into her head that she wasn't allowed to have a child of her own . . . because she'd lost Tamsin."

"That's—"

"Crazy? Yes, George, you're so right. Crazy is what it was. And it went on that way. I tried to keep her on an even keel. Maybe I didn't try hard enough. Or maybe I tried too hard. Maybe we both did. We got married. But that didn't help. In fact, it only made it worse. In the end, we felt tied to each other. Trapped. We were in Italy at the time. I accepted a job back in Turkey, knowing she wouldn't go with me because of what had happened there. She stayed on in Bologna. She hadn't actually been working in quite a while. Then she went back to England."

"When was that?"

"Autumn of 'ninety-eight."

"You were together a long time."

"Nearly seventeen years. She lasted less than a year on her own."

They must have covered a mile or more in silence before Sharp said, "Maybe the coroner was right and it was just an accident."

"Maybe."

"But who trails a fan heater on an extension lead into a bathroom on a summer's evening?"

"Exactly. Who does?"

"Blame yourself, do you?"

"What do you think?"

"I think it's handy in this case"—Sharp cast Umber a sidelong smile—"that you've got someone to share the blame with."

Blame had hung heavy in the air at Sally's funeral. Umber could remember the almost physical weight of it, pressing down on his shoulders. He had been tempted to plead pressure of work and stay away, but that would have been one desertion too many. So he had gone. And seen the accusations hovering in the eyes of the other mourners. And known that he could not rebut them. He should have saved her. He should have been capable of it. But in the end all he had managed to do was to save himself.

"When love fails, self-preservation takes over," Alice Myers, Sally's oldest friend, had said to him afterwards. She had not troubled to explain her remark. She had not needed to.

Umber had returned to Turkey the following morning. In simple terms, he had fled. He had been home since, of course. But only now, on this long drive across half of Europe, did he feel that his flight might at last be over.

It was after dark, in a service area near Aachen, over coffee and baguettes, that Sharp unveiled his plan.

"There's nothing very sophisticated about it. Checking facts and asking questions is what it amounts to. I want to know two things. One, who sent me the letter? Two, what *really* happened at Avebury on the twenty-seventh of July, 1981? Maybe that's basically the same question. We'll see. The great thing is to look on the passage of time as a blessing, not a curse."

"How can it be?"

"Because it means we can forget all that forensic crap. I never really trusted the white-coated brigade anyway. Fingerprints. Bloodstains. Fibre samples. They don't come into it. But *time*? That's a different matter. It reveals a pattern. What the people touched by the abduction of Tamsin Hall and the murder of Miranda Hall have done in the years since is the evidence we're going to sift."

"And what have they done?"

"Well, you and Sally—sadly—we know about. That brings us to the Hall family. How much do you know about them?"

"We heard the Halls had split up."

Sharp nodded. "It's not uncommon in cases like this. The death of a child. The loss of another. The parents cling together at first, then drift apart. Their lives are shattered. In the end, it becomes easier to rebuild them separately. The Halls divorced while I was still in Wiltshire. Jane Hall married a local wine merchant. Name of Questred. He used to keep a shop in Marlborough. With any luck, he still does. They had a child of their own, you know."

"Yes. I did know."

"A daughter."

"Sally had an aunt in Hungerford who seemed to think she needed to be kept informed about that sort of thing."

"When you'd rather she'd been allowed to forget the Halls."

"What about Oliver Hall? He didn't register on Aunt's radar. Banker, wasn't he?"

"Not sure, technically. Stockbroker. Financial consultant. Something like that. A money man. Retired to Jersey, I gather. That must make him a mega-money man. None of which brings his daughters back to him, of course. Also remarried. But no more children."

"And the son?"

"Went to live with his father after his mother remarried. That was before his father pulled the same trick. Then . . ." Sharp shrugged. "I never had any cause to find out. Until now."

"None of these people are going to want to talk to us, George."

"I can be very persuasive. You'll just have to follow my example."

"Who else do you intend to contact?"

"The other witnesses. If they're still in the land of the living. Collingwood was seventy-odd and shaky. I'll check, but I'm not optimistic. Nevinson's a better bet. Unless one of the stones has keeled over on top of him, I guess he'll still be hanging around Avebury. He and his sister lived with their mother on the council estate at Avebury Trusloe—where they put the villagers whose houses were pulled down in the fifties. Aside from nature taking its course where the mother's concerned I can't see much having changed there."

"But a nutter, by your reckoning."

"Sending me a letter made up of old Junius quotes could be right up his street."

"You reckon?"

"I don't know. It's a thought. Could Nevinson be Griffin?"

"Nevinson?"

The fellow had been there, at Avebury, with Umber, standing helplessly by the body of Miranda Hall, while they had waited for the emergency services to arrive. Customers from the Red Lion had joined them. Everyone, including those who had not seen the event itself, had been shocked, talking in soft, distracted undertones. The landlady had taken Sally and Jeremy into the pub, leaving Umber and Nevinson out on the road, watching the blood soak slowly through the blanket that someone had draped over poor dead little Miranda. They must have spoken to each other. They *must* have done. But Umber could remember nothing of what they had said.

"He can't be Griffin. I'd have recognized his voice."

"Sure?"

"Of course. I'd have been bound to. It was only two days since I'd spoken to Griffin."

"OK. Fine. But that leaves us with a problem."

"Who is Griffin?" Umber mused, versifying the words in the style of *Who is Sylvia?* "What is he?"

Umber left Sharp dozing in the passengers' lounge during the ferry crossing and went on deck to watch the patchy moonlight skittering across the Channel. It was a still, cold night. Dover glowed amber ahead, Dunkirk astern. He found himself remembering his one and only conversation with the mysterious Mr. Griffin, replaying it in his mind, as close to word for word as he could manage, so close, indeed, that he could almost swear they *were* the words, exact and verbatim.

Saturday afternoon, 25 July 1981. Umber was watching cricket on the television. He heard the telephone ring, but left his mother to answer it. Then she called to him, "It's for you, David." He watched one more delivery before ambling out into the hall.

"Hello?"

"David Umber?"

"Yes."

"You don't know me, Mr. Umber." The voice sounded silken, muffled, faintly effete. "My name is Griffin."

"Right."

"I'm in Oxford." The phrasing somehow implied that Oxford was not Griffin's normal stamping-ground. "I've heard about your ... Junian researches." This phrase too seemed loaded. The use of the adjective *Junian* suggested close familiarity with the letters and the controversy over their authorship.

"How did you—"

"I have something that may interest you. Something germane to your research."

"Oh yeah?"

"It's a rather unusual copy of the 1773 edition of the letters." That, as Umber was well aware, meant the second edition, incorporating an index and table of contents, for which Junius had told Woodfall he would wait before his bespoke copy was produced. "Vellum-bound and gilt-edged. Very handsome."

"Vellum-bound ... and gilt-edged?" Umber could not believe his ears.

"Quite so. Complete with an illuminating and more than somewhat surprising inscription."

"You're having me on."

"No. I'm in earnest, I assure you."

"But ... you *can't* be."

"I understand your incredulity. But I speak the absolute truth. I have what I describe. Would you like to see it?"

"What does the inscription say?"

"I can't discuss that over the telephone. If you're interested, I think we should meet."

"Of course I'm interested."

"Well, then?"

"I can come up to Oxford tomorrow."

"This is no business for the sabbath." Once again there came a hint of other-worldliness. It struck Umber that his caller sounded more like a man of the eighteenth century than the twentieth. "Would Monday suit?"

"Sure."

"But not Oxford. There are too many eyes and ears in this city. Do you know Avebury?"

"Yeah. Sort of."

"Let's meet at the village inn. The Red Lion. I'll be there at half past twelve."

"I can make that."

"Good. It won't be a wasted journey. I think I can promise you that."

"Look, Mr. Griffin, I—"

"Until Monday."

With that the line went dead.

And it had stayed dead for twenty-three years, subsumed and forgotten in the wake of the tragedy that had struck at Avebury two days later, engulfing all those who had been there to witness it. *"It won't be a wasted journey,"* Griffin had said. *"I think I can promise you that."*

Dover in the small hours of a chill March morning did not make for a gala homecoming. Sharp's doze aboard the ferry had left him taciturn and liverish. Umber was tired and dispirited. Leaving Prague suddenly felt like a huge mistake. Little was said as they followed the signs for the motorway and headed towards London.

Sharp stopped at a service area near Maidstone and announced he would be stretching out in the back of the van for the rest of the night. Umber retreated to the cafeteria.

Come dawn Sharp was as bright as a lark, tucking into a full English breakfast after a wash and a shave in the service area toilets. Umber was bleary-eyed and mentally drained. He did not even ask where they were going next. Somewhere between Maidstone and the M25, he fell asleep.

CHAPTER

FIVE

W e're there," Sharp announced, turning off the engine and opening his window to admit a gust of cold air.

Umber woke with a start. "What?" He coughed and blinked around him. "Where?"

"Avebury."

"Christ. You never said ..." Umber struggled to compose his thoughts. He had been to Avebury several times in the months following the tragedy and had driven through it, alone, maybe twice since. Sally's horror of the place had ruled out any other return visits, even if Umber had wanted to undertake them. They were in the High Street car park, he realized. Looking out of his window, he could see the village post office on the other side of the road. Straight ahead, the tower of St. James's Church was visible beyond the trees fringing the churchyard. "You never said we were coming straight here."

"Where better to start?"

"I feel sick."

"That's because you didn't have a proper breakfast. A breath of fresh air will set you right. Let's take a walk."

It was a cold, grey morning. A wind had got up, driving slashes of rain into their faces. A solitary customer emerged from the post office as they left the car park. Otherwise, they seemed to have the village to themselves.

Sharp led the way towards the Red Lion, but crossed the road before he reached it and took up position beneath the trees on the opposite corner. Moving slowly and reluctantly, Umber joined him.

"Nothing much has changed, has it?" Sharp asked rhetorically.

Umber took a deep breath and looked across at the Adam and Eve stones in the field behind Silbury House, at the gate in the fence through which Miranda Hall had run that day they were both replaying in their minds. Then he looked along Green Street, towards the other gate, through which Tamsin Hall had been carried to the waiting white van. And then, almost as an act of mercy, a lorry rumbled round the bend from the north, blocking his view.

"If you'd been standing here rather than sitting outside the pub," said Sharp, once the lorry had gone, "you'd have seen for certain whether there were two men in the van, or only one."

"There were two."

"Yes. Two." Sharp nodded thoughtfully. "Paedophiles don't generally work in pairs. And Tamsin was a lot younger than Radd's other victims."

"He was lying, George. You know it. I know it."

"But why?"

"I thought you reckoned he did a deal with your successor."

"Who'd not have been above such a thing, let me tell you. But what was the deal? There was nothing we could offer him. He was going away for life whatever he admitted to. So, what was in it for him?"

"You tell me."

"That's the point." Sharp looked round at Umber. "I can't."

To Umber's relief, they soon started back along the High Street. But they did not stop at the car park. Sharp had something other than a swift departure in mind.

"I thought we'd pay the Nevinsons a call."

"Now?"

"No time like the present."

"How about some other time, when I'm feeling more like myself?"

"Wait with Molly if you like."

"No. I'll come with you."

Sharp smiled. "Thought you would."

They crossed the churchyard and followed a narrow footpath between some cottages to the western edge of the old village. The
footpath headed on to a river-bridge, then continued to a field-gate.
There the tarmac ended, leaving Sharp and Umber to dodge muddy
patches the rest of the way to Avebury Trusloe, a huddle of utilitar-
ian brown-brick houses and bungalows straight ahead. An old man
carrying a shopping bag, bound presumably for the post office,
passed them on the way and nodded a wordless good morning.

The transplanted village was served by a lane off the main
road. Crossing it, Umber wondered why they had not driven round,
a thought he did not bother to utter, but which Sharp seemed to respond to anyway.

"I always used to cover the last few hundred yards to a suspect's
home on foot. Most of my colleagues thought I was mad. But the lie
of the land can be the key to the mystery. Understanding it can give
you an edge."

"So you've walked this route before?"

"No. I never have. Because Nevinson wasn't a suspect twenty-
three years ago. But he is now."

"And what has the lie of the land told you? Apart from the un-
likelihood of an early spring."

"That old man we passed."

"What about him?"

"Eighty if he's a day. Probably born in one of the cottages that
were demolished, then rehoused here."

"So?"

"Still goes back, doesn't he? They move the people out of the
village, but they can't move the village out of the people. Maybe I
should have looked for the answer to this . . . a lot closer to home."

Home for the Nevinsons was a poorly maintained semi-detached
house with windows in need of painting, an unkempt garden and a
fence with several pales missing. The neighbouring property was
not in much better condition, the only splash of colour in its garden
being a bright yellow toy car, lying on its side.

Sharp flung open the Nevinsons' gate and strode up the fissured concrete path to the door. He had given the bell two jabs with his forefinger before Umber caught up.

A woman answered, with surprising promptness. The sister, Umber assumed. Short and plump, clad in a voluminous sweater worn over tracksuit bottoms and ancient plimsolls, she had iron-grey curly hair framing a round, placidly smiling face. Sixty or so, he would have guessed. She might well have attended the inquest, if only to lend her brother moral support. But Umber had no memory of her.

She, on the other hand, appeared to have a memory of him—of both of them, in fact. A quizzical smile dimpled her cheeks. "Good morning," she said, a local accent wrestling gamely with Home Counties elocution. "I believe I know you gentlemen."

"I believe you do," said Sharp.

"But it's been a long time."

"It has."

"Chief Inspector Sharp, as ever is."

"Retired now, Miss Nevinson. Plain *Mr.* Sharp."

She looked intently at Umber. "And you'd be . . ."

"David Umber."

"Of course. Mr. Umber. The other witness. We were never introduced, were we? I'm Abigail Nevinson. Percy's sister." She held out her hand, which Umber stepped forward to shake. "What can I do for you?"

"We're looking for Percy," said Sharp.

"I suppose you would be." She treated them to an appraising squint. "You make a strange pair, if you don't mind me saying. Not a pair I'd have expected to find on the doorstep. Certainly not after all these years." A thought suddenly struck her. "You've not . . . found her, have you?"

"Found her?" Sharp seemed momentarily not to understand who she meant.

"The girl."

"No," said Umber, determined to stop this hare from running. "It's nothing like that."

"Oh. What a shame." And the expression on Abigail Nevinson's face suggested that it truly was a shame. "But it'll be about her you've called, I dare say."

"In a sense," said Sharp. "Is Percy at home?"

"I'm afraid not. He's off on his morning walk."

"Nice weather for it," said Umber.

"Oh, he pays no heed to the weather, Mr. Umber. It could be blowing a gale and he'd still head off."

"Will he be gone long?" asked Sharp.

"Hard to say. Could be back any minute, or gone till lunchtime. Would you like to step in for a cup of tea and see if he arrives meanwhile?"

"That's kind of you," Sharp replied. "We'd be glad to."

An eloquent glance over his shoulder at Umber as they entered suggested that Sharp's acceptance of the invitation was not prompted by an eagerness to socialize with Abigail Nevinson. The house was warm and comfortably furnished, albeit in a style several decades out of date. There was a brief discussion of milk and sugar requirements, then Abigail waved them into the sitting room and headed for the kitchen. Umber sat down in an armchair by the fire, while Sharp prowled around, inspecting the contents of a bookcase and a china cabinet.

"Has much changed here, George?" Umber enquired *sotto voce*.

"Nothing's changed at all." There was a rattling of cups and the singing of a kettle from the kitchen. "Except Old Mother Nevinson's not weighing down that chair you've parked yourself in."

"Great. What about Abigail?"

"Fatter and older. Like her brother, I expect."

"Are you going to tell her—or him—about the letter?"

"Not until I rule him out as the sender."

"How are you going to explain our visit, then?"

"Simple. I'll say it was your idea."

A few minutes later, Abigail arrived with tea and biscuits, frowning pensively. She went on frowning as she distributed the cups and plates, then sat down opposite them, looked solemnly at Umber and said, "I was very sorry to hear about your wife's death, Mr. Umber. We both were. It's terrible how that one day all those years ago ruined so many people's lives."

"Actually, it's on Sally's account that we're here." Umber

launched himself at once on his hastily prepared cover story. "Since her death, I've wanted to take another look at what happened and see if I can't . . . resolve some of the doubts she always had about the official version of events."

"I offered to help," said Sharp. "Least I could do."

"I thought the police had decided that dreadful man Radd was responsible," said Abigail.

"I don't go along with my former colleagues on that."

"No? How interesting. Neither does Percy."

"Oh? What's his theory?"

"You'd have to ask him, Chief Inspector. Percy has so many theories. About so many things."

"Including the stone circle, as I recall."

"Oh yes. He's quite the expert on that. It's been virtually a life-long study."

"You've always lived here?"

"Well, we used to live in the village proper, of course. But our cottage was pulled down and we were moved over here when Percy and I were children."

"The Nevinsons go back a long way in these parts, do they?"

"No. But the Bateses do. My mother's side of the family. *Did*, I should say. There are none left round here now."

"Except you and Percy."

"Except us."

"Last of the line."

"It's turned out that way, yes."

"Did you ever think of . . ."

"Marrying? I've had offers in my time, Chief Inspector, I can tell you. None I cared to accept, though. Besides . . ."

"There was always Percy to look after."

Abigail bridled faintly at that. It seemed to Umber that she had suddenly realized she was being drawn in a direction she did not wish to take. "Will you be . . . speaking to everyone involved in the tragedy?" she asked with conspicuous deliberation.

"If *they'll* speak to *us*," Sharp replied.

"The Halls got divorced, you know."

"I did know, yes."

"Mrs. Hall—Mrs. Questred as is—still lives locally."

"Do you happen to know where?"

"Over near Ramsbury. It's a picture-postcard house at the bottom of Hilldrop Lane. Swanpool Cottage. Not really what you'd expect her to make do with, pretty or no, but there it is. Her husband keeps a wine shop in Marlborough, so I suppose it's handy, though how she can bear to stick so close to Avebury I don't rightly know."

"You think she should live somewhere . . . grander?"

"Well, she *did* live somewhere grander when she was married to Mr. Hall, didn't she? And I suppose he'll have had to pay her a goodly sum to settle the divorce."

"Do you ever see her?"

"In Marlborough, from time to time. Shopping and such. She doesn't know me, of course."

"But she'd know Percy?"

"I suppose so. But I'm not sure she'd show it."

"Maybe she's trying to put it all behind her," suggested Umber, to an irritated frown from Sharp.

"Maybe she is," said Abigail. "No-one could blame her for that."

"No," said Umber. "No-one could."

Percy Nevinson had still not returned when, half an hour later, Umber and Sharp took their leave. Abigail had noted down Umber's mobile number and assured them she would ask her brother to ring them as soon as possible.

"I'll thank you not to undermine my questioning of suspects in future," Sharp complained as soon as they were clear of the estate.

"Abigail's hardly a suspect," said Umber.

"You know what I mean."

"You were pressing too hard, George. Do you want Percy on the defensive before you even speak to him?"

"I have a feeling he'll be on the defensive anyway. His sister's hiding something. Which means he's hiding something."

"You don't know that."

"I sense it. In this game, that's as good as knowing. If not better."

"If you say so."

"How many murders have you investigated, Umber?"

"Come off it, George."

"*How many?*"

Umber sighed. "None, of course."

Sharp nodded. "Exactly." And with that he quickened his pace.

Neither Sharp nor Umber looked much about them during this spat. As a result, they did not notice the figure in the telephone box at the corner of the lane that led them down to the footpath back to Avebury. He was a short, tubby man dressed in hiking boots, pale-green corduroy trousers and a faded brown anorak. The brim of a dark-green Tilley hat, worn low, obscured his features. He had his back turned as they passed and appeared as oblivious of them as they were of him.

He shifted his stance once they had reached the footpath, however, and could hardly have failed to see them as they moved ahead. A moment later, he put the telephone down, exited the box and headed into the estate, moving at an anxious clip.

CHAPTER

SIX

"Where are we going now, George?" Umber asked as they drove out of Avebury past the surviving stones of an ancient avenue that led south from the circle.

"Worried I'll go straight to Swanpool Cottage and antagonize Jane Questred, are you?" Sharp responded.

"Well . . ."

"Credit me with *some* sensitivity, Umber. I let her down twenty-three years ago. Badly. If she wrote me that letter, I could hardly complain. Doorstepping her on a Monday morning isn't the way to break the ice. Besides, Abigail only gave us her address to get us off Percy's case. I don't like being manipulated."

"So, what's the plan?"

"We'll drop in on Edmund Questred's wine shop and ask him— ever so politely—if his wife will talk to us."

"And if the answer's no?"

"It won't be." There was the briefest of pauses before he added, "Unless she's hiding something as well."

Marlborough was much as Umber remembered it. A gently curving High Street wide enough to turn a coach and four in was flanked by handsome buildings of several eras, mostly in brick, housing a genteel assortment of shops and cafés. They drove in past the teaching blocks and playing fields of Marlborough College, scanned for a parking space—and found one in the centre of the High Street.

Almost exactly opposite them, Umber noticed, was the arcaded, tile-hung frontage of the Kennet Valley Wine Company. And Sharp had noticed it as well.

"You a wine buff, Umber?" he asked.

"Not really."

"Nor me. More's the pity." Sharp clicked his tongue. "We'll just have to play it straight down the line."

A bell rang as they entered the shop. From an office at the rear, behind the counter, a tall, thin man with wiry grey hair and a neatly trimmed beard emerged, stooping to clear the lintel. He wore a soulful expression, his face set in lugubrious, bloodhound folds, and seemed instantly to sense that they were not there to buy wine, as their conspicuous failure even to glance at the ample array of middle-of-the-road whites and reds only confirmed.

"Mr. Questred?" Sharp enquired.

"Yes," Questred replied, cautiously.

"This is going to come as a bit of a surprise. My name's George Sharp. And my friend here . . . is David Umber."

A surprise it certainly should have been. But Umber felt, as Sharp's explanation of their visit proceeded, that it was a surprise Questred had somehow anticipated, even if only subconsciously. He seemed more disappointed than dismayed, as if they were fulfilling some gloomy presentiment that he only now recalled. When Sharp had finished, Questred went to the door, flicked the sign round to read CLOSED and slipped a bolt across to ensure they were not interrupted. Momentarily, he rested his forehead against the door frame. And then he sighed.

"We're sorry about this, Mr. Questred," said Sharp. "If I could find a different way to——"

"You want to speak to Jane." Questred turned to face them. "You want to go over the same old ground again with her."

"Just a few questions. That's all."

"All? I doubt you have any conception of what *all* really covers for her. She hasn't got over it, you know. She never will. But she's learned how to survive it."

"I'm sure you've been a big factor in that, Mr. Questred."

"I'd like to think so. I didn't know Miranda or Tamsin. Or Jane while she still had them. We have a daughter of our own now. We're happy. We have a good life. Jane doesn't need any reminders of the life she used to lead."

"She's moved on."

"If you want to put it like that."

"Except she hasn't moved on," put in Umber. "I mean, not physically. She still lives in the area."

"My business is here."

"You could have relocated."

Questred looked narrowly at Umber, as if paying him more attention than he had so far. "She didn't want me to. She doesn't run away from things."

"In that case, she surely won't mind speaking to us."

"But you'll be encouraging her to run away, Mr. Umber. From the truth."

"Which is?"

"That Tamsin's dead, just like Miranda. That she isn't coming back. That there are no miracles on offer."

"Does she believe Brian Radd killed her daughters?"

"What difference does it make who killed them? *Someone* did."

"It made a difference to my wife."

"Yes." Questred's glance fell. "I'm sorry."

"We could have gone straight to your home, Mr. Questred," said Sharp softly. "But Umber here insisted we consult you first."

"I should be grateful, then." But in Questred's voice there was far more resignation than gratitude. "I'll tell Jane you want to see her. I won't try to stop her. Or to force her It'll be her decision."

"When—"

"This evening. Good enough?"

Sharp nodded his acceptance.

"Are you staying locally?"

"We will be now."

"You'd better give me a number where she can contact you." Umber moved to the counter and began writing his mobile number on the back of a Kennet Valley Wine Company card. "*If* she wants to."

Sharp had evidently noticed the Ivy House Hotel on their way into Marlborough. It was a handsome red-brick Georgian building on the southern side of the High Street. He led the way across to it, haggled briefly over the tariff and booked them in for two nights each, with an option on a third. Then they headed back to the van and drove it round to the car park behind the hotel.

"I'm going for a walk after we've unloaded," he announced en route. "Want to come?"

"No, thanks."

"Need a break from my company, do you?"

"No, George. I just need a break."

A beer and a sandwich on room service, followed by a bath and a sleep, was the break Umber had in mind. He reckoned only after that would he be fit to assess whether they had accomplished anything so far or not. Sharp seemed optimistic, but Umber suspected that was because he was enjoying being back in harness, albeit unofficially. Maybe an ex-policeman was never happier than when asking questions, no matter what answers he got.

A lot sooner than he would have wished, Umber was woken by the warbling of his mobile. He had been tempted to switch it off, but had not done so in case Percy Nevinson called. This turned out to have been a wise precaution.

"Hello?"

"David Umber?"

"Yes."

"Percy Nevinson here." The voice was indeed faintly familiar—oddly pitched and breathily nervous, with the receiver held too close to the mouth, so that the P of Percy exploded in Umber's ear. "I gather you want to see me."

"If you don't mind."

"Not at all. Pleased to help. Naturally."

"Good."

"Where are you based, Mr. Umber?"

"Marlborough. Ivy House Hotel."

"Righto. Well, I can come into Marlborough this afternoon. Why don't we meet in the Polly Tea Rooms? Four o'clock, say?"

"All right."

"One thing, though."

"Yes?"

"Just you, Mr. Umber. I'll meet you. Not the policeman."

"There's really—"

"Not the policeman."

It was a measure of Umber's exhaustion that puzzlement at Nevinson's bizarre condition for their meeting did not prevent him falling back to sleep—after setting his alarm clock for 3:30.

Well before 3:30, he was once again roused abruptly, this time by a knock at the door.

It was Sharp, back from his walk. And he was none too pleased to hear Umber's news. "Bloody nerve of the man! I hope you told him where to get off."

"I didn't feel I could, George."

"Who does he think he is?"

"Someone whose cooperation we need, I suppose."

"Inflated idea of his own importance. That's his problem." Sharp ground his jaw in frustration. "All right. Let him have it his way. This time."

"He might be more likely to let his guard down with me."

"Maybe." Sharp eyed Umber with no great confidence. "I'll just have to hope you can take advantage if he does."

The Polly Tea Rooms were as close to the centre of Marlborough's small world as anyone could hope to penetrate at four o'clock on a Monday afternoon. Its doilied delights had drawn in a contented clientele, amidst which Percy Nevinson looked by no means out of place. When Umber arrived, on the dot of four, Nevinson was already ensconced towards the rear of the café. He was kitted out in a tweed jacket and dog-tooth-patterned sweater and was making rapid inroads into a large slice of fruit cake. He could have been an eccentric schoolmaster, it struck Umber, or a vicar in mufti. But an anonymous letter-writer? Yes. On balance, he could have been that too.

"Mr. Umber." Nevinson degreased his fingers as best he could and stood up. They shook hands. "It's been a long time."

"The years look to have been kind to you, Mr. Nevinson." It was true. The man seemed scarcely to have aged at all. He was balder, though not much. That was the only detectable change. They sat down. "It was good of you to come."

"Oh, any excuse to tuck into one of the Polly's fruit cakes. That's why I arrived early. In hopes of polishing off a slice before you joined me."

"Carry on."

"Thank you. And, please, call me Percy."

"OK. I'm David."

"Yes. Of course. It's odd, isn't it, to wait twenty-three years before getting onto first-name terms?"

"It was a brief acquaintance."

"But a memorable one."

"True." Umber broke off as a waitress approached. He ordered coffee. "It was certainly memorable." Nevinson had by now embarked on a last mouthful of cake, too large to permit coherent speech. "Your sister told you why Mr. Sharp and I are here?" Nevinson nodded affirmatively. "He retired from the Force years ago, you know. You have nothing to fear from him."

"A representative of the authorities never truly retires, David," Nevinson responded after a final swallow and a gulp of tea. "You should tread carefully."

"He's simply trying to establish whether there were any clues he missed—any leads he should have followed."

"I gather neither of you believes Brian Radd was responsible."

"Do you?"

"Certainly not. But who does, apart from the police? The authorities, you see. They're not to be trusted."

"Who is, Percy?"

"You and I, of course." Nevinson held up a hand to signal for silence as the waitress returned with Umber's coffee. Then he leaned forward in his seat and resumed, in a subdued tone. "We were there. We know what we saw. The question we must both consider—have both had to live with ever since—is what did it *mean*?"

"Mean?"

"Why was the child taken, David?"

"Because some sicko got it into his head to do such a thing."

"You believe that?"

"What else can I believe?"

"And your wife? Did she believe that? Please accept my condolences on your loss, by the way. She seemed . . . a charming person."

"She was. And thank you. As for what she believed, well, she could never quite bring herself to accept that Tamsin was dead."

"Perhaps she was right not to."

"Do you have some reason, Percy—some *good* reason—to say that?"

"I think I do, yes."

"Care to share it with me?"

"It's in your own best interests that I should." Nevinson pulled out a roll of thickish paper from the inside pocket of his jacket, slid off the rubber band securing it and spread out in front of Umber a large black-and-white photograph, which he proceeded to anchor down using the sugar bowl and the teapot.

It appeared to Umber to be an aerial photograph of some desert landscape, buttes and mesas widely spaced and varied by what looked like craters and a couple of strange conical formations. Most striking of all, however, was a mound close to the centre of the picture so contoured that it looked for all the world like a relief depiction of a human face.

"Ever seen this before, David?" Nevinson asked.

"I don't think so, no."

"What do you suppose you're looking at?"

"The desert somewhere. Egypt, maybe."

"Why Egypt?"

"The formations . . . don't look completely natural. And this . . ." He pointed to the face. "I don't know. I suppose it reminds me of the Great Sphinx in some way."

"Interesting you should say that. In fact, this is a photograph of the surface of Mars taken by the Voyager One orbiter in July 1976. It's a site in the northern hemisphere known as the Cydonia complex."

"Really?"

"Really and truly."

"So, these . . . shapes . . . are just freaks of nature." Sharp had warned him about Nevinson's Martian fixation, but he had not expected it to exhibit itself so swiftly. "Unless you're going to tell me they're not natural."

"You said as much yourself."

"I said they didn't *look* natural. That's not the same thing. This . . . face . . . could be an optical illusion caused by . . . the angle of the sun."

"What about this?" Nevinson pointed to a large circular rimmed depression near the right-hand edge of the photograph.

"A crater."

"And this?" Nevinson's finger moved to one of the conical mounds, below and slightly to the left of the crater.

"An extinct volcano?"

"NASA would be proud of you."

"Percy, what has this to do with—"

"Avebury? Simple. It *is* Avebury. What you call a crater and an extinct volcano are perfectly scaled representations of the stone circle at Avebury and the artificial hill at Silbury. Or vice versa. They are precisely proportionate and have the same geometric relationship. Trace a line due north from the centres of the volcano and Silbury Hill and you'll find that the centres of the crater and the Avebury circle are offset by exactly the same angle. Nineteen point four seven degrees. Does that ring any bells? 1947?"

"The Roswell incident." Umber's heart sank. This was worse than he had first thought. Far worse.

"July's been a busy month over the years. Roswell. Apollo Eleven. Voyager One. And our own strange experience."

Alien abduction. That was it, then. Nevinson's theory of choice to explain two men in a white van, one missing girl and one dead one. Umber sighed. "Do you really believe this, Percy?"

"I've been compelled to. The evidence is overwhelming."

"So . . . Tamsin was kidnapped by Martians?"

"Certainly not." Nevinson frowned pityingly at him. "Have you taken leave of your senses?"

Umber smiled grimly. "I'm not sure."

"Wessex is an encoded landscape, David. That's what you have to understand. Avebury. Silbury. Stonehenge. Woodhenge. The long barrows. The linking avenues. There're repositories of information—of ancient secrets. But not everybody wants those secrets to be uncovered." Nevinson's voice dropped to a whisper. "By the summer of 1981, I'd gone a long way towards cracking the code. I notified the authorities of my preliminary conclusions. I thought it my duty to do so. That was a mistake. Sadly, I fear Tamsin and Miranda Hall paid the penalty for my mistake."

"How do you figure that out?"

"I believe the incident was staged to demonstrate to me that innocent people would suffer if I continued with my researches. Of course, no-one was intended to die. The driver of the van simply panicked. But Miranda's death complicated matters. I believe it's the reason why Tamsin was never returned."

"What became of her, then?"

"I don't know. I imagine she's alive and well somewhere, with no conscious memory of what occurred that day. She was only two years old, after all."

"Did you tell Sharp any of this at the time?"

"I hinted at it. But I was left in no doubt that he'd been warned off by the powers that be. Hence the need for us to meet . . . *à deux*."

"I see."

"I suspect you've been manoeuvred into accepting his assistance. His role is to ensure you don't find what you're looking for. And, before you ask, I'm afraid I can't disclose what I've learned from my study of the henges. Naturally, I've continued to work on the subject since 1981. But to share my findings with others would only be to endanger them."

"Of course."

"I strongly advise you to abandon your investigation. If you must persist, do so alone. But be aware of the risks you'll be running. They're considerable. Although . . ."

Nevinson's voice trailed off into a silence Umber felt no inclination to break. The man was mad. That was clear. Not barking. But mad nonetheless. Yet his madness at least ruled him out as Sharp's correspondent. His obsession left no room for Junian diversions. Even Percy Nevinson could not suppose that Junius was a Martian.

"I don't really need to tell you, do I?" Nevinson appeared disappointed that some prompting was required. "Your wife's sad example is a salutary one."

"What do you mean?"

"Neither of us believes she died accidentally, do we? Or by her own hand. She must have strayed too close to the truth. How close, I assume you don't know, otherwise you wouldn't be here. The desire to avenge her is doubtless considerable, but—"

Umber stood up suddenly, pushing his chair back against the vacant table behind him with a thump. It stopped Nevinson in midsentence. He goggled up at Umber in surprise.

"What's wrong?"

"Nothing's wrong. I'm leaving. That's all." Umber plucked a fiver out of his wallet and tossed it onto the table. "Not sure that'll stretch to the cake, but I'll have to leave you to settle up, I'm afraid."

"But . . . we haven't finished."

"Oh yes, we have." Umber smiled stiffly. "I've heard enough."

Umber needed a walk to calm himself before reporting back to Sharp. In the course of it, he began to suspect that Sharp would criticize him for failing to confine Nevinson to practical issues. But there it was. The man was impossible. He was also, Umber felt sure, irrelevant.

As it turned out, Umber had more time to prepare his excuses than he thought. When he reached the Ivy House, he was handed a note from Sharp. *Have gone to Devizes. Back later.* As messages went, it was less than illuminating.

Wiltshire Constabulary Headquarters was in Devizes. That fact, once quarried from Umber's memory, lodged stubbornly at the fore of his thoughts as he awaited Sharp's return. Eventually, he quit the hotel in search of dinner. On his way back from the restaurant he wandered into the Green Dragon, a quiet, smoky pub, where he sat by the fire with a pint and did his level best not to imagine what conspiracy theories Nevinson might concoct if he knew of Sharp's unannounced journey. This exercise in mental discipline was itself partly designed to prevent his dwelling on Nevinson's absurd notion that Sally had been murdered. Down that road, Umber feared, lay his own brand of madness.

At some point he remembered, to his irritation, a question he had meant to put to Nevinson. What had he wanted to show Jeremy Hall at the Adam and Eve stones that day in July 1981? It was a magnifying glass Umber had seen flash in the sunlight. He knew that because he had noticed it clutched in Nevinson's hand as they stood together at the roadside. But what had he been using the glass *for*? What had he been looking at? Marks on one of the stones that he believed were Martian runes, in all likelihood, but—

"There you are, Umber." George Sharp loomed suddenly into view. "This is the third pub I've tried. Want a half in there?"

Taken aback as much by Sharp's unwonted jollity as his unheralded arrival, Umber mumbled his thanks and struggled to order his thoughts while Sharp bought the drinks. The pub was far from busy, however. Sharp was back within a couple of minutes.

"I've missed the Wadworth's up in Derbyshire," he announced, taking a deep swallow of 6X as he sat down. "But it must be nectar for you after that gnat's piss you've had to make do with in Prague."

"Was it the beer that took you to Devizes, George? The brewery's there, isn't it?"

"Very funny. I actually went to meet an old pal of mine. Johnny Rawlings. Just about the last serving police officer I still know. He's winding down to retirement with a desk job at Headquarters. He's the only one there I can be sure will do his best to help rather than hinder and will keep quiet into the bargain. I wanted to bend his ear about the Radd case. But we'll get back to what he told me later. What did you glean from Percy Nevinson?"

"What I *gleaned* was that his choice of fruit cake to sop up his tea was all too appropriate. He's convinced Tamsin was taken by government agents to frighten him into silence about his theory explaining the Martian origins of Avebury.'

"Still stuck in that groove, is he?"

"Never likely to emerge from it, as far as I can see."

"So, like I said, a nutter."

"Fully paid-up."

"Unless . . ."

"Are you going to suggest it's all camouflage, George? A plan to have us think him a nutter when he's really . . . what, exactly? A co-conspirator of Tamsin's abductors?"

"You obviously don't think that's what he is."

"No. I don't."

"Then we'll agree to put him on the back burner for the time being. Not off the stove altogether, mind. I mean to keep my eye on him. Now, as for Johnny Rawlings——"

"Why didn't you tell me you were going to see him?"

"Oh, it was a spur-of-the-moment decision. You were busy with the Man from Mars. I thought I ought to keep busy myself. Besides, I've been planning to drop in on Johnny. It was just a question of timing. I contacted him before I went to Prague, as a matter of fact. Asked a favour of him. Reckoned it wasn't too soon to check if he'd been able to swing it for me. When I phoned, he was up for an after-work pint, so I drove straight over."

"What was the favour?"

"Two favours, really. One, the low-down on Radd's confession. Was it solicited? Was there a deal?"

"You said there couldn't have been."

"Well, it seems I was right. Johnny's had a squint through the files. Radd confessed out of the blue. No-one here or at Thames Valley had even thought of pinning Avebury on him until he did it himself. And no-one can understand why he should have done— unless he was telling the truth."

"Which we know he wasn't."

"That brings me to favour number two. I asked Johnny if he could fix it for me to meet the man himself: Brian Radd. The best way to be sure if he's lying is to look him in the eye when he tells me his tale. Well, Johnny's come through with a visiting order. I'm in."

"When will you go to see him?"

"When it suits. Radd's in Whitemoor, up in Cambridgeshire. That must be a three-hundred-mile round trip. It'll have to wait until we've spoken to Jane Questred."

"She hasn't called."

"She will." Sharp grinned at Umber. "I'm banking on it."

CHAPTER

SEVEN

Jane Questred never made the call Sharp had so confidently anticipated. But she was in touch, via her husband, who phoned Umber during a late breakfast the following morning. Hearing Edmund Questred's voice, Umber at once expected to be told that she had refused to see them. But not so.

Two hours later, Sharp nosed the van through the open gate next to Swanpool Cottage and pulled up in front of the garage. The cottage was timber-framed and thatched, every bit as chocolate-box as Abigail Nevinson had claimed. A swag of wisteria obscured the gable end. The brickwork, where visible, was intricately patterned and immaculately pointed. Grand it might not have been, but beautiful it certainly was.

The front door opened as they approached and Jane Questred stepped out to greet them. A slim, elegant woman in her mid-fifties with grey-blonde hair and delicate features, she was dressed plainly in a dark top and black trousers. Her expression was studiously neutral. She looked less wary than cautious, self-controlled and better equipped to cope with an intrusion from her traumatic past than her husband's protectiveness had suggested.

"Mr. Sharp. Mr. Umber." They shook hands. "You found your way, then."

"Thank you for agreeing to see us, Mrs. Questred," said Sharp.

"Did I have a choice in the matter?"

The question went unanswered as she led them into a surprisingly large sitting room that looked as photogenic as the exterior, pastel-toned sofas and downland watercolours blending tastefully with exposed beams and a big, rough-hewn fireplace. There was an aroma of freshly ground coffee, explained by a cafetière standing with some cups and saucers on a table in front of the fire.

"I've just brewed some coffee," said Jane Questred. "Would you like some?"

They accepted. Coffee was poured. Seats were taken. Umber's armchair put him at eye-level with a silver-framed photograph of a blonde-haired teenage girl in riding kit, being nuzzled by a pony. She looked happy and carefree, unburdened by any sense that she had succeeded or replaced two other girls who had never reached their teens. He half-heard Sharp uttering some "Nice place you've got here" platitude. But it at once became obvious that Jane Questred had no intention of trading in platitudes.

"Edmund advised me not to meet you. I generally take his advice. In fact, the only reason I didn't in this case . . . was you, Mr. Umber."

"Me?"

"You're here for Sally's sake, I gather. Well, I'm seeing you for her sake as well. Oliver and I . . . eased some of our grief . . . by blaming her for what happened. I should have taken the trouble, if not at the time then later, to make it clear to her that I never truly held her responsible. If I'd been there instead of her, it would probably have turned out the same. When I heard she'd died . . . well, I'm so sorry . . . I neglected her feelings."

"They were your daughters, Mrs. Questred," said Umber. "It was only natural for you to blame Sally to some extent. She understood that—most of the time."

"I'm glad she did."

"What she couldn't understand was your willingness to accept Brian Radd's confession. She never wavered in her certainty that there were two men in the van."

"It's easy to be confused in such a situation. I'm sure Sally *believed* there were two men. Eyewitnesses often contradict each other. Isn't that so, Mr. Sharp?"

"It is, yes. But there's no contradiction here. There never were any eyewitnesses who swore there was only one man."

Jane Questred spread her hands on her lap. She had schooled herself to remain calm, Umber sensed, to become neither angry nor upset, to answer their questions coolly and rationally. "Why should Radd confess to something he hadn't done?"

"I mean to ask him that myself."

"You do?"

"Is there some reason I shouldn't?"

"No. It's just . . . I didn't realize you meant to take things that far."

"I should have made it my business to question Radd a long time ago."

"Do you really believe he did it, Mrs. Questred?" Umber asked.

"Yes." Her certainty was implacable. "I do."

"I've only seen a head-and-shoulders press photograph of Radd, of course, but he doesn't look much like the man I saw at Avebury."

"But you only had a fleeting glimpse."

"True. I couldn't swear it wasn't Radd. What surprises me is your confidence that it was."

"He confessed."

"Even so . . ."

"Your daughter, Mrs. Questred?" Sharp nodded towards the picture Umber had noticed earlier.

"Yes."

"Nice-looking girl. Takes after you."

"Thank you."

"How old is she?"

"Katy's fifteen."

"So, she must have been . . . a babe in arms . . . when Radd confessed."

"Yes. I suppose she was."

"You'd just made a . . . new start in life."

"What are you getting at, Mr. Sharp?"

"Just that . . . you might have been ready to . . . draw a line."

"Your colleagues were happy to assure me of Radd's guilt."

"They hadn't worked the case, Mrs. Questred. I had."

"What did your husband think about Radd?" Umber asked. "Ex-husband, I mean. Mr. Hall."

"He believed Radd's confession. Everyone did. Everyone still does."

"Sally didn't believe it."

"I meant . . . everyone around me."

"Your son too?"

"Yes."

"What does Jeremy do these days?" asked Sharp.

"He runs a surfing and sailing school in Jersey. He's done very well. I'm proud of him."

"It must be nice for his father, having him on the island."

"Are you going to speak to them as well?"

"Probably, yes."

"Jeremy didn't find it easy to cope with the loss of his sisters. How could he? His adolescence was . . . difficult. Oliver and I getting divorced didn't help. But Jeremy's put those troubles behind him now. I don't want him being forced to relive them all over again."

"We can't force anyone to do anything."

"You can rake up a lot of stuff he's better off forgetting. Speak to Oliver if you must. But, please, don't bother Jeremy."

Sharp seemed wrong-footed by the request. He had admitted to Umber that he should have done a better job of investigating the Avebury case. Perhaps the least he owed Jane Questred was to spare her son's feelings. "I'll, er . . . see what I can do."

"Does that mean you'll leave Jeremy alone?"

"It means . . . I will if I can."

"Do you see much of him, Mrs. Questred?" Umber asked in an attempt to defuse the moment.

"Not as much as I'd like. He's too busy to leave Jersey very often. And if *I* go to see *him*, well . . . there's his stepmother to consider. It's . . . not easy."

"I don't suppose it is."

"And people going over there to stir up the past to no purpose won't help one little bit."

"I wouldn't say to no purpose," put in Sharp.

"Wouldn't you? Then perhaps you'd like to tell me what you hope to achieve by going into all this again. I expected you to bring something to me, Mr. Sharp—some compelling reason for reopening old wounds that for some of us have never properly healed. But you've brought nothing. There's—" She broke off, aware that her self-control had faltered. "Why are you doing this?"

A better explanation than she had so far been given was clearly called for. Sharp cleared his throat and cast a darting glance at Umber—a warning glance, it seemed.

"I had an anonymous letter, Mrs. Questred. It said the truth about the Avebury case had never come out, but could still be uncovered if I was willing to make the effort. So . . ."

"You decided to make the effort."

"Yes."

"On the basis of an *anonymous* letter."

"Yes."

"May I see it?"

"I'm afraid not. I . . . destroyed it."

"*What?*"

"I threw it on the fire. It was . . . my instant reaction. Later, I . . . decided I ought to . . . do something about it."

"So, you haven't seen this letter either, Mr. Umber?"

"Er, no."

"How very convenient."

"It's not—"

"I don't believe you, Mr. Sharp. It's as simple as that. Destroying evidence would go against the grain even for a *retired* police officer."

"I can assure—"

"Either there was no letter and you've simply dreamt it up as an excuse or there *was* a letter, which you've kept and almost certainly shown Mr. Umber but aren't prepared to show me, because . . ." She looked Sharp in the eye. "Why, I wonder? Because you think I might have written it?"

"No. I don't think that."

"Then it must be because you think I might recognize the writing, but wouldn't tell you if I did."

"There's no question of that, Mrs. Questred. I—"

"I've heard enough." The words echoed those Umber had spoken to Percy Nevinson. And he could hardly say they were any less justified. "I must ask you both to leave." Jane Questred rose to her feet and glared down at Sharp. "I don't suppose there's anything I can do to stop you going on with this. But I'll try, believe me. For a start, I'll complain to the Chief Constable."

Sharp stood up slowly and returned her gaze. He seemed minded to utter some retort, but he must have thought better of it. With a twitch of his head to Umber, he turned towards the door.

"I'm sorry, Mrs. Questred," Umber murmured as he moved past her.

"Mr. Umber," she said softly.

"Yes?" He stopped and looked at her.

"Edmund said you seemed surprised that I hadn't moved out of the area."

"I was. A little."

"You shouldn't be. I have two daughters buried here, remember. Miranda, in Marlborough Cemetery. And Tamsin, somewhere in Savernake Forest. Oliver wanted to have Miranda cremated, but I insisted on burial. I knew instinctively Tamsin was in the forest, long before Radd confessed. I often go there to be close to her. And to the cemetery, of course, to be close to Miranda. I failed them in life. I mustn't fail them in death." She touched Umber's arm. "Let them rest in peace. Please. For everyone's sake."

"Not an entirely successful visit," said Umber a few minutes later, as they started back along the Marlborough road.

"I cocked it up," Sharp growled. "You don't need to rub it in."

"You shouldn't have lied to her, George."

"I had no choice. We can't show her the letter. Like she said, we wouldn't be able to trust her. She didn't send it. That's clear. But she might have good reason to protect whoever did."

"Perhaps we should do as she asked. Lay off."

"Not before I tackle Radd."

"When will you go?"

"Right away. It's just possible Mrs. Questred might be able to get me barred from the prison. There's no time to be lost." Sharp cocked his wrist for a view of his watch. "I don't know if I can make it up there before visiting hours end for the day. But I'm going to have to try."

Sharp was in a hurry. But Umber suddenly had time on his hands. After Sharp had dropped him off in Marlborough High Street he walked up to the cemetery, set high on the hills north of the town. It was not a large cemetery. It did not take him long to find the grave he was looking for.

MIRANDA JANE HALL
1974–1981
SUFFER THE LITTLE CHILDREN
TO COME UNTO ME,
AND FORBID THEM NOT: FOR OF SUCH
IS THE KINGDOM OF GOD

MARK 10:14

From where he was standing there was a clear view across the valley of the grey-green swathe of Savernake Forest. Whenever Jane
Questred visited Miranda's grave she could also see the place where
she believed Tamsin had been laid in the earth. And she had been
to the cemetery recently. There were fresh daffodils in the vase beneath the headstone. Perhaps she had been that very morning.

He walked slowly back down the hill into the town, turning
over in his mind the question of what he should do for the best.

He did not hear from Sharp until early evening.

"The traffic was hell. I was way too late for visiting. I'm going
to kip in Molly tonight and try my luck tomorrow."

"OK."

"Anything to report?"

"Nothing."

"I don't know when I'll get back to Marlborough. It could be
late."

"Understood."

"Until then, just sit tight."

"Will do."

But Umber had no intention of sitting tight.

CHAPTER

EIGHT

Umber's enquiries the previous afternoon had prepared him for a protracted and circuitous journey come Wednesday morning. The distance he had to travel was actually quite modest. But a man reliant on public transport cannot dictate his route. So it was that shortly after daybreak he was standing outside Ladbroke's betting shop on Marlborough High Street, waiting for the number 48 bus.

To his chagrin, the timetable required him to change buses at Avebury. He had no wish to go back there so soon, if only because he feared Percy Nevinson would somehow contrive to wander past the bus stop at some point during the seven-minute interval between the arrival of the 48 and the departure of the 49. But he had no choice in the matter.

In the event, Nevinson did not materialize during his brief visit to Avebury and the banalities of village gossip, as exchanged by the other two passengers waiting at the stop, kept assorted ghosts at bay. The 49 arrived on time. And Umber climbed gratefully aboard.

Just over an hour later he was pacing the platform at Trowbridge railway station, debating with himself once again whether there was any good excuse for the covert nature of his journey. His parents would not think there was if they ever got to know about it. But explaining to them why he had come back to England was something he was willing to go to considerable lengths to avoid. One thing could not be avoided, however. He needed to establish who the mysterious Mr. Griffin was—now more than ever, given that Sharp's approaches to the problem were generating more heat than light. Griffin brought him back to Junius—and the necessity to revisit all he had once known about that enigmatic, unidentified figure from two and a half centuries ago. Maybe he had missed some clue that would have taken him to Griffin long since. Maybe not. There was only one way to find out.

The train reached Yeovil at ten o'clock. It was a fifteen-minute walk from the station to the red-brick semi in which Umber had spent his youth and where his parents seemed content to spend their old age. They were creatures of habit. Mondays, Wednesdays and Fridays were shopping mornings. There was close to no chance of their being at home. And there was scarcely any greater chance that one of the neighbours would recognize Umber. The few who might remember him no longer lived in the area.

As it happened, the street was quiet and empty when Umber hurried along it to the front gate of number 36. A few steps took him to the front door. He let himself in and stood in the hall for a few moments, testing the silence. It was total. He was alone.

This was unusual, if not unprecedented, since he had moved out for good more than twenty years ago. The sensation was strange to the point of eeriness. There were ghosts here as well as at Avebury, albeit more benign ones. In many ways, they were ghosts of himself, of his several former selves, of turnings taken in life—and turnings not taken.

He ran up the stairs to the landing, opened the door of the cupboard straight ahead of him and lifted out a metal rod with a curiously fashioned hook on one end. Then he positioned himself beneath the loft-hatch, fitted the other end of the rod to the hatch fastening and turned it. The hatch fell open. He used the hook to pull down the loft-ladder, locked it in position and climbed up into the roof.

There was a switch to his left. When he pressed it, a fluorescent light above him flickered into life. The loft was much as he remembered, an elephants' graveyard of possessions his parents no longer had any use for but had failed to dispose of: plastic bags full of old clothes and blankets, tea chests crammed with books and redundant crockery, a gramophone, an ancient television, a dodgily wired convector, an unstable ironing board; and there, in the shadow of the water tank, the thing he was looking for.

It was a white cardboard box, fastened with string. When he pulled it round, he saw, written on the side in felt-tip block capitals, the single word JUNIUS. And the writing was his.

He dragged the box to the hatchway and, cradling it awkwardly in his arms, climbed down. He was panting with the effort by the time he reached the foot of the steps and had to sit on the box for a moment to recover himself. Then he scrambled back up to switch the light off before pushing the ladder back into place and closing the hatch. He replaced the rod in the cupboard, then carried the box down to the hall: mission accomplished.

It was going to be an arduous walk back to the station. The box was heavier than he remembered. But that could not be helped. He should be there in ample time for the 11:45 train. And his parents would be none the wiser.

He opened the front door, carried the box out and put it down on the doormat while he locked up. Then he turned and picked up the box again.

That was the moment at which Umber saw the man smiling at him from the front gate. He was tall, broadly built and middle-aged, wearing a dark suit and a sober tie, his grey-brown hair cut short, his tanned face split by a sparkle-toothed grin beneath darting, humorous eyes. His left hand was resting on the latch, his right was curled round the handle of a black briefcase. He opened the gate.

"Mr. Umber?" he asked, his voice neutral and low-pitched.

"Er . . . No."

"But this is the Umber house, isn't it? Number thirty-six?"

"Yes. But . . ." Umber reached the end of the path and rested the box on the gate between them. "They're not in."

"Right." The man looked quizzically at Umber. "Any idea when they'll be back?"

"Not really. I . . ." Some kind of explanation was clearly called for, preferably one close to the truth. "I'm their son. David Umber."

"I see. Of course. My name's Walsh. John Walsh. Lynx Aluminium Windows. I have an appointment with your parents at eleven thirty. Did they mention it to you?"

"No. But . . . I don't actually live here."

"Ah. That would explain it."

"Anyway, aren't you rather early?"

"Terribly. The truth is I had a previous appointment in the area which has just been cancelled, so I called round in the hope of bringing this one forward. Looks like no dice."

"Yes. It does. I'm sure they'll be back by eleven thirty if that's when they're expecting you."

"I'm sure they will."

"Actually—"

"Can I give you a hand getting that box to your car? It looks a real handful."

"I don't have a car."

'No? Well, can I give you a lift somewhere? I may as well, with this gap in my schedule. Besides, doing a favour for a potential customer's son can't be a bad idea, can it?"

"Okay. Thanks. I need to get to the station."

"Pen Mill?"

"Yes."

"No problem."

Umber was happy to accept the lift for a reason unconnected with the weight of the box. In the course of it, he needed to give Walsh a good and compelling reason not to mention their encounter to his parents. Such a reason began to shape itself in his mind as Walsh helped him load the box into the boot of his BMW and had attained its final, appealing form by the time they set off.

"There's another favour I need to ask you, Mr. Walsh."

"Oh yes?"

"Well, it's my father's eightieth birthday in a few weeks." (A few months was nearer the mark, but the distortion was necessary.) "We're planning a surprise party for him. I've been to the house making some . . . preparations. I'd be awfully grateful if you didn't . . ."

"Spill the beans? You can rely on me, Mr. Umber. Would it be better to say nothing about running into you?"

"It would."

"You coming out of the house lugging a heavy box. Me giving you a lift to the station. It never happened."

"Exactly."

"My lips are sealed."

"Thanks."

"I like surprises. They make life more interesting. What's in the box, then?"

"I, er . . ."

"No, no. Don't tell me." Walsh flashed a grin at Umber. "The less I know the better."

A few minutes later, they turned down the approach road to Pen Mill station. Walsh swung the car round in the forecourt next to the ticket-office entrance and stopped.

"Need a hand with the box?" he asked.

"I can manage, thanks," Umber replied.

"OK. Well, have a good journey. And don't worry. Your secret's safe with me."

"Thanks a lot." Umber climbed out, closed the door and walked round to the boot.

His thumb was about an inch from the boot-release when the car suddenly surged forward and accelerated away. It was out of sight round the bend before Umber had moved a muscle.

He started running after the car. But it was a futile effort. By the time he could see the top of the approach road, the BMW had vanished.

Umber stood where he was. It had happened, but he could not for the moment believe it had happened. Walsh had stolen his box of Junius papers. But the man was not really Walsh, of course. He did not work for Lynx Aluminium Windows. He had no appointment with Umber's parents. He had come to Yeovil for the same reason as Umber. And he was leaving with what he had come for. Umber took a few faltering steps and sat down on a metal stanchion next to the cycle rack. He slammed the heel of his hand against his forehead, then slowly spread his fingers down across the eyes, pressing them shut. "You fucking idiot," was all he could find to say to himself. And he said it several times.

The tortuous journey back to Marlborough gave Umber ample opportunity to contemplate his stupidity and to measure its cost. The word JUNIUS had been plainly visible on the box. Walsh could hardly have missed it. His theft of it meant he knew what was inside. Which meant that what was inside mattered. It was important. It held a clue. Umber had been right about that. But he had let the clue slip through his fingers.

He switched his mobile off. He did not want to speak to anyone, let alone Sharp. He stared morosely at the passing scenery. Time stood still. "What do I do now, Sal?" he murmured under his breath. But he heard no answer.

The 49 bus from Trowbridge got him to Avebury just after 1:30. He went into the Red Lion and bought a large scotch. While he was drinking it, he saw the Marlborough bus drive past the window. He did not care that he had missed it. He had no clear idea of what he would do when he reached Marlborough anyway. He finished his scotch and ordered another.

When he left the pub, he crossed the road and went through the gate into the Cove—the gate Miranda Hall had run through to her death. He stood by the Adam and Eve stones and stared about him. The circle was emptier than it had been that day. There was not a living soul in sight.

He walked out by the other gate into Green Street and headed east along the lane, through the enclosing rampart of the henge and on past Manor Farm. A keen wind was blowing ragged cloud across the downs. The air was cold and cleansing. The lane became a track as it steepened. He did not look back.

Two hours later, Umber was standing outside the Kennet Valley Wine Company shop in Marlborough High Street. The walk across the downs had cleared his mind. He had been stupid. But he did not have to go on being stupid. What Walsh had done he had been put up to do. And the list of people who might have put him up to do it was a short one.

The man Umber had seen enter the shop a few moments previously emerged, clutching a clinking carrier-bag, and headed off along the street. Even before the door had swung shut behind him, Umber was through it.

He closed the door, slipped the bolt and flicked the sign round. Then he turned to face Edmund Questred.

"What do you think you're doing?" Questred demanded, round-ing the counter.

"Making sure we're not disturbed."

"I have—"

With a shove in the chest, Umber pushed him back against the edge of the counter. "You had me followed to Yeovil, didn't you?"

"What?"

"Didn't you?"

"I don't know what you're talking about."

"Just tell me why."

"Why *what*?"

"Why Junius? What in God's name is it all about?"

"You're making no sense. If you don't leave—now—I'll—"

"Call the police? It's me who should be calling them. To report a theft."

"Have you come here . . . to accuse me of something?"

"No-one knows I'm in Marlborough except you, your wife and the Nevinsons. I don't see Percy or Abigail hiring someone like Walsh—or whatever his real name is. It has to be you—with or without your wife's knowledge."

"I've hired no-one."

"But he *was* hired."

"Are you serious?"

"I was followed to Yeovil and robbed. I think you know some-thing about it."

"I can assure you I don't."

"I don't believe you."

"That's up to you. But it happens to be true. All I want you to do is to leave Jane alone." Questred did not look or sound as if he was lying. Umber's confidence faltered. Maybe he was on the wrong track after all. "If someone's stolen something from you, you should tell the police. It's got nothing to do with me. Or Jane."

The telephone in the office behind the counter began to ring. The two men looked at each other. Then Questred pushed past Umber, strode into the office and picked up the telephone.

Umber expected to hear some brief and vapid discussion of a wine order. But what he actually heard was very different. "Kennet Valley Wine Company . . . Jane? . . . What's the matter, darling? . . . Who? . . . But what did he want? . . . Say that again . . . You're sure? . . .

I don't believe it . . . But this, on top of everything else . . . Yes, of course . . . I'll come straight away . . . Never mind that . . . Yes . . . Don't worry . . . I'll see you shortly, darling . . . 'Bye."

Questred slowly put the telephone down and stared into space. There was an expression of shocked confusion on his face.

"What's happened?" Umber asked.

"It doesn't make any sense," Questred murmured. "Why now? After all this time."

"*What's happened?*"

"Sorry?" Questred seemed to snap out of his brief reverie. His gaze focused on Umber. "Jane's had a reporter on to her. Asking for her reaction to the news. It was on the radio at lunchtime, apparently, but she hadn't heard. She's quite upset. I have to go home." He took his jacket down from a hook and put it on. Then he stopped and frowned at Umber. "Did you know about this?"

"Know *what?*"

"You didn't, did you? You really didn't."

"For God's sake, man, just—"

"Brian Radd's dead."

"*Dead?*" Umber gaped at Questred in amazement. "How?"

"They say he was . . ." Questred swallowed hard. "They say he was murdered."

CHAPTER

NINE

When Umber switched his mobile back on, he found a message from Sharp waiting for him. He already knew, of course, what Sharp had phoned to tell him.

"I heard the news in a pub at lunchtime. The locals were full of it. Radd's dead. Murdered by another prisoner, apparently. Details are sketchy at the moment, but I imagine all hell's broken loose at the prison. No point me staying here now. I'll head back. I don't know what to make of this, Umber, I really don't. We'll talk later. 'Bye."

Umber went back to the Ivy House and learned a little more from the Ceefax service on the television in his room. Radd had been found bleeding from a stomach wound, probably inflicted with a knife, in a toilet cubicle at the prison at about nine o'clock that morning. He had been rushed to hospital, only to be pronounced dead on arrival. A police murder inquiry was under way.

Umber stared at the words on the screen for several long minutes, shock giving way slowly to something closer to fear. The media would regard this as a fittingly violent end for a child murderer and rapist: rough justice dispensed by a fellow prisoner. But they were unaware of the pattern it fitted into. Even Sharp did not yet know what had happened that day in Yeovil and what both events seemed to imply. Someone was on to them. Someone had decided to stop their investigation in its tracks. And they were willing to kill to do it.

The trilling of his mobile fractured Umber's thoughts. He answered, guessing it would be Sharp, calling en route from Cambridgeshire. But he had guessed wrong.

"Hello?"

"David? Percy Nevinson here."

"What can I do for you?"

"I felt I had to call in view of the extraordinary turn of events. You've heard about Radd, I take it?"

"I've heard."

"Another mouth's been shut, it seems. There's no chance of him withdrawing his confession now, is there? At least this time no-one's in any doubt that it *was* murder."

"I can't talk about this, Percy. Not now."

"I understand your reticence, David. Perhaps you're wondering who to trust in such a situation. I can assure you—"

Umber switched the phone off. He could take no more of Nevinson. The report of Radd's murder was still there, on the television screen. He pressed the standby button on the remote. The screen went blank. He lay back on the bed.

He was not thinking about Radd any more, or the theft of his Junius papers. It was Sally's death five years ago and the circumstances surrounding it that filled his mind.

Umber had been in Turkey when it happened, roasting in the heat of Izmir. Sally had been living in a flat in Hampstead, lent to her by her friend Alice Myers. Late June had not brought tropical conditions to London. And Sally had always felt the cold more than most. The bathroom of the flat was unheated. It was possible to believe—just—that she had trailed a fan heater into the bathroom to warm it. There was a chair close to the bath, on which the coroner theorized she might have stood the heater, then somehow tipped it into the bath as she reached for a towel. Alternatively, she might have deliberately pulled the heater into the bath with her, fully knowing what the consequences would be. That was what most of her friends believed, grateful though they were to the coroner for not concluding as much. The absence of a note and Alice's testimony that Sally had been in better spirits than for some time sufficed for him to give her the benefit of the doubt. No-one had suggested murder, of course. No-one had considered such a possibility, nor looked for evidence of it. The idea would have been dismissed as absurd, not least by Umber. He had felt certain that Sally had taken her own life.

Now, five years later, he was certain of nothing.

He headed out for dinner, the thoughts still running round in his brain. Was it possible? Could Sally have been murdered? *"She must have strayed too close to the truth,"* Nevinson had said. Could he be right after all?

From the restaurant, Umber went to the Green Dragon. He had hoped to slink into a quiet corner, but the pub was staging a quiz night and there were no quiet corners. He swallowed one pint and left.

Back at the Ivy House, the receptionist told him Sharp had returned in his absence. He went straight up to Sharp's room.

He could hear a newscaster's voice through the door as he approached. In response to his knock there was a gruffly bellowed "Come in."

Sharp looked a weary man, slumped in front of the television with a glass of whisky, waiting for a report on Radd's murder to crop up on Sky News. He muted the sound and poured Umber a generous slug from the bottle of Bell's he had bought somewhere along the road.

"I didn't see this coming, Umber," he said. "It never crossed my mind."

"Child murderers aren't top of anyone's popularity list, George."

"That's not why he was killed and you know it."

"I do, yes. You could say I've had . . . independent confirmation of that."

Umber described his experiences in Yeovil, keen to have the anticipated outburst of scorn from Sharp over and done with. Drained of much of his pepperiness by his own experiences, however, Sharp merely grunted and growled and rolled his eyes during Umber's account. Then he topped up both their whiskies and switched off the television altogether.

"Shall I tell you where we are, Umber? Out of our bloody depth. That's where."

"You ought to know I'm beginning to think Sally may have been murdered."

"Yes. I suppose you were bound to. Which means you won't be prepared to drop it now, will you?"

"I can't."

"Thought so." Sharp rasped his hand round his unshaven chin. "Only you should bear in mind Radd may have been taken out in order to warn us off."

"I can't let that stop me, George. Not if they killed Sally."

"All right, then. We go on."

"You're not going to allow yourself to be . . . warned off?"

"Good God, no. What do you take me for? My professional pride's been dented. I need to hammer it back into shape. Starting with the question of who—deliberately or not—tipped off these people we're dealing with. Hardly anyone knew I was even thinking of going to see Radd."

"Your friend Rawlings knew."

"He promised to keep it under his hat. He wouldn't break a promise to an old mate."

"Are you sure about that, George?"

"A lot surer than I am about Jane Questred. She knew."

"Not until yesterday morning."

"No. But she said emphatically she was going to do whatever she could to stop us. So, let's find out *what* she did. And *who* she contacted."

"If anyone."

"Like you say. If anyone. But everything we try is a long shot. It's bound to be. Take Donald Collingwood for example. I stopped in Swindon on the way back and checked his old address."

"Dead and gone?"

Sharp nodded. "More than ten years." He mulled over that for a moment, then said, "A drop in the bucket compared with two hundred and fifty odd, though. What was in your Junius box that made it worth stealing?"

"I don't know. My Ph.D. research notes aren't exactly state secrets."

"No? Well, somebody wanted them, Umber. Badly. And since they were *your* notes, you're the only one likely to know why."

"There's no reason that makes any sense."

"What were they about?"

"Well . . ." Umber shrugged. "Junius."

"Can't you be a bit more specific?"

"All right." Umber rubbed his face. "Let's see. I'd started going through the list of candidates—all the people who'd ever been accused, even semi-seriously, of being Junius. There were fifty or sixty of them all told. My idea was to disprove each one conclusively before proceeding to the next. That involved checking their whereabouts at times when we could be sure where Junius was, based on the content of his letters, comparing their known political opinions with Junius's expressed views, examining examples of their handwriting and prose style for similarities to—"

"Hold on. What about that War Office clerk you mentioned as odds-on favourite? Did his handwriting match Junius's?"

"No. But then it's generally assumed Junius wrote in a disguised hand. There's also the possibility he employed an amanuensis."

"A what?"

"Someone to copy the letters for him before they were sent. There's a separate list of candidates for that role."

"Can you remember all the names on these lists?"

"Not after more than twenty years, no. But I could reassemble the lists. If I had to."

"And your notes too, I suppose."

"That would take months. I'd have to reapply for membership of several libraries for a start. You're not serious, are you?"

"No. But I was just thinking. Maybe the thief stole them to stop you looking at them rather than to look at them himself."

"Does it make any difference?"

"Not sure. But we should be grateful to him in one way."

"What way's that?"

"Well, Radd could have been killed because of a straightforward grudge between him and another prisoner. It's possible. Or it would be, but for your run-in with a double-glazing salesman impersonator the same day. We're on to something, Umber. We're definitely on to something." Sharp grinned ruefully. "It's just a pity we don't have the first bloody idea what."

It was agreed they would set off for Swanpool Cottage at nine o'clock the following morning. It was also agreed they would both benefit from an early night, though Umber for one did not anticipate a restful one. He watched the Ten O'Clock News report on Radd's murder. It told him nothing he did not already know. Then he switched his mobile on and checked for messages. There was one. And it was not from Percy Nevinson.

"This is Edmund Questred, Mr. Umber." He had spoken very softly, almost whispering into the receiver. *"We need to speak. Don't phone me. Come to the back door of the shop at eight thirty tomorrow morning. Please don't contact Jane in the meantime."*

Umber thought about phoning Sharp, then thought better of it. He might already be asleep. If so, it was a kindness to let him sleep on.

There was to be little sleep for Umber himself. He tossed and turned, counting Junius suspects like sheep, but to no avail. He made it to twenty or so, a long way short of the total. And then he thought about Sally. He had schooled himself for so long *not* to think about her death and the manner of it that it almost felt as if he was doing so for the first time. It was difficult to remember how weary he had been of her inability to put the past behind her; and how relieved he had felt in the months following their separation. The guilt that had swept over him the minute he heard she was dead—that was clear in his mind, however. He pictured her, lying lifeless in the bath, as Alice had found her. He had loved her. He had abandoned her. There had been no excuse. But maybe now there could be the next best thing to reconciliation—reparation.

There was no sign of Sharp in the breakfast room when Umber left the hotel next morning. He walked up past Marlborough Library and followed the lane round to the rear of the High Street shops. There was a small delivery yard at the back of the Kennet Valley Wine Company. The double doors leading to the storeroom behind the shop were ajar. He stepped through.

Questred was waiting for him inside. He was sitting on a wine box, smoking a cigarette and staring listlessly at a newspaper, folded open at an inside page. CHILD MURDERER SLAIN IN PRISON KNIFING ran the headline above the article he appeared to be reading. He did not rise at Umber's approach, merely looked up and nodded to him.

"You got my message, then."

"As you see."

"Jane reckons you and Sharp will be in touch with her today."

"Very likely."

"She reckons you'll have taken it into your heads that some-thing she did led to this." Questred held up the newspaper.

"Well, it's quite some coincidence, isn't it?"

"The only person she told about your visit was Oliver. She phoned him straight after you left the cottage. But he wasn't at home. She left a message, asking him to phone back as soon as possible. She didn't say why. And he didn't call until last night, so . . ."

"It really was a coincidence."

"You obviously don't think so."

"Do you?"

"No." Questred smiled grimly. "Does that surprise you?"

"Yes." Umber sat down on the nearest box. "It does."

"There's something I have to tell you. In confidence. I don't want it to reach Jane's ears. I'd deny saying it if it did, anyway, and she'd believe me over you every time. It's, er, about . . . your wife."

"Sally?"

"Yes. I . . . This Radd business has shaken me, I don't mind admitting. I don't know what to make of it. I—"

"What about Sally?"

"Yes. OK. Sally. Well, the day she died . . ." Questred rubbed his forehead. "That is, I realized later it was the day she died."

"What happened?"

"She phoned here . . . that afternoon."

"She phoned *here*?"

"Yes. She, er, wanted to speak to Jane, but she didn't have the number for the cottage and, er, well . . . I wasn't about to give it to her." Questred dropped the butt of his cigarette onto the concrete floor and ground it out with the toe of his shoe. "Anyway, she asked me to get Jane to phone her. She didn't give a reason. I didn't ask for one. To be honest, I, er, thought she sounded . . . overwrought. I told her I'd pass the message on. But, er . . ."

"You didn't."

"No. I didn't want her upsetting Jane. So, I said nothing about it when I got home. And I said nothing about it when we heard she was dead either. In fact, this is the first time . . . I've mentioned it to anyone. I, er, didn't think it mattered. Well, I persuaded myself it didn't. And maybe I was right."

"Or maybe not."

Questred looked cautiously at Umber. "I didn't expect you to take this so calmly."

"I've already done a lot of thinking about Sally's death. What you've just said only reinforces my suspicion she was murdered."

"Oh God. Do you really believe that's possible?"

"Yes. I really do."

"But that would mean . . ." Questred shook his head. "Christ knows what it would mean."

"I intend to find out."

Questred rose and moved to the door, where he stared out at the wedge of sunlight advancing slowly across the yard. "I'm frightened, Umber. That's the truth."

"So am I."

"Do you have to see Jane?"

"That's up to Sharp."

"How would it be if I arranged for Oliver to speak to you? He's got state-of-the-art security at his place in Jersey. You won't get past the gate if he doesn't want you to."

"In return for leaving Jane alone?"

"Yes."

"That'd be up to Sharp as well."

"But you could put it to him."

"Yes." Umber stood up. "I could."

And he did, over the breakfast he found Sharp polishing off back at the Ivy House.

"We only have his word for it that Jane didn't speak to anyone else," Sharp objected.

"He didn't have to tell me about Sally's call, George."

"True."

"And Hall could refuse to see us if he was so minded."

"Also true."

"So what do you think?"

"I think we'd better accept his generous offer." Sharp eyed Umber over a jagged triangle of toast. "Don't you?"

CHAPTER

TEN

It was unclear exactly how long it would take Questred to set up a meeting for them with Oliver Hall. Sharp gave him a twenty-four-hour deadline to concentrate his mind, then booked Umber and himself out of the Ivy House and headed for London.

"We can stay with an old pal of mine from the Met, Bill Larter, while we wait to hear from Hall," he announced as they drove towards the M4. "I gave him a call from the hotel. He'll be glad of the company. Not that he'll let you know it. Besides, he won't see much of us. We'll be busy. And this time you'll be calling the shots. Who can we talk to about Sally's activities in the days and weeks before her death?"

"Alice Myers was her best friend. She owned the flat Sally died in. Still does, presumably. If anyone knows what was going on in Sally's head at the time, it's Alice."

"We'll start with her, then."

"But there's a problem. Alice is anti-Establishment to her fingertips. Spent a whole winter in the eighties camped out at Greenham Common. Obstructs the police on principle. She'll clam up in front of you."

"What are you trying to say, Umber?"

"I'll get more out of her on my own, George. It's as simple as that."

"Huh." Sharp said nothing more for a mile or so, then resumed, the affront to his status evidently shrugged off. "All right. Leave me out of it. There's something else I need to do anyway."

"What's that?"

"Alan Wisby. Does the name ring any bells?"

"I don't think so."

"He was a private detective Oliver Hall hired when my investigation ran into the sand. You and Sally would have been in Spain by then, but if Wisby was doing a thorough job, which I—"

"Hold on. Yes. A private detective did come to see us. I can't remember his name. Insignificant sort of bloke."

"That would be Wisby. I can't blame Hall for going down the private route when it became obvious I was getting nowhere, but he could have done better than Wisby."

Umber was not going to argue with that. He recalled a short, thin, whisper-voiced chain-smoker, a pale streak of English winter in the Catalan spring. Sally had taken an instant dislike to the man. But he had not stayed long enough to become a nuisance. He had asked his questions, they had answered them and he had gone, with little or nothing to show for his trouble.

"I don't know how long Hall kept him on the case, but he'll have got bugger all for his money. Wisby was a wash-out. Anyway, according to *Yellow Pages*, he's still in business, so I was thinking of dropping by his office."

"Do you think you'll get anything out of him?"

"Shake a tree, Umber, and it's surprising what falls out. If Jane Questred didn't tip anyone off about our activities, you have to ask yourself: how were we rumbled?"

"And *Wisby's* the answer?"

"Probably not. But he's worth a visit. You see, it's occurred to me Junius may have sent the same letter I got to anyone else who was involved in investigating the case. And Wisby falls squarely into that category."

Sharp dropped Umber in Hampstead High Street and headed on his way. They had agreed to meet later at Bill Larter's home in Ilford. Umber had fewer qualms about his reception there than at Alice Myers' home, where he had last set foot, lingering for all of ten excruciating minutes, on the afternoon of Sally's funeral.

Alice lived in a tall, elegant Victorian house about halfway between the High Street and Hampstead Heath. She occupied the ground and first floors, where she worked as well as lived, while renting out the basement and the top floor. It was the top-floor flat she had given Sally the use of following her return from Italy. And it was there, on the evening of Thursday, 24 June 1999, that Sally had died by supposedly accidental electrocution.

Alice's multiple occupations of fabric designer, curtain-maker, cello teacher and political activist all had 22 Willow Hill as their hub. Umber was therefore confident he would find Alice in. But there his confidence ended.

There was no immediate response to the bell, but he hesitated to ring again. Then he heard a faintly vexed cry of "Coming." Alice, it seemed, was already preparing a less than fulsome welcome before she even knew who her caller was. A second later, the door was yanked open.

Umber never ceased to be surprised by Alice's size. Her name and her feathery voice created in the mind's eye an altogether slighter person than she actually was. Her outfit on this occasion—a baggy paint-spattered boilersuit—merely exaggerated her bulk. There were flecks of paint in her hair as well, flamingo pink amidst the pigeon grey, and one on the arm of her round, gold-framed spectacles, through which her large brown eyes regarded Umber with widening dismay.

"Oh my God," she said. "David."

"Long time no see," Umber responded, smiling uncertainly. "Can I come in?"

"Sure. I'm . . . in the middle of decorating." She led the way down the hall. They passed one room, bare of furniture, where a tide of pink had advanced halfway across the ceiling and a roller stood propped in a paint-tray against a stepladder. The next room contained the furniture displaced from the first room, crammed in with its own. By simple elimination, they ended up in the kitchen. "Do you want some tea?"

"All right. Thanks."

Alice filled the kettle and switched it on, then plucked two tea bags from a jar. "Green OK? Well, it's all I drink, so . . ."

"It's OK."

"You should've told me you were coming."

"What would you have said if I had?"

"That I was decorating."

"Anyway, it was a last-minute decision."

"Just passing through?"

"Not exactly."

Alice leaned back against the worktop and gave him a long gaze of scrutiny. "You look kind of strung-out."

"I feel kind of strung-out."

"I heard you were in Prague."

"I was."

"Home for good?"

"I doubt it."

The kettle boiled. Umber sat down at the kitchen table while Alice dunked the tea bags. A rumpled copy of the *Guardian* lay by his elbow, folded open at an inside page. There was a different headline from the one in Questred's paper, but the same grainy mugshot beneath it of Brian Radd, lately deceased paedophile.

"I owe you an apology, Alice."

"You do?" She glanced over her shoulder at him.

"Leaving like that. Without even saying goodbye."

"It was a tough day for everybody. Tougher for you than for most, I guess."

"I bet that's not what you thought at the time."

"It was five years ago. I'd just lost my best friend. I thought lots of things." She delivered the mugs to the table and sat down opposite Umber. "I'm sure I thought I'd never see you again, for instance. Certainly not here."

"Read this?" He turned the newspaper round to face her.

She frowned. "That's surely not what's brought you here."

"Do you know why I left so abruptly after Sally's funeral?"

"Afraid people would give you a hard time, I guess."

"I reckoned I deserved one. I felt ashamed for running out on her. Guilty for what had happened."

"It wasn't your fault."

"Whose fault was it, then?"

"No-one's. There's no blame . . . in situations like that."

"But what *was* the situation? I should have asked more questions. I should have forced myself to understand. We all should have."

"Things just got too much for her. There's nothing else to say."

"I think there is. Everyone was so eager not to challenge the verdict for fear we'd have to admit it was suicide that no-one asked whether it could have been . . . something else altogether."

"Such as?" Alice stared at him in bemusement.

He folded his hands together and looked at her over them. "Has it ever occurred to you, Alice, that Sally might have been murdered?"

"*What?*"

"It's occurred to me, you see. As a very real possibility."

"I don't believe this. I really don't." She shook her head to emphasize the point. "You turn up out of the blue after five years—five years of *silence*—and you tell me you think my best friend might have been murdered. In my house. Without me noticing. I mean, what did I do, David? Mistake the murderer for the plumber and let him in, saying hello, help yourself, you know where everything is?"

"Obviously not."

"Sally was alone when it happened. *On her own*. And you know what? It takes two to murder as well as tango. Give me a break."

"How do you know she was alone?"

"*How?*"

"Yes. It's a simple question."

Alice's expression suggested that it was less simple than stupid. "She was in the bath, David. Have you forgotten that? Where did this murderer suddenly spring from? There was no sign of a break-in, down here or up there."

"Perhaps he tricked his way in."

"And she decided to take a bath while he was still there? You know as well as I do how ludicrous that would be. Her problem wasn't people coming to see her. It was people *not* coming to see her."

"You said at the inquest she'd been in good spirits."

"*Irrationally* good spirits, I thought, when I looked back on it, though I didn't say so to the coroner, obviously. She'd broken her last appointment with Claire, you know."

"Who?"

"Claire Wheatley. Her psychotherapist. And a good friend of mine. She was at the funeral. I think you spoke to her. Don't you remember?"

"No." Such conversations as Umber had had at Sally's funeral he had done his level best to forget. "I can't say I do."

"Sally was supposed to see her earlier that week. She'd been doing well, according to Claire. They had regular Monday afternoon sessions. I remember seeing Sally set off at the usual time. She just never turned up at the other end. Well, that's not strictly true, but—"

"What do you mean?"

"She got as far as the waiting room at Claire's practice, then walked out a few minutes before she was due to go in. Claire couldn't get any kind of an explanation out of her over the phone, so she asked me to find out why. But I got nowhere. Sally told me not to worry about it. Airily dismissed the whole thing. She was in a hurry to leave when we had the conversation. I remember she said she was going to Wimbledon. The Championships had just begun, but, hey, when was she ever interested in tennis?"

"Maybe she wasn't going to the tennis."

"Oh, but she was. She told me so. I asked if she had a ticket and she said, 'I don't need a ticket.' It was all so unlike her. Claire thought she must have been yo-yoing by then—alternating between extremes of elation and despair. It was Wednesday morning when I spoke to her—the last time I *ever* spoke to her. By Thursday evening, she must have hit bottom."

"Hard enough to kill herself—by electrocution?"

"You know she had a horror of pills. Maybe it was the only way she could think of. When I found her the next day . . ." Alice looked away. When she spoke again, her voice had thickened. "I don't want to be reminded of this, David, I really don't. You could have asked me all these questions five years ago, but you chose not to. Why now?"

"Strange things have been happening."

She turned back to face him. "What kind of things?"

"The policeman who investigated the Avebury case got an anonymous letter recently, telling him Radd didn't do it. Now Radd's dead. And I've learned Sally tried to contact the Hall girls' mother the day she died."

"Are you sure?"

"Yes."

"What did she want?"

"I don't know."

"But you have a theory."

"I think she may have been getting close to the truth."

"The truth?"

"About what happened at Avebury."

"But she'd accepted what had happened—and Radd's part in it. Claire told me so. It was a measure of the progress they'd made."

"She never . . ." Umber stopped. He could not swear to what

Sally had come to believe in the last months of her life. He had made certain of that by walking out on her.

"You didn't know, David. You weren't here. I was. Sally wasn't chasing after answers. If anything, she was running away from them. You've got this all wrong."

"I don't think so."

"She wasn't murdered. That idea's plain crazy."

"This psychotherapist, Claire . . . whatever her name is . . ."

"Wheatley. Claire Wheatley. She's highly respected."

"Could you fix it for me to meet her, Alice?"

"For Christ's sake. What purpose could that possibly serve?"

"Well, you seem to think I'm crazy. Maybe I need some counselling."

"Maybe you do. But you can arrange that yourself. I take it you really want to see Claire so you can run your murder theory past her."

"If she's as good as you say she is, I'm sure she could cope with it."

"That's not the point."

"Isn't it? Look, Alice, you're right about me. I wasn't anywhere close when Sally most needed me. But let's be honest, you and Psychotherapist of the Month didn't exactly bring her through smiling and dancing either, did you?"

Alice compressed her lips, clearly determined not to start trading insults. There was a brief, fragile silence. Then she said softly, "All right. I'll ask Claire if she's willing to meet you."

"Thank you."

"I can't force her to agree."

"I don't expect you to try."

"But somehow I doubt you'll take no for an answer."

Umber shrugged. "Let's hope she says yes."

"Nothing you do can bring Sally back."

"Of course not."

"Why stir it all up, then—to no real purpose?"

"Oh, there's a purpose."

"Is there? Truly?"

"Remember what you said when I asked you what the point was of you and your peace sisterhood setting up camp at Greenham Common? 'Sometimes the right thing to do is the only thing to do.' That's what you said. I thought you were mad. But you know what? You were never saner. I just didn't understand what you meant. I understand now."

Reviewing his visit to Alice on the Tube into central London, Umber could not decide whether it had gone well or badly. Alice had reacted as all Sally's friends might be expected to react. Umber stood accused of deserting Sally in her hour of need. Querying the circumstances of her death five years later looked at best futile, at worst ghoulish. But that could not be helped. It was far too late to tread carefully. Alice had not agreed to plead his case with Claire Wheatley because he had asked nicely.

From Euston he walked the short distance to the British Library and joined the queue at the admissions office. His membership had lapsed long before the move from Bloomsbury. He did not know how quick or easy re-registering would be. In the event, he was browsing the catalogue in the Humanities Reading Room within an hour of his arrival. Within another hour, he had placed his order for half a dozen of the most obvious Junius-related books. It was too late to expect them to be available that afternoon. He settled for first thing the following morning.

Umber had switched off his mobile while he was in the Library. He switched it back on as soon as he was outside and checked for messages. There was one, from Oliver Hall. Hall could not have timed his call better if avoiding a telephone conversation had been his specific intention.

"*Mr. Umber, this is Oliver Hall.*" The voice was low-pitched and subdued, the enunciation surgically precise. "*Edmund's told me of your concerns. I'm willing to meet you. There's no need for you to come to Jersey. As it happens, I have to be in London on business next week. I'm flying over on Sunday. We can meet at my flat that evening. It's in Mayfair. Fifty-eight, Kingsley House, South Street. Would six o'clock be convenient for you and Mr. Sharp? Perhaps you could leave a message for me there on the answerphone. 020-7499-5992. Thank you.*"

Umber bought a coffee from the kiosk in the Library courtyard and sat on a bench, drinking it, while listening to the message over again. Oliver Hall sounded polite, even obliging. But his response was unmistakably calculating. Meeting in London rather than Jersey denied Umber and Sharp the opportunity to engineer an encounter with Jeremy. And giving them only the London number to reply to meant they could not argue about it even if they wanted to. Umber rang as requested and confirmed the appointment.

He was still sitting on the bench five minutes later, finishing his coffee, when his phone rang. Alice, it transpired, had wasted no time in keeping her promise.

"David, this is Claire Wheatley." The voice was faintly familiar, but Umber could put only the fuzziest of faces to it.

"Thanks for calling . . . Claire. Alice must have spoken to you."

"Yes. She has."

"Can we meet?"

"If you like. But to be honest—"

"I know you think it's pointless. So does Alice. Shall we just take that as read?"

"I actually suggested you come and see me when we met at Sally's funeral, David. You obviously don't remember."

"No. Sorry. I . . ."

"Look, I'm rather pressed for time. I'm going away for the weekend and I'm fully booked for Monday. But we could meet during my lunch break. How would that be?"

"Is that the soonest you can manage?"

"Yes." The clipped reply instantly made him regret asking.

"OK. Monday it is."

Oliver Hall and Claire Wheatley had both played for time. Umber turned the coincidence over in his mind during the train ride out to Ilford. They had agreed to meet him. But they had given themselves a breathing space. There was nothing he could do about that. He could force the issue, but not the pace. Besides, their delaying tactics were almost a vindication. They needed to prepare themselves. Which prompted an obvious question: what did they think they were preparing themselves *for*?

CHAPTER

ELEVEN

Umber reached Ilford with a trainload of weary commuters, exiting the station into a damp and windy twilight. According to his *A–Z*, Bengal Road was close by, but he contrived to follow a tortuously indirect route to it thanks to mistaking which side of the station he was on.

His destination was a street of terraced, bay-windowed, red-brick houses. Number 45 was one of very few whose front garden had not been converted into a car port. There were no lights showing at the windows. But there was a folded sheet of paper wedged in the letterbox.

It was a note from Sharp. *Gone to the pub. Turn right into Riverdene Road and follow it to the Sheepwalk.*

The Sheepwalk, it transpired, was the name of the pub. It was full to bursting at the close of the working week, the bar inaccessible through a smoke-wreathed ruck of drinkers. Umber blundered around aimlessly until he spotted Sharp at a fireside table in an alcove behind the blinking and beeping fruit machine.

Sharp's table-companion was a big, broadly built man of about the same age, with greased grey, centre-parted hair and a raw-boned, lantern-jawed face. He looked tall, even though he was seated, and had a red, bulbous nose that could as easily be owned by a boozer as a boxer.

"You made it, then," was Sharp's growled greeting. He looked glum and liverish. "Bill Larter. David Umber."

Larter gave Umber a crushing handshake as he sat down and a peremptory nod. "Want a drink, boy?"

"I'll get one in a minute. I just—"

"My local, my shout. Best bitter?"

"Er, yeah. Fine."

Larter unwound himself from his chair and drained his beer glass. "You ready for another, George?"

"Why not?"

Larter grabbed both glasses and steered a passage towards the bar, favouring his right leg as he went. Umber watched him go, then looked back at Sharp, whose expression suggested that his day had not gone well.

"To save you the trouble of asking, Wisby was a dead end."

"Not literally, I hope."

"Might as well have been. His ex-wife runs the business now, would you believe. Trades under Wisby's name on account of his reputation. Some people must have had a higher opinion of him than I did, that's for sure."

"He's retired, then?"

"Yes. But not to any traceable address. Plies the canals on his narrowboat, apparently. Grand Union. Leeds and Liverpool. Take your pick. He could be anywhere."

"Well, that cuts two ways, George. If we can't track him down, Junius can't have written to him, can he?"

"I suppose not." Sharp thought for a moment, then seemed to brighten. "How did you get on?"

"Do you want me to go into it all in front of Bill?"

"You can trust him with the secrets of your soul. He already knows a good few of mine."

"Fair enough."

Larter returned with the drinks part way through Umber's report of what, by comparison with Sharp's search for Wisby, constituted solid progress. It was obvious, though, that Sharp shared his suspicions of Oliver Hall. Hall was prepared to meet them, yes, but only at a time and place of his careful choosing.

"Business in London, my arse," was Sharp's succinct assessment. "He's trying to make sure we have no good excuse to go to Jersey."

"You can't blame him for that."

"We'll see about what we can and can't blame him for come Sunday."

"And until then?"

"Well, you'll be busy poring over the archives. There's not a lot *I* can do. Looks like you get your wish, Bill."

Umber watched the two old men exchange a smirk and waited for an explanation. Larter eventually supplied one after a lengthy swallow of beer.

"West Ham are playing at home tomorrow. George and me are going to take a stroll down memory lane."

Another pint later and Sharp and Larter had decided not to wait until Saturday to wander the byways of the past. Umber was left to sup in silence as they reminisced about crimes and colleagues of long ago. His attention drifted. He thought of Sally and their life together—and the short remainder of her life apart from him. He was tired and a little drunk by now. He could not seem to assemble all the implications of her death—and the manner of it—in his mind. He could not—

"Penny for them," said Larter suddenly, leaning close to his ear.

"What?" Looking up, Umber saw that Sharp had gone—to the loo, presumably.

"Not getting my old mate into more trouble than he can handle, are you, boy?"

"No more than he is me."

"That's what I was afraid of. The pair of you, egging each other on. There's no telling what you might bring crashing down on your heads."

"Reckon we should drop it, do you, Bill?"

"Bloody certain you should. But you won't. Not a chance. You've both got the same look in your eye."

"What look's that?"

"The damn-the-consequences look. But consequences can be treacherous. You should never damn them till you know what they are."

"I'll remember that."

"No you won't." Larter smiled. "Not until it's too late, anyway."

They returned at closing time to Larter's spotlessly clean and spartanly furnished house. Sharp took the bed in the spare room, leaving Umber the sofa in the sitting room downstairs. The arm at one end folded flat, which was a blessing, but the springs were pushing through the padding, squeaking and digging at every turn. And there was a lot of turning for Umber that night, as he dwelt on Larter's warning and all the good reasons why they should abandon their search for an elusive truth that they might not like much if and when they ever found it.

He did not feel a lot better come morning. But his determination was intact. Larter insisted on cooking him a bacon-and-egg breakfast to see him on his way. Sharp was still not up when Umber left. "Sleeping it off," was Larter's judgement as he walked him to the door. "And he's not as young as he used to be." To which the old man added, as Umber stepped out into a dank Ilford morning: "You should remember that as well."

Umber was not as young as he used to be either. A day's reading in the British Library proved a test for his eyesight as well as his concentration. It was also a sobering reminder of just how much he had forgotten about the subject he had once known so well, in every obscure detail.

Junius. The tormentor of politicians. The darling of the *Public Advertiser*'s readership. The tantalizer of his many hunters. Who was he? Who *could* he have been? The editor of the OUP's *Letters of Junius* provided a list of sixty-one names. It was essentially the list Umber had set himself to work through for his thesis. Most of them had had a book or pamphlet written in support of their claim. *Junius Discovered. Junius Identified. Junius Revealed. Junius Unveiled. Junius Unmasked. Junius With His Vizor Up.* It was a morass as well as a mystery. A researcher could sink without trace in the murky depths where half-forgotten candidates for the role were silted up for posterity. And nowhere amongst them, Umber greatly feared, would he find Mr. Griffin lying obligingly in wait.

He left when the Library closed, at five o'clock, with a sheaf of photocopied pages from various books and a bundle of notes. The copious note-taking with a pencil had given him a sore thumb, an aching wrist and a keen envy of those about him equipped with laptops. He had gone about his work the hard way, laboriously reassembling the basics of his long-lapsed mastery of all matters Junian, little good though it seemed to have done him. He could only hope that when he reviewed his findings with a fresh eye the next day something he had so far missed would reveal its hidden significance to him.

He was mentally drained and in no mood to hear Sharp and Larter describe their afternoon at the football. He drank a couple of pints in the pub opposite the Library, then, on a woozy whim, took the Tube to Green Park and made his way through the quiet streets of Mayfair to Kingsley House.

It was a five-floor red-brick apartment block, exuding an immaculately pointed air of reticent affluence. Quite why Umber had gone there he could not properly have explained. Oliver Hall had said he would fly over on Sunday, so there could be no question of catching him unawares. And yet, and yet . . . Umber stood on the other side of the road, gazing up at the few illuminated windows, wondering if he should try his luck. In the end, it seemed absurd not to.

He climbed the short flight of steps to the gleaming array of bell-pushes and pushed the one for number 58. He lingered for a few moments, expecting no response. Then there was a crackle and a female voice addressed him through the adjacent grille.

"Yes?"

"Mrs. Hall?" It was the best guess as to her identity Umber could make.

"Yes."

"Er, my name's David Umber."

"You left a message for my husband."

"Yes. So I did."

"He's expecting you tomorrow. He's not here yet."

"Tomorrow?" Umber decided to play dumb. "Oh, I see. I'm sorry. I thought . . . I must have got the day wrong."

"Yes. You must."

"Can I . . . perhaps . . ."

"You'd better come up." The door-release buzzed.

Why Mrs. Hall had let him in was a question he found no answer to during the brief lift-ride to the third floor. She could easily have sent him packing. But she had chosen not to. It was not as if he had done much to talk his way in. She had simply decided that she wanted to see him.

The door of flat 58 was ajar when he reached it. He stepped inside, closing it behind him. The flat was warm and softly lit, decorated as if for an interior-design shoot, with lots of empty space round sleek, oversized furniture. Guitar music was playing in the high-ceilinged drawing room, smoke from a cigarette drifting up sinuously into cedar-scented air. Next to the ashtray on a long, low table in front of the artfully faked fire was a slew of magazines—*Tatler*, *Vogue*, *Hello!*—and a chunky tumbler containing what looked like a very large gin and tonic.

Mrs. Hall had been peering into the huge oval mirror above the fireplace, removing an errant eyelash, when he entered. She was a slim, strong-featured, blonde-haired woman in her mid-forties, expensively dressed in a dark red shot-silk suit with high-heeled sandals. Umber assumed she was readying herself to go out. As she turned to greet him, he questioned his instant estimate of her age. Mid-forties was what she looked, but she could have been older. She was not a woman likely to deny herself whatever it took to maintain her appearance.

"There you are," she said, her voice poised and neutral, devoid of accent. "I'm Marilyn Hall." They shook hands. "Won't you sit down?"

"Thanks." He sat opposite the sofa where the positions of the ashtray and tumbler suggested she had been sitting.

"Would you like a drink? I'm having a G and T."

"The same for me would be fine."

"Great." She moved to a cabinet in the far corner of the room and poured his drink. The trim-jacketed, short-skirted suit flattered her. Umber could not fail to notice as much.

She returned with his drink and sat down. He half-raised the glass and sipped from it. "It was . . . good of you to see me."

"I could hardly turn you away when you'd come all this way." She took a long draw on the cigarette. "I often get confused over dates myself."

"I suppose I'm lucky . . . there's anyone here."

"I've been over doing some shopping. Oliver knows I have to hit Bond Street sooner or later. Jersey may be a tax haven. But fashion? Forget it."

"Did he tell you . . . why we've arranged to meet?"

"Oh yes. Jane's been on to him. Everyone's in the loop, David." The use of his first name sounded entirely natural, for all its suddenness. "Radd's murder"—she smiled—"has really put the cat among the pigeons."

"You think so?"

"What do you do for a living?" she asked, blithely ignoring his question.

"I'm kind of . . . between livings at the moment."

"Do you think that's why you've started down this road?" She gazed at him, defying him to be offended by her candour. "Too much time on your hands?"

"I don't believe Radd killed your husband's daughters."

"Somebody did."

"Does Oliver . . . talk about them much?"

"No."

"Do you ask him?"

"No."

"A closed subject, then?"

Marilyn shrugged. "Isn't that what the past should be?"

"I don't think so, no. Especially when we don't understand it."

"Ah. I see." She sipped at her drink. "But, then, Oliver tells me you're a historian, so I guess . . . that makes you biased."

"Not biased. Just . . . inquisitive."

"Well, inquire away. I can't help you. And you'll get nothing out of Oliver."

"Is that so?"

"Take it from one who knows."

"How long have you been married?"

"Long enough."

"How's your stepson?"

"Oh, Jeremy's fine. Just fine."

"It must have been difficult for you, marrying a man with so much tragedy behind him."

"Oliver's very resilient."

"He's needed to be."

"Are you in London for long, David?" Marilyn's ability to pose questions out of the blue was already apparent to Umber. Less apparent to him was the direction such questions were likely to take them in.

"Not sure."

"I'm here for at least another week."

"Really?"

"What's in the bag?" She nodded towards his holdall.

"I've been doing some research."

"Into what?"

"Eighteenth-century politics."

"Amazing."

"But true."

She chuckled. "I'm sure it is."

"Ever hear the name Junius?"

"No."

"Or Griffin?"

"Some sort of . . . dragon?"

"Some sort. Yes."

"Oliver tells me you're a widower as well as a historian."

"That's true."

"Being alone . . . after years of love . . . can't be easy."

Umber could find no response to that. He was in truth surprised by the degree to which Marilyn had taken him aback. He stared into his glass and swallowed some gin.

"If you are alone . . . that is."

He managed a smile. "More or less."

"Would you like to go to the theatre with me next Thursday?"

"What?"

"I have a couple of tickets. It's Shakespeare. Your sort of thing, I imagine. And Oliver's. But he's not going to be able to make it. It seems a pity to waste the seat."

She was asking him out. It seemed barely credible. But it was true. She was a mature and attractive woman, unafraid to hold his gaze. She knew what she was doing. What she had said merely skimmed the surface of what she meant. An offer of some kind was on the table. Who ran the bigger risk—she by making it, he by accepting it—was far from clear. But in that uncertainty, her half-smiling expression implied, lay the object of the exercise.

Umber cleared his throat and swallowed some more gin. "Which play?" he asked.

Marilyn leaned back in the couch and blew some smoke towards the ceiling. "Does it matter?" she said softly.

CHAPTER
TWELVE

Umber said nothing to Sharp about Marilyn Hall's theatre invitation. He told himself this was because it was not entirely clear he had accepted it and, besides, it was even less clear he would still be in London come Thursday. "Call me on the day," Marilyn had ambiguously concluded. She had been casting frequent glances at her wristwatch by then, as if this visit was threatening to make her late for something. It had been time for him to leave. Though there had been just time enough for Marilyn to pose a parting question.

"Would you prefer me not to mention your visit to Oliver?"

"Why should I?"

"Oh, just because . . . he might not believe you'd mistaken the day."

"But won't it be rather awkward for us to pretend we haven't met?"

"Not really. I won't be here, you see."

"No?"

She had smiled. "Oliver's choice."

"Well . . . in that case . . ."

"I'll say nothing."

"It was a bloody stupid idea to go there in the first place," Sharp complained when Umber reached Ilford and reported what had happened.

"Maybe," Umber admitted. "But, as it turns out, I've got the better of Oliver Hall without him being aware of it. He didn't want us to meet Marilyn, did he? Well, now one of us has."

"And what have we got out of you meeting her?"

"The knowledge that she and Oliver don't trust each other."

"We might have been able to work that out anyway. The question you should be asking yourself is whether *you* can trust Marilyn Hall to keep her mouth shut."

"I think so."

"You *think*?"

"Time will tell, George."

In that regard, time was bound to tell. In terms of Umber's Junian researches, it seemed much less likely to prove revelatory. He spent most of the daylight hours of Sunday sitting at the table in Larter's dining room sifting through the notes and photocopied extracts he had brought back from the Library—to little avail.

The sixty-plus candidates for Junius's identity resolved themselves to fewer than twenty serious possibilities. Those were the ones Umber had concentrated on for his thesis. Yet there were, he now recalled, objections to all of them. Some of the objections were weightier than others. But none were insubstantial.

Umber wrote out his shortlisted names on a fresh sheet of paper, in strictly neutral alphabetical order. There were sixteen in all. He then struck out the names eliminated by strong circumstantial evidence, usually their absence abroad at times when Junius was writing chatty notes to Woodfall to accompany his public letters, containing information available only to someone actually resident in London. That reduced the list to eleven. Next to go were those who died before Junius wrote his last private letter to Woodfall in January 1773, emphasizing he would never go into print again. The list was pruned to nine. Next went those with whom Junius had engaged in private correspondence, writing to oneself to divert suspicion being a plausible tactic only if done publicly. The list was shortened to six: Edmund Burke, Lord Chesterfield, Philip Francis, Lauchlin Macleane, Lord Temple and Alexander Wedderburn. But Burke and Wedderburn were both lawyers by training. They would surely have avoided the legal blunder Junius made during his attack

on Lord Chief Justice Mansfield in his last public letter. The list
shrank to four.

Umber knew that if he worked at it he could reduce the figure
to zero. Philip Dormer Stanhope, 4th Earl of Chesterfield, was a
septuagenarian relic of a bygone political age when Junius began
writing his letters. He was plainly too old and too ill to have been
responsible for them. Philip Francis was an obscure War Office
clerk, too young, some would say, and too low in the pecking order
to be the author. Lauchlin Macleane was an unprincipled Irish-
Scots adventurer with a taste for political intrigue. The Scots were,
however, routinely abused by Junius and Macleane himself attacked in a letter generally reckoned to have been written by Junius
under a different pseudonym. Richard Grenville, 2nd Earl Temple,
shared many of Junius's prejudices, but was the brother of George
Grenville, with whom Junius engaged in private correspondence
without any apparent fear of recognition.

Modern historians had settled on Philip Francis. His opinions,
his character and his whereabouts fitted Junius like a glove. A
computer-aided stylo-statistical analysis had also fingered him as a
habitual user of Junian phrases and constructions. His youth and
his junior station counted for little in the face of that. Case closed.

Not quite. The handwriting was the problem. There was no similarity at all between his and Junius's. This was explained away by most
experts as evidence of Francis using a disguised hand when writing as
Junius. Fine. But Junius wrote fluently and elegantly, while Francis
scratched away crabbedly all his life. The disguised hand should logically have been inferior to the real thing, not the other way round.

Amanuenses entered the argument at this stage. And certainty
went out by the opposite door. Francis seemed too secretive a man
to have employed an amanuensis and nobody could suggest who he
might have chosen for the role in any case. Meanwhile, some
graphologists detected a similarity between Junius's handwriting
and that of Christabella Dayrolles, wife of Lord Chesterfield's godson Solomon Dayrolles. Thus, bizarrely, the finger of suspicion took
a late swing back towards its least credible target—a half-blind,
stone-deaf and largely bedridden old nobleman, who had died two
months after Woodfall's receipt of Junius's very last letter.

———

Christabella Dayrolles. The name chimed distantly in Umber's memory. Yes, that was it. She was the subject he had been working on at the end of the Trinity term at Oxford in 1981. She was the seemingly trivial point his researches had arrived at, never, in the event, to progress beyond. He could recall little of what he had learned about her and there was nothing in any of the books he had consulted to assist him. If he still had his boxful of Junius papers, it would be a different matter. But he did not. Christabella Dayrolles was, for the moment, out of reach.

"What *do* you know about her?" Sharp demanded when Umber explained the problem to him during their drive to Mayfair late that afternoon.

"Precious little. Her husband was a career diplomat and a favourite of his godfather. Chesterfield's letters to Dayrolles are a treasure trove of information on Georgian politics and court life. Mrs. Dayrolles was . . . Dayrolles's wife. Mother of his children. Keeper of the domestic flame. Stereotypical eighteenth-century female. Or not. I don't know."

"But her handwriting resembles Junius's?"

"Yes. Superficially, I seem to remember. More than Philip Francis's does, that's for sure. But Chesterfield as Junius? I could never buy that."

"What about her husband, then?"

"Dayrolles? He's never been in the frame."

"Why not?"

"Because . . ." Umber hesitated. It was a good question. And there was a good answer, he felt certain, though he could not for the moment recall what it was. He had been trying to connect Mrs. Dayrolles with Junian suspects other than Lord Chesterfield when he had abandoned his researches in the summer of 1981. His efforts had taken him nowhere—as far as he knew at the time. But perhaps they had taken him closer to the truth than he could ever have suspected. "I'm going to have to go back into it, George. That's all I can tell you."

"Well, maybe you won't have to. if Oliver Hall gives us a lead."

"Yeah," said Umber half-heartedly. "Maybe."

Umber did not expect anything to have changed at 58 Kingsley House. But Marilyn's absence and Oliver's presence turned out to constitute more than a simple swap of hosts. The atmosphere was cooler, almost chill. There were fewer lights on. There was no music. The tone of everything was palpably different.

Umber remembered Oliver Hall as a quiet, reserved, smartly suited man in his early forties. He had less hair than a couple of decades before and what there was of it was grey. He had developed a slight stoop and a turkey neck. He was wearing what Umber took to be his idea of casual dress—razor-creased trousers, cashmere sweater, check shirt. He looked neither relaxed nor nervous. He did not offer them a drink. He made no overtures. They had his attention. That was all.

"I never expected to see either of you again," he said when they had sat down. "It's doubly surprising . . . to see you together."

"I assume you've spoken to your former wife about our visit to her," said Sharp.

"Oh yes. I'm fully apprised."

"What about Sally's attempt to phone her just before she died?" put in Umber. "Did Questred tell you about that?"

"You can assume I know everything I need to know," Hall replied.

"She didn't by any chance try to phone you as well, did she?" asked Sharp.

"Not as far as I know."

"Can't you be sure?"

"No."

"Why not?"

"Because she might have phoned me, got no answer and failed to leave a message."

It was a precise and incontrovertible answer. Hall's lawyer would have been proud of him. It gave nothing away—except, of course, his reluctance to give anything away.

"Has Radd's murder made you doubt his guilt, Mr. Hall?" Umber asked.

"No."

"It's made Questred doubt it."

"I can't say that surprises me. Edmund's a rather woolly thinker."

"What about your son?" asked Sharp. "How does he feel about it?"

"The same as I do, I imagine."

"You *imagine*?"

"We haven't actually discussed the matter."

"Don't you think you should?"

"I'm sure we will. At some point. Jeremy clearly isn't concerned about it. Otherwise he'd have contacted me."

"You don't see a lot of each other, then?"

"As much as we both want, Mr. Sharp. Neither more nor less."

"Relations with a step-parent can be difficult, I'm told. Maybe your remarriage . . . put some distance between you."

Hall smiled faintly as if amused by the blatancy of Sharp's attempt to prod a nerve. "No. It didn't."

"How does he get on with . . . Mrs. Hall?"

"Very well, thank you."

There was a magazine lying on the table in front of Umber. It was the *Culture* supplement of the *Sunday Times*, folded open at the theatre reviews page. The RSC production of *All's Well That Ends Well* at the Gielgud had been given a chunky write-up. He could not stop himself glancing down at it before he looked across at Oliver Hall, who was already looking straight at him. "Has she come over with you?" Umber asked in as idle a manner as he could contrive.

Hall nodded. "Marilyn's in London with me, yes." Once again the studied accuracy of his statements was apparent. She had not come over *with* him. He had not claimed as much. But it was the inference he would happily have let Umber draw.

"Sorry we've missed her," Sharp remarked.

"Your business is with me," said Hall. "There's nothing Marilyn can tell you."

"There doesn't seem to be much you can tell us either."

"True, I'm afraid. But . . ." Hall leaned back in his chair and spread his hands in a gesture hinting at conciliation. "I accept your motives are honourable. I believe you're mistaken, though. Radd was responsible for my daughters' deaths. There's nothing any of us can do to bring them back. I've learned to accept that." He fixed his gaze on Umber. "Others must learn to accept their own loss. The idea that Sally was murdered . . ." He shook his head. "It's simply not credible."

"I believe it," said Umber, with quiet emphasis.

"So do I," said Sharp.

"I see." Hall looked at each of them in turn. "Well, let me tell you what I have in mind, then. I have business in the City tomorrow and the day after. I still sit on one or two boards. I can't get down to Marlborough until Tuesday night. That's really the soonest I can manage. It'll take time to talk all this through with Jane. And with Edmund, of course. But that's what we need to do. Discuss your concerns . . . calmly and rationally. Then . . ."

"Yes?" Sharp prompted. "What then?"

"Report back to you, Mr. Sharp. What else? If a joint discussion leads any of us to question the official view of the case, I can promise you our full support in reopening the inquiry."

"You can?"

"Absolutely. I believe we already know the truth, dismal and tragic though it is. If I'm wrong, or if everyone else *thinks* I'm wrong . . ."

"All bets are off?" suggested Umber.

"Yes." Hall smiled at him. But the smile did not reach his eyes. "If you want to put it like that."

Nothing was said during their ride down in the lift. For no logical reason, Umber felt unable to speak freely until he was off the premises. Sharp evidently felt much the same. They were in fact halfway between Kingsley House and the van before either of them broke the silence.

"He thinks he's got us where he wants us," said Sharp.

"And has he?"

"This trip to Marlborough he's oh-so-reasonably agreed to take is just for show. He'll come back after a couple of days and tell us they're all singing from the same hymn-sheet: Radd guilty; Radd dead; end of story."

"What can you do if that's the plan, George? You can't stop him going. Or dictate what he says to the Questreds when he gets there."

"No. I can't."

They reached the van and climbed in. Sharp started away promptly and did not speak again until they were turning into Berkeley Square.

"I don't have to sit around twiddling my thumbs while he plays his little game, Umber. And I don't intend to."

"So what *do* you intend to do?"

"I'm going to Jersey."

"You are?"

"No better time to size up Jeremy Hall than when his father isn't there to interfere."

"You promised his mother you'd leave him out of it."

"If I could. Well, I can't. Not any longer."

"When do we go?"

"*We* don't. *I* do. I'm driving down to Portsmouth tonight. I've booked Molly and me on tomorrow morning's ferry. We sail at nine."

"You've already booked the ferry?"

"Yup."

"But . . . you couldn't have known . . . what Oliver Hall was going to say."

"I could have cancelled if he'd proved more open-minded than I expected. Doubted he would, though. And I was right."

"What am I supposed to do?"

"Go see Sally's therapist. Knuckle down to your research on Mrs. Dallyroll. And cover my tracks if Hall or the Questreds get in touch before we're ready for them."

"When'll that be?"

"No way to tell." Sharp braked to a halt at the traffic lights on Piccadilly and glanced round at Umber. "Let's just hope it's before *they're* ready for *us*."

THIRTEEN

Irritated though he was at Sharp for booking his passage to Jersey without telling him, Umber could not deny that it made sense for one of them to go while Oliver Hall was out of the way. Umber was not free to leave London, so there was no choice: it had to be Sharp. His excuse for keeping Umber in the dark was that it had spared him from lying to Hall. Umber reckoned it was more likely Sharp feared he might give the game away. Since he had not been entirely open with Sharp about his dealings with Marilyn Hall, however, he was in no position to complain.

With Sharp aboard the ferry to Jersey, due to dock in the late afternoon, Umber spent Monday morning at the British Library. He ordered a further batch of books, which were certain to take several hours at least to be fetched, then worked his way through various entries in the *Dictionary of National Biography* in search of background information on what he now remembered referring to in his original researches as the Dayrolles Connection.

The known facts were tantalizingly meagre. Solomon Dayrolles was the nephew and heir of James Dayrolles, British Resident at The Hague for many years until his death in 1739. The date of Solomon Dayrolles's birth was unrecorded, but could hardly have been later than 1710 and was very possibly earlier, given that his first diplomatic appointment was as secretary to Lord Waldegrave, Ambassador to Vienna, a post Waldegrave held from 1727 to 1730. Dayrolles's uncle obtained the position for him through the influence of the young Lord Chesterfield, who was Solomon's godfather, despite the fact that he was born in 1694 and could therefore have been no more than a youth at the time of Dayrolles's birth.

Chesterfield was at this period winning his spurs as the great wit and cynic of Georgian political life. He had been a favourite of George II when the latter was still Prince of Wales, but offended the King after his accession by his attacks on the Prime Minister, Sir Robert Walpole. Chesterfield drifted into the opposition camp and the circles of the new Prince of Wales, George's hated son, Frederick.

Dayrolles meanwhile became a wealthy man on the death of his uncle and bought Henley Park, a country estate near Guildford, as his English residence. When the fall of Walpole restored Chesterfield's political fortunes and he was appointed Lord-Lieutenant of Ireland, Dayrolles accompanied him to Dublin as his secretary.

In 1751, Dayrolles married the eighteen-year-old Christabella Peterson, daughter of an Irish colonel. The couple had four children—a son and three daughters—and the marriage in no way affected his relations with Chesterfield, who had by then retired from active politics.

Chesterfield's old age was afflicted by tragedy—the sudden death of a beloved son—and illness. When he died, in March 1773, his godson-cum-friend was at his bedside. The Earl's last words were reported to be: "Give Dayrolles a chair."

Solomon Dayrolles died in March 1786, his widow Christabella in August 1791. Not until William Cramp produced his book *Junius and his Works compared with the Character and Writings of the Earl of Chesterfield* in 1851 did anyone suspect or suggest that Mrs. Dayrolles might have written the letters of Junius at Chesterfield's dictation. Cramp's theory was generally ridiculed on account of the Earl's age and infirmity, the similarities between Mrs. Dayrolles's handwriting and that of Junius dismissed as insignificant.

The handwriting. That was the nub of it. The similarities were too striking to be rejected without further study. Umber could remember thinking that when he had inspected some examples for himself, wildly improbable though Chesterfield's authorship of the Junius letters nevertheless seemed. He had learned what more he could about Christabella Dayrolles, though it had not been much and it had taken him nowhere. But where had he learned it *from*? There was no clue in the DNB entry for her husband.

Or was there? Umber read the two columns devoted to the life of Solomon Dayrolles again. Then he recognized a long-forgotten name. Ventry. The Dayrolleses' eldest daughter, also called Christabella, had married, in 1784, the Hon. Townsend Ventry. There were some documents, categorized as the Ventry Papers, lodged in a county records office somewhere. Umber had gone to take a look at them.

But *where* had he gone? The dusty interior of one records office was much the same as another. He recalled an airless Midlands town on a hot afternoon. Derby. Nottingham. Leicester. Somewhere like that. But it was all he *could* recall.

Nor did he have time to dwell on the point, a glance at the Reading Room clock reminding him that he would be late for his appointment with Claire Wheatley if he did not stir himself. He made a hasty exit and headed for the street.

A taxi ride got him to his destination with several minutes to spare. Claire Wheatley's practice was not in Harley Street, but it was close enough to the medical heartland to count. She shared a smart address in Wimpole Street with an acupuncturist and a reflexologist.

The first-floor waiting room was empty and the door to the room beyond ajar. Somebody on the other side of it was playing back telephone messages. Umber half-pushed, half-knocked, at the door and went in.

Claire Wheatley was sitting at a desk, with her feet propped on one end, munching a sandwich between sips from a small bottle of mineral water. Umber did not recognize her. She was thinner and shorter-haired than the woman he had persuaded himself he remembered and looked several years younger, big-eyed and pixie-faced. She was dressed all in black: zip-fronted top, pleated miniskirt, tights and suede boots. Her legs were long and shapely and hard not to notice, given how prominently they were on display. Her spikily cropped hair was black as well, though most of the colours of the rainbow glistened in her dangling ear-rings. They swayed kaleidoscopically as she put down the bottle, switched off the answerphone and swung her legs to the floor.

"Sorry," she said, swallowing a mouthful of sandwich. "I'd planned to have finished this before you arrived."

"We did say one fifteen, didn't we?"

"Yeah. But my noon appointment ... kind of overran." She packed the rest of the sandwich back in its wrapper and stood up. "Do you want to sit down?" She gestured towards a pair of soft leather armchairs as she rounded the desk. "What about a cup of tea or coffee?"

"I'm fine, thanks."

"You don't look it."

"Sorry?" He stopped and stared at her.

"You don't look fine." She smiled blithely. "I'm just telling it like it is."

"Do you take that line with your patients?"

"They're clients, not patients. And no, I don't. But this is my lunch hour. So, you get the real me, not the therapist. Please. Sit down."

He lowered himself into one of the armchairs. Oddly, Claire made no move to sit down herself. She stood behind the chair opposite him, leaning over its back and frowning at him. "Well," he said, with an effort at ingratiation, "it *was* good of you to agree to see me. Thanks."

"What have you been doing since Sally died, David?"

"Teaching, mostly. In Prague for the last two or three years."

"Prague's a beautiful city."

"So it is."

"I'd have looked you up when I was there, if I'd known."

"When was that?"

"Summer before last." She grimaced. "Not good timing, actually."

"The floods."

"Exactly. Of course, I was just a visitor, so there was a kind of grim fascination about it. How did it affect you?"

"I was in England at the time. My flat had the Vltava flowing through it and there wasn't a thing I could do."

"Lose much?"

"Not much. Just everything."

Claire nodded thoughtfully, then walked slowly round the chair and sat down in it. She straightened her legs and leaned forward slightly, her hands clasped between her knees. She fixed him with her round-eyed gaze. "Alice seems to think you're out of work. Is that right?"

"Yes and no."

"It doesn't take a psychotherapist to spot the equivocation in that answer, David."

"How I make a living is irrelevant."

"Not really. You lost your wife five years ago. You lost most of your possessions—including most of your tangible reminders of Sally, I assume—eighteen months ago. Now you've lost your job. Sounds like there's a gaping hole where most people your age have a family, a career and a fairly clear idea of the direction they're headed in."

"A hole you think I'm trying to fill by chasing after Sally's ghost?"

"That's not exactly how I'd put it."

"How would you put it, then?"

"Are you sure you want to know?"

"I can take it, Claire." Umber forced a smile. "Remember. It's your lunch hour."

"OK." She smiled too, gently acknowledging the riposte. "I have the advantage of knowing you quite well already, you see, through Sally. And through Alice too. Of course, that doesn't neces-sarily give me a balanced view, but even Alice admits you have some redeeming qualities. You're not a monster in anyone's eyes. You left Sally because you were worn out by her. Maybe you'd have gone back to her eventually. We'll never know, will we? Because Sally's dead. She committed suicide, David. You know it. I know it. Those left behind tend to blame themselves for not doing enough to prevent a suicide. We know that as well. Because we've both blamed ourselves for not saving Sally. But if she didn't kill herself—if she was murdered—well, we wouldn't be to blame, would we? We'd be off the hook."

"Did Alice tell you *why* I think Sally was murdered?"

"Yes."

"It obviously didn't impress you."

She shrugged. "I saw Sally at weekly intervals during the last months of her life. You didn't."

"You never suspected she might do away with herself, though, did you?"

"I was aware we were . . . treading a thin line. I thought we were the right side of it. I was wrong."

"Why do you think she did it?"

"Because she'd spent eighteen years believing in the possibility that Tamsin Hall wasn't dead, but couldn't go on believing it. Because she'd lost you for the sake of that fantasy and ruined her life in the process. Because, in the end, she'd run out of hope."

"Not a success story for your style of therapy, then?"

"All right. I'm not going to hide behind some elaborate conspiracy theory so I can deny failing her. I should have done more. I should have intervened."

"Why didn't you?"

"It's not always easy to spot the warning signs."

"Maybe there weren't any."

"Perhaps there weren't enough. The change in her behaviour was certainly sudden. It became irrational by anyone's standards. You've spoken to Alice. You know what I mean."

"She might have walked out on her appointment with you because she'd suddenly realized you weren't doing anything for her."

"OK." Claire smiled weakly. "I guess I deserved that." She leaned back in the chair. "I admit our last meeting went badly."

"The appointment before the one she broke, you mean?"

"No. I saw Sally the day she died."

That stopped Umber in his tracks. He stared at Claire in silence for a moment, then said, "Alice didn't mention that."

"She doesn't know. I guess I was too ashamed to tell her. Though I'd have told you, if you'd given me the chance . . . after the funeral."

"You've got the chance now."

"Yes. That's really why I agreed to see you, to be honest. Even psychotherapists need to unburden themselves sometimes. And hearing how she was that day . . . may help you understand."

"Go on."

"Well, I was worried about her. It's as simple as that. Nothing I'd heard from Alice had reassured me. And I couldn't get Sally to speak to me on the phone. So, I went to Hampstead to see her. As it turned out, I never got to Alice's house. I spotted Sally sitting in a coffee shop near the Tube station. This was about . . . ten o'clock in the morning. I went in and tried to talk to her. It didn't go well. Truth is, her attitude annoyed me. Stupid of me to let it happen. Very unprofessional. But there it is. I asked her about the broken appointment and she just dismissed the subject. "Something else cropped up." That was her answer. Which made no sense, obviously. Then I spotted the magazine she'd been reading. It was from my waiting room. My PLEASE DO NOT REMOVE sticker was still on the cover. That riled me. Such a petty thing, too. Anyway, I asked if and when she was planning to return it. I must have sounded so pompous. She got up, threw the magazine at me and walked out. 'You don't need to worry about me any more,' she shouted. Those were the last words she ever spoke to me. I should have realized, of course, what they really meant."

"Which was?"

"That I needed to worry about her like never before." Claire rubbed her hands together, then parted them in a gesture of helplessness. "I'm sorry I let her go like that, David. Sorry I didn't . . . save her from herself."

"Don't be."

"Because it wasn't herself she needed saving from? That won't wash. You know it won't."

"Maybe something else really had cropped up. Maybe *something else* is why she was murdered."

"The truth about what happened at Avebury twenty-three years ago?"

"Exactly."

"Don't you think Oliver Hall would have uncovered that, given the lengths he went to?"

"Sally told you about the private detective he employed, did she?" Claire frowned. "No. How could she?"

"We're taking about Alan Wisby, right? The guy Oliver Hall hired when he gave up on the police investigation. The guy who came out to Barcelona to question Sally and me."

Claire was still frowning. "Wisby was his name, yeah. But he came to see me a few months *after* Sally's death."

"He did?"

"Yes. I had no idea he'd been working for Hall from way back. He never said so."

"But he did say he was working for Hall *then*?"

"Yes. He explained that Oliver Hall wanted to find out why Sally had killed herself in case it had some bearing on his daughters' deaths."

Wisby had still been on the trail five years ago. That meant Oliver Hall had been on the trail. Why would he have been? He had claimed only yesterday to have accepted Radd's guilt long since. Had Sally been in contact with him, despite his assurances to the contrary? "What did you tell Wisby?" Umber asked, hastening to catch up with the lie he had caught Hall out in.

"Nothing. I don't discuss my clients with passing strangers. I'm only discussing Sally with you because you were married to her."

"So you gave Wisby the brush-off?"

"I told him his employer had no reason to enquire into the matter."

"Wisby accepted that?"

"He asked a few questions. When he realized he wasn't going to get anywhere, he gave up and left."

"What sort of questions?"

"He wanted to know what had been on Sally's mind in the months before her death. He quoted a name at me. Asked if Sally had mentioned it. Well, she hadn't and I said so. It seemed the easiest way to get rid of him."

"What was the name?"

"Gosh, I can't remember now. Somebody linked with the Avebury case, I suppose. I didn't recognize it."

"Nevinson?"

"He was the other witness, right? No. That wasn't it."

"Collingwood?"

"No."

"Sharp?"

"The policeman? No."

Umber hesitated, then threw out one more name, sure in his own mind of the answer Claire would give. "Griffin?"

"Yes," she said, confounding him. "That was it."

C H A P T E R

FOURTEEN

Half an hour later Umber was walking fast along South Street. The probable futility of his journey to Mayfair had not restrained him. He stood a better chance of finding Oliver Hall at home in the evening, but he could not wait till then. He knew himself well enough to understand that he could not return to the British Library without first trying his luck at Kingsley House.

He recited to himself as he went the multiplying significances of what Claire Wheatley had told him. Oliver Hall did not believe Radd had killed his daughters. He did not believe Sally had killed herself. He did not even believe both of his daughters were necessarily dead. Wisby had been working for him all these years: probing, enquiring, ever seeking the answer. And the answer had something to do with Griffin.

"Yes?" It was Marilyn's voice, responding just when Umber had convinced himself there would be no answer.

"David Umber here."

"David?"

"Yes."

There was a fraction of a second's pause. Then the door-release buzzed.

The door of the flat was ajar, as before, and the warmth had been restored to it. The music was back, more wallpapery this time, soothingly electronic. Marilyn walked along the passage from the bedrooms to greet him, towelling her hair as she came. She was wearing fluffy mules and a peach-coloured dressing gown, belted at the waist. The material of the gown was soft and clinging. She did not look to be wearing anything beneath.

"This is a surprise," she said. "I thought you'd wait till Thursday."

"I was looking for your husband "

"In banking hours? Here?"

"Sorry if I . . . disturbed you."

"That's OK." She smiled. "I was just taking a shower. London's such a dirty city, isn't it?"

"Er, yes. Yes, it is."

"Coffee? Tea? Something stronger?"

"No thanks. I won't stop."

"That's a pity."

"When will he be back?"

"Oliver? Hard to say. Six? Seven? I don't know." She tossed the towel over a radiator and padded past him into the drawing room. He followed, a few paces behind. "Do you want to leave a message for him? I think we'd better come clean about your visit this time, don't you? We don't want to push our luck." She caught his gaze in the mirror above the fireplace.

"You could tell him I've found out about Wisby."

"Who?"

"The private detective he's hired "

"First I've heard of it. What was the name?"

"Wisby. Alan Wisby."

"Are you sure about this, David?" She turned to look at him directly. "How long has this man been working for Oliver?"

"More than twenty years, off and on."

"And what's he been investigating? Or is that a stupid question?"

"Anything but, given how certain Oliver said he was that Radd was guilty."

"I see. Well, I'll certainly tell him. Of course, he may deny employing the man."

"I expect he will."

"Then, what do you gain by asking him? If he's been using a private detective, he's been doing it without my knowledge. So, he's pretty well certain to deny it. And if he hasn't, he'll deny it anyway. Either way, you won't believe him."

"I can prove Wisby's been working for him."

"How?"

"Wisby approached Sally's psychotherapist on Oliver's behalf."

"Really?"

"Claire Wheatley. She's a disinterested professional. And she was emphatic on the point. Wisby made it clear to her he was working for Oliver."

"Perhaps he was lying."

"Somebody's lying."

"If it's Oliver, he's not likely to stop now. Are you sure you want me to tell him you know about Wisby—assuming there's anything to know?"

Suddenly, Umber was far from sure. Marilyn's casual cynicism regarding her husband's honesty was strangely disarming.

"This trip he's taking to Marlborough—wouldn't you be better off challenging his *word* after he's had his *tête-à-tête* with Jane?"

"Whose side are you on, Marilyn?"

"Whose do you think?"

"Not mine."

"You could be wrong about that."

"Could I?"

"Tell you what. I'll make you an offer. As a sign of my . . . intentions."

"What kind of offer?"

"I stand a much better chance than you do of finding out for certain whether Oliver's had this man Wisby on some kind of long-term retainer—and, if so, why. As a matter of fact, I *want* to find out. In case I'm one of the subjects he's been enquiring into."

"Surely not." Umber could not resist playing Marilyn at her own game to some degree.

"Stranger things have happened."

"And the offer?"

"I'll pass on everything I learn to you."

"Why would you do that?"

"Because I know nothing about this, David. And Oliver isn't supposed to have any secrets from me. If he has, well, I might need an ally. Someone I can trust."

"Think you can trust me?"

"Yes." She smiled. "Of course I do."

"I'm not sure you can."

"Well, maybe hope's a better word, then."

"Ever heard of somebody called Griffin?"

"No."

"Sure?"

"I think I am." She gazed at him in silence for a moment, her eyes narrowing slightly. Then she said, "Or is hope a better word again?"

Umber felt both encouraged and disturbed by his visit to Kingsley House. He sat in a coffee shop in Curzon Street, trying to sift the good from the bad in his mind. He had a lead, of sorts, and a spy in the enemy camp whose reliability was questionable to say the least. The Halls were pursuing different and conflicting strategies, for reasons Umber was a long way from understanding. He was entangled in both. And entanglement with Marilyn, tempting though it undeniably was, seemed certain to lead to disaster. He could not trust her. But he could not afford to ignore her. By rights, he should agree on his next move with Sharp. But Sharp was still en route to Jersey, phoneless and infuriatingly out of touch. For the moment, Umber was on his own.

The British Library was open until eight o'clock on weekdays. The books Umber had ordered could wait a while. Sensing he would not be able to concentrate on them until he had explored at least one other avenue where Wisby was concerned, he headed for Green Park Tube station.

His destination was Southwark, where Wisby Investigations Ltd. operated out of an address in Blackfriars Road. Umber had learned this much from Claire Wheatley's telephone directory. He had also learned the phone number, of course, and could have spared himself the risk of a wasted journey by calling ahead, but he wanted to see just what sort of an operation it was, so he decided to try his luck in person.

171A Blackfriars Road was a first-floor office above a shoe-repair business. 221B Baker Street it was very far from. A young, yawning Asian woman was the sole occupant. She broke off from typing on a word processor that looked about twenty years old to tell him, "They're all out," without apparently feeling the need to explain who *they* were.

"I'm looking for Alan Wisby."

"He's retired."

"I don't think so."

"Oh yes, he has. Since before I started here."

"When was that?"

"Nearly a year now. Monica Wisby's in charge. She's out at the moment."

"When will she be back?"

"I don't know. Could be soon. Could be ... late. Do you want to leave a message?"

"For what it's worth, yeah."

She grabbed a notepad and pen. "What's your name?"

"Umber. David Umber. Monica's already—"

"You're David Umber?" She looked surprised.

"Yes."

"Can you . . . prove it?"

Umber took out his wallet and placed his brand-new British Library reader's card on the desk. The young woman looked at the photograph on it, then up at him, then down at the photograph again. "Satisfied?"

"Sorry. I had to be sure."

"Any particular reason?"

"Monica said you might turn up, but I wasn't to hand it over or even mention we had it—unless you had some ID."

"What are you talking about?"

"This letter." She opened the desk drawer and took out a sealed buff envelope. "It's for you." She handed it over.

Umber stepped back to the doorway before opening the letter, unsure how to react to such a turn of events.

His name had been printed on the envelope using an old-fashioned typewriter in need of a change of ribbon. There was one sheet of paper inside, so thin that some strikes of the keys had perforated it. It bore neither address nor date, but was signed at the bottom *A. E. Wisby*.

> Dear Mr. Umber
> Monica apprised me of Sharp's visit to my old place of business. He gave her your name and mobile number for me to contact. I don't trust phones *or* policemen, so we'll keep this between ourselves if you don't mind. I'm willing to talk to you as long as you come alone. I'm on the Kennet and Avon at present, between Newbury and Kintbury. You'll recognize the boat's name when you see it. Don't leave it too long, or I'll have moved on.

Umber made it to Paddington in time to catch a crowded five o'clock commuter train bound for Bedwyn, stopping just about everywhere en route, including Newbury and Kintbury. From the guard he learned that Kintbury station was right next to the canal, which clinched his choice of destination. He somehow doubted Wisby would have moored in the centre of Newbury anyway.

The train reached Kintbury at 6:30. The sun had set by then, behind dark clouds rolling in from the west. A still, greying twilight filled the air. Umber lingered on the platform, watching the other passengers who had got off leave the station. The canal was separated from the railway line by the width of the small station car park. The village of Kintbury lay to the south, the lane into it crossing the canal over a humpback bridge. There was a pub on the other side of the bridge. One of the departing passengers was making straight for it. The others were clambering into their waiting cars.

The guard blew his whistle. The train rumbled off into the dusk. The level-crossing gates rose. The vehicles they had been holding back drove on. The car park emptied. Within a few minutes of the train's arrival, there was no-one left in sight. Umber was alone in the descending silence and gathering gloom. He headed for the towpath.

It was plainly foolish to set off on such a search in failing light. But the truth was that biding his time had simply not occurred to him until he was on the train. He doubted he would have found the patience to wait until morning in any event. Besides, Wisby was more or less certain to be aboard his boat come evening. To that extent, this was exactly the right time to go looking for him.

On the other hand, it had to be five or six miles to Newbury and it would be pitch black long before Umber got there. He was pinning his hopes on finding Wisby's boat within the first couple of miles. There were no boats moored ahead that he could see, but that was not far on account of the canal's winding route. He walked faster and faster, breaking occasionally into a jog as the sky darkened.

Wisby's choice of the Kennet and Avon Canal was not a matter of chance, of course. Umber was keenly aware of that. Marlborough lay no more than ten or twelve miles to the west, an easy bus-ride from Bedwyn, the canal's closest approach to the town. Wisby was in the area for a reason and was content to let Umber guess what that reason might be. He could hardly know about the towpath walk Umber had taken with Sally after the inquest all those years ago, but the memory of it was hovering close to Umber. Nor was it the only memory crowding in on him. He was a man fleeing the past as well as pursuing it.

The silence was suddenly broken as a high-speed train roared into view beyond the wood-fringed fields to his left. The brightly lit carriages sped past in a barrage of sound—and were gone. Umber stood listening to the fading note of the engine. Then he pressed on.

A few minutes later, rounding the next bend, he saw a humpback bridge ahead and the pale line of a track leading up from it across the sloping field on the other side of the canal. And then he saw the dark shape of a boat moored just beyond the bridge. He stepped up the pace.

The bridge served only the track. There was no road in sight. An old wartime pillbox was half-buried in the undergrowth beside the towpath just beyond the bridge. The mooring was quiet and inaccessible. Umber could see no signs of life as he approached the boat. There were no lights showing at any of the windows. It was a smartly painted, well-maintained craft, roped fore and aft to stakes driven into the bank. Its name was lettered boldly on the prow: *Monica.*

Umber stepped into the bow area and voiced a hopeful "Hello?" But the doors to the cabin were padlocked shut. Wisby was obviously not there. Umber peered in through one of the glazed panels in the doors, but could see nothing.

Then, as he stepped back, the padlock suddenly fell to the deck with a thump. Umber stared at it in bemusement. The loop had been snapped clean through. The pierced edges glinted up at him. Someone had cut through the lock, then replaced it loosely on the hasp. Umber's movements had been sufficient to dislodge it. It had been rigged to appear secure, whereas in reality . . .

He flicked the hasp back and pulled the doors open. The cabin was in darkness, the twilight seeping through the half-curtained windows scarcely penetrating the deep, jumbled shadows. He felt for a light switch, but could not find one. His fumblings did chance on a torch, however, hanging just inside the doorway. He unhooked it and switched it on.

The torch beam revealed what seemed at first to be an immaculate interior of polished wood and burnished brass, with nothing out of place. Then, about halfway down the cabin, the light fell on a slew of papers across the floor. They lay at the foot of a three-drawer metal filing cabinet—an incongruous sight aboard a narrowboat. There were discarded folders amidst the scatter of papers. Someone had ransacked the cabinet.

Umber was about to step into the cabin when he felt the boat lurch beneath him. As he turned, he saw a gap opening between the boat and the bank. A man in a black tracksuit was standing on the towpath, staring straight at him—a man he knew from their encounter in Yeovil as John Walsh. Beside him, the stake was still planted firmly in the ground. But there was no rope tied around it.

For a second, Umber froze, his thoughts and reactions scrambled. Where had Walsh come from? The pillbox, perhaps? He could have hidden inside it as Umber approached. He must have broken into the boat, failed to find what he had been looking for, then lain in wait for Wisby. But it was not Wisby who had walked into his trap.

Walsh had untied the rope and shoved the boat away from the bank. But the rope at the other end of the vessel was still fastened, causing it to drift out diagonally across the canal. There was already too wide a gap to jump from the bow. Umber would have to reach the stern to get off. But he did not for a second believe Walsh meant to let him do that.

"You shouldn't be here," Walsh shouted, shaking his head. "You really shouldn't." His gaze shifted suddenly away from Umber. In the same instant, there were heavy footfalls on the roof of the cabin.

Umber turned just in time to see a burly, camouflage-clad figure looming above him. He glimpsed the blurred arc of a base-ball bat swinging towards him. He raised his arm to protect him-self, the torch still clasped in his hand. The bat was aimed at his head, but the rubber barrel of the torch took the direct force of the blow.

Of this, Umber was in no real sense aware. Something had struck him a stunning blow. That was all he knew. Then something else struck the back of his head as he fell. And the rest was dark-ness.

CHAPTER

FIFTEEN

Umber was cold. God, was he cold, shivering as he woke to a damp patter of rain on his face. Dreaming and consciousness collided in a jolt of blurred memory. He moved, wincing as a pain throbbed through his head. Slowly, he pulled himself up into a sitting position.

The night was inkily black. He could see virtually nothing. He put his hand behind his head and felt a tender, oozing lump. Then he noticed a feeble glimmer of light nearby and stretched towards it. It was the torch, its batteries all but exhausted. He switched it off.

He was still aboard the *Monica*. That was about all he could be sure of. The boat was rocking gently beneath him, the cabin doors creaking on their hinges. There was another sound, of wood thumping dully against wood.

He clambered awkwardly to his feet, his every movement slowed by dizzying pulses of pain in his head. The boat must be adrift, he reasoned. For all he knew, it was in the middle of the canal. But no. There was that thumping again. And he could make out the shadow of something beyond and above the cabin. A bridge, perhaps? No. It was too low. A lock gate, then? Yes. That had to be it. The *Monica* had drifted down to the next lock.

He felt his way round the bulwark to the side he had boarded by and reached out blindly into the darkness. Nothing. Then he scrabbled around the deck until he found the broken padlock. He tossed this in the direction of where he thought the bank should be and heard it fall to earth rather than into water. He pulled the

left-hand cabin door wide open and, grasping its handle, stretched
out farther into the void, flapping his arm as best he could in
search of a hold. Still nothing. He slumped back against the door,
head pounding.

It was hopeless. He was going to have to phone for assistance:
the police or an ambulance. He reached into his pocket for his mobile. Not there. It must have slipped out onto the deck. He lowered
himself to his knees and felt around for it. The bow area was small.
It did not take long to cover. But the phone was nowhere to be
found. Then he understood. It was not there because Walsh had
taken it, either to deny Umber the use of it or to listen to any messages left for him.

He crouched where he was, gathering his resources. To get off
the boat, he was going to have to reach the stern. He could go
through the cabin, but the aft door was bound to be locked. Walsh
would hardly have broken in at both ends. No, the only ways off
were along the outside of the cabin or over the top. There was a
ledge either side of the cabin, Umber vaguely recalled, but it was
desperately narrow. The roof was a marginally better option. He
scrambled to his feet, waited for the ache in his head to subside,
grasped what felt like a rail fixed to the roof, put one foot on the
bulwark and pulled himself up.

In the same instant, the boat bounced against something, pitch-
ing Umber forward. His hand slipped from the rail. He lost his balance and fell.

It was the ground he hit, not water. The *Monica* had drifted
into the bank. A jarred shoulder and a red mist of pain behind his
eyes were worth it to feel mud and grass beneath him. He levered
himself slowly upright and blundered forward like a blind man until he reached the jutting balance beam of the lock gate. He leaned
against the beam for a minute or more, recovering his breath and
what was left of his wits. He looked at his wristwatch. The lumi-
nous dial told him the time was a few minutes before nine. He
would have guessed it was the middle of the night. But then so, in a
sense, it was—for him.

The shaly surface of the towpath crunched beneath his feet as
he took a few tentative steps away from the beam. Logically, if he
kept to the path, with the canal to his right, he would make it to
Newbury in the end. Kintbury was probably closer, but the fright-

ening possibility that Walsh and the man who had attacked him were still waiting for Wisby by the bridge meant Newbury it had to be. He started walking.

He never made it to Newbury. A slow, stumbling mile or so later, he reached another lock, and a road-bridge over the canal. He was feeling worse than when he had left the boat by now. Nausea and dizziness were sweeping over him ever more frequently. Seeing the lights of a house a short distance along the road, he headed towards it.

A bloody-headed stranger staggering in out of the night would alarm many a rural resident. But the couple whose door Umber knocked at responded with genuine concern and practical assistance, never once querying his explanation that he had injured himself in a fall on the towpath. The woman disinfected his wound as best she could, then her husband volunteered to drive him to hospital for a check-up. Umber accepted the offer with more gratitude than he could express—and slept like a baby throughout the journey.

The speed with which he was processed through Casualty gave Umber his first indication that he might actually be seriously ill. Concussion, the doctor told him after stitching the gash at the back of his head, should not be taken lightly. He could have suffered a brain injury whose full effects were not yet apparent. They would have to take him in for observation. He did not argue. He did not have the strength to.

Before being admitted, however, he did force himself to make a phone call—to Bill Larter.

"Where are you, boy?"

"Royal Berkshire Hospital, Reading. Knocked myself out in a fall."

"Knocked *yourself* out?"

"I'll tell you about it when I get back."

"When will that be?"

"Not sure. Tomorrow, I hope. Have you heard from George?"

"Not yet."

"Shouldn't you have done by now?"

"Maybe the ferry was delayed. Maybe he's trying to get through at this very minute. He'll like as not call you first anyway."

"He can't. I've lost my mobile."

"How'd that happen?"

"Never mind. Tell him not to call me on that number."

"All right. Though he'll want to—"

"Got to go, Bill. I'll be in touch. 'Bye."

A nurse gave him some painkillers once he was on the ward. Maybe they were more than just painkillers. He certainly knew very little after taking them until morning. Even then, connected thought seemed beyond him. He knew he should feel angry about what had happened, but relief that he was still alive blotted out everything else. He asked if there had been any phone calls for him and was told there had not. He asked when he would be allowed to leave and was told that was for the doctor to decide. He asked no more.

The doctor came to see him around midday with the news that his X-rays had shown no abnormalities. Since he was conscious, coherent and complaining of nothing worse than a headache, he could leave provided a friend or relative came to pick him up and kept an eye on him for the next twenty-four hours.

This was easier stipulated than accomplished. Larter had no car. Sharp was in Jersey. Umber considered phoning his parents, but soon rejected the idea. In the end, he could think of only one person to ask.

"Are you sure you're well enough to be discharged?" was Alice's less than encouraging greeting when she arrived several hours later. "You certainly don't look it."

"Thanks for coming."

"What happened to you?"

"Long story."

"Yeah? Well, judging by the amount of traffic heading into London on the M4, I'll have plenty of time to hear it. Let's go."

Fobbing off Good Samaritans and night-shift nurses with a story about hitting his head on a canal-lock balance beam had been surprisingly easy. Umber had no intention of trying the same trick with Alice. Indeed, he was happy to tell her the truth in the hope it would persuade her he really was onto something. In that, however, he was to be disappointed.

"Why didn't you tell the police about this?"

"They'd probably have arrested me for breaking into Wisby's boat."

"Which you didn't do."

"No, Alice. I didn't."

"And where is Wisby?"

"Haven't a clue."

"But you went to the canal basically because he invited you?"

"Yes. He sent me a letter. You want to see it?"

"Not really."

"You can ask Claire about Wisby. She'll vouch for his existence."

"Maybe I'll do that."

"You think I made all this up?"

"No."

"Then, what *do* you think?"

"I don't know, David. I just don't know."

"Don't know was made to know," Umber muttered under his breath. But she did not hear.

It was nearly six o'clock by the time Alice delivered him to 45 Bengal Road, Ilford. Larter was not at home. Umber had little doubt as to where the old man could be found, but Alice, having accepted a degree of responsibility for his welfare, insisted on driving him to the Sheepwalk to check on the point.

The pub was less crowded than on Friday. Larter was installed with a pint at his favourite fireside table. He surprised Umber by appearing pleased to see him, though he added a suitably grouchy, "You look like death warmed up." He volunteered nothing more in Alice's presence, seeming to sense her ingrained suspicion of policemen, even retired ones. She declined a drink and did not linger.

"Strange people you're mixing with," she said when Umber walked her out to her car.

"Just people I can rely on, Alice."

"I came and got you, didn't I?" she snapped, bridling at the implied contrast.

"You did. And I'm grateful."

"You should get some rest, David. You really should."

"So the doctor said."

"Going back to Prague might not be a bad idea."

"I'll think about it."

"Oh yeah?" She climbed into her car, slammed the door and lowered the window. "Do something for me, will you?"

"What?"

"Take more care."

"Who was she?" Larter demanded as soon as Umber returned to the pub.

There was a pint waiting for him and Umber took a long and healing swallow before answering. "An old friend of my wife's."

"How much does she know?"

"More than she wants to."

"Did you tell her George was going to Jersey?"

"Of course not."

"Did you tell anyone?"

"No. Why?"

"George is in trouble."

"What sort of trouble?"

"The big sort. The Jersey police stopped him as he was leaving the ferry last night and searched the van. They found a bag of heroin inside each wheel arch."

"You're joking."

"Wish I was, boy. George is in the slammer. No joke."

"Bloody hell."

"The duty solicitor who got his case phoned me a few hours ago. George was up before the magistrates this morning. They remanded him in custody on smuggling charges. He's looking at a few years inside if he can't talk his way out of this, you know."

"They fitted him up."

"Someone did, yeah. Planted the drugs in transit, then tipped off Customs at St. Helier. That's how I read it, anyhow. Happen to know who that someone might be?"

"I wish I did."

"I don't suppose I'd be far out in guessing they had something to do with whatever scrape you got into last night, though, would I?"

"No. You wouldn't."

"I'd better give you the message George's solicitor asked me to pass on to you, then."

"Message?"

"From George. You're not to go to Jersey. Under any circumstances."

"Not go?"

"I reckon he thinks it'd be too dangerous. Look what's happened to him."

"I can't just . . . abandon him."

"It's what he's telling you to do." Larter took a thoughtful sup of beer. "Of course, George never has been the best judge of what's good for him. Not by a long shot. So . . ." He looked expectantly at Umber. "When do you leave?"

C H A P T E R

SIXTEEN

Booking a flight to Jersey was the easy part. The hard part for
Umber—much harder—was knowing what to do when he
got there. Sharp's plan had been to put some pressure on
Jeremy Hall while his father was away and see what resulted.
Whether the people who had framed Sharp for drugs smuggling
had anticipated such a move was unclear. What *was* clear was that
they must have followed Sharp to Portsmouth and hence had probably been following him for some time. The same might apply to
Umber himself, despite his certainty that no-one had followed him
to Kintbury. Walsh had seemed surprised to see him aboard Wisby's
boat, but that could have been play-acting, at which the man was
something of an expert.

In the final analysis, it hardly mattered. They could easily guess
how Umber would react to news of Sharp's arrest. He could not seriously hope to travel to Jersey undetected. He was not sure he even
wanted to. Stealth and caution had landed Sharp in prison and
Umber in a predicament he could see no obvious way out of. It was
time to step into the open—and see who might be waiting for him.

"Make sure they don't pull the same stunt on you," was Larter's
farewell piece of advice the following morning. "Don't let anyone
near your bag or your pockets."

Crossing London at the start of the working day made it
virtually impossible to follow such advice, but Umber reached

Victoria confident no-one had planted anything on him. The painkillers he had taken and the beer he had drunk the night before were ganging up to undermine his watchfulness, however. He fell comprehensively asleep aboard the Gatwick Express and stumbled onto the Airport Transit in a daze, conducting a fuddled search of himself and his bag as he went.

Two hours later, he was hurrying through an unattended Green Channel on arrival at Jersey Airport. He exited the terminal into more of the dazzling sunlight and chilling breeze he had encountered on leaving the plane and made straight for the head of the taxi rank.

Umber had never been to Jersey before. The view he had from the taxi during the drive to St. Helier was of an undulating, daffodil-spattered English landscape, with French place names and architectural styles grafted on—a pretty island, but a small one nonetheless: that had been apparent from the air. Oliver Hall had settled there because of its tax-haven status, but maybe he had found another kind of haven in the process and his son along with him. And maybe now their seclusion was about to come to an end.

The approach to St. Helier was a busy main road round a wide, south-facing bay, with the rooftops of the town, the lofty ramparts of Fort Regent and the piers and derricks of the harbour growing ever closer ahead. Umber had asked to be taken straight to the offices of Le Templier & Burnouf of Hill Street. He had not thought much further ahead than what he meant to do there, which included learning all he could about Sharp's prospects. He had a strong suspicion they were far from bright.

It was lunchtime in St. Helier, the pavements crowded, the traffic thick. The taxi stopped and started and eventually reached Umber's destination: a brass-plaqued legal practice in an elegant Georgian building opposite the Parish Church.

Umber had half-hoped Sharp's solicitor, Nigel Burnouf, might be lunching in the office and would agree to see him there and then, but it was not to be. The receptionist told him to come back at 2:30.

He filled the hour and a bit this left him with by booking himself into the nearest hotel—the Pomme d'Or in Liberation Square—and doing a small amount of research on the Halls. Oliver was not listed in the Jersey telephone directory, which came as no surprise. But Jeremy was less shy. His entry gave an address in Le Quai Bisson, St. Aubin, an address he shared, according to the *Yellow Pages*, with Rollers Sail & Surf School. The map lodged with the stationery in Umber's room showed St. Aubin to be a village a few miles back round the coast. And the timetable in the bus station right opposite the hotel promised a half-hourly service in that direction. Tracking down Jeremy Hall would clearly not have tested Sharp—if he had ever had the chance.

Back at Le Templier & Burnouf promptly at 2:30, Umber was sent straight into Nigel Burnouf's office.

Burnouf was a plump, placid, middle-aged man with sandy hair, gold-framed spectacles and a reassuring air of unflustered efficiency.

"I was a little surprised when Janet said I was to expect you, Mr. Umber," he said after they had shaken hands and sat down. "Didn't you get my message?"

"Oh, I got it, yes."

"And proceeded to ignore it. Well, I confess the possibility you might do so had occurred to me. As I suspect it has to Mr. Sharp."

"I'm here to do whatever it takes to get him out of trouble."

"That's rather a tall order, I'm afraid. He was caught red-handed. We need a witness who saw a third party plant the material on his van—or a confession by said party. I'm not holding my breath."

"You do understand he was definitely framed, don't you?"

"It's what he tells me. And he's certainly an unlikely candidate for drugs smuggling. But facts are facts. It would help me if you could suggest who might have framed him—and why."

"Hasn't George come up with a name?"

"No. Though I have the feeling there *is* a name. Could you enlighten me, perhaps?"

Sharp had said nothing about the Halls. It seemed, in fact, that he had said nothing at all beyond protesting his innocence. Umber had guessed it would be so. In the circumstances he could only follow Sharp's lead. "There's nothing I can tell you at the moment. I need to . . . make a few enquiries."

"Thus exposing yourself to those risks Mr. Sharp is so anxious you shouldn't run?"

"I'll be careful."

"Do you want me to tell him that? Or will you do so yourself? I can arrange for you to visit him."

"I'll hold off on that, thanks. In fact . . ."

"You'd rather he didn't know you were here?"

"Well . . . yes."

"You're not asking me to deceive my client, are you, Mr. Umber?"

"No. But you don't have to volunteer information, do you?"

Burnouf considered the question for a moment, then said, "I suppose not."

"He'd only worry about me."

"And he already has plenty to worry about. Point taken."

"How is he?"

"Much as you'd expect. Imprisonment comes hard to a man of his age and former occupation. On the other hand, La Moye isn't Pentonville. His problem is time. It hangs heavy. And it's likely to go on doing so. He'll reappear before the magistrates next week, when a further and lengthier remand in custody is more or less inevitable."

"No chance of bail?"

"Realistically, none. Drugs smugglers are notorious for jumping bail, I'm afraid."

"And when will the case come to trial?"

"Not for several months at least." Burnouf leaned forward. "The best way to help your friend in the meantime, Mr. Umber, is to let me have any information that's even marginally relevant. For instance, if Mr. Sharp didn't come to Jersey for the purpose of trafficking in drugs, why did he come?"

"What does he say?"

"Nothing." Burnouf smiled wanly. "Rather like you."

"I do have something that might help, as a matter of fact."

"You do?"

"This." Umber took a sealed envelope out of his pocket and placed it on Burnouf's desk.

"What is it?"

"A statement, I suppose you'd call it. My record of certain recent events not unconnected with what's happened to George."

"You want me to read it?"

"No. That is, not unless . . . I should happen to meet with a fatal accident."

Burnouf's eyes widened. "Aren't you being rather . . . melodramatic?"

"I hope so. But I have good reason to doubt it. So, just in case . . ." Umber patted the envelope. "The contents may be enough to get George off. I'm not sure. They'll give you some material for his defence, anyway."

"I see." Burnouf picked up the envelope. "Or, rather, I don't."

"I'm sorry I can't say any more."

"So am I."

"You'll hold onto the statement for me?"

"If those are your instructions."

"They are."

"Very well, then." Burnouf took a roll of Sellotape out of his desk drawer, tore off a strip and stuck it over the flap of the envelope. Then he tore off a couple more strips and stuck them over the envelope's seams. "Sign across the seals, would you, Mr. Umber?" He proffered a pen. Umber obliged. "Your receipt." Burnouf hastily filled in a form and handed it over. "All done."

"Thanks." Umber rose to leave.

"Where are you staying?" Burnouf asked as he saw him out.

"The Pomme d'Or."

"Nice hotel. Quite a history attached to it, actually. If you go along to the Occupation Museum, you can see film of the crowds gathered outside the Pomme to celebrate the end of German rule, with British troops sitting on the balcony waving—" Burnouf broke off. "Sorry. I'm talking as if you're a tourist."

"Jersey's changed a lot since the War, I imagine," said Umber, feeling he had to respond in some way.

"Enormously. And not necessarily for the better, according to my father and quite a few of his generation." Burnouf smiled. "Tax exiles from the mainland are the problem, apparently. They've brought a lot of money to the island. And lucrative employment for the likes of me. But they've brought their troubles with them as well." He looked Umber in the eye. "I have a funny feeling you know that, though."

Umber had not enjoyed holding out on Burnouf, but he did not regret it either. He did not know exactly what to allege or who to allege it against. He needed evidence. And only the truth seemed likely to furnish it. But the truth was as elusive as ever. The statement he had lodged with Burnouf proved nothing. Yet it was all he had to show for his and Sharp's efforts. He had to learn more—and soon.

The number 15 bus dropped him in the centre of St. Aubin, a smart, bustling seaside town clustered round a harbour filled with yachts and motorboats clinking at their moorings in the late-afternoon sun. He asked directions of a passer-by and was pointed along the harbourside boulevard to the first turning.

Le Quai Bisson was a narrow side-street leading to several old stone warehouses functioning as small business premises. The doors of Rollers Sail & Surf were firmly closed, the small office to the rear locked and unattended. The place had a pre-season look about it, with last year's tide tables still displayed in the office window.

A steep flight of steps led up beside the warehouse to a higher road. Halfway up the steps was the entrance to the flat which the roof area of the building had been converted into. Umber could hear the bass output of an amplifier within. He took an optimistic stab at the bell. No response. He tried again, adding a rattle of the letterbox for good measure.

The door opened suddenly to a gust of heavy metal and a blank stare from a slightly built young woman dressed in black combat trousers and a purple T-shirt. Dark, straggly hair fell either side of her narrow face, in which a vermilion slash of lipstick was the only trace of colour. The shadows beneath her eyes and the pallor of her skin did not suggest sailing and surfing were recreations she often indulged in.

"Hi," she said with a lop-sided grin.

"Jeremy in?"

"Not right now."

"Are you expecting him back soon?"

"Yeah. But that doesn't mean it'll happen. Is this . . . business?"

"Not exactly. He knows me from a long time back. I'm David Umber."

"Umber? You said Umber?" She looked genuinely incredulous.

"That's right."

"Fuck me. The Shadow Man."

"What?"

"Never thought you'd show up. Bloody hell. I'm Chantelle, by the way." The name went some way, Umber supposed, to explain the hint of a French accent. "Do you want to come in?"

"OK. Thanks." He stepped into a narrow hallway. A tiny kitchen and a scarcely bigger bathroom were to the right. To the left was a large lounge-diner-bedroom with dormer windows to either side and a Catherine-wheel window set in the gable at the front of the warehouse, through which there was a sparkling blue glimpse of the harbour between the opposite rooftops.

"Fancy a tea?" asked Chantelle.

"Sure."

"I've just made some." She stepped into the kitchen to fetch her mug and fill one for him. It was easy to believe, given the state of the bed and the dining table, that the tea had been intended to round off her breakfast. Umber edged his way to the hi-fi tower perched amidst the general chaos and nudged down the volume.

"There you go." She was waiting with his mug as he turned round. He took it from her with a sheepish grin. "Sorry the place is such a mess."

"Don't worry about it."

She cleared a drift of magazines and CDs from the couch so that he could sit down, then folded a blanket back over the unmade bed and plonked herself on the end of it, mug cradled in both hands as she looked at him with almost comic intensity.

"What's this about Shadow Man?" he asked.

"Oh, it's what Jem calls you. On account of your name. Umber. From the Latin for shadow, isn't it?"

"Yes. It is. But I'm surprised . . . Jem . . . talks about me at all."

"Are you really surprised? I mean, it was quite a thing, what happened to his sisters. It stays with him. He likes to talk about it sometimes. Can't stop himself, to tell the truth. Not that I want him to."

"How long have you known him?"

"About six months." She smiled. "Best six months of my life."

"That's nice to hear."

"Yeah." She looked bashful, then said, "So, what's brought you here?"

"It's, er, complicated. No offence intended, but it'd be best if I spoke to Jem about it."

"Understood. But you could tell me about yourself, I suppose." She grinned. "Unless that's classified information."

Umber chuckled. "Boring, but not classified."

"Great. So——" She broke off as the throaty roar of a motorbike engine half-drowned the music. "Hold on. That sounds like him now." She leaned across the bed for a view through the nearest window. "Yeah. Thought so."

A few moments later the front door opened and a tall, broad-shouldered man entered at a slight stoop, then froze in mid-stride at the sight of Umber.

Jeremy Hall was barely recognizable as the small boy Umber had first seen at Avebury twenty-three years previously. He was in his early thirties now, a tanned and muscular figure in red and black motorcycling leathers, his fair hair curlier than in childhood, his eyes a greyer shade of blue. There was certainty in his steely gaze. He knew who Umber was. Alarmingly, there was also a simmer of anger. He knew—and he was far from pleased.

"Guess who," chirruped Chantelle.

Jeremy set down his crash helmet and gauntlets on the hall table, then stepped slowly into the room.

Umber rose cautiously from the couch. "I'm sorry not to have phoned ahead," he ventured. "This must be a bit of a shock for you."

"Aren't you going to say hello, Jemmy?" put in Chantelle, her smile stiffening. "It's the——"

"Shadow Man." Jeremy's voice was cold and hard. "I know. David Umber." He nodded. "I've been expecting him."

Chantelle blinked in surprise. "Expecting him? You never said."

"Do me a favour, sugar." Jeremy took a coin out of his pocket and flicked it onto the bed. "Pop down to the shop and buy an *Evening Post.*"

"My tea will get cold."

"Just go."

Chantelle flinched at the harshness of his tone and blushed slightly. She leaned forward and picked up the coin. Then, without looking once at Umber, she put down her mug, stood up and walked out of the room. She glanced at Jeremy as she passed him and laid a hand gently on his arm, but he only jerked his head towards the door.

A second later it had closed behind Chantelle, leaving the two men alone together.

"I had a call from the old man," Jeremy cut in before Umber could say a word. "Warned me you might pull something like this."

"I only want to—"

"Dig up a load of stuff that's best forgotten. I know what you *only* want."

"It's far from forgotten by you—according to Chantelle."

"Leave her out of it."

"Suits me."

"There's nothing I can tell you about Sally."

"Who said I meant to ask you about Sally?"

"What, then? *No.*" Jeremy shook his head. "I'm not getting into this. Not here. Not now."

"I don't know what your father said, but—"

"Here's the deal. The only deal you'll get from me. You're staying in St. Helier?"

"Yes."

"I'll meet you there tomorrow afternoon at La Frégate. It's a café on the seafront, shaped like a capsized boat. You can't miss it. Be there at four."

"All right. But why can't we—"

"Shut up." Jeremy levelled a threatening finger at Umber. "We're playing to my rules, not yours, OK? It's tomorrow or nothing."

"OK." Umber tried to sound calmer than he felt. Why his unannounced visit had so enraged Jeremy he did not understand. But he could imagine that rage tipping over into violence all too easily. And his experiences of Monday night had left him with a strong sense of

his physical vulnerability. He had not realized how acute that sense
was until this moment. "Tomorrow afternoon it is."

"Now . . ." Jeremy moved to the front door and yanked it open.
"Get out."

Umber noticed a tremor in his hands as he walked past Jeremy's
motorbike and out beside the warehouse towards the harbour. The
encounter had affected him more than he would have expected. He
would have to pull himself together before he met Jeremy again.
Seizing the initiative from the younger man would otherwise be beyond him.

He turned onto the Boulevard and made for the bus stop. It lay
just beyond the road junction in the centre of the town. As he
neared the junction, he spotted Chantelle making her way across it,
a newspaper clutched in her hand. In the same instant, she spotted
him and pulled up abruptly, then swivelled on her heel and headed
for the higher road that would take her to the top of the steps above
the flat.

By the time Umber reached the junction, she had vanished
from sight.

CHAPTER

SEVENTEEN

Back in St. Helier, Umber was forced to admit to himself that he could not brush off his tangle with Walsh and baseball-bat man as readily as he had supposed. His nerves were fragile, his physical resources diminished. He could only hope a good dinner and an early night would hasten their recovery.

When he woke the next morning, he felt, if not quite his old self, then at least a closer approach to it. He had slept for ten solid hours and was momentarily uncertain where he was, until a distant shriek of gulls in the harbour told him that, yes, he really had come to Jersey.

He stumbled into the bathroom, emerging half an hour later showered, shaved and reassuringly alert. There was not even the trace of a headache, although the stitches in his wound tugged at his scalp occasionally to remind him of what had happened sixty hours or so ago.

He pulled back the curtains to confront a wide blue sky across which a strong wind was blowing fluffy bundles of cloud. Only then, with sunlight filling the room, did he notice, as he turned away from the window, the envelope that had been slid beneath his door.

The envelope was blank. Inside was a slim mail-order catalogue, advertising the pick of the stock of "Jersey's premier antiquarian and second-hand-books dealer"—folded open at the page devoted to the eighteenth century.

Quires, of Halkett Place, St. Helier (established 1975, proprietor Vernon Garrard), was clearly the place of first resort for Jersey bibliophiles: a multi-roomed glory-hole of *Punch, Wisden,* Whitaker's, Dickens, Scott, Austen, Defoe, Pepys, Shakespeare *et al.* When Umber arrived mid-morning, there were only a couple of other customers, none of them in the main room, where Garrard was conducting a telephone conversation at the cluttered cash desk in the corner.

The scene was about as safe and humdrum as could be imagined, but it did not appear so to Umber. The sense of being manipulated was not so very different from the feeling of being watched. He had no idea who might have slipped Garrard's catalogue under his door, but he knew what he had been supposed to infer. There were no editions of the *Letters of Junius* listed, but Junius was why he had been sent to Quires. There could be no other reason. Just as, for all his doubts and reservations, there could be no question of ignoring the clue he had been supplied with.

The eighteenth-century shelf in the antiquarian section, which lay within close view of the desk, was an unremarkable if well-bound selection of Pope, Swift, Hume, Goldsmith and Dr. Johnson. Umber fingered his way slowly along the spines, wondering if he would chance on an uncatalogued Junius. But, no, he did not. Then he heard the telephone go down behind him and the sound of a chair being pushed back. He turned to find Garrard bearing soft-footedly down on him.

A balding, round-shouldered man of sixty or so, Garrard wore the dusty tweed and corduroy uniform of his trade and the resigned expression of one well aware that browsers outnumber serious customers in the second-hand-books world by a depressing margin. "Can I help you?" he lethargically enquired.

"Not sure," Umber replied. "I was wondering if you had any editions of the *Letters of Junius.*"

"Junius? No. I'm afraid not. He doesn't crop up very often."

"Ever?"

"Well . . ." Garrard scratched his cheek. "Now and then. I had a nice Junius in a few months back, as a matter of fact." He smiled weakly. "Snapped up, I'm afraid."

"Was that a first edition?"

"Er, no. Second, as I recall."

"The 1773, you mean?"

"Do I? Probably. It sounds as if you'd know better than I would."

"A two-volume set?"

"Yes."

"How was it bound?"

"Handsomely, if . . . slightly unusually. Most Juniuses you see are in calfskin, but this was—"

"Vellum."

"Yes." Garrard frowned at Umber. "So it was."

"If you don't mind my asking, how did you come by it?"

"Rather oddly, as it happens. I never even knew I had it until a customer took it down from the shelf and asked to buy it. My brother Bernard sometimes minds the shop for me. He must have taken it into stock. We have sellers as well as buyers who call in. Bernard can be infuriatingly neglectful of record-keeping, I'm afraid."

"So, its origin is . . . a mystery."

"You could say so, yes."

"And the person who bought it?"

Garrard smiled. "What would you like to know?"

"Well, their name and address, if you have the information."

Unaccountably, Garrard loosed a dry but hearty laugh. His eyes twinkled mischievously. "Oh dear, oh dear. Here we go again."

"I'm sorry?"

"Your name would be Umber, I assume."

"What?" Umber stared at the bookseller in frank astonishment. "How do you know that?"

"I've been down the Junius road with someone else only last week."

"Who?"

"A Mr. Wisby."

"*Wisby?*"

"Yes. He phoned me this morning and said you might call round. This is an entertaining charade, though a baffling one from my point of view. I'm sure you both know what you're about. Still, I've no wish to go on acting as go-between. If I give you his number, I trust that'll be the last I hear of the matter."

Umber rang Wisby from the first call-box he came to after leaving Quires. The promptness of Wisby's answer suggested he had been waiting for the call.

"Mr. Umber." The susurrous voice was unmistakable, even after more than twenty years.

"Mr. Wisby."

"The very same."

"I thought you didn't trust phones."

"Needs must. Besides, communicating with you by letter didn't turn out very satisfactorily, did it?"

"What the hell's going on?"

"Not a hundred per cent certain. But I probably know more than you do. If you want to talk about it, join me in Royal Square in ten minutes."

It took Umber less than ten minutes to thread his way through the pedestrianized part of the town centre to his destination: a sedate, flagstoned piazza overlooked by the handsome nineteenth-century buildings housing Jersey's parliament and principal court, with a gilded statue of George II tricked out as Caesar presiding at one end.

In the centre of the square, seated on a bench and reading a newspaper, was a lean, round-shouldered man in a brown raincoat and navy-blue trousers. He was smoking a cigarette—and Alan Wisby he had to be.

He looked much as Umber remembered, though greyer, in skin as well as hair, and perhaps even thinner. There was a grizzled moustache too which he might or might not have previously sported, but then he had always possessed a strangely insubstantial quality. He was someone easily forgotten, someone who had refined the art of not being noticed and applied it to his professional purposes. He looked up as Umber approached and nodded an unsmiling greeting. Umber sat down beside him.

"Have you read yesterday's *Jersey Evening Post*, Mr. Umber?" Wisby asked, holding up the newspaper.

"No."

"Tiny article on page five took my eye. Drug smuggler caught coming off the ferry from Portsmouth Monday night was up before the beak. Name of Sharp. George Sharp."

"I'm not here to play games, Mr. Wisby."

"Good. Though it's strange you should say that, actually. I'm told someone's been playing games with *Monica*. My narrowboat, I mean. She was set loose from her mooring on the Kennet and Avon Canal Monday night. Safe in the boatyard at Newbury now, you'll be glad to know. Busy old night, Monday, it seems."

"I went down to Kintbury at *your* invitation. You weren't on the boat. Two people were waiting for you, though. Worse luck for me."

"I spotted them earlier in the day and decided to make myself scarce. I didn't set you up, Mr. Umber, if that's what you thought."

"I didn't, actually."

"Good."

"They'd broken into the boat and been through your files."

"They were welcome to. I'd already removed what they were looking for."

"And what was that?"

"Well, that's the sixty-four-thousand-dollar question, isn't it? The what, the why and the wherefore."

"Are you going to answer it?"

"I'm going to try. Where shall we begin?"

"Oliver Hall. What's he been paying you to do?"

"Nothing. I took a look at the Avebury case for Hall back in 1982. That was the last time I had any dealings with the man."

"I know that's not true. You told Claire Wheatley—"

"I lied." Wisby smiled fleetingly and flicked away the butt of his cigarette. "Loose ends have always niggled at me, Mr. Umber. When I handed over the day-to-day running of the business to Monica—the other Monica—I revisited a few cases that had left me . . . dissatisfied. Avebury was always going to be one of them. Your wife's sudden death brought it to the front of the queue. I thought her psychotherapist likelier to cooperate if I led her to believe I was working for Hall. Didn't get much out of her, though."

"Get much out of anyone?"

"I've made some headway recently. Thanks to Junius."

"You had a letter too, did you?"

"The same one as Sharp received, I assume. "It is the misfortune of your life that you should never have been acquainted

with the truth with respect to the Marlborough murderers."
Etcetera, etcetera. Familiar?"

"Word for word."

"Sharp had you down as prime suspect, I take it."

"Initially."

"That's the trouble with policemen. They think in straight
lines. Of course, he lacked a crucial piece of information I turned
up five years ago. The letter brought it centre stage."

"What might that be?"

"All in good time, Mr. Umber. Let's not rush our fences." Wisby
lit another cigarette. "I was over here last week double-checking a
few points. I hadn't planned to do anything on the strength of my
conclusions straight away, but the arrival of the heavy mob canal-
side forced my hand. That's why I'm back. What about you?"

"George was intending to speak to Jeremy Hall. Someone went
to considerable lengths to stop him. So, I reckoned I ought to pay
Jeremy a call. But how did you know I was on the island?"

"It stood to reason, with Sharp here as well. I tried a few hotels
and struck lucky at the Pomme d'Or. Bringing his van to Jersey
wasn't a smart move on Sharp's part. He was asking for trouble. I
flew. Like you, I imagine. Have you seen Jeremy yet?"

"Yesterday afternoon."

"How was he?"

"Not a happy bunny. Threw me out."

"Understandable. He's under a lot of pressure. I should know,
since I'm the one applying it. That's why I steered you towards Quires.
So we could get together before you queered the pitch for me."

"Who bought the vellum-bound Junius? Was it Jeremy?"

"Yes. I had to pay Garrard over the odds for an unreadable
history of Jersey before he'd give me a decent description of the
customer, but there was no doubt who it fitted. Of course, I could
have guessed that anyway. The really important question isn't who
bought the book, but where it came from."

"Garrard said he didn't know."

"I don't think he does. But it's a vital link in the chain that
connects Griffin with Jeremy Hall. *We* have to know."

"How do we find out?"

"By forcing Jeremy to tell us. Which brings me to your part in the
proceedings. You're the historian, not me. Part of my deal with

Jeremy is that he hands over the Junius and in return I don't tell his father he stirred up all this trouble for his family by sending anonymous letters to Sharp and me and God knows who else."

"Jeremy sent them?"

"I think his purchase of the book proves he did. And the book proves something else. If it's authentic. That's where you come in. I was going to have to back my own judgement but I don't need to with you tagging along. You'll be able to say for certain if it's the copy Griffin promised to show you at Avebury."

"Well, yes, I can. But—"

"How did it get to Jersey, hey?" Wisby turned to look Umber in the eye. "And what does it mean? I think I know. I think I have it all worked out."

"Planning to let me in on the secret?"

"Yes—as soon as we have the book."

"Tell me now."

Wisby shook his head. "Too risky. There's a chance you might try to do your own deal with Jeremy and cut me out. Got a meeting arranged with him, have you?"

"Yes. I have. Why shouldn't—"

"When is it?"

"This afternoon."

"Time and place?"

"A café on the seafront. La Frégate. Four o'clock. Come along if you don't believe me."

"Oh, I will. That's where and when *I'm* meeting him too." Wisby laughed, setting off a phlegmy cough. He discarded his cigarette in apparent disgust. "Quite a comedian, isn't he? He obviously thinks we're in cahoots. As we are now, I suppose."

"Are we?"

"Might as well be." A second bout of coughing came and went. "Don't you reckon?"

C H A P T E R

EIGHTEEN

Partnering up with Wisby did not leave Umber with a pleasant taste in the mouth. But he could not see, even when he reviewed matters back at the hotel, how he might have managed their encounter any differently. They stood a better chance of extracting the truth from Jeremy Hall by joining forces. Theirs was only a temporary alliance. Umber told himself. Once they had learned the truth—whatever it was—different rules would apply.

He phoned Larter during the empty few hours that separated him from their meeting with Jeremy. He should have made the call sooner, as Larter forcefully reminded him. The truth was that he had felt safer with no-one knowing his exact whereabouts. But it was not a feeling he could afford to indulge.

"What are you up to, boy?"

"Can't go into details, Bill."

"Onto anything promising?"

"Depends what you mean."

"I mean something that will get George out of choky."

"I might be."

"I had him on the blower yesterday."

"*George?*"

"Prisons ain't what they used to be. Inmates are allowed all sorts these days—including phone calls."

"How did he sound?"

"Down in the mouth."

"Did he ask about me?"

"Of course he asked about you. I told him you'd scarpered, intentions unknown. He didn't believe me, though. I could tell. He never said as much, but I got the feeling he reckons you'll have ignored his message. That's why he's keeping his lawyer in the dark. To give you a clear run."

"I'll try and make the most of it."

"You better had, boy. You better had."

La Frégate was a café housed in an artful representation of the inverted hull of a wooden ship, beached on St. Helier's breezy seafront. The chill edge to the breeze had driven its few customers inside, with the solitary exception of Alan Wisby. He was sitting at one of the outdoor tables, hunched over a cigarette and a cup of tea, when Umber arrived. There was nearly a quarter of an hour to go till their appointment with Jeremy Hall, but beating Wisby to any rendezvous was clearly next to impossible.

"Couldn't wait, hey?" said Wisby by way of greeting.

"Like you, it seems."

"No, no. I got here early for the sea air. Ozone's good for the brain, they tell me."

Umber did not pursue the point. He went into the café and bought a coffee. By the time he came back out, a way to wrongfoot Wisby had presented itself appealingly to his mind. He sat down and looked at Wisby, who had angled his chair to face the dual carriageway heading into St. Helier from the west—the direction Jeremy Hall would come from.

"We should hear him coming even if we don't see him," Wisby said. "Unless he's already in town. As he may well be, if, as I suspect, he's been keeping the books in a safe-deposit box somewhere."

"You can tell me about your theory now."

"No, no. Not until the books are in our hands."

"You refused to tell me earlier on the grounds that I might cut my own deal with Jeremy. Well, it's too late for that now, isn't it? So, there's no need for you to hold out on me."

Wisby squinted round at Umber in the dazzling sunlight. "No need for me not to, either."

"Oh, but there is. Particularly if you want to be able to rely on my say-so as to whether the Junius he brings with him is the one Griffin promised to show me at Avebury. And that's central to your theory, isn't it?"

"Yes," Wisby hesitantly and reluctantly agreed.

"So you need to be certain. Absolutely certain. And for that you need to give me something in advance."

"Don't you trust me, Mr. Umber?"

"Not at all."

Wisby drew smilingly on his cigarette. "Well, it's good to know where we stand, I suppose."

"What's your theory?"

Wisby sat in thoughtful silence for a moment, then said, "All right. I'll tell you. Since my good faith's being questioned. Griffin *is* central. Why didn't he turn up at Avebury?"

"I don't know. I've never known."

"It's a mystery."

"Yes. A total mystery."

"Perhaps not. If he *did* turn up."

"What do you mean?"

"Donald Collingwood was already dead when I went back over the case five years ago. That turned out to be to my advantage. I went to see his widow. She was in an old people's home. With Collingwood six foot under, she didn't mind telling me something she'd never have breathed a word about while he was alive. Seems Collingwood came into money straight after the Miranda Hall inquest. Not a fortune, but a tidy sum. He spun his missus a yarn about a lucky bet on the horses, but she never believed him. Just like she never believed he drove through Avebury on the twenty-seventh of July, 1981."

"What?"

"Seems there was no reason for him to have been on that road."

"And you're saying . . . he wasn't?"

"Exactly."

"But—"

"He came forward three weeks into the inquiry to account for the car that followed the van. Don't you see? He was put up to it. Paid . . . to cover Griffin's tracks."

"Griffin?"

"He was the car driver, not Collingwood. Griffin saw what happened and, good citizen that he was, set off after the van. Well, I think he caught up with it. Or was allowed to, once the driver realized he was tailing them. I think he was murdered to stop him telling the police where the van had gone. Plus its registration number, of course. Plus . . . who knows?"

"Can you prove any of this?"

"Not yet."

"What about a body? If Griffin was murdered . . ."

"I've checked the records carefully. There were no unclaimed corpses within any feasible radius of Avebury in late July of 'eighty-one. And no missing-person report anywhere for anyone called Griffin. If there had been, Sharp would have picked up on it straight away."

"Sounds like you've gone a long way to proving yourself wrong, then."

"Not if Griffin was using an assumed name and/or his body was carefully disposed of."

"Come off it. You're stretching."

"Wait till you hear what Jeremy Hall has to tell us, Mr. Umber. The key is how—and in whose hands—the book got from Avebury twenty-three years ago to Jersey a few months ago. I don't believe for an instant Jeremy found it on the shelf at Quires by chance. I reckon—"

"Mr. Umber?" Both men turned at the call. "One of you two Mr. Umber?" It was the serving girl leaning out through the door of the café. "There's someone on the phone for you."

Umber exchanged a glance with Wisby, then stood up and hurried into the café. The girl pointed towards the telephone at one end of the counter, receiver dangling off the hook. Umber picked it up.

"Hello?"

"That you, Shadow Man?" It was Jeremy Hall. There was, of course, no-one else it could have been. His voice was slightly slurred, as if he had been drinking.

"Yes. It's me. Why aren't you here?"

"Wisby with you, is he?"

"Yes. As you arranged. I repeat: why aren't you here?"

"I thought about it and decided we ought to meet somewhere more . . . private."

"Where?"

"The old man's place. With him and Marilyn away, it's nice and quiet. I'm there now. Wisby knows where it is. Come on over. I'll wait for you."

"OK. But, Jeremy, you ought to know Wisby and I aren't—"

"Save it. I don't want to hear. Remember the day we first met, do you?"

"Of course."

"There was a kestrel above us. I saw it. Turning and turning in the sky. Did you see it?"

"I don't think so."

"Predator or prey. We're one or the other. You want your Junius, Shadow Man? You come and find him."

Wisby had parked his hire car on the other side of the harbour. By the time they had reached it and got onto the dual carriageway heading out of town, twenty minutes had passed, testing both men's patience.

"I smell a rat," said Wisby as he accelerated well beyond the sedate island-wide speed limit of 40 mph. "He never intended to meet us in St. Helier, did he?"

"Maybe not. But what difference does it make?"

"If he's planning to play some kind of trick on us . . ."

"What kind *could* he play? I thought you had him where you wanted him."

"I do. But despite that he seems to be calling the shots. Which is worrying. Distinctly worrying."

They turned inland halfway round the bay and headed north along a winding road through a tree-filled valley—Waterworks Valley, according to Wisby, named on account of its several reservoirs.

Sunlight sparkled on the still blue water and the bright yellow drifts of daffodils in the roadside meadows. Oliver Hall had chosen a picturesque corner of Jersey to retire to.

Wisby slowed as they rounded a bend. A gated driveway led off the road to the left, climbing through landscaped grounds towards a large house set amongst trees. A sign at the foot of the drive identified it as Eden Holt.

"This is it," said Wisby. He pulled up in front of the gates, lowered his window and pressed a button set next to an intercom grille on a post. "Let's see if he's going to let us in."

He was—without even bothering to confirm it was them. The gates swung slowly open. Wisby drove through and started up the slope towards the house.

Most of the building had been out of sight from the road. It was set on a shelf of land halfway up the side of the valley, commanding an expansive view of the rolling Jersey countryside. An elegantly meticulous recreation of a three-storeyed Queen Anne mansion, with porticoed entrance, mullioned windows and high, slender chimneys, its clean-cut grey stone glistened opulently in the sunshine.

The drive ran between the house and a wide, oval lawn towards a tree-screened triple garage. Jeremy's motorbike was standing in front of the garage, propped at an angle, sunlight shimmering on its petrol tank. Wisby stopped short of the balustraded steps that led up to the front door and turned the engine off. They climbed out into crystalline air and suspended silence, which the slamming of the car doors pierced like muffled gunshots. The two men exchanged a glance of mild puzzlement that Jeremy had not come out to greet them, but, as they started up the steps, they saw that the broad, green, dolphin-knockered door was ajar. It *was* a greeting—of sorts.

Wisby pushed the door open, giving them a view of the hall—a vast chequerboard of black and white marble tiles leading to a curving staircase. Doors stood open to ground-floor rooms on either side. But Jeremy did not step out of any of them, aware though he must have been that they had arrived.

"Where is he?" muttered Wisby. "What's he—"

"Look," Umber cut in. "Look, man."

Umber's gaze had drifted round to the console table standing against the wall a little way along the hall—and had gone no farther. There was a silver tray on the table, intended for post, perhaps. There were no letters lying on it. But it was not empty.

Two small books, held together by a rubber band, had been placed on the tray. The books' smooth white covers identified their binding as vellum. And the gold-lettered titles on their spines identified them as particular, exclusive and unquestionably unique.

"That's them, isn't it?" Wisby asked, glancing at Umber.

"Oh yes." Umber nodded. "That's them." And it was. There could be no doubt. There had only ever been one vellum-bound gilt-titled Junius, specially prepared to the author's specification and left for him by Woodfall at one of their secret coffee-house delivery points early in the month of March, 1773. Left—and later collected. "At last," Umber added, in a creamy murmur. "At long— What was that?"

He whirled round at a sound behind him: a sharp, metallic ping. Almost at once, there was a second ping and, this time, he saw what had caused it. A small pebble struck the roof of the car as he watched and bounced off. Another pebble followed.

Umber rushed down the steps onto the driveway and looked up, backing away towards the lawn as he did so. There were dormer windows set in the grey-slated roof, their lower halves obscured by a parapet running round the edge of the roof. In the centre of the parapet, directly above the front door, was a pediment. Jeremy Hall was leaning nonchalantly against its sloping left-hand side. He nodded, as if satisfied now he had got some attention, and tossed the remaining pebbles into the gully behind the pediment. Then he propped one foot on the parapet and gazed down.

"Spotted what's waiting for you in the hall, Shadow Man?" he called.

"Yes," Umber replied.

"Take them. They're yours."

"We want more than the books," shouted Wisby as he caught up with Umber. "You know what my terms are."

"Oh yes," Jeremy shouted back. "I know."

"Come down. Let's talk. Like we agreed."

"Like you demanded, you mean. Remember the kestrel, Shadow Man?"

"Yes. But—"

"Predator or prey. We're one or the other. Never both." He seemed to look beyond them, into the distance. "There's so much air up here. So much sky. And everything's so very, very simple."

"Come down," shouted Wisby.

"All right," Jeremy responded. "I will."

In that second, Umber knew what Jeremy was going to do. He stepped forward. And so did Jeremy. Out into the empty air beyond the parapet. Out into a place he could see so clearly. Out—and down.

Umber closed his eyes an immeasurable fraction of a second before Jeremy hit the ground. But the sound of the impact—the squelching thud of flesh and bone on tarmac, the fricative last gasp of breath forced from Jeremy's mouth—was no easier to bear than the sight of it would have been. Umber could not keep his eyes closed for ever. When he opened them, he knew what he would see. And already, before he did so, he knew of the other death it would call to his mind. The mangled body; the wine-dark blood; the stillness and the silence: as it had been for the sister so it was now for the brother.

Umber opened his eyes.

By a small, scant miracle, Jeremy had fallen with his face angled away from them. Only the tide of blood seeping from his smashed body, carried towards Umber by the camber of the drive, declared his death as an unalterable fact.

Umber stepped back onto the lawn before the stretching red fingers reached him. He sank to his haunches and stared at the lifeless, crumpled figure in front of him, at Jeremy's tousled blood-flecked hair, at the upturned palm of his nearest hand, cradled as if to receive some gift.

Umber thought of Jane Hall, standing in the cemetery above Marlborough, mourning her daughters and comforting herself with the knowledge that at least she still had a living, breathing son. Soon, all too soon, she would have that comfort snatched away from her.

Umber had done nothing to save the daughters. And now his action, for reasons he did not properly understand, had destroyed the son.

"Oh God," he murmured. "Oh dear God."

The car engine burst suddenly into life. Umber looked round and saw Wisby reversing the car away from him. It bumped up onto the lawn, then Wisby slammed it into forward gear, swerved round onto the drive and accelerated down the slope towards the gates.

Umber's reactions were addled by shock. He could not comprehend what was happening. Where was Wisby going? What in God's name did he think he was doing?

The probable answer hit Umber like a blow to the face. He jumped up and, skirting the pool of blood that had spread from Jeremy's body, ran across the drive and up the steps to the front door.

It was wide open. In the hall, on the console table, the silver tray stood empty.

Wisby had stopped at the foot of the drive, waiting for the gates to open after the car had crossed the sensor-cable. The gates swung slowly and smoothly. The car idled. Umber started running down the drive, certain he would be too late, but running anyway, his feet pounding on the tarmac.

The car started forward as soon as there was a large enough gap between the gates for it to pass through. Wisby pulled straight out onto the road and put his foot down. The car sped away. It was out of sight before Umber reached the gateway.

Umber's last few strides carried him out onto the road. He stared despairingly in the direction the car had taken—back the way they had come earlier. The gates were fully open by now. A few seconds later, they began to close again.

Umber had still not moved when they clanged shut behind him.

CHAPTER

NINETEEN

Umber walked south along the Waterworks Valley road through the encroaching dusk. Forward motion was the only strategy he was able to settle on. He had set off from Eden Holt telling himself he would flag down a car or call at the next house he came to in order to raise the alarm. He had done neither. He could have climbed the gates and phoned the police from Eden Holt, of course. Failure to do so had already set his course for him.

Jeremy Hall was dead. Nothing could restore him to life. The ugly truth was that Umber's dread of the consequences of Jeremy's death was stronger than the duty he felt to report it. Naturally, he *would* report it. But not from the scene. Not there and then. Not in any way that required him to account for his part in it. As yet, he was unable to do that even to himself.

After two or three miles, he reached the village of Millbrook, where Wisby had turned off the coast road on their way from St. Helier. There was a call-box by the junction. Umber went in, dialled 999 and asked for the police.

"There's been a suicide at Eden Holt, a house in Waterworks Valley," he said, ignoring requests for his name and location. And then he promptly rang off.

He crossed the road and waited at the bus stop. He knew he was on the route of the half-hourly service to the Airport. And he knew for a rock-solid certainty that the Airport was where Wisby would have headed, fearing an encounter with Umber if he lingered on the island. He had what he wanted, after all. Not all of it, of course. Not the full explanation he might have been able to extract from Jeremy Hall. But he had the vellum-bound Junius. And no doubt he was determined to keep it.

The bus route to the Airport, as Umber also knew, ran through St. Aubin. He did not get off, telling himself it was better if Chantelle heard the news from the police. That way, she could happily assume for a few more hours at least that Jeremy would return to her. Umber could only pray he would not see her in the street as the bus passed through. And his prayer was answered.

There was no sign of Wisby in the check-in area at the Airport. A word at the information desk revealed there were several flights to various British destinations he could already have left on. No doubt he had taken the first available one, whether it was to Gatwick, Bristol or even Manchester. But had he left at all—rather than returned to St. Helier, if only to collect his belongings from his hotel? Umber prowled the car park, inspecting numerous lookalike hire cars, until he found one whose rear tyres were smeared with mud and grass from a recent lawn-skid. That clinched it. The bird had flown. Perhaps he had checked out of his hotel earlier, guessing he might need to make a hasty getaway after their meeting with Jeremy. Umber suspected Wisby had intended all along to spring some kind of double-cross as soon as the Juniuses' authenticity had been confirmed. A glance at the books from ten feet away was hardly sufficient for Umber to do that, but Wisby had clearly decided to settle for it in the suddenly and savagely altered circumstances.

Umber had been so close to laying his hands on the fabled special copy of the 1773 Junius and reading what Griffin had described to him twenty-three years previously as *"an illuminating and more than somewhat surprising inscription"* that he could scarcely believe he had let the opportunity slip through his fingers. He knew why, of course. He knew the reason only too well. The sight of Jeremy Hall lying dead in a spreading pool of blood burst into his mind whenever he closed his eyes. It had not been enough to stop Wisby, however. It had not been enough even to make him hesitate.

It was the galling thought of Wisby studying the inscription over an in-flight drink that suddenly alerted Umber to the one question above all he should have put to Vernon Garrard—but had failed to. He rushed back into the terminal building and made for the payphones.

It was way past Quires' probable closing time. But a book dealer is always open to offers. The recorded message at Quires gave an out-of-hours number to try. Umber rang it—and Garrard answered.

"David Umber here, Mr. Garrard."

A sigh. "I rather thought our business was concluded, Mr. Umber."

"There's a question I forgot to ask. Just one."

Another sigh. "Very well. What is it?"

"What was the inscription in the Junius?"

"Inscription?"

"You must have inspected the book before selling it. Especially since you hadn't even known it was in stock."

"Ah. I see. Well, yes, I cast my eye over it, naturally, as you say, if only in order to set a price."

"And?"

"It's rather odd, actually. Both you and Mr. Wisby neglected to raise the point."

"Exactly. But now we've been able to compare notes. So, what was the inscription?"

"There wasn't one."

"No inscription?"

"None."

"You're sure?"

"I'm sure there *wasn't*. But as to whether there *had been* . . ."

"What do you mean?"

"The fly-leaves had been torn out of both volumes, Mr. Umber. *That's* what I mean."

Umber booked a seat on a morning flight to Gatwick and took the bus back to St. Helier. It was Thursday evening. A glance at his watch reminded him that he could even then have been sitting with Marilyn Hall in the theatre, watching *All's Well That Ends Well*, with her stepson alive and none the wiser. But there was only one rule in the game of consequences: you could never go back. Jeremy Hall was dead. And his death made one thing certain. All was not going to end well.

Umber should have phoned Larter and warned him of his return, but could not bring himself to, knowing that, if he did, he would have to explain why he was leaving Jersey. It was not as if he had made any progress towards securing Sharp's release from prison. He was, however he chose to present it, fleeing the scene of a crime. What the nature of the crime was he could not exactly have said. But to inflict the loss of another child on Jane Questred and Oliver Hall was unforgivably cruel. They would certainly not forgive him when they learned from Chantelle of the part he had played in driving Jeremy to his death. They would travel to Jersey as soon as the news reached them. Umber must not be there when they arrived. He could not look them in the face and tell them what had happened—how he had watched, helplessly but culpably, their son's self-destruction. He could not. And he would not.

He took a taxi to the Airport in the morning, rather than a bus, thereby avoiding a diversion through St. Aubin. Once inside the terminal building he behaved almost like a fugitive, fearing Oliver Hall might fly in before he left, improbable though that was. It did not happen. Umber boarded the flight to Gatwick and watched Jersey shrink behind him as the plane climbed away to the west. Then it turned, kestrel-like, across the sky. And the island vanished from his sight.

It was nearly one o'clock when Umber reached Ilford. He checked the Sheepwalk on his way to Bengal Road from the station. Larter was not there. Nor did he seem to be at home. There was no answer to the bell. Umber stood on the doorstep, wondering how long the old boy might be gone.

"David!"

He turned, half-recognizing the voice before he saw who had called to him, but surprised nonetheless when he actually set eyes on Claire Wheatley. She was standing by a sleek blue TVR, holding open the driver's door on the opposite side of the street. He hurried across to join her.

"Surprised to see me?" There was an edge to her tone, of hostility or anxiety—he could not decide which.

"Yes, I *am* surprised. What's brought you all the way out here, Claire?"

"You. I got the address from Alice."

"What have I done?"

"I don't know. You tell me."

"I'm not with you."

"Where have you been since Tuesday?"

"Why do you want to know?"

"Alice told me about picking you up from the hospital in Reading, David. And why she had to. Your run-in with the people who were looking for Wisby. Remember that?"

"Of course I remember it."

"It seems to have sparked something off."

"Oh yes?"

"Get in the car. I'll tell you on the way."

"On the way where?"

"Whipps Cross Hospital. You'll be wanting to visit your friend, Bill Larter. According to one of his neighbours, that's where he is."

"Bill's in hospital?"

"The house was burgled last night, apparently. He tackled the burglars and got beaten up. The neighbour didn't know how badly. Shall we go and find out?"

Umber was too shocked to argue even if he had wanted to. Before he could articulate a response to Claire's news, she had hustled him into the car and driven away. And then she had started to tell him the rest of her news.

"The practice was broken into on Wednesday night. The police reckoned the intruders were looking for drugs and didn't have the brains to realize a psychotherapist isn't a psychiatrist. They certainly made a hell of a mess. But I think that was just camouflage. They went through my client files, yet nothing was taken. Do you know what they were looking for, David? Of course you do."

"Your notes on Sally," Umber responded glumly.

"Has to be, doesn't it? I destroyed them a year after Sally's death, as it happens, so they went away empty-handed. Last night they tried their luck here. That's three break-ins, counting the raid on Wisby's boat. So, what exactly are they after, David?"

"I'm not sure."

"Try guessing."

"All right. At a guess, I'd say they're trying to figure out how close Sally was to the truth. And whether any of us know as much as she knew."

"That's my guess too. So, thanks for dragging me into this. It's all I was short of. I've had to move in with Alice in case they come to my house, though I'm not sure *her* house is much safer in the circumstances. My life's been turned upside down since you called round for a confidential lunchtime chat. The way I see it, you were either followed or you told someone about me—someone you shouldn't have trusted."

"Marilyn Hall," he murmured. The sequence of events assembled themselves with sickening logic in Umber's mind. He had mentioned Claire when he had called at Kingsley House in search of Oliver Hall. He had mentioned Wisby too. "I *am* sorry, Claire. Really. I'm afraid things are worse than you think."

"How can they be?"

"Easily. As you'll understand when I tell you what I've been doing since Tuesday."

Claire had pulled into the car park at Whipps Cross Hospital by the time Umber had finished his account. She turned off the engine and said nothing at first, tapping her nose against a crooked index finger, her lips parted, her gaze unfocused. When eventually she spoke, it was in a pensive undertone.

"I guess I owe you an apology, David."

"What for?"

"Denying you were onto something. Insisting Sally couldn't have been murdered. Advising you, even if not in so many words, to pull yourself together."

"We're even then. I never intended to drag you into this."

"No? Well, I'm in it now."

"I doubt you really need to worry. The raid on your practice was probably just a precaution. Like you said, they drew a blank. They can't afford to attract too much attention to themselves. I think they'll leave you alone from now on."

"You do, do you?" She turned to look at him.

"I hope so."

"Me too." She sighed. "Go and see your friend, David. I'll wait here."

Umber had to claim a blood relationship with Larter before he was allowed in to see him. The old man was in poor shape, broken ribs having led to a collapsed lung. He had a suction tube in his chest and oxygen on tap to aid his breathing. A split lip was a further obstacle to speech and the sister instructed Umber to keep their conversation to a minimum.

"Lucky . . . I didn't have . . . my teeth in," Larter wheezily joked. "I'd probably have had them . . . knocked down my throat."

"Were there two of them, Bill?"

"Yeah. Smug-looking geezer . . . and some shaven-headed bruiser . . . with a baseball bat."

"Did they say what they were after?"

"Not *what* . . . *who*." Larter pointed a shaky finger at Umber. "Thought I could . . . take them on." He managed a weak grin. "Bloody stupid of me."

"I'm sorry, Bill. This is all getting way out of hand."

"Yeah." Another grin. "I'll have them . . . keep a bed for you . . . Maybe George is better off . . . where he is."

"Yes. Maybe he is."

"Word of advice, son."

"What?"

"Don't hold back. . . . It's too late . . . for that. It's them . . . or you."

Before leaving the hospital, Umber promised Larter he would board up the window Walsh and baseball-bat man had broken during the break-in. He had the keys to the house and permission to stay there as long as he needed to. As it turned out, however, Claire had other ideas about his accommodation.

"I've just spoken to Alice. She suggested you stay at her house for the duration."

"There's no need for that."

"Isn't there?' Claire's look suggested otherwise.

"Safety in numbers, you mean? All right. If Alice insists."

"It's more than that. We have to decide what to do for the best, David. I don't want to have to schlep out to Ilford to talk it over with you."

"We can talk it over now."

"No. I have to see a man about a new lock. Tonight, at Alice's, the three of us: *that's* when we'll talk."

At 45 Bengal Road, Umber found some chipboard and tools in the garden shed, as Larter had said he would. He knocked out the broken glass from the smashed pane in the back door and covered the gap as best he could.

Then he busied himself on the telephone. The one meagre consolation he could take from what had happened in Jersey was that Wisby had got away with less than he must have reckoned on. The inscription had been removed from his stolen Junius. There had to be a reason for that—a reason that might reveal some of what Jeremy Hall could have told them had he chosen to. The only advantage Umber possessed over Wisby was his historical training. There was still a trail he could follow that might lead to Junius— and the secret contained in the inscription.

Several phone calls later, he had established that the Ventry Papers were held at the Staffordshire County Record Office. Not Derby, Nottingham or Leicester, then, but Stafford. With the weekend looming, he would have to wait until Monday to inspect them. That felt like a preposterously long time in his present state of mind, but Monday it would have to be.

It was late afternoon when he left Ilford, but he did not go straight to Hampstead. Guilt and anxiety were gnawing at him as sharply as ever. From Liverpool Street he took the Tube to Bond Street and walked down to Kingsley House. A damp dusk was descending on Mayfair. It was more than dark enough for the lights to be on in the Halls' apartment. But none were. Umber risked a word with the porter manning the desk in the lobby.

"Mr. and Mrs. Hall have gone away, sir."

"That must have been sudden. I told them I might drop by this evening. They didn't say anything that suggested they mightn't be here."

The porter smiled tightly. "Perhaps they changed their plans."

"Have they gone to Jersey?"

"I couldn't say, sir."

But Umber could. He knew exactly where they had gone. And why.

"Do you want to leave a message in case they phone?" the porter asked.

"No." Umber turned towards the exit. "No message."

C H A P T E R

TWENTY

Dusk had given way to night by the time Umber reached Hampstead. He walked up Willow Hill, steeling himself for the accusations Alice and Claire had every right to throw at him. He had no adequate response prepared, nor any course of action to suggest that might lead them out of their difficulties. George Sharp in prison, Bill Larter in hospital and Jeremy Hall dead: they were the bitter sum of his achievements to date.

"Good of you to join us," was Alice's sarcastic greeting. She had been hitting the gin, to judge by the half-empty tumbler of something with lemon clutched in her hand as she opened the door of number 22, not to mention the heaviness of her tread as she led him into the drawing room.

An aroma of fresh paint still lingered in the room. Redecoration was evidently complete. Some platitudinous enthusing over the colour scheme died on Umber's lips. Claire, who was sitting by the fire with a mug of green tea, rolled her eyes at him as Alice pulled round a chair.

"Would you like some tea, David?" Claire asked.

"I expect he'd prefer a beer," said Alice.

Umber shrugged. "Whatever."

"Either way, it's in the kitchen. Help yourself."

Umber shrugged again, this time for Claire's benefit, and made his way to the kitchen. He found a bottle of Grölsch in the fridge.

While he was hunting down a glass, he caught a drift of words from the drawing room, but could not make them out. Claire was speaking, in an undertone. Only Alice's response was audible. "Why should I?"

"It goes without saying that I'm sorry for dragging you both into this," Umber ventured as he rejoined them. "I never intended to cause you any trouble."

"What did you intend to do?" Alice snapped.

"Learn the truth." He sat down and countered her glare with a level gaze. "If I could."

"Find one more to your liking, you mean."

"There's only one truth, Alice. And it's not what we thought."

"I'm not going to start believing Sally was murdered just because you've stirred up a hornets' nest."

"I think you may have to."

"I was here when it happened. You weren't. Sally was alone when she died. There was no intruder. No murderer."

"You can't be absolutely certain of that, Alice," put in Claire.

Alice tossed her head pettishly. "Not you too."

"We need to consider every possibility."

"OK, then. Consider this. How did the murderer get in?"

"Perhaps Sally invited him in."

"Then promptly took a bath? Get real, for God's sake."

"It was a summer's evening. She'd have had the windows open, presumably."

"Yeah. But her windows happened to be on the second floor."

"He could have swung down from the roof and through the open top half of the sash," said Umber, reasoning as he went. "Then just let himself out of the flat and left by the front door."

"Who are we talking about here? The SAS?"

"A professional of some kind. That's who we're talking about."

"I think David's right," said Claire, calmly but firmly. "Recent events don't really leave much room for doubt, to my mind. Sally was onto something. And somebody was determined to stop her bringing it into the open."

"That's not what you said at the time."

"I had no reason to think it. *Then*. But this is now. David's provoked a response. We may wish he hadn't. But we can't ignore it. Think about it, Alice. If Sally really was murdered . . ."

"She wasn't."

"But if she was . . . do you want to let her killers get away with it?"

"Of course not."

"OK, then. We have two options as I see it. One, tell David to go back to Prague and let his policeman friend take his chances in court, then hope everything blows over, as it probably will, Jeremy Hall's suicide notwithstanding. It's the line of least resistance. It's the safest and simplest thing to do."

"But it's not the option you favour, is it?" Alice's tone was almost fatalistic.

"No. It isn't."

"Better give us number two, then."

"Do all we can to find out what Sally may have uncovered."

"If anything."

"Yes. If anything."

Alice took a deep swallow of gin and looked sceptically at Claire and Umber in turn. "You've left it five years too late. If there were any clues, they're long gone. Assuming there was something for there to be clues *to*."

"What happened to her possessions?"

"Ask David."

Umber winced. Alice had urged him to take whatever keepsakes he wanted when he had flown in from Turkey for the funeral. But guilt, grief and a secret, simmering anger at Sally for running away from life had deluded him into believing he wanted none. Alice had more or less forced him to take Sally's wedding ring. Everything else he had left. "I don't know what happened to them," he said hoarsely.

"Her parents took some stuff," Alice stated matter-of-factly. "The rest—clothes and such—went to Oxfam."

"Were there any papers?" Claire asked. "Notes? Diaries? Documents?"

"It was hardly my place to sort through it," Alice replied. "And David declined to. So I can't say. Whatever there was . . . her parents removed."

"We'd better contact them, then."

"They'll probably have got rid of it all by now."

"Let's hope not." Claire looked at Umber. "Do you know where they live, David?"

"Unless they've moved, yes. They have a bungalow on the Hampshire coast. Near Christchurch."

Umber had assumed till now that Reg and Peggy Wilkinson had left his life for good and all. He had few happy memories of his parents-in-law, as few as he suspected they had of him. Reg had never troubled to disguise his disapproval of Umber's rootless and pensionless existence. And what Reg thought, Peggy always went along with. It had never been a harmonious relationship. Sally's death had ended it as badly as could be imagined. But not, it seemed, as completely.

"There's something you should understand, Claire," he said hesitantly. "The Wilkinsons and I . . . er . . ."

"What he means," put in Alice, "is that they hate his guts. They aren't likely to give him the time of day, let alone the chance to root through whatever they have left of Sally's."

"It's not as bad as that," Umber protested. But, almost instantly, it struck him that pretence on the issue was pointless. "Well, maybe it is."

"Yes," said Claire dispassionately. "Bearing in mind what Sally told me about how things stood between you and her parents, I should imagine it might well be. Which is why Alice and I will go to see them without you."

"Excuse me?" spluttered Alice.

"Tomorrow," Claire breezed calmly on. "I think we can all agree there's no time to be lost."

Several hours and an awkward little supper party later, Alice took herself off to bed none too soberly, leaving Claire to load the dishwasher, while Umber sat at the kitchen table with a mug of black coffee.

"She'll be fine in the morning," said Claire, with a wry smile. "Stress affects people in different ways."

"You seem to be coping all right," said Umber, understating the case if anything, given her consistent *sangfroid*.

"It's just a technique. I break problems down into small, soluble portions. That way I can kid myself nothing's beyond me, as long as I can take it one logical step at a time."

"Do you teach the technique to your patients? Sorry. I mean clients."

"Well remembered. And yes, I do. Or at any rate I try. But psychotherapy isn't really that simple."

"I imagine not."

"It can be helpful, though." She pushed the dishwasher door shut and started the machine going, then turned to look at him. "It can resolve a lot of issues."

"Think I could benefit from a course?"

"I'm sure you could." She sat down at the table opposite him. Her shoulder-bag was hanging from the back of the chair. She delved into it and plucked out a pack of cigarettes and a disposable lighter. "Just now I recommend something a bit more basic, though. You want one?"

Umber shook his head. "I didn't know you smoked."

"Only in emergencies." She lit up and piloted a spare saucer into the centre of the table to serve as an ashtray. "What about you?"

"Never got the taste for it."

"Nor for resolving issues?"

"I've taken that up late in life."

"With what results?"

"Mixed. Decidedly mixed."

"Alice suggested something to me before you arrived this evening. And before the gin hit her bloodstream. She said the two of us ought to go away together. She had South America in mind. An adventure holiday. A couple of middle-aged girls on a spree."

"Sounds like fun."

"Think we should go?"

"You could do worse."

"Like staying in London, you mean?"

"The people we're dealing with, Claire, whoever they are, whatever their motives—"

"Aren't kidding around?" She held his gaze through a plume of cigarette smoke.

"No. They're not."

"So, if we succeed in finding out what Sally knew . . ."

"You may wish you'd taken that trip to South America."

C H A P T E R

TWENTY-ONE

The bloated Saturday edition of the *Guardian* arrived in Alice's hallway with a loud thump, though it was probably the higher-pitched rattle of the letterbox that roused Umber from an uneasy sleep in the rear drawing room. Alice's sofa-bed was several comfort points up on Bill Larter's, but that had hardly been sufficient to provide him with a good night's rest. The stitches in his scalp were becoming more of an irritant the longer they stayed in. And the demons inside his head never paused for slumber.

He struggled into his clothes, collected the *Guardian* from the door-mat, then headed for the kitchen—and the coffee jar.

The kettle had not even come to the boil when his idle leafing through the newspaper took him to a headline he had hoped against false hope not to see. TRAGEDY RETURNS TO MURDER FAMILY 23 YEARS ON. He anxiously scanned the paragraphs below, relieved at least not to find his own name—or George Sharp's—staring back at him. But that was the full extent of his relief. Events at Avebury in July 1981 were back in the public eye. And its gaze was unblinking.

Less than two weeks after the murder in prison of Brian Radd, the serial child killer held responsible for the deaths of Miranda and Tamsin Hall in 1981, the girls' brother, Jeremy Hall, has been found dead at his father's house in Jersey.

A police spokesperson said Mr. Hall, who was 33, had died as the result of a fall from the roof of the house. He had been alone at the time and the circumstances surrounding the incident were as yet unclear.

The dead man's father, Oliver Hall, aged 66, said Jeremy's loss had come as a great shock to him and to Jeremy's mother. He appealed to the media to respect their privacy at 'this terrible time.'

The original murder case has dogged many of those involved in it. Five years ago, the children's nanny, Sally Wilkinson, died in what was officially ruled an accidental electrocution. She was among those who had cast doubts on Brian Radd's confession, which he volunteered shortly before his trial on multiple murder charges in 1990. Jeremy Hall's death will only fuel speculation that—

"The press were bound to pick up on it," said Claire, causing Umber to jump with surprise as she leaned over his shoulder to examine the article. She was dressed in a navy-blue tracksuit and mud-spattered trainers. Her hair and face were damp with sweat. Umber had supposed himself to be awake before the rest of the house, but that was clearly not the case. "You must have seen this coming, David. Surely."

"I didn't think they'd make such a splash of the story."

"Coming hard on the heels of Radd's murder? They were never going to ignore it."

"They even mention Sally."

"But they use her maiden name, I see. Maybe you should be grateful for that."

"Will the Wilkinsons be grateful?"

"Only one way to find out. Isn't there?"

Claire and Alice set off for Hampshire in Claire's TVR at 10:30. There was no guarantee the Wilkinsons would be at home, of course. But the risk of a wasted journey was preferable to the possibility that Reg would forbid them to come if they phoned ahead. Alice predicted he would not let them past the door even without Umber for company, but her pessimism was partly a symptom of her hangover. Claire seemed altogether more confident. "They'll be happy to talk about Sally. Silence is never golden for bereaved parents." The professional had spoken.

As far as she and Alice were concerned, Umber was planning to spend the day at the British Library, boning up on Junius. He had, of course, already established that the Ventry Papers, which represented his only remaining lead to Junius's identity—and hence Griffin's—were lodged in the Staffordshire Record Office. It was therefore unnecessary for him to do any more research in London and, in fact, he had no such intention. Alan Wisby had given him the slip in Jersey, cunningly and clinically. That did not mean he could go on doing so. *Monica* would remain in the boatyard at Newbury, deserted by her owner. Umber had no doubt Wisby would stay well away from her. But the man had to stay somewhere. And that put another Monica in the frame.

Umber's trip to Southwark was little more than a fishing expedition. He did not seriously expect to find anyone in the office at 171A Blackfriars Road on a Saturday morning. His ambitions were fixed no higher than extracting a home address or telephone number for Monica Wisby from the shoe-repair man in the ground-floor shop. He turned the handle of the door leading to the stairs up to the first floor fully expecting to find it locked.

But it was not.

A tall, broad-hipped, big-bosomed woman in tight jeans and a clinging sweater was fingering her way through a set of bulging folders in one of the middle drawers of a battered filing cabinet when Umber stepped into the room at the top of the stairs. She had a mane of bottle-blonde hair and a raw-boned face done no favours by cigarettes and a career of private inquiring.

"Monica Wisby?" he ventured, already certain it was her.

She started violently, scattering cigarette ash down her sweater as she turned. "Who the fuck are you?"

"David Umber."

"How did you get in?"

"The door was open."

"Bloody well shouldn't be. We're not open for business." She hip-barged the drawer of the filing cabinet shut. "Come back Monday." Then recognition of his name kicked in. "Hold on. Did you say Umber?"

"Yes. You know. The guy you were holding a letter for last week on your ex-husband's behalf."

"Yeah. That's right." She had absorbed the surprise of his arrival by now and Kleenexing the ash off her sweater gave her a few more moments for tactical thought before she looked him in the eye. "Well, what about it?"

"Where is he?"

"Alan?"

"He and I need to meet. Urgently."

"He obviously doesn't agree. Otherwise you wouldn't be asking me. But you got it spot-on. *Ex*-husband. Ex as in gone, separated, finished—for good."

"I know you keep in touch with him."

"No. *He* keeps in touch with *me*. When he wants to. Which he currently doesn't seem to. Tried the boat?"

"You're joking, of course. I'm sure he's told you what happened when I 'tried the boat.'"

"I've heard nothing from Alan since he sent me the letter for you. And that was only a few words on a covering note."

"He didn't get everything he wanted in Jersey, Mrs. Wisby. Small matter of a missing inscription."

"I don't know what you're talking about."

"Maybe not. But he will. Tell him I've got the missing pages." A lie designed to smoke out Wisby counted as a white one in Umber's book. "He can't do anything without them."

"Tell him yourself. You're more likely to get the chance than I am. And you can give him a message from me if you do. He's supposed to be retired, for Christ's sake. I'm fed up having to explain to his clients that his freelance activities have nothing to do with me. He seems to be doing more work now than when he was supposed to be in charge of the business. First there was that pensioned-off policeman. Then you. And then . . . what's his name?" She grabbed a scrap of paper from the nearest desk and squinted at it. "Nevinson."

"What?"

"Know him, do you?"

"Percy Nevinson?"

"He didn't give me a Christian name and I didn't ask for one. But he's been on several times this week." She held out the note for Umber to read. He assumed it had been written by the secretary for Monica's attention. *Mr. Nevinson called again for Mr. Wisby. Please call with any news. 01672-799332.*

"Mind if I use your phone?"

"Haven't you got one of your own?"

"No. I lost my mobile on your ex-husband's boat, as a matter of fact. I'll pay you for the call if it's such a big deal."

Monica looked as if she wanted to refuse on principle but was unsure what the principle might be. "Oh, be my fucking guest, then," she said with a toss of the head.

Umber picked up the telephone and dialled. There was a distant, old-fashioned ringing tone. Then Abigail Nevinson answered.

"Miss Nevinson? This is David Umber."

"Mr. Umber. I was just thinking about you."

"You were? Why?"

"Oh, it doesn't matter. What can I do for you?"

"Is Percy there?"

"No. Percy, er . . . Well . . . He's gone away. To one of his . . . ufological conferences."

"Where's it being held?"

"I'm . . . not sure."

"How would you get in touch with him in an emergency?"

"It would be difficult. I'd . . . have to wait for him to contact me."

"Is that normal when he goes to one of these things?"

"Well . . . No. Not really. It's a little . . . concerning, I have to admit."

"When did he leave?"

"Early this morning. Before I was up."

"And when's he due back?"

"I'm not sure. I imagine it's just a weekend event, though. They normally are. Unless . . ."

"What?"

"I've just read about Jeremy Hall in the paper, Mr. Umber. I suppose you know what's happened."

"Yes."

"You don't think Percy's trip . . . has anything to do with that, do you?"

Umber did think so. In fact, he felt certain of it, though what dealings Nevinson might have had with Wisby were a mystery to him. That applied to a good deal else as well. Every step he took led him further into a labyrinth of lies. For every one he nailed there was another waiting to deceive him.

From Blackfriars Road he walked aimlessly towards Tate Modern, pausing amidst the ambling tourists on the Millennium Bridge to stare downriver and wrestle in his mind with the confusions and contradictions that threatened to swamp him. Nevinson had gone to Jersey. Umber's every instinct told him so. The Halls and the Questreds were there and so were the clues to what had driven Jeremy Hall to suicide. Maybe Wisby had gone back there as well. And maybe Umber should follow. But what could he accomplish there? What could he hope to achieve? There was still no trail he could follow that promised to lead him to the truth.

Umber ended up walking most of the way back to Hampstead. Physical exhaustion seemed to be the only brake on the enervating whirl of his thoughts. He took a decision of sorts during the long trudge through Finsbury and Camden Town. It involved misleading Claire and Alice. But he reckoned he would be doing them a favour— just about the only favour he had in his gift.

They had already returned from Hampshire when he reached 22 Willow Hill, his arrival time handily consistent with the studious hours he had supposedly spent in the British Library. He expected to be told they had learned nothing from the Wilkinsons. The assumption had been factored into his decision. But it was an assumption that was to be rapidly confounded.

"Alice is busy upstairs on her computer," Claire said as she let him in and led the way towards the kitchen. "We got back half an hour ago."

"Empty-handed?"

"No." She glanced over her shoulder at him. "We found something all right, David."

He recognized the object as soon as he saw it lying on the kitchen table: a spiral-bound crimson-covered scrapbook. "My God," he said. "I never thought I'd see that again."

Sally had amassed a collection of newspaper cuttings relating to Miranda Hall's murder and Tamsin Hall's presumed murder. Triggered by Radd's out-of-the-blue confession nine years after the event, she had bought a scrapbook and pasted the cuttings into it, along with new ones reporting Radd's trial. Umber had urged her to throw them away, but that had only fired her determination to preserve them. The book was a testament to her belief that 'Somebody has to keep a proper record in case they fiddle with the facts and hope we won't notice.' It was around then that Umber had begun to understand the intractability of her plight. Time had hardened Sally's wounds, not healed them.

"You've looked through it?" Umber asked, laying his hand lightly on the cover.

"Yes," said Claire from behind him.

"Morbid reading, isn't it?"

"Yes."

"And Sally did read it. All too often."

"Unlike her parents, then. I don't think they'd ever brought themselves to open it."

"No?"

"Not her mother, anyway. Reg Wilkinson had a stroke the year after Sally died. He's virtually mute, so there's no way to tell what he might or might not have made of it."

"And Peggy?"

"She's fit and well. Sent you her love."

Umber swallowed hard. "Did she?"

"She was happy to let us borrow the scrapbook if it helped to make any sense of Sally's death."

"Can't see how it could do that. There's nothing in these cuttings we don't already know."

"That's not strictly true, David. Turn to the back of the book."

Umber opened the book at the last page, which, like several before it, was blank. A sheet of paper had been slipped inside the cover: a page torn out of a glossy magazine. Under the heading INSIDE STORY was an assortment of paparazzo-snapped celebrities, most of whose names registered, if only dimly, in Umber's consciousness. It was a page from *Hello!*, of course. That, he knew at once, was the point.

"As soon as I saw it I remembered," said Claire. "When I had that stupid row with Sally in the coffee-shop the day she died and she threw the magazine at me. You know? I told you about it."

"Yes?" He looked round and frowned at her.

"I'd forgotten, until I saw that. Sally tore a page out of the magazine *before* she threw it at me."

"And this is it?"

"Has to be."

"But what does it mean?"

"It means she saw something significant in a month-old copy of *Hello!* she was looking at in my waiting room. That's why she walked out. Because what she saw made a counselling session with me . . . suddenly irrelevant."

Umber looked at the page again and turned it over. More INSIDE STORY zoom-lensed pictures of movie stars out shopping in sunglasses and baseball caps or sunbathing in cellulite-revealing swimsuits. "I don't get it," he said. "What's *significant* about any of this?"

Claire flipped the page back over. "There," she said, pointing to a spread of three photographs of what looked to be a friendly game of mixed-doubles tennis on a red-clay court featuring an actor and actress Umber had never heard of on one side of the net and a tennis player he *had* heard of, plus girlfriend, on the other. According to the captions, the actor and actress were taking a break from promoting their latest blockbuster at the Cannes Film Festival. The bronzed, honed, raven-haired tennis star entertaining them on a local court was Monaco-based Michel Tinaud, of whom great things were expected at the forthcoming French Open. "He's why Sally went to Wimbledon that week," Claire continued. "Remember what she said to Alice? "I don't need a ticket." Don't you see? She wasn't going to watch tennis. She was going to speak to a tennis player."

"Why?" Umber already knew the answer, but the question was apt nonetheless. He knew. But he did not understand.

"It has to be the girlfriend," said Claire.

And so it did. Unnamed by *Hello!* presumably because unidentified, Tinaud's playing companion was dressed in a red T-shirt and white tennis skirt. She had long fair hair tied in a ponytail and featured in only one picture, biting her lower lip and wrinkling her brow in concentration as she waited to receive service.

"Recognize the expression?" Claire slipped the *Hello!* cutting out onto the table, then turned to a page nearer the front of the scrapbook, where one of the Halls' photographs of Tamsin had been reproduced in a newspaper a few days after her abduction. The two-year-old Tamsin was wrinkling her brow at the camera and biting her lower lip.

"It's a common gesture," Umber murmured. "It doesn't mean—"

"Sally saw something. Probably more than just the expression. She was the girl's nanny. She knew her as closely as her mother did. She knew her well enough to recognize the child in the woman. The girl on the tennis court looks about twenty to me. What do you think?"

"Probably."

"The right age."

"Like thousands of others."

"But *not* like thousands of others—in some way that convinced Sally she'd found her."

"You can't be sure."

"Sally was sure."

"Was she?" Umber knew the answer to his question better than Claire could hope to. He was playing for time—the time he needed to think. Because he had seen something too. Not a tantalizing resemblance to a missing, presumed-dead two-year-old girl. But an unmistakable similarity to someone he had met only recently. The hair was a different colour, worn in a different style. The clothes were a bizarre contrast. The environment was alien to her. But there was absolutely no doubt in Umber's mind. Michel Tinaud's girlfriend . . . was Chantelle.

CHAPTER

TWENTY-TWO

The decision Umber had taken was, in the event, merely re-inforced by what Claire had shown him. Amid his general bemusement, he held on to the conviction that the only way he could atone for endangering innocents and bystanders and blameless friends alike was to ensure that he did not lead any of them further down a road whose end he could not foresee. He slipped the *Hello!* page back into the scrapbook and closed it. As he turned towards Claire, he saw Alice walk in through the door behind her.

"You look like you've seen a ghost," she said, cocking her head at him. "Think you have?"

"Maybe."

"We reckon Sally was more certain."

"So Claire tells me."

"I've just been catching the latest tennis news on the Web. Tinaud's career isn't what it was in 'ninety-nine. He's just gone out of the Nasdaq Open in Miami in the first round."

"Oh yes?"

"The next big tournament in the calendar is the Monte Carlo Masters. Home ground for Tinaud. So, I guess he'll already be back there."

"And you're going to suggest we go see him?"

"I was sceptical about this whole thing, David. You know that. But I'm convinced now. Sally went to Wimbledon the day before she died to confront that man. We've got to find out what happened."

"Do you agree?" Umber looked at Claire.

"It's the obvious next step. The *only* next step. We have to go."

"No," he said quietly.

"What?"

"I thought it all through while you were down in Hampshire. Sally's dead. We can't bring her back to life. All we'll do by chasing after answers to questions no-one's forcing us to ask is to put ourselves in unnecessary danger. We have to give it up."

"You don't believe that."

"I do. I'm taking your option one, Claire. I'm going back to Prague. I'm bowing out."

"You can't."

"I can. And I will. What's more, I advise you to follow my example."

"What about George Sharp?"

"I'm not responsible for what happens to George. He dragged *me* into this. He'll have to drag *himself* out."

"Jesus," said Alice, staring at him with a mixture of surprise and contempt. "It didn't take long for you to revert to type, did it? I thought you'd finally found some moral fibre. But no. It was just a passing phase. This is the real you, isn't it? The man I urged Sally to have nothing to do with. The spineless shit she should never have—"

"Alice." Claire glared round at her friend, commanding her silence. Then she turned back to Umber. "You're not serious about this, are you, David?"

"Never more so."

"We've just uncovered the biggest clue going to what Sally was up to. And you want to walk away from it?"

"Self-preservation, Claire. That's what it comes down to. Like Alice said. This is the real me. Someone who believes, at the end of the day, in looking after number one."

"I don't think that's the real you at all."

"Well, you'll have to start getting used to the idea. I'm not going on with this. It's as simple as that."

"We'll go on with it."

"You shouldn't. You really shouldn't."

"Because of the risks?"

"Obviously."

"Help us minimize them, then. Come with us."

"No."

"David, I—"

"You're wasting your breath, Claire," said Alice. "He's got it all worked out. Sometimes the wrong thing to do is the only thing to do. Isn't that so, David?"

Umber shrugged. "Sticks and stones."

"Yeah." Alice nodded grimly. Her low opinion of him made the deception all too easy to carry off, Umber realized. She wanted to believe in his loss of nerve too badly to question its genuineness. "You're the living proof of words never hurting, David. You know that?"

"Yes." He gave her a stoical little smile. "I suppose I am."

It took Umber no more than a few minutes to pack his belongings. He hoped to make it out of the house without further debate. Certainly Alice seemed too self-righteously angry to spare him even a parting gibe. But Claire, still worryingly unconvinced by his change of heart, cornered him in the hall.

"How soon are you going back to Prague?" she asked with pragmatic coolness.

"Not sure. Within a couple of days I . . . thought I'd go and see my parents before I left."

"Are you going down to Yeovil now?"

"Yes," he replied, altogether too quickly.

"I'll give you a lift to Paddington."

"No need. I'll . . . take the Tube." He brushed past her to the door and opened it. " 'Bye."

"This isn't goodbye, David." She followed him out, ostentatiously pulling the door shut behind her. "We both know that."

"I'm quitting, Claire. OK? I'm *out.*"

"Mind if I walk with you to the Tube?"

"I'd rather you didn't."

"Accept my offer of a lift, then."

"No."

"You've fooled Alice," she said, lowering her voice. "You haven't fooled me."

"I'm not trying to fool anyone."

"Fine. Have it your way. But I'll go back indoors and persuade Alice to see it *my* way—unless you stop arguing and get in the car."

Umber stopped arguing. The truth was that Claire left him little choice in the matter. A few minutes later, they were heading towards Swiss Cottage in her TVR. And Claire was doing all the talking.

"Let's cut the crap, shall we, David? Alice believed you because she's prejudiced against you. But I don't share her prejudice, so it won't wash with me. You took an important decision while we were down in Hampshire, but chickening out wasn't it. My guess is you decided to go it alone, probably out of some warped sense of chivalry, which I personally find more offensive than flattering. You think we'll be safer if you leave us out of whatever it is you're planning to do. I suspect you've worked something out you're not telling us about. And I reckon that something involves Michel Tinaud's girlfriend."

Umber shook his head. "You've got it all wrong, Claire."

"You thought we'd get nothing out of the Wilkinsons. That was the basis on which you took your decision. But we came back with a genuine lead. Yet you didn't change your mind. You didn't even hesitate. You ploughed straight on with your cover story. That can only be because you already knew about Tinaud and the girl."

"How could I?"

"I don't know. Unless—" She braked sharply to a halt, throwing Umber forward in his seat against the lock of the seatbelt. A car behind them blared its horn. Claire held up a hand in apology, then pulled into a parking space at the side of the road and turned to stare at Umber. Her eyes were sparkling with the satisfaction of a sudden insight. "You've seen her, haven't you? Or at any rate you know where she is."

"Of course not."

"Look me in the eye and tell me I'm wrong."

He looked her in the eye. But he said nothing. He knew she would see through any lie he told. In fact, she already had.

She turned off the engine, her gaze still fixed on him. Then she said, calmly and quietly, "There's no guarantee she's still with

Tinaud. Given the lifestyle of the average top tennis player, it's quite likely she isn't. But Tinaud can tell us what happened when Sally tracked him down, as I'm sure she did. It makes sense to ask him. He may also be able to tell us where the girl is. And he can certainly tell us who he believes her to be. There's every reason to go and see him. And I will. Unless you're prepared to tell me why I shouldn't."

Umber sighed. "Look Claire, I—"

"Just tell me. OK?"

"OK." He surrendered the point. "The reason's obvious. The reason is what happened to Sally when she got too close. I don't want that to happen to you. Or Alice." He ventured a smile. "But especially you."

"So you take all the risks?"

"Sally was my wife. And I was at Avebury when they took Tamsin. I have to take the risks. You don't. I can't let you. Give me a few days, Claire. You can stall Alice that long. A few days is all I ask."

"To accomplish what?"

He shrugged. "As much as I can."

The pretence was over. Claire dropped him at the next Tube station. An hour and a half later, he was at Gatwick, buying a ticket for the first flight next morning to Jersey. He booked into the cheapest of the airport hotels for the night and slept surprisingly well.

CHAPTER

TWENTY-THREE

British Airways flight 8035 hit the runway at the States Airport just before 9:30 on a cool, breezy Sunday morning. Umber had accepted an inclusive car-hire deal when he booked the flight. After a few minutes of form-filling, he was on his way from the terminal to the waiting Peugeot. And a few minutes after that, he was on the road to St. Aubin.

All was quiet at le Quai Bisson. Nothing had outwardly changed at Rollers Sail & Surf. The parking space in front of the office was empty. There was no sign of life, nor yet sound of it. As Umber mounted the steps to the door of the flat, no rock music was pounding through its walls. Chantelle, he felt certain, was not there. He had come more in hope than expectation, knowing that the only other step open to him—going to Eden Holt to confront Jeremy's parents with his suspicions—was a step into the profoundest unknown.

He pressed the bell. There was no response. He pressed it again, with the same result. He lowered himself onto his haunches and pushed up the flap of the letterbox. The bare wall at the end of the hall and part of the bathroom doorpost met his gaze unrevealingly. Leaning forward, however, he could glimpse some letters lying on the mat, where they had presumably lain since Saturday morning. Chantelle must have left as soon as she heard of Jeremy's death.

The purr of a car engine behind and below him seeped almost

unnoticed into his consciousness. Only when it stopped did he realize that it was *directly* below him. He glanced round to see the driver's door of a sleek navy-blue Mercedes SL open—and Marilyn
Hall climb out.

She was dressed in jeans, leather jacket and polo-neck sweater,
the unisex look of a piece with the cool, unastonished, appraising
stare she gave him before slamming the car door and starting up
the steps as the locking system beeped behind her.

"Who did you expect to find here, David?" She threw the
question at him like a challenge. "A ghost?"

He nodded, determined to seem unabashed. "In a sense. I was
looking for Chantelle."

"*Who?*"

"You must know about her."

"No."

"Really? Why don't you seem surprised to see me, then?"

She frowned at him in apparent puzzlement, then plucked a key
out of one of the zip-pockets of her jacket. "We can talk inside."

She unlocked the door and he followed her in, stepping over the
waiting post. Already, the flat had an indefinable air of desertion
about it. The living room was tidier and emptier than he remembered. A sense of absence was everywhere.

Marilyn strode halfway down the room towards the Catherine-
wheel window, then stopped and turned to face him. "Oliver
wanted me to pick up a couple of things," she explained. "He
hadn't the heart to come himself." She was sombre and unsmiling,
the flirtatiousness buried deep. Yet there was a guardedness about
her too. She seemed unsure of her ground—as Umber was of his.
"Lucky for you it was me he sent."

"Why lucky?"

"Because I'm the only member of the family who knows you
were at Eden Holt when Jeremy died." She held his gaze. "You're
not going to deny it, are you?"

"How did you find out?" he asked, as calmly as he could.

"That can wait. Tell me about Chantelle."

"She was here. When I called round last week. Living here, I
mean. I thought she was Jeremy's girlfriend. Well, I suppose they
let me think that."

"But you don't think that now?"

"No."

"What, then?"

"You don't know?"

"I've never heard of such a person. There *was* a girl in Jeremy's life. But they split up more than a year ago. And she wasn't called Chantelle."

Some instinct held Umber back from telling Marilyn who he believed Chantelle really was. Their exchanges were hedged about with half-truths and evasions. He could not afford to show his hand until he knew what she held in hers.

"If she *was* living here," Marilyn resumed, "where is she now?"

"I don't know."

"I don't see any sign of her, do you?" Marilyn looked around. "Just Jeremy's bachelor stuff."

"She was here."

"Let's try the bathroom."

Marilyn strode past him. He followed meekly and watched as she first opened the door of the airing cupboard, then peered into the tiny cabinet above the handbasin. But the sight of a single toothbrush propped in the mug on the end of the bath told its own story.

"No knickers or bras, David," said Marilyn matter-of-factly. "No girlie toiletries." She folded her arms and gazed at him. "No Chantelle."

"She's gone. She must have left . . . as soon as she heard about Jeremy."

"Why would she do that? And how would she hear? The police contacted Oliver and no-one else. They were on the scene promptly." She arched an eyebrow. "Thanks to an anonymous phone call." She walked past him, back into the living room. He followed and there they faced each other once more. "Are you sure Chantelle isn't just a figment of your imagination?"

It was a faintly odd choice of phrase, odd enough to make Umber read into it a disturbing double meaning. "Are you suggesting I made her up? Or do you think I'm suffering from delusions?"

"I can't say. But Wisby didn't mention her. And I think he would have."

The name plunged into Umber's thoughts like a spike into a gearwheel. *"Wisby?"*

"That's how I knew you were there when Jeremy threw himself off the roof. Wisby told me what happened."

"When? When did he tell you?"

"Yesterday. He came up to me as I was parking my car in St. Helier. He'd followed me from Eden Holt. He'd been waiting for the chance to speak to me alone, he said, and guessed he'd get it sooner or later. The atmosphere at the house . . . well, you can imagine. Jane's barely coherent. And Oliver's as close to broken as I've seen him. I had to get away. Shopping for essentials was a decent excuse. Wisby had banked on me doing something like that. There's a lot of the rodent about him, don't you think? Including a sharp little brain."

"What happened was his fault. Did he tell you that?"

"It hardly matters whose fault it was, David. I can tell you who Oliver and Jane and her was-out of a husband will blame if they ever find out you were there at the time. And it isn't Wisby."

"Why haven't they found out?"

"Because Wisby's put me in a difficult position." Disarmingly, she smiled. "He's blackmailing me."

"With what?" But even as he asked the question, Umber guessed the answer.

"Junius. Your speciality, I believe."

"The vellum-bound edition?"

"Yes."

"What's that to you?"

"Nothing. But it was in Jeremy's possession, wasn't it? Wisby can prove that. Which as good as proves Jeremy sent the letters to Wisby and Sharp that stirred all this up. And that he clearly didn't believe Radd was his sisters' murderer. Jeremy's death has been a savage blow to Oliver. And to Jane. If they learn their son didn't trust them . . . well, I'm not sure either of them could cope with that, I'm really not. And I don't intend to find out."

"Wisby's selling the books to you?"

"That's what it comes down to, yes. Without them, he can't back up his allegations. And he won't want to, anyway. He'll have turned a big enough profit to keep his mouth shut."

"He's alleged more than that Jeremy sent the letters, Marilyn, hasn't he?"

"Some crazy stuff about the man who originally owned the

books being murdered, you mean? Oh, he fed that into the works as well, yes. I didn't know what to make of it—what it really amounted to. As far as I can see, though, it would only make everything worse for Oliver. My priority is limiting the damage you and Wisby caused by pressurizing Jeremy. God knows, it's bad enough already. I don't want it to get any worse."

"For your husband's sake?"

"And mine. My life with Oliver runs on smooth and predictable lines. I like it that way. I want to *keep* it that way."

"It's a funny thing, Marilyn." Umber took a step towards her. "The more candid you are with me, the more duplicitous I suspect you of being."

"Duplicitous?" Her eyes twinkled. "There's a big word for a Sunday morning."

"How much are you paying Wisby?"

"A hundred thousand."

Umber failed to suppress a gasp. "That's a hell of a lot of damage limitation."

"It's loose change, actually. Thanks to Oliver. He's always been very generous to me."

"Is that why you married him?"

"It was a consideration," she replied, with unblinking coolness. "Do you want a cut of that generosity, David?"

"What?"

"I didn't tell you about my dealings with Wisby to make myself feel better, you know. Finding you here was actually . . . fortuitous, to say the least." Was it *merely* fortuitous? Umber asked himself. Within one set-up might lie another. He could be certain of nothing. "I've been worrying he might try to trick me into accepting duplicates of the Junius, leaving him free to go ahead and do what I'll already have paid him not to. He strikes me as the type to want the penny *and* the bun."

Wisby had obviously not mentioned the missing fly-leaves to Marilyn. It would have undermined his bargaining position to do so. Umber knew better than to mention them himself. It was not hard to guess why Marilyn had told him about Wisby's blackmail pitch. She meant to ask a favour of him, enabling him to ask one in return. "You want me to authenticate the Junius for you?"

"Yes. In fact . . ." She hesitated.

"What?"

"I want you to conduct the exchange for me. Never having to see or speak to Wisby again would suit me rather well."

"Wouldn't that be a little risky, Marilyn? I might take off with the Junius myself and do my worst with it."

"And what would your worst be? You're hardly likely to inflict the truth on Oliver and Jane when you come out of it so badly yourself. Besides, you lack Wisby's cruel streak. I don't mind you hanging on to the Junius. It's no use to me. I only want it out of Wisby's hands. I only want to be sure it isn't going to come back to haunt Oliver and me."

Umber paused for a momentary show of reflection before he responded. Then he said, "All right. I'll do it. As long as you do something for me in return."

She looked long and hard at him. "What did you have in mind?"

"I want the keys to this place. All the keys. Including those for the office and the boat store."

"Why?"

Umber allowed himself a smile. "And no questions asked."

"Think Chantelle will come back, do you?"

Umber did not think that. But he did think there might be clues to her whereabouts to be found on the premises. And he needed time to look for them. Alone. "Like I said, Marilyn. No questions."

"Who is she?"

"No-one, according to you."

"Very cute." She leaned against the chair-back behind her. "You're a nicer person to negotiate with than Wisby, David. Much nicer. We have a deal."

"Can I have the key you used to get us in, then?"

"I'm afraid not. I took it off the bunch Jeremy had in his pocket. If Oliver or Jane change their minds and decide to come here after all, I can hardly tell them I've given the key to you. But I can have duplicates of all the keys cut for you tomorrow. You can have them when I see the Junius."

"What are your arrangements with Wisby?"

"The exchange is fixed for noon tomorrow. I can't get the money until the banks open. Do you have a car with you?"

"Yes."

"All right. You know the Pier Road multi-storey in St. Helier?"

"Beneath Fort Regent?"

"That's the one. Drive up past it to Mount Bingham. You'll see a small car park next to a play area with a view of the harbour. I'll meet you there at eleven, deliver the keys and the cash and tell you where Wisby will be waiting. He's going to phone me around then with his choice of rendezvous." She raised her eyebrows. "He seems to feel the need to behave like some character in a spy novel."

"Perhaps he doesn't trust you."

"We'll agree then how to meet up afterwards," she went on blithely. "I have to take my own precautions. Oliver's not paying me a lot of attention at the moment. But I can't go missing too often."

"I'm sorry, you know." He looked her in the eye, needing to be sure she believed him, about this if nothing else. "For what happened to Jeremy. Sorrier than I can say."

"We're all sorry." She moved suddenly away and across the room, to the chest of drawers beside the bed. She picked up something that had been lying next to the alarm clock: an expensively chunky wristwatch. "The Rolex Oliver gave Jeremy for his eighteenth birthday," she explained, flexing the metal strap between her fingers. "One of the things I was sent to collect. He wasn't wearing it, you see. Didn't want to smash it in the fall, I suppose. Which means he'd already made up his mind to kill himself when he left here on Thursday afternoon. You didn't push him off the roof, David. He jumped. You didn't force him to send those letters. He did it on his own. He brought it all on himself." She frowned. "Unless you think . . . Chantelle was in it with him."

"What else did you come for?" Umber asked, evading the point.

"There should be an address book." She pointed. "By the phone, maybe?"

Umber stepped over to where the telephone sat amidst crooked stacks of CDs in the lee of the hi-fi tower. There was indeed a dog-eared address book sitting beneath it. Umber slid it free.

"We need it to notify Jeremy's friends." Marilyn held out her hand.

"Mind if I take a look?"

"Go ahead."

Umber opened the book speculatively at T—T for Tinaud. There was no such entry, of course.

"You've gone way past C," said Marilyn.

"So I have."

"Do you know her surname?"

"Whose?"

"Maybe we should stop playing games, David."

"Too late for that, don't you think?" Umber closed the book and handed it to her.

"I've got what I came for. We ought to leave."

"You go ahead. I'll let myself out."

"Nice try. But there's no deadlock on the door. I can't leave the flat unsecured. We leave together. After tomorrow, you can come and go on your own. But you'll have to be careful. If Oliver finds you here . . ."

"I'll have a lot of explaining to do."

"And he won't be as easily fobbed off as me."

"I don't think you're easily fobbed off at all, Marilyn. I think you're just tolerant of other people's secretiveness . . . on account of your own."

"You really know how to sweet talk a girl, don't you?" She gave him a fleeting, enigmatic little smile. "Let's go."

Marilyn took the accumulated post (an electricity bill and credit card statement) with her as they left, locked up carefully and led the way down the steps. Umber felt frustrated at having to walk away from the chance to search the flat for something—anything—that might lead him to Chantelle. But the chance was merely postponed and so gift-wrapped that it could not be spurned. He had got what he wanted and more then he expected. But, strangely, he sensed Marilyn had too.

"Where are you parked?" she asked, as she opened her car door.

"Behind the parish hall."

"Jump in. I'll run you round there."

"It's only a two-minute walk."

"Jump in anyway. There's something else I want to say to you."

Umber did not argue. Marilyn reversed out and turned right onto the Boulevard, planning, he assumed, to take a roundabout route to the car park—as roundabout as it needed to be, anyway.

"Wisby told me about Sharp's arrest," she said as they cruised slowly past the harbourful of moored yachts, their bare masts clustered like winter saplings. "You must be worried about him."

"He was fitted up."

"No doubt. But what are you going to do to get him *unfitted*?"

"What *can* I do?"

"Pull a few strings. It's the Jersey way. Get someone to have a word in the right ear. Sharp's not going to get off scot-free. But a light sentence—maybe suspended—*could* be arranged. If you set about it in the right way."

"And what is the right way?"

"Royal Channel Islands Yacht Club," she said, pointing to an imposing building ahead of them at the end of the Boulevard. "A good place to start."

"I'm not a member."

"Neither am I." Marilyn took the sharp bend by the club entrance at a crawl. "But Oliver is." The road narrowed as it climbed between the cottages of an older part of town. "Through him, I've met most of the people who matter on this tight little members' only island. There are ways and means of achieving what you want, David. But they aren't written down anywhere. They aren't even spoken about. You just have to move in the right circles."

"Do you move in the right circles, Marilyn?"

"Oh yes. I make a point of it."

"Could you help George?"

"I'm sure I could. In fact, I'd be happy to."

"Why?"

"Because this is getting messy." She turned back towards the centre of town, along the higher, inland route. "And I don't want it to get any messier." She glanced round at him. "We should all walk away from this, David. We really should."

C H A P T E R

TWENTY-FOUR

Walking away as soon as they had extracted the Junius from Wisby probably would be the prudent course. Umber conceded as much to himself as he strolled out along St. Aubin's harbour wall and gazed back towards the Boulevard. If he had done that when Sharp had approached him in Prague, however, he would still be frittering away his days there—safely, dully, deludedly, believing Sally had committed suicide, believing Tamsin Hall had been murdered, believing . . . all that he believed now to be false.

He was not about to walk away.

He did not even intend to stir far from St. Aubin. He had told Marilyn openly that he suspected her of duplicity and it was true. What form it took he had no way of determining, but her ignorance and indifference where Chantelle was concerned could have been feigned. He proposed to keep a close eye on the flat in case anyone tried to conduct a search before he could—or, against the odds, Chantelle returned.

He had noticed from the harbour wall that there was a small hotel on the Boulevard just beyond the turning into le Quai Bisson. A prowl round past Rollers Sail & Surf revealed there were first-floor rooms at the back of the hotel with a view of the boat store and flat above. The receptionist, used to people requesting a sea-facing room, had no difficulty accommodating him. He booked himself in.

Then he went along to the supermarket in the centre of town, bought some sandwiches and bottled water and returned to the hotel to keep watch.

He had bought a day-old copy of the *Jersey Evening Post*, along with the food and drink. In the privacy of his room, he bleakly perused its coverage of the "Eden Holt Tragedy." The family background was given more detail than in the nationals. Jeremy's contribution to Jersey life was emphasized, with a photograph of him being presented with a cup for winning some local regatta. There was a photograph of Miranda and Tamsin as well—the one all the papers had used back in 1981. And there was a quote from the police, appealing for the anonymous caller who had alerted them to Jeremy's death to come forward. But there was, Umber knew, no prospect of that.

Nobody went near the flat all day. Umber thought he saw a movement at one of the windows midway through the afternoon and dashed round to investigate, but there was no sign of anyone and he eventually concluded that what he had seen was merely the reflection of a seagull in flight.

When nightfall came—late, thanks to the clock change for summer time—Umber relaxed, reasoning that no-one would visit the flat once they had to switch on lights to see what they were looking for, because it would signal their presence to anyone who might be watching.

If anyone was even planning to, of course. *If* there was anything to find. *If* . . . But ifs were all Umber had to bet on. He spent a couple of hours in a pub farther along the Boulevard, then walked out to the Yacht Club and back by the higher route, cutting down to Quai Bisson by the steps past the flat.

All was in darkness. All looked to be undisturbed. It seemed he was waiting for something that was never going to happen. He stood for some minutes by the door of the flat, turning over in his mind the possibility that somehow he had deceived himself. How sure was he that Chantelle and the girl in *Hello!* were one and the same? How likely was it that she had left anything there that would enable him to trace her? Just how slender a chance was he chasing?

Nothing changed next morning. A modest weekday bustle took hold of St. Aubin. But it did not spread to Rollers Sail & Surf. At ten o'clock, Umber imagined Marilyn presenting herself in a marbled banking hall with a coolly phrased request to withdraw £100,000 in cash from an account that presumably held a great deal more. At 10:30, he set off for St. Helier.

He spotted Marilyn's Mercedes in the car park by the play area at the top of Mount Bingham as he crested the rise from Pier Road. As he pulled in beside it, he saw she was speaking to someone on her mobile. She signalled to him to wait until she had finished, so he sat where he was, looking down at the docks and the ferry terminal spread out below him, at Elizabeth Castle and the causeway linking it to the shore, exposed by the retreating tide. His gaze came to rest on a vast, sleek-lined private cruiser heading in slowly from the sea lane away to his left. The pallid sunlight glistened on its polished silver-grey hull.

"Penny for them," said Marilyn as she pulled open the passenger door and slipped in beside him. "Well, rather more than a penny, actually."

She was wearing a short-skirted dark-blue suit and pearl-buttoned blouse. Resting on her knees was a black leather briefcase that looked new enough to have been bought for the occasion. She plucked off her sunglasses and looked at him.

"Are you all right?"

"Fine," he replied. "Just fine."

"This is the money." She snapped open the case to reveal neatly stacked wads of £20 notes. "All Bank of England issue, no Jersey currency, as Wisby specified." Then she closed it again. "And here are the keys." She handed him an assortment of Yales and mortises held on a ring. "You'll have to sort out which is which, I'm afraid."

"OK. Thanks."

"That was our man on the phone."

"I thought it had to be."

"You're to meet him at La Rocque. It's a village on the coast about five miles east of here."

"I've got a map. It came with the car. I'll find the place easily enough."

"There are parking spaces by the harbour just after you pass the martello tower. He'll be waiting for you there."

"Does he know *who* he'll be waiting for?"

"I told him I was sending someone."

"It could be quite a shock for him, then."

"I imagine the contents of the case will help him get over it."

"What about afterwards? You'll want to see what you've got for your money."

"Oliver is taking Jane to see the undertaker at three o'clock. My presence is . . . not required." There was something in her tone that implied resentment of the degree to which Jeremy's death had brought his parents together, but Umber had no thoughts to spare for such an issue. "I'll meet you at the flat then."

"Suits me."

Marilyn slid the briefcase across to him; their fingers brushed as he took it from her. "You'll be careful, won't you, David?"

"Of course."

"Only . . . Wisby outwitted you last time you met, didn't he?"

"Is that what he told you?"

"Isn't it true?"

"No. Not really." That was not how Umber saw it, anyway. Wisby had simply been cold-blooded enough to seize the advantage Jeremy's death-fall had given him. There would surely be no such advantage for him to seize this time.

"Well, in case you need it, good luck."

"Thanks."

To his surprise, she leaned forward and kissed him lightly on the mouth, then climbed swiftly out of the car.

"I'll see you later, Marilyn," he said as she held the door briefly open.

"Right," she said, smiling tightly. Then she slammed the door, hurried round to her own car, climbed in and started up.

Umber was watching her as she reversed out of the bay and drove away. But she never once glanced at him.

Umber followed the coast road out through St. Helier's straggling eastern suburbs. The retreating tide had revealed great stretches of grey-brown reef, so extensive that the sea was a mile or more from the shore. The weather was a mix of winter grimness and spring cheer—ambiguous, uncertain, on the cusp of the seasons.

He sighted the first of several martello towers marked on the map as he neared Le Hocq. He pulled in there and waited. When only five minutes remained till Marilyn's noon appointment with Wisby, he drove on.

It was barely another mile to La Rocque. He slowed as he passed its martello tower, scanning the arc of parking spaces facing the harbour. He was looking for a hire car similar to his own. And he saw one almost immediately, his eye drawn to the H-prefixed numberplate. There was a single occupant, staring straight ahead at the harbour, in which assorted craft lay beached at their moorings. The profile was Wisby's.

He pulled in to the left of the car and looked round, meeting Wisby's gaze, in which there was not the merest flinch of surprise, though a surprise it must have been—and a big one.

Umber climbed out, carrying the briefcase with him. He opened the passenger door of the other car and eased himself in beside Wisby, cradling the case in his lap.

"Mr. Umber," Wisby said neutrally, with no hint of fear or hostility. "We meet again."

"Not in your game plan, I dare say."

"No. But I wasn't to know you'd got into bed with Marilyn Hall, was I?"

"She thought you might try to trick her," Umber replied, refusing to be provoked. "A chap with your track record must expect that."

"Well, I should congratulate you, I suppose. You get the Junius after all. And Mrs. Hall pays for it. Sorry I left you in the lurch at Eden Holt, by the way. It was nothing personal."

"Did you really do all this just for a fat pay-off?"

"No. But I've decided to settle for one. You too, I imagine."

"I'm getting nothing out of this."

"Really? I can't believe you haven't cut a deal with Mrs. Hall. Why else should you be acting as her go-between? What have you gone for? Cash . . . or kind?"

"Where are the books?"

"Ah. Is that it? A late revival of your historical career. Junius: the truth at last. I might have a minor disappointment for you on that front."

"I know the fly-leaves are missing, Wisby. I checked with Garrard. Like you should have."

"I should. You're right. But you said yourself the vellum-bound 1773 edition is unique. Even without the fly-leaves, it proves my case. A case Marilyn Hall can't afford to let me go public with."

"Exploiting the Hall family's grief is beneath contempt."

"That's what you think I'm doing, is it?"

"What would *you* call it?"

"How much do you know about Marilyn Hall? I wonder. Less than me, I suspect. A lot less. I've enquired into her background, you see. I've done my research." Wisby smiled thinly. "Like you should have."

"And what have you learned?"

"Enough to make me worry I may have settled for too modest a sum."

"Are you going to tell me what you're getting at?"

"No." Wisby squinted out towards the distant ocean. "I'll let you find out in your own good time."

"Where are the books?" snapped Umber, losing patience with the game-playing.

"You can have them when I have the money."

"How about when you *see* the money?" Umber flipped up the lid of the briefcase, giving his companion a clear view of the contents. There was a gleam of satisfaction in Wisby's eyes and a greedy little swipe of his tongue along his lower lip. He reached out for the case. But Umber held on. "The books. Remember?"

Wisby looked at him and grimaced, as if giving up what he had come to trade genuinely pained him. "They're in the glove compartment. In front of you."

Umber stretched one hand forward to open the compartment. Its door flopped down. And there were the books, vellum-bound and gilt-edged, held together by a rubber band as he had seen them before. The spines were facing him. He angled his head to read the gold-lettered titles. Not *Junius's Letters I* and *Junius's Letters II*, like every other edition he had come across, but simply JUNIUS 1 and JUNIUS 2.

"The money, Mr. Umber," said Wisby. "If you please."

Umber surrendered the case and took the books out of the glove compartment. It was strange—surpassingly strange—to lay his hands at long last on the prize Griffin had promised to deliver to him at Avebury twenty-three years previously. He peeled off the rubber band and opened the first volume.

A few jagged scraps close to the binding were all that remained of the fly-leaf. But the title page was untouched. The name of Junius appeared at the top in bold Gothic capitals. Umber's gaze shifted to the bottom. *Printed for Henry Sampson Woodfall, MDCCLXXIII.* The date was right. And the binding was right. It *was* Junius's personal copy.

He looked round at Wisby, who was checking his way through the money, fanning each wad of notes and counting roughly as he went. Then he looked back at the Junius, shaking his head: £100,000 was a high price to pay for two mutilated old books. Nor was it by any means the highest price to have been paid for them. They were not worth Jeremy Hall's life. Yet he had lost his life because of them. Volume two fell open in Umber's hands at the last paragraph of Letter LVIII, encouraged to do so, he guessed, by being pressed flat on a photocopier some weeks before. There was the fateful phrase Jeremy had chosen near the end of the letter. *"The subject comes home to us all."* And so it did.

The snapping shut of the briefcase interrupted Umber's thoughts. "It seems to be all here," said Wisby, with a flicker of a smile.

"Did you doubt it would be?"

"I doubt everything."

"Yes. I suppose you would."

"Why were the fly-leaves removed, do you think?"

"You tell me."

"It's obvious, isn't it? To break the evidential link with Griffin. Without them they're just another copy of Junius's letters."

"Not quite."

"No. But they'd seem so, other than to an expert. And having removed the fly-leaves, where better to lose the books, so to speak,

than an antiquarian bookshop? I doubt Garrard's scatterbrained
brother bought them. I suspect they were simply slipped onto the
shelf. Not by Jeremy, obviously. Perhaps by someone who was trying
to keep them *from* Jeremy. By implication someone Jeremy knew,
resident on the island. Someone . . . close to him."

"Like you say, Wisby. You doubt everything." The man's logic
was as seductive as it was disturbing. But Umber had no intention of
acknowledging as much. "Are we done?"

Wisby nodded. "I believe we are."

A few minutes later, Umber sat in his hire car, watching Wisby
drive away. Wisby was heading west, probably making for the
Airport. He had every right to be well pleased with his day's work.
But Umber's work was far from done. He skip-read his way through
Junius's grandiloquent *Dedication to the English Nation* at the beginning of volume one of the *Letters* till he had given Wisby the
ten-minute start he had agreed to. Then he started the car and
headed in the same direction.

CHAPTER

TWENTY-FIVE

Umber reached St. Aubin with more than an hour to spare before his appointment with Marilyn. He parked the car at his hotel, headed round to le Quai Bisson and let himself into the flat.

Everything was as it had been the previous day. The keys Marilyn had given him would permit access to the office and boat store on the ground floor as well, but the flat was the obvious place to begin his search. Once he *had* begun, however, he realized how frail a prospect he had pinned his hopes on. A systematic search of the lounge-diner-bedroom was likely to prove time-consuming as well as futile. Umber did not really know what he was looking for and could devise no subtler method of setting about the task than moving everything to see what might or might not be concealed by pillows, cushions, magazines, books, CDs and the like. Nothing was the answer.

By the time he had trawled through the bathroom and kitchen with similar results, three o'clock—the hour set for Marilyn's arrival—was no longer comfortably distant. He decided to try his luck in the Rollers Sail & Surf office. Hurrying down to it, he found the right key after a couple of tries and went in.

It was a cramped, single-windowed room furnished with a desk, swivel-chair, filing cabinet and cupboard which looked as if they had been bought as a job lot second- or third-hand. A communicating door leading into the boat store stood half-open, explaining the faintly salt-tinged mustiness that filled the air.

Umber glanced through the doorway into high-roofed gloom,

where he could make out little beyond the shrouded shapes of wintered vessels. They did not interest him. The office held infinitely greater promise. He decided to start with the filing cabinet. He walked over to it and pulled the top drawer open.

Whether he heard something first or merely sensed movement behind him he could not afterwards have said. Perhaps his instincts gave him some fractional forewarning. Or perhaps the breath Chantelle took as she lunged across the room at him, knife in hand, was sharp enough to be audible.

He threw himself to one side. The blade of the knife struck the metalwork of the drawer at an angle but with enough force to dent it and throw out a scatter of paint fragments. He heard her cry out "Shit!" in pain at the jarring of her wrist. The knife fell from her hand and clattered to the floor. Umber glimpsed its blade—long, pointed and gleaming. Then he looked up into Chantelle's eyes. Fear and hatred and desperation burned back at him.

"You bastard," she screamed. "You fucking bastard." She stooped for the knife.

His foot got there first, stamping down hard across the handle. She grabbed his ankle and tried to pull him off, but she was physically no match for him. He grasped her waist and swung her off her feet, whirling her round into the angle of filing cabinet and wall, where he pinned her by his own weight.

"Let go of me," she shouted, flailing at him with her fists. "Let fucking go of me."

He caught her wrists and forced her arms back above her head. Their faces were no more than a couple of inches apart now. He could feel her hot, racing breaths against his chin, could see deep into her staring, wide-pupilled eyes. And they were a different colour, he suddenly realized. Not the dark brown that he recalled, but a pure cornflower blue. "Listen to me, Chantelle," he shouted. "I know who you are. But I've told no-one. *No-one.*"

"I don't care who you've told. I just want to make you suffer for what you did to Jem."

"I did nothing. He took his own life. I don't really know why."

"Yes you do, Shadow Man."

"To protect you, I guess, but—"

"You boxed him into a corner. You left him no way out." Her face crumpled. She closed her eyes. Tears flowed down her cheeks. "No way out at all."

"Wisby was the one threatening him, Chantelle. Not me."

She reopened her eyes and stared at him through her tears. "You're lying. Wisby and you are in it together. Jem said so."

"I know he thought that and I understand why. But he was wrong. And I can prove it. Wisby's gone. Left the island. He wouldn't have gone if he knew about you. But he doesn't. He never met you, did he? He never had the chance to put two and two together. Only I had that chance. I give you my word, Chantelle. No-one else knows what I know. And no-one else can protect you now Jeremy's dead. Trust me. Please. For my sake as well as yours. *Trust me.*"

Her arms slackened. Her expression altered fractionally. "Give me one good reason . . . why I should."

"Because you have to. Because I'm your only hope. And you're mine."

"You haven't told anyone about me?"

"I told Marilyn I'd met Jeremy's girlfriend here. A girlfriend she knew nothing about. But I didn't tell her what I really think you and Jeremy were to each other."

Chantelle swallowed hard and sniffed. "What d'you really think we were?"

"Brother and sister," Umber whispered. Then he took a step back, releasing her wrists. Her arms fell to her sides. She did not move. Her mouth was open. But she did not speak. She stared at him, barely blinking. A frozen moment passed.

Then she said, "Fuck." And that was all she said.

"Why have your eyes changed colour, Chantelle?"

"I haven't got the brown lenses in. They were Jem's idea. Part of my . . . disguise."

"It's a good disguise."

"Not good enough, though. Is it?"

"I'd never have seen through it."

"How did you rumble me, then?"

"I didn't. Sally did. My wife."

"I know who she is. *Was.* Sorry."

"She left a clue. I only came across it recently. A magazine cutting."

Chantelle closed her eyes and sighed. "That fucking magazine. Changed my life. My whole life."

"Why don't you—"

Chantelle's eyes flashed open, wide and alarmed, at the sound of a car drawing near. Umber grabbed her by the shoulders and hurried her from the room, through the doorway into the sheltering darkness of the boat store, where they stood listening as the car drew nearer still, into the parking space in front of the office—and stopped.

"Don't worry," Umber whispered. "It's Marilyn. She's come to see me. I can get rid of her." They heard the clunk of a car door closing. "She'll go up to the flat. I'll follow and speak to her there. All you have to do is wait here. Will you do that?"

"OK," said Chantelle in a quavering voice.

"Don't move from here. All right?"

"All right."

There was another clunk above them: the flat door closing. A floorboard in the hall creaked. "I'll be as quick as I can. Just stay still and silent."

"OK."

He squeezed her shoulder, then slipped out through the office.

And there he stopped. The car was not Marilyn's. It was a charcoal-grey BMW. And Umber would have sworn on his life he had seen it before—in Yeovil.

Too many thoughts tumbled through his brain for him to sort into any pattern that made sense. It was Walsh's car. Which meant Walsh, not Marilyn, was waiting for him in the flat. Which also meant Walsh knew of his appointment with Marilyn. Umber had clearly been set up.

Set-up or no set-up, he had no choice but to climb the steps to the flat and go in. If Walsh came down, he would find Chantelle, with consequences Umber dared not contemplate. He pulled the office door shut and ran up the steps two at a time.

A few seconds later, he was in the flat, the door slamming behind him as he rushed into the hall, expecting to see Walsh standing expectantly in the middle of the main room. But the room was empty.

"Umber!" came Walsh's voice from the kitchen.

Umber turned. Walsh was leaning casually against the fridge, arms folded, dressed as if for golf, in mustard-yellow polo shirt, generously cut chocolate-brown trousers and two-toned brogues.

"I was just going to come and look for you. Thanks for saving me the effort."

"What are you doing here?"

"Marilyn sent me." Walsh smiled his gleaming smile. "Well, that's not strictly true. *I* sent *her* yesterday. And now I've come myself."

"What do you want?"

"These, obviously." Walsh picked up the Juniuses from the work-top where Umber had left them. "For starters."

"Starters?"

"The main course is Chantelle. What do you know about her, Umber? What have you found out?"

"Nothing."

"Worse luck for you if true, which I doubt. Let me explain the situation to you. Then you'll understand why you've no choice but to cooperate." Walsh glanced at his watch. "Wisby will have been picked up at the Airport by now. By the police, I mean. Acting on a tip-off. That money you gave him? Hot. Very hot. The serial numbers of the notes match those on a vanload of cash stolen from Securicor in Essex six months ago. Wisby will have a lot of explaining to do. As will the man videoed delivering the money to him at La Rocque earlier today. If and when the film comes to the attention of the police, that is. You catch my drift?"

"I catch it."

"So, what can you tell me about Chantelle?"

"Like I said: nothing."

Walsh dropped the Juniuses back on the work-top, pushed himself upright and took two slow steps towards Umber. "You know who she is, Umber. You've worked it out. And according to what you told Marilyn you've recently met her. Well, I'd like to meet her too. Very much. So would one or two other people I know. Can you arrange that for us?"

"No. I can't. I wouldn't know how to."

"I find that hard to believe."

"Many things are."

"Too true."

The man moved like a snake striking. Umber had half-expected something of the kind, but his reactions were far too slow and Walsh was far too quick. The next thing Umber knew was that his face was pressed against the frame of the door to the main room, the edge of the wood grinding against his cheekbone, his right arm doubled up behind him several degrees beyond its natural limit.

"You're a lucky man, Umber," Walsh rasped in his ear. "Knowing more about Chantelle than anyone else means you get the chance to wriggle out of this situation. But don't push your luck. I'd be happy to reopen those stitches I can see in the back of your head with a few taps against this doorpost. More than happy. So, I suggest you start talking. I really do."

"There's nothing . . . I can tell you."

"Wrong answer. You're going to have to—"

"*Stop!*"

It was Chantelle's voice. Umber could not see her, but he heard the front door bounce against its stop, setting the letterbox rattling, and glimpsed her shadow in the hallway from the corner of his eye.

"Let go of him."

"Happy to." Walsh released Umber's arm and moved back. "Now you're here."

Umber turned in time to see Chantelle advancing towards Walsh, her right arm tucked behind her, and guessed in that instant what she was about to do.

"Good to see you again, Cherie," said Walsh. "It's been far too—"

The blade plunged into his stomach, deep and hard. He rocked on his feet, clutching at her as she pulled the knife up, tearing through his flesh and innards and the fabric of his shirt, blood spilling and spreading between them. His mouth opened wide. But no words came. Only more blood and a clotted, strangulated groan.

He lolled forward against her. His weight pushed her back. The knife came out of him. There was yet more blood. And something thicker and darker, sagging from the wound. He dropped to his knees, then fell sideways into the kitchen doorway.

He moaned and pressed his right hand to his stomach. The sound in his throat became a gurgle. His feet scrabbled at the thin mat beneath them. Then, suddenly, they stopped. His body slackened. His hand slid away from his stomach. He twitched twice. And then he was still.

CHAPTER

TWENTY-SIX

"What are we going to do?"

It was the third or fourth time Chantelle had asked the question and Umber was no surer how to answer it. They were sitting on the bed, facing the Catherine-wheel window, neither caring to glance back at the shape in the kitchen doorway. Umber had covered Walsh's body as best he could with the hall mat, though that did nothing to conceal the pool of blood on the tiled floor of the kitchen or the patches of it on the hall carpet. Chantelle had removed her blood-smeared T-shirt and trousers and was now enveloped in Jeremy's dressing gown, but bloodstains remained on the trainers she would at some point have to put back on. Walsh's death and her responsibility for it were facts they could not ignore.

"What are we going to do, Shadow Man?" Chantelle's voice was tremulous and plaintive. But the *we* was important. Umber had asked her to trust him. And now it seemed she did.

"We can't stay here," he said, forcing his brain to reason its way through the shock of what had happened. "They'll come looking for him sooner or later. And you know who *they* are, don't you, Chantelle? Or should I call you Cherie?"

"Chantelle's my name now. And I don't know who they are. Or *what* they are. The people my parents work for, I mean. My foster parents, I ought to call them. My *false* parents. That man . . ." She gestured with her chin towards the door.

"Walsh?"

She shook her head. "Waldron. Eddie Waldron. Uncle Eddie, he wanted me to call him. But I never did. I was always frightened of him."

"You don't have to be frightened of him any more."

"He'd have forced you to tell on me. When I saw his car and realized it wasn't Marilyn who'd come . . ." Her head sank. "I knew it was him or me."

"We've got to get out of here, Chantelle. That's about all I'm certain of. We've got to get out."

"I was going to make a run for it," she went on, hardly seeming to hear him. "I wasn't sure of you. I reckoned it was safer not to trust you. But when I saw the car . . . I went back for the knife. I thought, finish Uncle Eddie this time, girl. I thought . . . stop him ever hurting you again."

"You did that, Chantelle. You truly did."

"You're not going to let me down, are you, Shadow Man?" She looked up at him, her eyes moist and red-rimmed. "I don't think I can . . . go on alone."

"We'll get out of this. Together."

"How?"

"Is there anything in this flat or the office or the boat store to lead them to you?"

"No. Nothing. Jem was always careful about that."

There were questions—a host of them—Umber longed to put to her. But they would have to wait. The need now was to act. And to make sure they acted for the best. "My car's just round the corner. We'll walk to it and drive away."

"What about Eddie?"

"We leave him here. He'll be found soon enough, but I'm betting those who find him won't want to set the police on us. On *you*, anyway."

"I can't walk down the street looking like this."

"Could you put some clothes of Jeremy's on?"

"I suppose."

"Do that. And fast. We should go as soon as we can. But there's something I have to do first."

She made no move and merely went on staring at him.

"Please, Chantelle. *Do it.*"

She flinched at the forcefulness of his tone, which he instantly regretted. But it had its effect. "Sorry," she murmured, rising unsteadily and stumbling across to the chest of drawers. "Sorry."

Leaving her to it, Umber jumped up and hurried out into the hall. Taking a deep breath, he pulled the rug clear of the body of the man he now knew as Eddie Waldron. Deliberately avoiding a glance at the bloody, oozing mess of the fatal knife wound, he unclipped the small bunch of keys he had seen hanging from one of Waldron's belt-loops. The remote for the BMW was among them. Noticing the bulge of a wallet in Waldron's hip pocket, he took that as well. Then he folded the rug back into place.

He pocketed the wallet and keys and stepped gingerly into the kitchen, keeping clear of the pool of blood. There he hunted down a tea towel, Sellotape and a roll of black plastic rubbish sacks. He took these out into the hall, wrapped the knife in the tea towel, put the bundle inside one of the rubbish sacks, folded it over and taped down the ends. Then he returned to the kitchen one more time—to collect the Juniuses.

"I'm ready," said Chantelle, watching from beside the bed as he edged past the rug-shrouded shape. She was wearing jeans baggy enough to cover all but the toes of her bloodstained trainers, even though they were rolled up several inches at the ankle, and a navy-blue sweater, with some kind of yachting motif on it, that hung to just above her knees. Only the tips of her fingers were visible beneath the sleeves. Umber saw her glance fall to Waldron's feet protruding from the rug. "Christ," she murmured. "I really did it, didn't I?"

"Don't think about it," said Umber. "We're leaving now. OK?"

There was a long silence. Finally, she wrenched her gaze back to Umber. "OK."

"Put your clothes in this." He peeled off a second rubbish sack and tossed it to her, then moved to the front door and edged it open. There was neither sight nor sound of movement on the steps. He waited a few seconds to be sure. Then he stepped back and signalled to Chantelle. "Come on."

She hesitated, then hurried out to join him by the door, the sack containing her discarded clothes clutched in one hand.

"Go down to the office and wait there. I'm going to check his car. It won't take long. Then we'll go."

Chantelle nodded and headed past him. With a parting glance behind, Umber followed, pulling the door shut as he left. Chantelle was already out of sight as he descended the steps. He flicked the remote at the BMW. The sensor behind the rear mirror flashed. The door locks released. There was no-one close by. The nearest passers-by were on the Boulevard and were paying events in le Quai Bisson no heed. He glanced into the car, but could not see what he was looking for. He strode round to the boot and opened it.

Inside was a smart-looking camcorder, nestling in an unzipped shoulder-bag. And there, to his astonishment, towards the rear of the boot space, was a white cardboard box, fastened with string. The word JUNIUS stared at him in his own, long-ago handwriting. He shook his head in disbelief and smiled despite himself.

"What is it?" called Chantelle, frowning at him from the door-way of the office.

"Something I never expected to see again." He hauled the box out and dropped it on the ground, wedged the black plastic bundle under the string and hoisted the camcorder-bag onto his shoulder. "Come on."

Chantelle hurried over. Umber handed her the Juniuses, then picked up the box. The strap of the bag slipped off his shoulder as he did so. Chantelle hoicked it back into place, squinting in puzzle-ment at the titles on the books she was holding and the word on the side of the box.

"I'll explain later. Let's get moving."

The walk to the hotel was brief and uneventful. Conspicuous though they felt, no-one in fact paid them any attention. They loaded everything they were carrying into the boot of Umber's hire car, then he went into the hotel and booked out.

"Where have you been staying?" Umber asked Chantelle when he returned to the car.

"A small hotel on the other side of St. Helier."

"Right. We'll drive there, pick up your stuff, pay your bill and make for the Airport. There should be an evening flight to Gatwick we can get a couple of seats on."

"We're leaving Jersey?"

"The sooner the better."

Umber's every instinct told him they would be safer off the island. What they were going to do back in England he had literally no idea. The next step was all he could focus on. The step after that lay beyond his power to imagine.

"Where did you grow up, Chantelle?" he asked as they headed round the coast road towards St. Helier through ever thickening traffic: the rush hour was upon them.

"South Africa. Hong Kong. Gibraltar. We moved about a lot. My parents—" She broke off. "Roy and Jean Hedgecoe. That's what they're called. Not Dad and Mum to me any more. Roy and Jean."

"What did they do for a living?"

"Good question. I never really knew. Roy was in import-export, whatever that meant. He had business with . . . strange people."

"Like Eddie Waldron?"

"His sort, yeah. All his sort."

"Any brothers or sisters?"

"No. Just me. Carted around the world by . . . Roy and Jean. When I was sixteen, we moved to Monaco. A new opening, they said. More like a reward, I guess. For looking after me so carefully. We lived high there."

"And you met Michel Tinaud?"

"Yeah. He thought he was God's gift. So did I. I was pretty stupid back then. I had no idea what was going on. Any of it, I mean. Not just what was *really* going on. I was a different person. Not me. Not this me, anyway. Some . . . other girl they'd brought me up to be. Only it didn't work out. I was crazy about Michel. I didn't really think about much else. I went to Paris with him. Then Wimbledon. And that's when everything changed. Because of Sally. Your wife. How long were you two married?"

"Eight years. But we were together a lot longer than that."

"You want me to tell you what happened when she tracked me down, don't you?"

"Yes. I do."

"Do you blame me for her death?"

"Of course not."

"Maybe you should." She gazed ahead for a long, vacant interval, then said, "Can I tell you later? I just . . . don't want to talk about it right now."

"OK."

"But I *will* talk about it." She glanced at him. "I promise."

They entered St. Helier and drove through the Fort Regent tunnel, then followed the main road out to the east until Chantelle pointed out the Hotel Talana ahead of them. Umber pulled into the car park at the rear and Chantelle went in to change her clothes, pack her few belongings and check out.

While she was gone, Umber fetched the camcorder from the boot and unloaded the cassette. The tape was only part-used, as good a confirmation as he needed that it held the recording of his meeting with Wisby. He dropped the cassette onto the ground and stamped on it several times, smashing the plastic case and the spools inside. He dragged the tape out of the wreckage and shoved it into his pocket for later destruction. At least he did not have to worry about being fitted up as Wisby's accomplice now, though there was no telling what Wisby would say about him to the police. For that reason if for no other, an early departure from Jersey was essential.

Back in the car, Umber checked through Waldron's wallet. It turned out to contain several hundred pounds and a couple of credit cards, one for John E. Walsh, the other for Edward J. Waldron. There was nothing else.

It was only as he closed the wallet that a thought caught up with Umber relating to Wisby. And a disturbing thought it was.

Wisby had no way of knowing Umber was not party to the plot against him. He would in fact assume Umber was very much a party to it. His best hope of persuading the police to believe he had been framed was to tell at least some of the truth about his reasons for visiting Jersey and to finger Umber as a treacherous accomplice. As matters stood he could not prove Umber had played any part in blackmailing Jeremy Hall, but he *could* prove Umber had been working with George Sharp, another self-proclaimed victim of a frame-up. If the police then learned there had been a killing at Jeremy's flat, they would eventually go to see Sharp's solicitor. Burnouf would probably be sufficiently alarmed by what had hap-

pened, and genuinely concerned for the safety of a client he had
heard no more from since the previous week, to give them sight of
the statement the client had left with him—a statement in which
Umber had made it very clear he was in Jersey to extract information from Jeremy Hall by whatever means he could devise.

Umber glanced at his watch. It was nearly six o'clock. If it was
not already too late for conducting business at Le Templier &
Burnouf, it surely would be by the time he got there. So, either he
left the statement where it was . . . or he was not leaving Jersey as
soon as he wanted to.

Another quarter of an hour had passed before Chantelle returned to
the car. She must have read Umber's heightened anxiety in his expression, because the first words she spoke to him were, "What's
wrong?"

Plenty was the answer. But what Umber actually said was,
"There's been a change of plan."

CHAPTER

TWENTY-SEVEN

I'm not going alone."

It was the third or fourth time Chantelle had said so and Umber had reluctantly concluded that she meant it. They were sitting in Umber's hire car in a desolate corner of the Airport car park, watching the light fade slowly beyond the terminal building as the last flights of the day came and went. Chantelle's refusal to leave without him that night would soon become unalterable, because leaving that night would soon become impossible.

"Jem put me on a ferry to St. Malo on Thursday and told me he'd join me there the next day. But he was dead by then. I waited for him. But he never came. I don't want to do that again. I've spent too much of the past few years alone, Shadow Man. I can't do it any more."

"It's too risky to stay, Chantelle."

"*You're* staying."

"Because I've got to get that statement out of Burnouf's office. I have no choice."

"Fine. Get the statement first thing tomorrow. Then we'll go."

"OK," said Umber, glumly accepting the reality of her decision. "Have it your way."

"Do you think they'll have found Eddie's body yet?"

"Maybe."

"And do you think they'll be looking for us?"

"If they've found him, for certain."

"Better not stay here, then, had we?"

"Where do you suggest we go, Chantelle? It's a small island."

"But not too small to hide in. Let's get moving."

Trade was slack at the Prince of Wales, the hotel overlooking the beach at Grève de Lecq on Jersey's north coast. Postcards for sale at reception depicted the bay in all its kiss-me-quick, bucket-and-spade summer jollity. The story on a windy night at the end of March was rather different. A couple of rooms were readily to be had at a knock-down rate.

Umber tried to persuade Chantelle to eat something, but she insisted she was not hungry and in truth he had no appetite himself. After booking in, they walked down to the beach and stood among the deserted cafés and souvenir stalls as the sea crashed in, the surf a ghostly grey rim to the blackness of the night-time ocean.

"You saw me that day, didn't you, Shadow Man? The day my first life ended. The life I don't even remember. You were at Avebury on the twenty-seventh of July, 1981."

"Me and a few others, yes."

"But most of them are dead, aren't they? My sister. My brother. Your wife. All gone now."

"What about the day your second life ended, Chantelle? Can you bear to tell me about that?"

"Reckon I've got to."

"It'd be good if you wanted to."

"I do. But it's like . . ." She looked round at him, her expression indecipherable in the darkness. "Jem never thought you'd team up with Wisby. That was a real shock to him, y'know."

"I didn't team up with him."

"No. Guess you didn't. But it looked like you had. And that tore something out of Jem. He'd thought of you as a . . . fellow-victim. He didn't blame you. He only sent the letters to people he blamed . . . for not getting it right."

"Why *did* he send the letters, Chantelle? I mean, really, *why*?"

"Why didn't I stop him's a better question. But that's starting at the wrong end. I have to tell you about Sally first." She shivered. "Let's go inside."

———

There was a trayful of paraphernalia for making tea and coffee in Umber's room. He turned the radiator up to maximum while the kettle was boiling and went to pull the curtains, but Chantelle asked him to leave them open. He did not argue.

He sat on the bed and Chantelle took the only chair, which she dragged close to the radiator. Energy was failing her almost visibly now. She looked drained and haunted and, somewhere deep inside, damaged. She sat hunched in the chair, holding her mug of coffee in both hands, sipping from it as she spoke, her voice barely above a whisper.

"I suppose I knew from my early teens there was something iffy about the way Da——" She broke off for a second, then resumed. "About the way Roy made a living. And about the people he did business with. I never came out and asked. That wasn't encouraged. I was spoiled rotten and I liked it. We had it soft in Monte Carlo. Big duplex looking straight out onto the Med. Everything I wanted. Plus loads of things I didn't even *know* I wanted. Except . . . background. There was no family. No grandparents, aunts, uncles and cousins like my friends had. Unless you counted Uncle Eddie, which you can bet I didn't. Just a blank. Only children of dead only children. That was Roy and Jean's story. And they were sticking to it.

"It didn't bother me anyway. I was having too much fun. After I finished school, they wanted me to go to university and I thought, great, that'll be in England. But no. They didn't want that. Easy to see why now. At the time, I thought they were just being . . . overprotective. They were keen on Nice, so I could come home at weekends. My French was certainly up to it. We argued. In the end, I went nowhere. That pissed them off. I went with boys they didn't approve of. That pissed them off some more. Then I met Michel and it was, like, all is forgiven. He was perfect as far as they were concerned. Even when I went to Paris with him.

"Then came the Wimbledon trip. They couldn't really object after going such a bundle on him. He *was* a tennis player, after all. And I didn't know there was any reason why they *should* object. A fortnight in Paris had been no problem. So, what did they do? They came with us. Michel got them tickets for the tennis, of course. He more or less had to. He'd rented a flat near the club and I stayed with him there. Roy and Jean booked themselves into a plush hotel on

Wimbledon Common. I thought—I honestly did—that they were just using my trip as an excuse to visit London. We saw some of the sights together while Michel was busy practising. Everything was OK. I mean, I'd have preferred them not to be there, but it wasn't so bad. They didn't crowd me. Though now, when I look back, I see what they really did was . . . mind me. Keep an eye on me. Make sure that whatever they couldn't help worrying *might* happen *didn't* happen.

"But it happened anyway. Despite them. Despite all the precautions they'd taken over the years; all the things they'd ever done to prevent me asking or checking or finding out or wondering or somehow, against the odds, *remembering* . . . why there were no photographs of me as a baby, why we had no relatives, why that was the first time I'd ever been to England, why . . . why . . . why . . ."

"Wednesday evening, it was. June twenty-third, 1999. Michel was still at the club, warming down after his second-round match. I'd gone back to the flat. Hadn't been there more than a few minutes when Sally arrived. She'd followed me from the club, she said, after waiting all afternoon for me to leave. She told me who she was. Then she told me who I was.

"I thought she was mad. Well, what else *would* I think? Michel thought the same when he arrived. More or less threw her out. Told me to forget about her. She was a crazy woman trying to get to him through me. Typical of him to decide it was all about *him*. We rowed. I went for a walk to clear my head. I didn't believe Sally. But I didn't exactly *dis*believe her either, even then. What she'd said made a horrible kind of sense. It slotted into those holes in my life. It wasn't something I could just ignore, however much I wanted to.

"Sally hadn't gone far, of course. She was waiting for me at the corner of the street, as I suppose I'd half-hoped she would be. Mad or sane? I didn't know. But I wanted to hear more.

"It was still light. I walked with her to Southfields Tube station. I listened as she talked. I even . . . let her hold my hand. I made a deal with her. I'd think about what she'd said. I'd ask my . . . 'parents' . . . some questions and see what answers I got. I'd meet her on Friday morning, while Michel was with his coach, to talk some more. We agreed the boating lake in Wimbledon Park as a rendezvous. She kissed me and went into the station. There were lots of people about, trickling home from the tennis. I lost sight of her in the crowd. And I never saw her again.

"I never got the chance to put any questions to Roy and Jean either. Michel had called them while I was out and they were at the flat when I got back. They were the ones asking the questions. Why had I let her in? Why had I talked to her? Why had I *encouraged* her? I was gobsmacked. It was like I'd done something wrong— *really* wrong. And I had, of course. Just when it ought to have been impossible, too late, way past any danger—I'd learned the truth.

"I didn't know that then, of course. I only knew their reaction was all wrong. It was so out of proportion *if* Sally was just a nutter. They were taking me back to Monte Carlo right away, they said. Michel sided with them, said he couldn't concentrate on his tennis with so much going on. I saw through him that night as well. I didn't bother to argue. I could tell it was a waste of breath. I said OK, fine, we'll go. They were happy with that. They believed I meant it. They believed most things I said, actually. Just like I believed most things *they* said. Until then.

"Roy and Jean went back to their hotel, saying they'd collect me in the morning. I decided there and then I wasn't going to be collected. I started another row with Michel, knowing he'd react by storming out and driving round London in his sponsored Ferrari. He was a pretty predictable kind of guy. Once he was out of the way, I packed as much as I could into a rucksack—and left.

"I walked all the way into the centre of London. It was a warm night. I remember sitting on the Embankment at dawn thinking you've done it now, girl, you really have. I wasn't short of money, of course. I wasn't homeless, like other people my age I saw on the streets. I bought breakfast, tried to stop feeling sorry for myself and asked a policeman where I could look up back copies of national newspapers. He said he'd never been asked that one before. But he knew the answer.

"So, I ended up spending most of the day in the Newspaper Library at Colindale. As soon as I saw one of the photographs of Tamsin Hall, I knew. Sally had told me the truth. I read every report there was to read on the case. I stayed there till closing time. I went in as Cherie Hedgecoe. I came out . . . as someone else.

"I spent that night at a hotel opposite Euston station. Early next morning, I went back to Wimbledon. It was risky, of course. I knew that. But I had to see Sally again. I had to tell her I believed her and ask her . . . what the fuck I was supposed to do next. I waited for her in the park for hours. Hours and hours. She never turned up, obviously. She was already dead by then. I didn't find that out till I read it in the paper next morning, though. I was checking through it to see if I'd been reported missing. It looked like I hadn't. Then I saw Sally's photograph and the words in the headline: FOUND DEAD.

"They'd killed her. I was certain of that. Not Roy and Jean. But whoever they'd told about her. Whoever was behind the whole crazy fucking thing. They'd ordered her death like they'd ordered Tamsin's abduction—*my* abduction. Eddie Waldron might have carried out the order. If not him, then someone like him. But who actually did it doesn't matter. What matters is who *gave* the order. And why.

"I still don't know the answer. And back then I didn't even want to find out. I was so frightened. So alone and so frightened. There was no-one I could trust. Sally had said my real parents had been suspiciously eager to believe Radd's confession and that's how it looked to me too. Like they might be in on it as well, whatever *it* was. I couldn't fit all the possibilities inside my head. I was just . . . running scared.

"So that's what I did . . . I ran. For a long time. For years. India. Hawaii. South America. All over. I went wherever I wouldn't be known. A guy I met in Nepal fixed me up with a fake French passport and I became Chantelle Fontanet. I'll always be Chantelle now, Shadow Man. Never Cherie. Never even Tamsin. Chantelle is them added together. Them transcended.

"But not forgotten. You can only run for so long. Sooner or later, pretending you don't care what the truth is about your life doesn't cut it any more. Last summer, or winter where I was, in Brazil, I came face to face with the realization that I couldn't leave the mystery alone any longer. That I had to try . . . to find the real me . . . and the answers to all those questions.

"Sally had told me Oliver and Jane were divorced. She'd also told me Jeremy was living with his father here in Jersey. Whatever was behind my abduction, however much my real parents knew, I felt sure Jeremy had to be innocent. He was only ten years old at the time, after all. I reckoned he was the one member of the family I might be able to trust. *Might*. I had to check him out first. I came to Jersey and tracked him down to St. Aubin. I watched him going out with his sailing classes. I spied on him at the flat. I hung around, trying to work up the courage to approach him.

"As it turned out, I didn't have to. *He* approached *me*. He'd noticed the attention I was paying him and one day he surprised me on the steps up to Market Hill. Demanded to know what I was up to. I ummed and ahhed a bit. And then . . . then he said he recognized me. What would you call it? Sibling instinct? I don't know. But it was true. I saw it in his eyes. Just as he saw something in mine. "It's you, isn't it?" he said. "You've come back." And I had.

"Jem was on pretty poor terms with Oliver by then. He didn't quite trust him any more. Or Marilyn. Things had never been the same since Radd's confession, he said. There was no good reason to believe Radd was telling the truth. But they did. That left Jem out in the cold. The way he saw it, my turning up was his reward for keeping the faith. He was . . . exultant. High on the joy of it. So was I. Those first few months, last summer and autumn . . . were the best. Just the absolute best.

"We rented a flat in St. Malo. It seemed safer to spend most of our time together in France. Once the sailing season was over, Jem was hardly ever here. I had him all to myself. We were careful. I dyed my hair. And we never used mobiles. Too easy to trace, Jem said. He came up with the idea of coloured contact lenses as well. And he taught me to stop doing that thing with my lower lip that had caught Sally's eye in *Hello!* People must have taken us for boyfriend and girlfriend. I suppose that's how it felt to us too, in a way. It was a kind of romance. A voyage of rediscovery, Jem called it.

"But there were still those questions, niggling away at us, itching to be asked . . . and answered. It seemed worse for Jem than for me. Our parents were two people I'd never known. But he'd loved and trusted them implicitly. He needed to know the truth more than I did. He couldn't let it go.

"It was Marilyn he was most suspicious of. She was spending more and more time in London. Oliver and her were virtually separated. When I described Eddie Waldron to Jem, he thought it sounded like a man he'd once seen Marilyn with, at the marina in St. Helier. She came over for Christmas. Jem was expected to spend the holiday at Eden Holt and it would have looked odd if he'd refused, so off he went. He got into a row with them about Radd, he told me afterwards. And he asked Marilyn a lot of pointed questions about how she and Oliver had met.

"He got more of a reaction then he'd bargained for. He was due to join me in St. Malo on New Year's Eve. The day before that, when he was shopping in St. Helier, he spotted Marilyn on the other side of the road, hurrying out of a bank, with a brown-paper parcel in her hand, looking . . . furtive, he reckoned. She didn't notice him and he followed her into Royal Square, where he hung back and watched as she sat down on a bench and unwrapped the parcel. Inside were two small antique books. Well, Marilyn's no book collector, is she? Jem didn't know what to make of it. But he was more than curious. He was suspicious. Specially when she tore the front page out of each of the books and folded them away in her handbag. Then she put the books into a carrier-bag, chucked the wrapping paper in a bin and headed off.

"Jem followed. And you can guess where he followed her *to*. Quires, in Halkett Place. He watched her through the window from behind a delivery van on the other side of the street and saw her slip the books out of the bag and *onto* the shelf. Then she left.

"Jem let her go, then went into the shop and took a look at the books. When he saw what they were, he knew he had to buy them. They were evidence. Evidence Marilyn had been eager to get off her hands. He'd got hold of a transcript of the original inquest at the time of Radd's confession to check for contradictions. So, he knew what you'd told the coroner about Griffin and the special edition of the Junius letters. And there they were. Minus the fly-leaves. The fact that Marilyn had torn them out clinched it for him. His probing over Christmas had panicked her. She'd decided to cover her tracks. Maybe she'd meant to get rid of the books for years but hadn't bothered to. Maybe the distance opening up between Oliver and her was a factor. Maybe she didn't expect to be back in Jersey that often. It doesn't matter why she made her move that day. What matters is that Jem caught her in the act.

"I wish to Christ now he hadn't. He'd still be alive. We'd still . . ." She swallowed hard. "Sorry. Can't stop now, can I? Can't go all weepy on you.

"The Junius letters were clearly the key to it all, but Jem didn't really understand why. He couldn't get the idea out of his head of using them in some way to expose the truth—and to punish Marilyn for her part in it. Eventually, he decided to construct a message out of words and phrases in the letters and send it to three people outside the family he hoped could be goaded into going back into the case. Sharp. Wisby. And Hollins—the policeman who put Radd away. Looks like Hollins ignored the letter. But Sharp and Wisby didn't. They rose to the bait.

"Jem didn't kill himself because he was afraid you'd expose his campaign to his parents, y'know. He did it to shield me. To draw a line, with me on the safe side of it. He was spooked by the ruthlessness of whoever's behind all this. He felt guilty for stirring up trouble for me. He didn't quite believe they'd killed Sally, y'see. But when they killed Radd? Then he believed. He didn't know where they'd stop. He wanted the truth to come out. All he got for his pains was unwelcome attention from you and Wisby. And he was worried who might follow after you. You meeting me was the last straw, I reckon. He was determined no-one else would get the chance. So, he sent me to St. Malo, knowing he never would meet up with me there. And then he went to finish it with you and Wisby the only way he could.

"I'm alone now, like I guess I always have been. Miranda, the sister I can't even remember. Jem, the brother I had for a few precious months. They're gone. It's just me left. I don't know what to do. I can't run. I can't stay. I can't hide. I can't show myself. I want a mother and a father who don't lie to me or betray me or insist I'm dead or someone else or Christ knows what. I want justice for Jem. And for myself. I want everyone to face the truth. And I want to know what the truth is. But I don't expect to get what I want. I don't *expect* at all. I can't see the future. Any future. I can't see a way out. Or ahead. Or even back." She paused, frowning into what remained of her coffee. Then, for the first time since she had begun speaking, she looked Umber in the eye. "Can you, Shadow Man? Tell me honestly, can you?"

Chantelle had not had much of an answer to her question when she went back to her room. She was so clearly exhausted by then that Umber hoped she would sleep for the rest of the night. He held out no such hope for himself. He lay on his bed, not even bothering to undress, staring into the darkness above his head. And darkness was all he saw.

He rose at dawn and slipped out of the hotel, carrying the knife in its bundle of black plastic. He fetched the bag containing Chantelle's bloodstained clothes from the boot of the car and followed the coast path as it climbed the hill to the west. *Cliffpath to Plémont,* the sign at the bottom had promised. But soon, infuriatingly, it turned inland. He had to cut through a small copse and a bank of bracken beyond to reach the edge of the cliff. He tossed the bag and the bundle over. They fell amongst rocks and foaming sea, lost to the eye almost at once. Safe enough, he reckoned. He headed back.

CHAPTER

TWENTY-EIGHT

When they left Grève de Lecq next morning, Umber shunned the obvious route back to St. Helier, preferring to head east and approach it from the north, across the middle of the island. There was no good reason for such an elaborate precaution. They would only really be in danger of discovery once they were in St. Helier. And there was no way of avoiding that danger if he was to retrieve his statement.

But the danger, he assured Chantelle, was actually minimal. It was just too soon for the police to have thought of contacting Burnouf. And Waldron's associates had no reason to. It was a simple errand, swiftly and easily accomplished. Nothing would go wrong.

That did not stop him telling Chantelle what to do if something *did* go wrong, however. They sat in the car in the Pier Road multi-storey, facing a concrete wall in the gloom of one of the lower floors, as nine o'clock ticked round. She had said she would not go alone. But the contingency Umber was determined to prepare her for was one in which she would have no choice in the matter.

"If I'm not back by ten, leave without me. Take the Juniuses with you and get off the island any way you can. Go to London. Phone this woman." He passed her Claire Wheatley's card. "There's a mobile number on the back. Claire was Sally's psychotherapist. You can trust her. Tell her everything. She'll know what to do for the best."

"But you *will* be back by ten, won't you?"

"I fully intend to be."

"So, no need to worry, then."

"None at all." He scraped off the time on the parking paycard and propped it on the dashboard. "I'll see you soon." Then he gave her a parting smile and climbed out of the car.

It was only a few minutes' walk down Pier Road and along Hill Street to Le Templier & Burnouf. The receptionist was drinking coffee and sorting through the post when Umber arrived and took a while to absorb the message that he wanted the envelope he had left with Burnouf back and he wanted it now. She rang Burnouf on the internal line and he agreed to spare Umber five minutes.

Five minutes was as long as Umber wanted to spare Burnouf, as it happened, though he did not say so. The ever placid solicitor was still on the internal phone, instructing the receptionist to fetch the envelope from the safe, when Umber hurried into his office.

"Thank you, Janet." Burnouf rang off. "Good morning, Mr. Umber. Bright and early, I see."

"Sorry to burst in on you. I, er . . . well, there's been a . . ."

"Promising development?"

"No." Umber was temporarily nonplussed. "What made you think that?"

"Well, you left your . . . statement . . . with me as a precaution, so I understood. Retrieving it suggests precautions are no longer necessary."

"I've . . . changed my mind about it. That's all."

"I see."

"I'm allowed to do that, aren't I?"

"Of course. It's just . . ." Burnouf frowned. "Mr. Sharp reappears before the magistrates this morning. I tried to reach you at the Pomme d'Or to discuss his prospects, but they said you'd checked out."

Umber smiled weakly. "I found somewhere cheaper."

"Do you still wish me to say nothing to him about your activities on his behalf?"

"I'll leave that for you to decide."

"Really? You seem, if I may——" There was a tap at the door. The receptionist came in with the taped and sealed envelope. She delivered it to Burnouf and left. "Thank you, Janet," he called after her.

"There's the receipt," said Umber, whipping it out of his pocket and placing it on the desk. "May I?" He held out his hand.

"By all means." Burnouf passed him the envelope. "There's space on the receipt for you to confirm retrieval. Would you mind signing?" He proffered a pen. Umber signed. "Leaving Jersey, Mr. Umber?"

"Did I say I was?"

"No. It's just . . . an impression I have."

"I'll be in touch."

"What about the Halls? Will you be in touch with them?"

"Sorry?"

"Jeremy Hall's suicide prompted a lot of publicity. One of the newspaper articles I read mentioned a previous suicide by someone linked with the Avebury case. Sally Umber. Not a common surname. Not common at all. I took a flick through the archives. Found you—— and Mr. Sharp. I visited him yesterday and asked him about it."

"What did he say?"

"Nothing. Absolutely nothing."

"Well, that's my line too."

"I rather thought it might be. Though whether the police will be content with it . . ."

"The police?"

"They're bound to follow up the connection sooner or later. I wondered if that was why . . . you'd called in this morning." Burnouf glanced pointedly at the envelope in Umber's hand.

"Thanks for this," Umber said stiffly. "I've got to go." He turned and made for the door, but before he reached it something stopped him. He looked back at Burnouf. "Perhaps you could pass a message to George for me after all."

"I'd be happy to."

"Tell him . . . it isn't over."

How Sharp would take such a message Umber did not know. His thoughts were fixed now on getting himself and Chantelle off Jersey as quickly as possible. He hurried out of Le Templier &

Burnouf and started back the way he had come, glancing at his watch as he went. It had just turned half past nine. He was comfortably on schedule. His gaze returned to the street ahead.

And he found himself looking into the eyes of Percy Nevinson.

"David! Well, well, well." Nevinson beamed at him. "How very nice to see you. And how very unexpected."

Umber's heart sank. Silently but eloquently, he cursed his luck. "Percy, I—"

"We shouldn't be too surprised, though. This is a small island. And I assume we're bound for the same destination this morning."

"Where might that be, Percy?"

"The magistrates' court." Nevinson winked. "Mr. Sharp's hearing. It should prove interesting, I think. Of course, you may be able to tell me how he finds himself in such a position. The gamekeeper poached, so to speak. Why don't we step in somewhere for a cup of coffee? You can fill me in on the background."

"Sorry. I'm in a rush. Can't stop."

"Well, I'll walk with you and we can talk as we go. You see, I can hardly believe Mr. Sharp's predicament is unconnected with the latest tragedy to strike the Hall family. Jeremy Hall's suicide is actually what prompted me to come to Jersey. I imagine you can tell me a good deal about that as well, if you've a mind to."

"But I don't have a mind to, Percy. That's the point. Get out of my way."

Nevinson bridled. "There's no need to take that tone."

"Oh but there is. Now I—"

The events of the next few seconds were compressed into a bewildering jumble in Umber's mind. The flank of a white Transit van appeared suddenly at the edge of his vision. The vehicle bounced up onto the pavement and lurched to a halt a few inches from him, the side-door sliding open fast as it did so. He was grabbed from behind by someone on the pavement, his arms pinned to his sides, the envelope plucked from his hand. A second figure loomed above him and grasped his shoulders. Then he was hoisted off his feet and into the van.

He was face down on an oily blanket covering the floor as the door slammed shut. Two men, strong enough to handle him like a child, were above and around him. There was a shout of *"Go!"* then the van surged forward, left the pavement with a jolt and accelerated away. Umber could see the thick neck and shaven head of the driver through the wire-mesh screen between him and the cab.

It was to be no more than a glimpse. His head was yanked up. A blindfold was slung across his eyes. The cloth pressed painfully into them as the knot was fastened. He cried out. But the cry was stifled by a strip of duct tape, slapped across his mouth and pressed tight against his skin. His hands were crushed together behind his back, then cords twined round his wrists and tightened. He tried to struggle up, but a boot descended heavily on his neck, forcing him down again.

Then came a rasping voice close to his ear. "Lie still or we'll break every fucking bone in your body."

They were on the road for about half an hour, Umber estimated. His shock faded slightly, but his fear only increased. Reasoning as best he could, he deduced they had been following Nevinson in the hope he would lead them to Umber, as, by pure and malign chance, he had. Nevinson had presumably been left to goggle at the departing van. He was not important. They had got the man they wanted. But what they meant to do with him he did not know. All he knew for certain was that he did not want to find out. The only consolation he had to hold on to was that they had struck too soon. He might have led them to Chantelle if they had held off. But they did not know about her. That was his only advantage. And he had to make the most of it.

Eventually, the van came to a halt. The engine died. The side-door slid open. He was pulled upright and bundled into the open air. He felt the coolness of it against his skin at once. The wind stirred his hair. There was stony ground beneath his feet. "Start walking" came the instruction. He was frogmarched forward. They covered about twenty yards. He heard a burble of conversation nearby, but could not catch the words. Then: "Get in the car." He was pushed through an open car doorway, a hand pressing down his head to clear the frame. The door clunked shut behind him.

He could smell new leather and a residue of cigar smoke. There was an armrest to his left. With his hands tied behind him, he had to lean forward slightly in his seat. He sensed there was someone beside him. He heard an envelope being torn open. There was a rustling of paper. A few minutes of silence followed. Then the man beside him spoke, in a soft, moist, sticky tone, as if he was sucking a toffee.

"Listen to me carefully, Mr. Umber. I'm going to offer you a deal. And you're going to accept it. That's the way it is. That's the way it has to be. We want Cherie. Or Chantelle, as I gather she calls herself now. You're the only one who's seen her recently. The only one alive, anyway. So, you know what she looks like these days. And we believe you can find her for us. We could persuade you to tell us what you know about her and go after her ourselves, but we're concerned about our profile. It's been worryingly high lately. So, you get the job. Congratulations. There's a time limit, naturally. Three days. I'm going to put a card in your pocket." Umber felt something being slipped into his shirt pocket. "There's a telephone number on it. Ring us by noon on Friday with details of where and when we can collect the girl. In return, we'll arrange for a reliable witness to tell the police he saw the drugs being planted on Sharp's van and we'll refrain from sending them this incriminating document you've kindly supplied us with. We cleaned up after you at the flat in St. Aubin, but there's a body waiting to be found in an abandoned car at Noirmont Point which fingerprints and DNA would tie you to for certain *if* the police were pointed in the right direction. Wisby's likely to throw all sorts of accusations your way. You really do need to be in a position to refute them. There'd be other kinds of retribution if you defied us, of course. For you and Ms. Wheatley and Ms. Myers. And we'd find Cherie in the end anyway, so you and your friends would be sacrificed in vain. But I don't need to spell it all out for you, do I? You're an intelligent man. You can see there's no choice. It's open and shut. So, just nod your head to confirm we have a deal. That's all you have to do. That and deliver the girl, of course." There was a pause. "Well?"

A moment slowly passed. Then Umber nodded.

"Thank you, Mr. Umber. It's been a pleasure doing business with you."

A signal of some kind must have been given. The car door opened and he was pulled out. His captors led him back to the van, loaded him aboard and dumped him, as before, face down on the floor. They set off once more.

It was a shorter drive this time, or perhaps it merely seemed so to Umber, who no longer feared for his life, at least in the short term. The knowledge that he would soon be set free relaxed him to a degree.

The van made slower going as the journey continued. At one point, it stopped and reversed to the sound of roadside branches scraping against the bodywork, then went on again, as if passing another vehicle in a narrow lane. Eventually, it pulled over and came to a halt, with the engine running. The side-door slid open. Umber was hauled into a sitting position in the doorway, his feet resting on the ground. "Stand up," he was told. He did so. "Take one step forward." He did that too. Then his hands were untied, the door slid shut behind him and the van pulled away, accelerating hard.

By the time Umber had released the blindfold and his eyes had adjusted to the light, the van was out of sight. He was standing a few feet from a five-bar gate into a field. On the other side of the gate a herd of Jersey cattle were grazing contentedly on rich green pasture. One of them cast him a mildly curious glance, then returned her attention to the grass. Even the cry he gave as he pulled the strip of tape away from his mouth did not distract her further.

Umber started walking along the lane in the direction the van had taken, reasoning fuzzily that a main road was likely to be closer ahead then behind. His throat was dry, his lips were sore from the tape, his eyes were aching from constriction by the blindfold and the wound on the back of his head was throbbing. One of his knees was also paining him, having taken some kind of knock while he was being bundled into the van in St. Helier.

Unfortunately, none of these discomforts had the merit of taking his mind off the deal he had notionally struck. He was lost in the Jersey countryside and part of him would have been happy to stay lost. Within three days, he was required to betray Chantelle to her pursuers, something he had no intention of doing. But what was he to do instead? Who was he to betray in her place? He plucked the card he had been given out of his pocket and looked at the number printed on it. There was no clue to be found there, no message but the one already conveyed to him, calmly, clearly and implacably. An answer was required of him by Friday. And only one kind of answer would suffice.

CHAPTER
TWENTY-NINE

A limping forty-minute hike through a maze of lanes took Umber to the village of Maufant, where he had to wait more than half an hour for a bus back to St. Helier. It was gone one o'clock by the time he was delivered to Liberation Square. Limping now more heavily than ever, he hurried up Pier Road to the multi-storey, hoping on balance he would find the hire car gone—and Chantelle with it.

But the car was where he had parked it. As he caught sight of it in the bay ahead of him, he hardly knew what to expect to find inside. Surely Chantelle could not still be waiting for him, more than three hours beyond the deadline he had set for his return.

She was not. It was a relief in a way, though also a disappointment. He did not like to consider what thoughts would be going through her head. She would be frightened, alone and uncertain what to do. And she had good reason to be frightened. The reason was, if anything, better than she knew.

The car was unlocked, the key still in the ignition. She must have left on foot, which worried him, since driving straight to the Airport would have been her best bet for a swift departure. He opened the boot. Her bag had gone, along with the Juniuses. His bag—and his box of Junius-related papers—remained.

Where had she gone? What would she have decided to do once it had become clear he was not coming back? She might have gone to look for him at Le Templier & Burnouf. If so, she would have drawn a blank. What then? The absence of the Juniuses suggested she had paid at least some attention to what he had said. Logically, she must have resolved to leave Jersey. But why not take the car? Perhaps, it occurred to him, she simply could not drive. Stupidly, he had not bothered to check the point. Or perhaps, it also occurred to him, she had left by ferry. St. Malo was only an hour and a bit away.

He drove down to the Harbour, frustrated by the slowness of the lunchtime traffic, parked in front of the ferry terminal and hurried inside. The girl at the Condor information desk told him a ferry had sailed for St. Malo at noon; the next one sailed at six. His description of Chantelle rang no bells.

The timings proved nothing anyway. It was equally possible Chantelle had taken a bus to the Airport and flown out. Umber had to assume she would do as he had told her and make for London. If so, she would contact Claire. He decided to call Claire himself and forewarn her.

But all he got on her practice number was the answerphone. And her mobile was switched off. He got no response from Alice's home number either. He left a message on none of them; there was no telling who might end up hearing it. Then he went back to the car and headed for the Airport.

He knew the BA flight times to Gatwick, having phoned an information line before leaving Grève de Lecq that morning. He was too late for the 1:30, though Chantelle of course would not have been. The next flight was at 5:30. There was no way he could be in London before early evening.

It was a quiet and orderly afternoon at the States Airport. Umber parked the car, heaved his bag and box of notes out of the boot and carried them into the terminal building. He dropped off the keys, then made for the BA desk.

There was no queue and the woman on duty was chatting with a female colleague as he approached. One of them had a newspaper open in her hands. The name 'Jeremy Hall' reached Umber's ears an instant before they noticed him and he peeled off to inspect a rack of leaflets, remaining within earshot as their conversation continued.

"The coffin was on the one-thirty flight. His mother was

aboard. I saw her in the club lounge waiting for take-off. Like a ghost, she was. So pale."

"Was the father with her?"

"Not sure. There was a man. But he didn't look like this picture of Oliver Hall."

"The second husband, then."

"I suppose so."

"It must be dreadful for all of them. Just dreadful."

Umber had heard enough. He interrupted and booked himself onto the 5:30 flight. His eye strayed to the newspaper they had been reading. It was that afternoon's *Jersey Evening Post*. He could see photographs of Jeremy and Oliver Hall beneath the headline MURDERED GIRLS' BROTHER TO BE BURIED IN ENGLAND. It seemed that in one way at least he had had a narrow escape. But what about Chantelle? Was it possible she had been on the same flight as her mother—and her dead brother? He felt sick at the thought, unable to imagine what the consequences of such a coincidence might be.

After checking-in his box of notes as hold luggage, Umber headed back to the news stand and bought a copy of the paper. He sat down and read the article through.

An inquest was opened and adjourned yesterday into the death last week of Jeremy Hall, proprietor of Rollers Sail & Surf, St. Aubin, and brother of the two girls slain in the infamous 1981 Avebury murder case. Jeremy was found dead at the Waterworks Valley home of his father, Oliver Hall, who told the *Post* after the hearing that he was very grateful for the many messages of sympathy he had received since the news broke. Mr. Hall said Jeremy would be buried next to his sister Miranda in Marlborough, Wilts, in accordance with his mother's wishes. Mr. Hall also said he knew of no connection between his son's death and the arrest in St. Helier earlier last week on smuggling charges of a retired police officer said to have been prominently involved in the 1981 murder inquiry.

The article only heightened Umber's fears, formless though many of them were. He made for the payphones and called Claire again. It was the same story: recorded messages at the practice and Alice's house and no joy on Claire's mobile. Nor did the story change at the second, third, fourth or fifth time of trying. Eventually, he gave up.

The flight, short as it was, felt agonizingly protracted to Umber. Several drinks failed to quell the whirl of his anxious thoughts. It was too late to expect an answer from Claire's practice by the time he made it through baggage reclaim and Customs at Gatwick. But she or Alice really ought to be answering on the Hampstead number. Except that they were not. And the mobile was still switched off.

Umber's only recourse now was to head for Hampstead and hope to find them in when he arrived. Even if he had not been in a hurry, he would have taken a taxi after the Gatwick Express had delivered him to Victoria; the box he was carrying seemed to weigh more every time he picked it up. Even so, the journey contrived to take longer than the flight from Jersey and it was gone 8:30 when the taxi pulled up outside 22 Willow Hill.

The hall light was on, but the ground and first-floor rooms were in darkness. Claire's TVR was not parked nearby. The auguries were far from good. Umber had wheedled an undertaking out of Claire to dissuade Alice from going to Monte Carlo to grill Michel Tinaud. But it was beginning to look as if they had both overestimated her powers of dissuasion. Or perhaps she had simply tired of waiting to hear from him. He had asked for a few days' grace and, technically, that is what he had already had.

The lights *were* on in the top-floor flat. It was occupied by an articled clerk called Piers. Alice had made several references to him, though Umber had not actually met him. Telling the taxi driver to wait, Umber clambered out, hurried to the door and pressed the bell next to the neatly printed label PIERS BURTON.

There was no intercom system and consequently no way to tell whether Piers was going to respond or not, until, just as Umber was about to give the bell a second prod, the door opened. A sleepy-eyed, curly-haired young man in fogeyish casual wear regarded him through owlish, black-framed glasses and ventured a wary hello.

"Piers, right?"

"Yes. I—"

"I'm David." Some instinct deterred Umber from volunteering his surname, sharing it as he did with a deceased former tenant of Piers's flat. "I'm, er . . . a friend of Alice's. I was staying here at the weekend."

"I was out of town."

"Well, we'd probably have bumped into each other if you'd been here."

"Probably."

"Look, the thing is——"

"Alice isn't here."

"So I see. Has she gone away?"

"Yes. Last-minute decision, apparently. There was a note waiting for me when I got home this evening. She's taken off with her friend Claire. *She's* been staying here. I know that." There was a hint in his tone that Claire's presence in the house was something he could vouch for, whereas Umber's was altogether more debatable.

"Did the note say where they'd gone?"

"No. Maybe she didn't want to make me feel envious."

"What about for how long?"

"Open-ended, apparently. A few days. A week. She wasn't sure."

"Right." Monte Carlo it had to be. Claire's mobile had probably been switched off during the flight. If Chantelle had tried to contact her, she would not have succeeded. The fail-safe Umber had supplied her with had proved to be useless. "Well, thanks."

"No problem."

No problem to Piers, perhaps. For Umber the situation was much more complicated. He went back to the cab and climbed in.

"Where to now, guv'?" the taxi driver prompted, when ten seconds or so had passed without a destination being supplied.

"I . . ." Umber thought of what Chantelle had done after fleeing Tinaud's rented apartment in Wimbledon five years ago. It was possible—just—that she had done the same after trying to speak to Claire. "A hotel near Euston station."

"There are quite a few, guv'."

"Near as in opposite."

"There's a Travel Inn on the other side of Euston Road. That'd be more or less opposite."

"Then that'll do."

It was a long shot and Umber was disappointed but not surprised to be told there was nobody called Fontanet—or even Hedgecoe—staying at the Euston Travel Inn. Fast running out of options, he booked himself in for the night. He thought about trying Claire's mobile again, then thought better of it for reasons that had only just begun to take shape in his mind.

He did some more thinking in the large and noisy pub a few doors along from the hotel. There was nothing Claire could do for Chantelle in Monte Carlo. If she and Alice were intent on confronting Tinaud, it might be better, in fact, if they knew as little as possible about his errant former girlfriend's whereabouts.

But that conclusion left Umber alone and resourceless. If he was no better placed come Friday, the roof would fall in on all of them. He had to do something. He had to seize the initiative. But how? With what? There was nothing: no answer; no hope.

Then, quite suddenly, around the time a tsunami of cheers burst over him following a goal in the football match splashed across the pub's widescreen TV, the glimmer of an answer came to him. And with it a sliver of hope.

Junius held the key. Chantelle had said as much and maybe she was right. Wisby believed Griffin had been done away with by Tamsin's abductors. His special edition of Junius's letters had ended up in the hands of Marilyn Hall. Did that make her one of the abductors? If so, it was a chink in the armour of whoever she had been acting for—the juicy-voiced man in the car for one. If Umber could pin Griffin's murder on her, it would give him a bargaining chip, maybe a decisive one. It was a tall order. It required him to trace the previously untraceable Griffin. And that brought him back to the hunt for Junius himself, a hunt in which he had made only faltering progress. But something had changed now. Something had been returned to him. And it was time to remind himself what it contained.

THIRTY

Opening the Junius box returned Umber for the duration of a sleepless night to a long unremembered past: *his* past, before Avebury, before the last Monday in July, 1981. His life had been so simple then, so unfettered. A sense of that freedom reached him from every eagerly scribbled note, every neatly labelled batch of papers. They were the work of a younger, keener-eyed, sharper-brained man, a man who believed academic zeal was the best and surest way to prise a secret from its history.

Separate bundles of notes and photocopied documents recalled to Umber the time and effort he had devoted to each. THE CHATHAM SPEECH. If, as Junius implied, he was in the House of Lords gallery when Lord Chatham made a speech attacking Lord Mansfield on 10 December 1770, who among the Junian candidates did that date and location eliminate? THE FITZPATRICK CONNECTION. A French spy reported to Louis XVI that Junius was actually Thady Fitzpatrick, smooth-tongued man about town, an idea scotched by Fitzpatrick's death several months before the letters stopped. But who among his boon companions might be a more plausible suspect? THE GILES LETTER. In December 1771, a Miss Giles of Bath received an amorous poem from an anonymous admirer, accompanied by a note of commendation in a hand now commonly agreed to be Junius's, although the poem itself was in a different, less distinctive hand. With how many Junian candidates could Miss Giles and her family be linked? THE HIGHGATE SOURCE. Examination of postmarks revealed that a significant number of the Junius letters were despatched to the *Public*

Advertiser by penny post from the Highgate Village post office. Which of the candidates lived in Highgate or had friends or relatives who lived there? THE JUNIA EXCHANGE. Goaded by a provocative letter from a woman calling herself Junia, printed in the *Public Advertiser* on 5 September 1769, Junius replied in flirtatious vein two days later, then almost immediately wrote to Woodfall asking him to print a denial that the reply was his work, blaming the lapse on "people about me." Did this raise the serious possibility that the letters were collaborative compositions and, if so, could such collaborators be found among the Junian candidates? THE COURIER QUESTION. Junius began a letter to Woodfall on 18 January 1772 with the tantalizing statement "The gentleman who transacts the conveyancing part of our correspondence tells me there was much difficulty last night." Woodfall's letters to Junius were always left at one of several pre-arranged coffee-house drops around the Strand. So, did Junius always use the same courier for their collection? Was that person also responsible for posting Junius's letters *to* Woodfall? And, if so, was there any evidence as to his identity? THE FRANCISCAN THEORY. Would an exhaustive analysis of the known movements and activities of the hot favourite among the candidates, War Office clerk Philip Francis, reveal any occasion on which he was quite simply in the wrong place and/or at the wrong time to be Junius? THE AMANUENSES. What were . . .

Ah yes. The amanuenses. They were the point Umber's researches had arrived at towards the end of the Trinity term of 1981. And there was what he was looking for, in a clutch of papers labelled *Christabella Dayrolles.* He sifted eagerly through them, in search of the notes he knew he must have made during his inspection of the Ventry Papers, likely repository of any clue that Christabella Dayrolles had written the letters at Junius's dictation.

But Umber had forgotten less than he thought. He had evidently examined everything there was to be examined on the uncelebrated doings of the wife of Lord Chesterfield's friend, godson and confidant, Solomon Dayrolles. The truth was that this amounted to very little. Christabella Dayrolles had stubbornly refused to emerge from her husband's shadow. If she *was* Junius's amanuensis, he had clearly chosen wisely. Her discretion alone had survived her.

As for the Ventry Papers, there was the briefest of notes, written by Umber, it seemed to his older self, in a mood of some exasperation. *Staffs Record Office, 16/7/81. Ventry Papers. Tedious screeds of*

estate correspondence. Family refs almost all to Ventry side. Prob a
dead end, but worth checking Kew ref in sister's letter to Mrs. V of 19
Oct 1791.

What was the Kew reference? The note did not say. It had not
needed to, of course. Umber had intended to follow it up long before there was any danger of forgetting it. But eleven days after his
visit to the Staffordshire Record Office, something had happened to
put such matters out of his mind. Which is where they had remained. Until now.

The choice had been made for him. He had to go to Stafford and nail
down the reference. It might be a waste of precious time, but he could
not know that without going. He had intended to go before now and
been sidetracked. He was not about to let himself be sidetracked again.
Waldron had probably glanced at the contents of the box and decided
he could safely ignore them. It would be good to prove him wrong.

In attempting to do so, Umber was also trying to prove himself
right. Junius was unfinished business in more ways than one. His
instinct was to pursue the Ventry lead to the finish. Too often in the
past he had failed to follow his instincts. This time would be different. It had to be.

He caught an early enough train from Euston next morning to be
in Stafford by nine o'clock, booking a second night at the Travel Inn
before he left. Lack of sleep caught up with him disastrously somewhere around Watford, however. He did not wake until the train
was pulling into Crewe, the stop *after* Stafford, two hours later. He
then had to wait another hour for a train back to Stafford and did
not arrive at the County Records Office until gone eleven o'clock.

It was an infuriatingly bad start. But the staff at the Record
Office were soothingly efficient. The Ventry Papers were in his
hands within half an hour.

They had been bound in several marbled leather volumes by a
Ventry of the Edwardian period, who had added a comprehensive
table of contents. Umber steered a straight course through boundary disputes, rent-rolls and local Hunt politics to the letter of 19
October 1791.

It was written by Christabella Ventry's younger sister, Mary Croft, from her home in London. She dwelt on family affairs that would be known to both parties: cousins, aunts, uncles, in-laws. There were several references to their 'dear departed mother' (Christabella Dayrolles), who had died two months previously. And then came the reference to Kew.

> The depth of feeling expressed by so many since Mother's passing is a testament to the nobility and generosity of her character. I was more affected than I can say to receive a letter this week past from her dear and troubled friend at Kew, who confesses himself sorely afflicted by the loss of her counsel and acquaintanceship.

That was it. There was nothing else. A friend at Kew, known to both daughters. It amounted to hardly anything. Yet there was just enough, in the description of the friend as "dear and troubled," in the mention of their mother's role as his adviser, in the faintly suspicious way that Mary Croft avoided naming him, to draw Umber in.

There was no quick or easy way to follow it up, however. Umber admitted as much to himself as he sat aboard the lunchtime train back to London. That was probably why he had made no immediate attempt to do so in July 1981. An unnamed man living in Kew two centuries before was effectively untraceable. Logically, Umber would have to search for him by indirect routes—exploring any connections with Kew, however apparently tenuous, that he could find in the affairs of Lord Chesterfield and Solomon Dayrolles.

But such researches could last for weeks, if not months. Umber had two days, not even enough time to scratch the surface. It was, quite simply, a hopeless task.

A powerful sense of that hopelessness clung to Umber when he got off the train at Euston. He did not know what to do or where to go. He had very little time to act in. And no idea what action he should take. Largely by inertia, it seemed to him, he drifted down into the Underground station. And there he bought a ticket to Kew.

On the Tube, Umber tried to apply his mind to the problem like the historian he had once been. What did he know about eighteenth-century Kew? Not much. But not nothing either.

It was a place with royal connections. George II, when still Prince of Wales, lived at Richmond Lodge, which he retained when he became king. His son Frederick, the next Prince of Wales, settled with his wife, Augusta, at Kew House, just to the north. After Frederick's death in 1751, Princess Augusta pursued his ambition to transform the estate into the famous botanical gardens. Frederick's son, the future George III, grew up at Kew under the combined influence of his widowed mother and her trusted adviser, the Earl of Bute. Junius reserved a particular venom for both parties, insinuating that they were lovers and cruelly relishing the news when it came of Augusta's fatal throat cancer.

It had not occurred to Umber until now that Junius's loathing of Augusta and Bute might have been heightened by their being, as it were, his neighbours. His knowledge (and disapproval) of George III's upbringing could then be seen, if the point was stretched, as the fruit of personal experience.

But it *was* a stretch, as Umber well knew. He walked out of Kew Gardens station that afternoon into the heart of a Victorian suburb that had not existed when Mary Croft wrote a letter to her sister in October 1791. His own previous trips to Kew had either been to tour the Gardens or to visit the National Archives, which had been massively and modernistically extended since 1981, to judge by his glimpse of the riverside complex from the train. Two hundred years previously, documents now stored at meticulously maintained levels of temperature and humidity would have been mouldering in a Chancery Lane cellar. Such was the scale of all the changes through which Umber knew it was fanciful to suppose he could somehow thread a path.

He wandered into a bookshop that caught his eye as soon as he left the station and bought a pocket history of the area: *The Story of Kew.* He leafed through it over a cup of coffee in a café a few doors along, lingering on the chapters devoted to the Georgian period. The account of the origins of the Botanical Gardens held no surprises. Nor did much of what followed concerning the persistent rumour

that George III, while still Prince of Wales, had secretly married a
Quakeress called Hannah Lightfoot and fathered by her a son, who
should legally have counted as his heir but was instead banished to
South Africa. The theft of the parish registers from St. Anne's
Church, Kew, in 1845 was held to be related to this, though oddly the
stolen registers did not cover the period of the alleged marriage,
which would obviously not have been recorded anyway. The motive
for the theft was therefore a mystery.

Then, as Umber turned the page, a name leapt out at him from
the print. Dr. James Wilmot was the clergyman supposed to have sol-
emnized the marriage. And Dr. James Wilmot was on the long-list of
Junian candidates. There *was* a connection between Junius and Kew.

It was a frail one, however. As far as Umber could recall,
Wilmot was never a serious contender, his candidature resting on
airy claims made by a niece after his death. What Umber could not
recall was any suggestion of a link between Wilmot and the
Chesterfield-Dayrolles clan. Besides, Wilmot had never been Vicar
of Kew, no matter what marriage ceremonies he may have con-
ducted there. He could not have been the friend of Christabella
Dayrolles referred to in Mary Croft's letter.

Umber left the café and headed towards Kew Green. A map of
1800 reproduced in *The Story of Kew* showed the whole area east of
the Gardens as fields. There were only two small areas of housing:
one centred on the Green, at the northern end of the Gardens, the
other lining the opposite bank of the Thames either side of Kew
Bridge. Logically, Christabella's friend had to have lived in one of
these locations.

It could not have been the Green. Umber sensed rather than deduced this as he prowled across it, scanning the elegant Palladian
frontages of the surrounding houses. In 1791, they would have been
the residences of princes and princesses—George III's aunts,
uncles, brothers and sisters—plus assorted hangers-on. Surely
Christabella's friend could not have dwelt literally amongst them.
To fit Umber's hazy image of him, he needed to be at one remove—
an observer from a safe distance.

Umber crossed Kew Bridge and turned right along Strand-on-the-Green, a riverside path running east round a curve of the Thames past well-kept fishermen's cottages and gentlemen's villas clearly dating from the eighteenth century. This, he reckoned, was more like it. Humbler than Kew Green, but still smart enough, and within easy reach.

But it was only a hunch, of course. He was in no position to back it up. He would have to probe the history of every house if he was to mount a serious search for Christabella's friend. Even then he might fail to find him. It was academic in any case. There was simply not enough—

Umber came to a sudden halt on the path and stared at the building in front of him. It was a small yellow-brick cottage squeezed between two grander residences. The front door was undersized, accessed by a short flight of steps. It looked as if the entrance had been modified as a precaution against flooding, which Strand-on-the-Green was presumably prone to. Above and to one side of the door was a stone-carved likeness of a mythical beast, acting as a lampholder. The creature had the wings and head of an eagle, set on the body of a lion. It was a griffin.

Umber pressed the bell, staring into the stone eye of the griffin as he did so. He had no idea what to expect if and when the door opened. He had no expectations of any kind. He could only let chance and circumstance take their course.

"Good afternoon."

The door had been opened by a tall, lean, weather-beaten man of sixty or so with wavy grey hair and a ruggedly handsome face. The chinos and guernsey he was wearing gave him a maritime air, suggesting his stooped posture had been acquired from long acquaintance with cramped ships' cabins, his squinting gaze from the scanning of many horizons.

"Can I help you?"

"I . . ." Umber did not know what to say, or at any rate how to begin to say it. "I'm looking for . . . a Mr. Griffin."

The man smiled. "Well, you've found him."

CHAPTER

THIRTY-ONE

Umber's use of the indefinite article proved prescient. He had found a Mr. Griffin, not *the* Mr. Griffin. But nonetheless he had found more than he could ever have hoped. The irony was that back in 1981 he would have approached the problem more systematically. He would never have ambled through Kew expecting the answer to leap out at him. And consequently he might never have found his way to the cottage with the griffin lampholder.

He sat in the small bachelor-spruce drawing room and explained himself as best he could. He had got no further than the bizarre truth that he had come in search of someone he had been due to meet twenty-three years previously, when his host, who had introduced himself as Philip Griffin, interrupted.

"Sounds as if you're talking about my brother Henry, Mr. Umber. Before we go any further, I ought to tell you that 1981 was the last year anyone ever saw or heard of him. I was out of the country at the time. I didn't find out Henry had gone missing till I got back here thirteen years later. So, when and where did you have this appointment with him? And what was it about?"

"Avebury. Twenty-seventh of July, 1981."

"Avebury? 1981?" Griffin's brow furrowed. "Haven't I read something recently about a murder at Avebury in 1981?" He snapped his fingers. "That's right. The bloke they got for it was murdered in prison a couple of weeks ago. And somebody connected to the case committed——"

"Suicide. I know. You could say that's what brought me here."

"I don't understand. What's Henry got to do with all this?"

Umber answered the question as fully as he could allow himself
to. He summarized the events of 27 July 1981 accurately enough
and emphasized that his theory about what had happened to Henry
Griffin was just that: a theory. He said nothing about Chantelle,
however. He did not even suggest he subscribed to Sally's belief in
Tamsin's survival. Not that Tamsin—or Sally—much interested
Philip Griffin. His attention was focused on the fate of his long-
missing brother.

"I'm sorry to be the bearer of bad news, Mr. Griffin. I suppose
you must have hoped he was still alive somewhere. And that *is* possible, of course. I—"

"It's OK. I wrote Henry off a long time ago. He and I didn't
really see eye to eye. That was one of the reasons I left Father and
him to it after Mother died and took myself off round the world. I
lost touch with them completely. And I didn't come back for nearly
twenty years. When I did, I found Father going gaga with this
house collapsing around his ears—and no trace of Henry. They'd
fallen out long since, according to the old man, though he was too
far gone to remember why—or so he pretended. Henry had left on
account of their disagreement, whatever it was about, and good rid-
dance was the gist of his ramblings. Not a warm-hearted man, my
father. He's dead and gone himself now. The neighbours said it was
the summer of 'eighty-one when Henry vanished from the radar.
So, it sounds as if your theory fits the facts, doesn't it?"

"Yes. I suppose it does."

"And it also sounds as if Henry died trying to be a good citizen,
which is some consolation. But there's one thing you still haven't
mentioned, Mr. Umber. The *reason* for your appointment with
Henry."

"Ah. Well, I was at Oxford in 1981, studying for a Ph.D. Your
brother phoned me out of the blue, saying he had a book—
technically, a pair of books—relevant to the subject of my thesis
which he was sure would interest me. We agreed to meet at the pub
in Avebury—the Red Lion—that Monday, the twenty-seventh of
July, so that I could take a look at them."

"What books were these?"

"A special edition of the letters of Junius."

"Junius?" Griffin's expression suggested surprise rather than incomprehension. "Well, well, well."

"You've heard of him?"

"Oh yes. Growing up in this house, you could hardly fail to, even if you were a duffer at history. Which I was. Unlike Henry."

"Is there some connection, then, between your family . . . and Junius?"

"You could say so. The Griffin family legend, we'd better call it. Junius . . . and our claim to the throne."

"What?"

"Laughable, isn't it? But Henry believed it. So did Father. And his father before him."

"Your . . . *claim to the throne?*"

Griffin smiled ruefully. "Don't worry. I'm not about to serve a writ on the Queen and demand the keys to Buckingham Palace. But it's entertaining stuff in its way. Want me to fill you in on it?"

"Yes, please."

"Well, before I do, let's get back to these books. How special were they?"

"Very. A uniquely bound copy of the letters printed for Junius's own use."

"I see."

"Which means—"

"No need to spell it out, Mr. Umber. I know what it means and it ties in with something Father said a couple of times, now I think back. He called Henry a thief. But he never said what he was supposed to have stolen. I think I understand now. Father must have kept the books hidden away. And Henry must have found them." Griffin rose to his feet. "Wait here, would you? There's something I want to show you. But it might take me a few minutes to lay my hands on it."

Umber was happy to wait. He needed a few minutes alone to settle in his mind the limits of what he could or should tell Philip Griffin. He had learnt nothing so far that amounted to the proof he needed of Marilyn's complicity in Henry Griffin's murder. And the crackpot details of the Griffins' claim to the throne, however entertaining, were unlikely to supply it.

Close to ten minutes passed, during which the sounds of drawers
being opened and closed in an upper room reached Umber's ears in-
termittently. Then Griffin returned, clutching a stapled sheaf of
papers.

"There was a lot of Henry's stuff left here when Father died. I
chucked most of it out. But I kept this, if only because it's as handy
an account of the family legend as you could ask for. As you'll see,
Henry hoped to get it published. But it wasn't to be." He passed the
papers to Umber. "Take your time. I'll make some tea."

So, almost immediately, Umber was alone again. He looked at
the papers in his hand. The top sheet was a letter to Henry from the
editor of *History Today*, dated 16 April 1980. It was a rejection letter for an article Henry had submitted, entitled *Junius, the Royal
Family and the Griffins of Kew*. The editor described the piece as
"diverting," but crushingly added, *"I am sorry to say that you provide no supporting evidence for any of your extraordinary asser-
tions."* He returned the article therewith. And it was still attached,
typed out by Henry on double spaced, generously margined pages.
The poor chap could not be faulted for presentation, however un-
substantiated the contents. Umber settled down to read it.

My family has lived in Kew for nearly two hundred years.
Strangely, the founder of our family was a man none of us
is related to. This man, Frederick Lewis Griffin, is histori-
cally very important, though history has nothing to say
about him. The time has come to put that right.

Frederick Griffin was born in Covent Garden, London,
on 29 June 1732. He was an illegitimate son of Frederick,
Prince of Wales, by the actress Sarah Webster. His mother
gave him the surname Griffin because the Prince had been
known in his childhood in Hanover as *"Der Grief"*—the
Griffin, a beast he was supposed to resemble.

By the time of the boy's birth, Sarah Webster had already been supplanted as the Prince's mistress, but the
Prince paid her a generous allowance for his son's upbringing. He continued to do so after his marriage to Princess
Augusta of Saxe-Gotha in 1736. When Sarah Webster
died, in 1740, the Prince arranged for his friend the Earl of

Chesterfield to look after the boy, who was given an excellent education.

Frederick Griffin was an undergraduate at Oxford when the Prince died suddenly on 20 March 1751, aged 44. Some said his death was caused by the aftereffects of a blow from a cricket ball. Others said he had caught a fatal chill while working in his beloved gardens at Kew in wet weather. Still others whispered that he had been poisoned by his wife because he had discovered her long-standing affair with his Lord of the Bedchamber, the Earl of Bute.

Princess Augusta immediately cancelled the allowance paid to Frederick Griffin, who was forced to leave Oxford. Lord Chesterfield obtained a position for him in the East India Company and he spent the next ten or twelve years in India. He returned to England at some point in the mid-1760s a moderately wealthy man. He bought a small house at Strand-under-Green (now Strand-on-the-Green) on the north bank of the Thames, opposite Kew, and lived there for the rest of his life.

It has always been believed in my family that he chose to live at Strand-under-Green because of its proximity to the royal residences of Kew Palace and Richmond Lodge. He had heard the rumour that Princess Augusta had murdered his father. He had heard another rumour concerning his half-brother, King George III, who had succeeded to the throne in 1760. This was that George, while still Prince of Wales, had secretly married Hannah Lightfoot, a Quaker, and who had a son by her, known as George Rex. Once on the throne, George had put Hannah aside and contracted a politically more expedient though technically bigamous marriage to Princess Charlotte Sophia of Mecklenburg-Strelitz.

Frederick Griffin was appalled by such conduct and the deleterious effect he believed it to be having on the moral fibre of the nation. Thus he began his letter-writing campaign under the name of Junius, protesting at corruption in the high offices of government. Princess Augusta, the 'odious hypocrite,' as Junius called her, came in for particularly harsh criticism. The King, a 'consummate hypocrite,' fared little better. The letters appeared in the pages of the *Public*

Advertiser for a little over three years. They came to an abrupt end early in 1772, when Princess Augusta's death deprived Junius of his principal target.

Frederick Griffin lived on at Strand-under-Green and at some point befriended the young George Rex. Very little seems to be widely known of the life of George Rex prior to the year 1797, when he was appointed Notary Public to the Governor of Cape Colony in South Africa. This lucrative appointment was subject to two unusual conditions: firstly that he should never return to England; secondly that he should never marry. The intention was obviously to ensure that his legally irrefutable claim to the throne died with him. He abided by these conditions to the extent that he remained in South Africa until his death in 1839 and left no legitimate issue there.

We must now move forward to the famous theft of the parish records from the robing room of St. Anne's Church, Kew, during the night of 22/23 February 1845. This has never been satisfactorily explained, although it has often been alleged that the Royal Family required the removal of the record of a marriage or baptism which they found embarrassing. George III's marriage to Hannah Lightfoot and the birth of George Rex predate the records stolen (marriages after 1783, burials after 1785, baptisms after 1791) by many years and cannot have been the reason.

It has always been believed in my family that the theft was actually organized at the behest of Prince Albert to nullify a potential threat to the legitimacy of Queen Victoria's claim to the throne. The threat was posed by the fact that George Rex married a local woman called Mary Ann Leavers at St. Anne's Church on 30 December 1796. Frederick Griffin was one of the witnesses. The officiating priest was Dr. James Wilmot, who had also officiated at George III's marriage to Hannah Lightfoot more than thirty years previously.

When George Rex's marriage became known to the King, he took steps to have the couple separated and banished his son to South Africa. What George Rex did not know when he took ship for Capetown in the summer of 1797, however, was that his wife was pregnant. A son, John, was born on 3 January 1798. His mother did not survive the birth. Honouring a promise given to her with such an eventuality in mind, Frederick Griffin became the boy's guardian and sought to protect his identity by conferring his own surname upon him.

Frederick Griffin died on 25 August 1815, aged 83. This information was recorded on his gravestone (now removed) in the churchyard of St. Anne's, Kew. The written record of the burial was among those stolen from the church in 1845, along with the record of his ward's baptism and the marriage of his ward's parents.

John Griffin, rightful heir to the throne of England and, following his father's death in 1839, rightful King, led a quiet and private life. He died on 8 October 1870, aged 72.

John Griffin was my great-great-grandfather.

Philip Griffin had brought in the promised tea by the time Umber had finished reading the article. "What do you think of it?" he asked. "As a historian, I mean."

"Like the editor said. There's no evidence."

"Could any of it be true?"

"It could *all* be true. The Hannah Lightfoot–George Rex story is semi-official history these days. But it can't explain the theft of the registers, because George Rex was already dead by then, supposedly without an heir to take his place as a threat to Victoria. Your family legend, on the other hand, accounts for it perfectly. Unfortunately, without supporting evidence that's all it is: a legend."

"Could the special edition Junius have changed that?"

"It depends on the inscription. 'Illuminating and more than somewhat surprising.' That's how your brother described it. I only wish I'd seen it for myself. I only wish I'd met your brother."

"Me too."

"I suppose he was hoping my work on Junius would beef up his case into something the likes of *History Today* would have to take seriously. And maybe it would have. The Chesterfield connection certainly ties in with some leads I was following."

"Father always said something called the Royal Marriages Act meant the Griffins' claim to the throne failed on technical grounds."

"It's a good point. Since the act was passed—in 1772, I think—

members of the Royal Family have needed the monarch's consent before they can marry. Without such consent, their marriage isn't valid. George the Third obviously learned something from his youthful indiscretion. The effect is that either George Rex wasn't a member of the Royal Family, in which case his marriage to Mary Ann Leavers doesn't matter, or he was, in which case it doesn't count."

"Something and nothing, then?"

"I wouldn't say that. It's a humdinger of a story. If I'd been able to dig up some hard evidence, it might have turned my file-and-forget thesis on Junius into a bestselling book. With your brother as co-author."

Griffin smiled. "Henry would have liked that."

"So would I." A thought suddenly struck Umber. "What sort of car did your brother drive, Mr. Griffin?"

"Sorry?"

"Your brother's car. The one he was travelling in to Avebury. What type was it?"

"I don't know. He used to run a . . ." Griffin struggled with his memory for a moment. "Triumph Herald estate. Yes, that's right. Phenomenal lock—it could turn on a sixpence—but a bit of a rust-wagon. Whether it was still on the road in 'eighty-one . . ." He shrugged. "Henry wouldn't have traded it in unless he had to, that's for sure."

"What colour was it?" Umber asked, replaying in his mind's eye the glimpse he had had of the car that had followed the van out of Avebury that day in July 1981, past the small, broken body of Miranda Hall.

"Dark green."

"Of course." Dark green it was. Dark green it had to be.

Dusk was coming on when Umber left Strand-on-the-Green and wandered back towards Kew. He was more or less at the halfway point of the three days he had been given to find Chantelle and hand her over. But his search for her and for ammunition to use against those who wished her ill had so far yielded nothing.

That was not strictly true, of course. He had traced Henry Griffin. He had learned what Griffin had meant to tell him at

Avebury. And he had established Griffin's murder by Tamsin Hall's abductors as a virtual certainty. But none of that made any difference. In a sense, it only made it worse. Twenty-three years ago, David Umber the budding historian had been cheated of an encounter that might have changed his life. Yet his life had changed anyway. It had taken the course leading to the evening of solitude and despair that was opening out before him. It had led inexorably to where he was. And where it would lead next he preferred not to imagine.

But imagine he had to. The strange tale of the Griffins of Kew, which would once have delighted and fascinated him, was no help in his predicament. It left him as powerless to obey as to defy those who required an answer of him by noon on Friday. Yet an answer of some kind he would have to give.

CHAPTER

THIRTY-TWO

Alcohol put Umber to sleep that night. It was more like oblivion than slumber. He woke, dry-throated and gritty-eyed, with the stitches in his head tugging sharply at his scalp. Dawn was edging its grey fingers between the curtains of his room at the Travel Inn and the traffic on Euston Road was only just beginning to thicken. He stared out at it through the tinted glass of the window as he sipped a two-sachet black coffee, wondering not so much what he should do as what, almost independently of his own reasoning, he was going to do.

The answer came to him in the shower, as cold water sluiced over him. Chantelle had said she could not go on alone and there was no reason to disbelieve her. Failing to contact Claire, she would have sought some other way out of the waking nightmare her life had become. It was quite possible she had flown to England on the same plane as her dead brother and the mother who thought she was dead too. Even if she had not, their destination must have drawn her as well. Home. The place where it all began. The unremembered start of her journey. There was nowhere else she was likelier to have gone. And there was nowhere else for Umber to go in search of her.

He had to do his best by others before setting off, however. He tried Claire's mobile again as soon as he was out of the shower. And this time there was an answer.

"Hello." Her voice sounded husky and slightly slurred, as if she had just woken up.

"Claire. It's me. David."

"David. Where are you?"

"London. Sorry if I woke you. I thought you'd already be up. You're an hour on in Monaco, aren't you?"

"You must have been out to Hampstead, if you know where we are."

"I thought you were going to wait until you'd heard from me, Claire."

"For a few days. That's what we agreed. And that's as long as I *could* wait. Alice would have come without me otherwise. And I didn't reckon that was a good idea."

"Have you spoken to Tinaud?"

"Not yet. His PA's blocking us. I haven't pushed it. I've been hoping you'd call and say there was no need. *Is* that what you're going to say?"

"In a sense."

"Care to explain?"

"Can't. I'm in over my head, Claire. I know too much. I don't want to put you in the same position. Don't speak to Tinaud. And don't come back to London until you've heard from me again."

"What?"

"Now would be a good time for that girls' jaunt to South America. It really would. Talk Alice into it. Talk yourself into it."

"What's happening, David?"

"I don't know. But, whatever it is, I *will* know. All too soon."

"You're not making any sense."

"If only that were true. If you never trust me in anything, trust me in this. You'll learn nothing from Tinaud I don't already know. But speaking to him may get you the attention of some very dangerous people. Don't do it. And don't come back here. At least for a few days."

"We're back to a few days, are we? A *few* more days for you to go it alone."

"The last few. I can promise you that."

"You're going to have to—"

"Goodbye, Claire." He put the phone down, certain, because he had withheld his number, that she would not be able to call him back.

He skipped the Travel Inn breakfast, checked out, took a cab to Liverpool Street station and boarded a train for Ilford. The only place he could think of to store his box of Junius Papers was 45 Bengal Road. He planned to leave a note for Larter, then head west.

But his plan had taken no account of the pressure on beds in the National Health Service. Larter had been patched up and sent home, with stitched lip, reinflated lung and slowly healing ribs. He was moving gingerly around the kitchen, preparing a bacon-and-egg start to the day, when Umber let himself in.

"Where have you been hiding yourself?" was the old man's wheezily barbed greeting. "And what's in that bloody box?"

"Some old research papers of mine. I was hoping you could hold on to them for me."

"Till when?"

"Not sure."

"You've got a nerve."

"I boarded up the window for you, Bill." Umber glanced at the back door. "I see you've had it re-glazed."

"Yeah, well, that was a kindness, I suppose. But this box . . ."

"No-one's going to come after it. I promise."

"Better hadn't." Larter hoicked an old cricket bat out from beside the fridge. "I'll be ready for them this time."

"Remember the one you called a smug-looking geezer?"

"What about him?"

"He won't be coming. Here or anywhere else. I can tell you that for a fact."

Larter eyed Umber suspiciously. "Do I want to know how you can be so sure?"

"No, Bill. You don't."

"Spoke to George yesterday. Said he'd had a . . . message from you. 'It isn't over.' Right?"

"Right."

"How long before it is?"

"Not long at all. One way or the other."

"Shall I put in an extra rasher for you?" Larter gestured at the frying pan with his spatula.

"Can't stop."

"Please yourself." Larter nodded at the box. "You can leave that if you've a mind to. It'll be good practice in case I have to go into left luggage to top up my pension."

"I'll be in touch." Umber dropped the spare set of keys Larter had given him on the table. "Thanks, Bill."

"Don't mention it."

"I'll be off now."

"Righto." Then, after the briefest of pauses, he added, "Good luck, son."

Back to Liverpool Street, round the Circle line to Paddington, then a fast train to Reading. Door to door from 45 Bengal Road, Ilford, to the Royal Berkshire Hospital took Umber nearly two hours. Time was sliding through his fingers like sand. If the stitches in his head had not been causing him almost as much discomfort as his troublesome knee, he would probably have given the out-patients' clinic a miss, but, as the whims of the NHS would have it, he did not have to wait long for the stitches to be removed and felt instantly better for it, despite the nurse's less than encouraging assessment.

"How are you feeling, Mr. Umber? You look a little under the weather."

"I'm fine, thanks." Which he was not, of course. But under the weather? No. That description did not do his condition any kind of justice.

By noon he was back at Reading station, waiting for a train to Bedwyn. And one and a half hours later, he was clambering off the connecting bus in Marlborough High Street. He had a plan. He knew what he was going to do. What it would achieve, however, was quite another matter.

His first port of call was W. H. Smith, where he grabbed a copy of the local weekly newspaper. He was still in the queue, waiting to pay for it, when he found what he was looking for among the funeral notices.

> HALL, Jeremy. Died tragically in Jersey, Thursday 25th March, aged 33. Dearest son of Jane and Oliver, fondly remembered by Edmund and Katy. A service of celebration for his life will be held at Holy Cross Church, Ramsbury, on Friday 2nd April at 11 a.m., followed by interment at Marlborough Cemetery at noon. Family flowers only.

Umber reread the notice after he had left the shop. It had to be a coincidence, of course. But it did not feel like one. Jeremy Hall was due to be buried on the day and at the hour when the deadline Umber had been set to hand over Chantelle expired. The burial of the brother and the betrayal of the sister were paired events in a possible version of the all too near future.

He entered the Kennet Valley Wine Company little expecting to find Edmund Questred manning the till. In truth, he was faintly surprised to find the shop open at all. But Questred had found a stand-in—a plump, bespectacled, middle-aged woman with an engaging smile.

"Good afternoon," she said. "Can I help you?"

"I'm looking for Mr. Questred."

"I'm afraid he's not in today. There's been a family bereavement."

"I know." He held up his copy of the *Gazette & Herald*. "A terrible business."

"Yes, indeed."

"I knew Jeremy as a boy. Nice lad. I, er, taught at his school."

"Really?"

"Do you happen to know which undertaker is handling the funeral? The notice didn't say and I, er . . ."

"*Umber.*" The office door beyond the counter opened by a foot or so and Edmund Questred stared out through the gap. "Come in here." He glanced at the woman. "It's OK, Pam. We know each other."

Umber edged round the counter and moved through into the

office. Questred closed the door behind him, then gestured for Umber to follow as he led the way out into the storeroom and switched on the lights. Fluorescent tubes flickered pallidly into life above the assorted boxes of wine.

"What are you doing here?" Questred looked and sounded too tired to summon up much in the way of overt hostility. "And why do you want to know which undertaker we're using?"

The answer was that Chantelle might want to see Jeremy one last time before the funeral. But it was not an answer Umber could afford to give. "I'm not sure. Just trying to draw something out, I suppose."

"Haven't you the decency to drop all this now Jeremy's dead?"

"It's not a question of decency."

"Are you going to tell me you think Jeremy was murdered, like you reckon your wife was?"

"No. I'm not. Though, as I recall, you agreed Sally's death was suspicious last time we spoke."

"I agreed nothing."

"Have it your way."

"Is Sharp with you?"

"No." Questred did not seem to know about Sharp's arrest. Nor did he appear even to suspect that either Sharp *or* Umber had been in Jersey the day Jeremy had died. "I'm on my own."

"At least one of you has realized you ought to back off, I suppose."

"I'm sorry about Jeremy. Truly. How's your wife taking it?"

"How do you think?"

"Hard, I imagine."

"And then some." Questred frowned. "You're not planning to show up at the funeral, are you?"

"Would it be so awful if I did?"

Questred shook his head, as if despairing of Umber's sensitivity altogether. "You have no idea, do you? Jane's lost three children. *Three.* Jeremy's suicide has brought back the grief of Tamsin and Miranda's deaths as well. If it weren't for Katy, I'm not sure Jane would be able to get through this. But I'm sure seeing you won't help. I'm *absolutely* sure of that."

"She won't see me."

"Do I have your word on that?"

Umber looked Questred in the eye. "No. You don't. All I can say is ... she won't see me unless I feel she has to."

"What's that supposed to mean?"

"Why do you think Jeremy killed himself?"

"The best guess is ... Radd's murder sparked something off in his mind. Seeing his sisters killed in front of him ..." Questred shrugged. "Maybe he never really got over it."

"He only saw one of his sisters killed, actually."

Questred squinted at Umber in genuine bafflement. *"What?"*

"Do Jeremy's friends in Jersey say he was depressed?"

"No. Well, not exactly. He'd been keeping himself to himself a lot lately, apparently. He hadn't been seen around. Maybe that was the start of it. Even before Radd."

"Maybe it was."

"You didn't speak to him, did you? You or Sharp, I mean. If Jane thought ..."

"Would it make it easier having us to blame?"

"It might."

"Then, tell her whatever you think it's best she believes."

"Don't make tomorrow any more difficult than it has to be, Umber. Please don't do that to her."

"I won't."

"Is that a promise?"

"Yes." It was one promise Umber was sure he could keep, if only because the events of tomorrow were so comprehensively beyond his control. "It is."

C H A P T E R

THIRTY-THREE

Umber left Questred to puzzle over his intentions and headed along the High Street to the Ivy House Hotel, where he booked himself in for the night. Before going to his room, he borrowed the local Yellow Pages from behind the desk and hunted down the addresses and telephone numbers of Marlborough undertakers.

There were only two, so it seemed easier to walk round than phone ahead. As it happened, the first one he tried, a short walk away at the eastern end of town, was the firm handling the Jeremy Hall funeral.

He had harboured no wish to view the deceased, but felt bound to ask if he could do so, if only to camouflage his curiosity about who else had been to the chapel of rest for the same reason. The receptionist had been well schooled in the arts of discretion, however. She was giving nothing away, other than a coolly framed confirmation that he was the first person from outside the family to make such a request—which happened to be exactly what he wanted to know. So much for his hunch that Chantelle would not be able to stay away. Unless, of course, she had claimed to be a relative. A cousin, perhaps. Something like that. Anything, in fact, but what she really was.

He had seen Sally only a few hours before her funeral, at a chapel of
rest in Hampstead. He had wished later that he had not seen her, so
hard did it prove to rid his mind of the memory of her white,
drained, lifeless face. This time he knew better than to linger by the
coffin. He prowled the room for a few minutes, just long enough to
suggest he was a sincere mourner, which in one sense he was. He
did no more than glance at Jeremy Hall. The young man's face was
unmarked. Either that or the marks his fatal fall had left on it had
been expertly masked. You could imagine he was at peace, if that
was the way your imagination worked. It was not the way Umber's
worked, however. He hurried out.

The cemetery was his next destination. Chantelle's sister was
buried there, after all. And men were at work digging the grave, not
far from Miranda Hall's, where Jeremy Hall would be laid to rest
tomorrow. There was a good chance Chantelle would go there.

But there was no sign of her. She could have been and gone, of
course. She might be planning to visit later, when the gravediggers
had finished their work. Or she might be determined to stay away.
She might be miles away—thousands of miles, even. In a part of
his mind, Umber hoped she was. But in another part, the part
where hope held no sway, he knew she was not.

He walked out along the Ridgeway, then on across the downs towards Avebury. The afternoon began to fade into evening. The light
was pearly grey, the air cool but barely moving. He could hear skylarks singing above him, but he could not see them. Once he saw a
larger bird that might have been a kestrel, hovering away to the
north. But he could not be sure. He pressed on through the broad,
rolling landscape.

He had acknowledged the probable futility of his journey long before he reached Avebury. The simple truth was that even if he was
right about the places Chantelle would feel drawn to, he had no way
of calculating when or even if she would actually visit them. If he
found her by this method, it would be pure luck.

But he had no other method to apply. Passing Manor Farm and cresting the last hillock before the henge came into view, he half-expected he *would* see her, walking slowly along one of the banks, head bowed, lost in thought, her slim, dark-clad figure silhouetted against the wide, pale sky.

But she was not there. Umber walked most of the way round the north-eastern bank, from which he had a clear view of the Cove. No-one was loitering by the Adam and Eve stones. Visitors to Avebury were few at this hour of the day. Umber could see nobody even remotely resembling Chantelle.

He doubled back and completed a slow half-circuit of the henge, passing one dog-walker and a pair of hikers on the way. He finished up in the High Street of the village with nothing to show for his efforts but a renewed ache in his injured knee. It was growing cold now. The place was different, utterly different, from how it had been that blazing day of high summer twenty-three years ago. But still it was the *same* place. The ghosts remained, whether they showed themselves or not.

Umber headed along the High Street towards the Red Lion. Chantelle might be waiting till dusk to put in an appearance, he told himself, till it was safe to follow in her own forgotten footsteps. He would wait at the pub, as he had waited before.

But someone had got there before him. As Umber rounded the front gable of the pub, he saw a figure seated at one of the tables set in the angle of the L-shaped building, a figure muffled up against the encroaching chill, anorak collar turned up, Tilley hat brim turned down.

"Good evening, David," said Percy Nevinson. "Thank goodness you've arrived. It's getting decidedly nippy out here."

"Percy." That was all Umber could find to say. There had been a risk of bumping into Nevinson. He had realized that. But the pub was not the man's natural territory. And it was clear that this encounter, unlike their last, was not a product of chance.

"Shall we go inside? Perhaps I could buy you a drink?"

"All right." Umber struggled to recover himself. If Chantelle did turn up, the last person he wanted for company was Nevinson. Getting rid of the man would be next to impossible, however. Maybe it was safer for them to be inside the Red Lion than out. "Let's do that."

The bar was quiet. Nevinson bought Umber a pint and another half for himself. They sat at a table by the window, Umber taking the chair facing it, so that he had a view of the road and the stones of the henge's southern inner circle. Nevinson took off his hat and ruffled his hair, smiling at Umber with irritating mildness.

"You came to no harm in Jersey, then," he said after a sip of beer.

"As you see."

"When Abigail came back from shopping in Marlborough this afternoon, she told me she'd spotted you from the bus. I felt sure you'd come out here sooner or later if I waited long enough."

"And you were right."

"Gratifyingly so. Our last meeting was . . . rudely interrupted. It's good to have this opportunity to take up where we left off."

"Look, Percy, I—"

"It's no good claiming to be in all kinds of a hurry this time, David. The last bus to Marlborough left at six fifteen. Even if you phoned for a taxi now, we'd have least twenty minutes to chat."

"All right. Let's chat." Umber smiled grimly and flung himself into an attempt to lead the discussion, since discussion there clearly had to be. "Talking of Abigail, did you tell her why you went to Jersey? Or are you sticking to the ufological-conference line?"

Nevinson pursed his lips. "A white lie to spare my sister's feelings, nothing more. Naturally, I've . . . come clean since returning home."

"*Completely* clean, Percy?"

"Well, I . . ."

"Did you mention hiring Wisby?"

Nevinson grimaced. "That would only have confused her."

"Why *did* you hire him?"

"I didn't. Not really. I asked him . . . to share his findings with me, that's all. Which he never did, beyond what he judged sufficient to extract an exorbitant fee from me."

"Slippery character, Wisby."

"Indeed."

"What about standing idly by while I was grabbed off the street by a couple of heavies in St. Helier? Did you mention *that* to Abigail?"

"There again . . ."

"You didn't want to confuse her."

Nevinson grinned nervously. "Exactly."

"As a law-abiding citizen, shouldn't you have phoned the police? You'd witnessed a kidnapping, after all."

"Is that what it was, David? To be honest, I considered the possibility that it was—how shall I put it?—staged."

"Staged?"

"For my benefit, I mean."

"*Your* benefit?"

"Besides, in a sense, I *did* consult the police. *A* policeman, that is." Nevinson's grin broadened. "Well, a *retired* policeman."

"What are you talking about?"

"I'm referring to Mr. Sharp."

"You visited George?"

"There was no need to visit him. I spoke to him at the magistrates' court after his hearing. Well, *near* the magistrates' court, to be strictly accurate."

"Near?"

"Yes. There's a pleasant little park just round the—"

"Never mind the bloody park. How come you've been strolling around St. Helier with George? He's in custody."

"Not since Tuesday. He was granted bail, you see."

"What?"

"Bail. In consideration of his status as a retired police officer, apparently. A thousand pounds and the surrender of his passport. The conditions seemed very—"

"George is out?"

"Yes. That's what it amounts to. Out. Pending trial." Nevinson's grin acquired a sickly thinness. "I'm rather surprised you didn't know."

Nevinson's surprise was nothing compared with Umber's. Larter had not breathed a word about this. Yet he must have been aware of it. He had actually mentioned speaking to Sharp only yesterday. For some reason, the two men had decided to keep Umber in the dark. "Are you sure about this, Percy?"

"How could I not be? I was there when the magistrates said their piece. And I certainly didn't imagine our conversation in the park. We were standing by the statue of General Don. According to my Jersey guidebook, he was responsible for——"

"Forget General Don. What did George say?"

"Well, he was surprised to see me, naturally. But he rapidly deduced that news of Jeremy Hall's death had brought me to the island. He was very interested by what I had to tell him about you. And about Wisby, of course. It was at his request that I took the matter of your apparent kidnapping no further. He said he'd deal with it."

"Deal with it?"

"I confess I'm not entirely clear what he meant by that."

Neither was Umber. What in God's name was Sharp up to? How had he wangled bail, which Burnouf had said was next to impossible? And where had he been since? Where—and why?

"Wisby was up before the magistrates himself on Tuesday," Nevinson went on. "Caught trying to leave Jersey in possession of stolen money, apparently. No bail for him, of course. I think Mr. Sharp meant to visit him before leaving Jersey himself."

"He said he was going to visit Wisby?"

"Not in so many words."

"And what about leaving Jersey?"

"I took it as read. Why would he stay when the next stage in the Hall family drama is about to unfold here in Wiltshire? Lack of a passport is no bar to travelling from Jersey to England, after all. Just as I'm surprised you hadn't heard about his release, however, I must confess to even greater surprise that he hasn't been in touch with you since, given your previous . . . collaboration. You look, if I may say so, more than a little dismayed yourself."

"How very perceptive of you, Percy."

"Why would he be avoiding you, I wonder?"

"I'm wondering the same myself."

"Could it be that Wisby has told him something that causes him to doubt your loyalty? If so, he may suspect you weren't really kidnapped at all. Or that you were but subsequently struck some kind of deal to secure your release."

"Suggest that to him, did you?"

"By no means. But the possibilities could have occurred to him. As I'm forced to admit they did to me."

"Well, you can take it from me it wasn't a put-up job. And I've done no deals."

"I'm happy to take your word on both scores, David. Despite all the evidence to the contrary."

Umber would have felt angrier with Nevinson if he had not been so bewildered by the turn of events. "What evidence?"

"Your current state of unfettered liberty, of course. Which I note you've conspicuously failed to explain."

"Now just a—"

"None of my business, I'm sure. We must all shift for ourselves in this world. It was only a matter of time, after all."

"What was?"

"Your removal from the chessboard." Nevinson leaned forward, fixing Umber with a stare and lowering his voice to a conspiratorial whisper. "The powers that be have decreed there can be no queening of pawns in this game."

The only way to shake off Nevinson, it became clear, was to return to Marlborough. And Nevinson had been uncannily accurate about the likely delay until a taxi arrived. Before he could make an exit, Umber had to endure a further twenty minutes of the man's infuriatingly smug assumption that he had in some way sold out.

Umber stopped listening once Nevinson had veered off onto his favourite topic: the role of the intelligence community in stifling research into the Martian origins of the stone circles and avenues scattered around Avebury. Umber's mind filled instead with doubts and questions concerning Sharp's activities since Tuesday.

He began to suspect that Nevinson was right. Sharp had concluded he could no longer be trusted. That was why he had sworn Larter to secrecy about his release. Umber's unannounced visit to Ilford, none the worse for his supposed kidnapping, must have seemed like confirmation of his treachery.

He had lied to Nevinson in one crucial regard. He *had* done a deal, albeit one he did not intend to fulfil even if he got the chance. There *were* good reasons to believe he might have gone over to the opposition—whoever the opposition might be. The fact that he had not was no help. He could not prove his good faith. He could only demonstrate it. As long as Chantelle continued to elude him, there was no way he could do that. And maybe, even if he found her, there would still be no way.

"Will you be attending the funeral tomorrow?" was Nevinson's parting question as he accompanied Umber out of the pub to the waiting taxi when it eventually arrived. "Mr. Sharp may be intending to, don't you think?"

Umber offered no reply as he nodded to the taxi driver and opened the door.

"For that reason alone, you may prefer not to, of course," Nevinson continued, catching Umber's eye. "I suppose it boils down to a question of who can be warned off—and who can't."

"Goodbye, Percy."

Umber did not glance back at the pub as the taxi joined the main road and headed south. Instead, he looked over his shoulder at the dwindling shapes of the Adam and Eve stones, at the empty quadrant of the henge where he had first set eyes on Sally and the Hall children.

The view was a fleeting one, rapidly blanked off by the houses at the eastern end of the village. The face the past had briefly shown him turned away, leaving him with no choice but to turn away likewise.

During the drive back to Marlborough, a suspicion somehow more disturbing even than the possibility that Sharp had written him off as a traitor formed in Umber's mind. Maybe Sharp was the one who had done the deal. Maybe his release on bail had been a *quid pro quo*. If so, Umber was more isolated than ever and the danger to Chantelle was all the greater.

Umber could do nothing about that. Tomorrow would tell. And he greatly feared it would tell against him.

THIRTY-FOUR

The taxi dropped Umber outside the Ivy House, but he did not go in. Instead, he walked along the High Street to the Green Dragon and took the edge off his anxiety with a couple of pints and double whisky chasers.

The drinks, numbing though they were, only nourished his suspicions of Sharp. His silence since Tuesday, it seemed ever clearer to Umber, was the real giveaway. A week in prison could have sucked all the pride and determination out of a man of his age and former occupation, leaving him all too susceptible to whatever deal had been offered him. Release on bail might have been the down payment, a dropping of the charge held out as the ultimate reward, in return for . . . what? Had Sharp been set the same task as Umber? Could that be it? Were they each insurance against the failure or defiance of the other?

It was gone ten o'clock when Umber made his woozy way back to the Ivy House. He had no plan now beyond a few hours' sleep. He did not expect it to help. He did not expect anything at all. He was no longer thinking about tomorrow. He could not bear to.

"Message for you," said the receptionist, handing him a note along with his key. "Could you phone this number? Urgent, apparently."

Umber stared at the piece of paper in his hand. A mobile

number was written on it. And that was all. "There's no name," he blearily objected.

"He didn't leave one. Declined to, actually. I did ask."

"When did he phone?"

"Around eight o'clock. Then again about half an hour ago."

"Old? Young?"

"Not young. Polite. Well-spoken. But . . ."

"What?"

"Edgy. You know? Definitely edgy."

Umber dialled the number on the phone in his room. It was answered before the second ring.

"That you, Umber?"

It was not the voice Umber had expected to hear. Despite the receptionist describing the caller as well-spoken, which was hardly a perfect fit, he had convinced himself during the short walk along the hotel corridors that the message was from Sharp; that the old man had seen sense and decided they should rejoin forces. But the message was not from Sharp.

"Know who this is?"

"Of course."

"We need to meet. Tonight."

"Why?"

"Want the truth? The whole truth? And a way out of it?"

"Yes."

"Then don't argue. I'll pick you up at midnight. Wait in front of the Town Hall."

"How did——"

"Will you be there?"

"Yes. All right. But——"

"See you then." The line went dead.

Umber put the phone down, hoisted his feet up onto the bed and lay back against the pillows. He stared up into the shadows angled across the ceiling, his mind struggling with the implications of what had just happened. Oliver Hall wanted to see him. Oliver Hall was willing to tell him the truth. Oliver Hall was offering him an escape route. It was too good to be true. It was too alluring to be anything but a trap. And maybe it was a trap deadlier than any of those he had so far blundered into. But he had agreed to go. And he would. He could not ignore the summons. He could not resist the bait. He could not avoid the trap.

Umber got to the Town Hall several minutes early. Marlborough was quiet, the High Street largely empty. It had occurred to him by now that leaving an anonymous message at the Ivy House and nominating a pick-up point a little way from the hotel showed just how determined Hall was to avoid leaving any evidence that they had conversed, let alone met. Such precautions did not augur well. But there was of course no reason why they should. Umber waited, sitting on the steps that led up to the Town Hall entrance, staring along the curve of the High Street.

He had no way of knowing Hall would approach from that direction, of course. In the event, shortly after St. Mary's Church clock struck twelve, a gleaming blue-black Bentley purred round the sharp-angled bend to Umber's left and pulled in.

Oliver Hall nodded at him through the driver's window, then jerked his head towards the passenger's door. Umber stood up, walked round and climbed in.

"You came, then." Hall was dressed in a Barbour, open-necked shirt and dark trousers. His face was sallow in the filtered amber lamplight, his eyes hooded and weary, his brow furrowed, his mouth set in a grim, charcoal-shadowed line.

"I said I would."

"You *said* you'd wait to hear from me before visiting Jeremy. You didn't, though, did you?"

"Sharp's arrest forced my hand."

"Did it really?"

"Yes. It really did."

"Were you surprised to hear from me this evening?"

"What do you think?"

"It doesn't matter. You're here. That's what counts. Let's go." Hall started away.

"Where are we going?"

"Not far. Not far at all." He swung the car round into Kingsbury

Street and headed up the hill Umber had climbed earlier on his way to the cemetery.

"How did you know where to find me?"

"Edmund told me you were in Marlborough. It was a fair bet you'd stay at the Ivy House again."

"Where are *you* staying?"

"Worried about how close Marilyn is, are you, Umber?"

"Should I be?"

"No. She's still in London. I'm here on my own. On my own initiative, you might say." Hall followed the road round to the right at the top of the hill. The cemetery, then, was not their destination. "High time, you might also say. And you'd be entitled to. Don't think I'm not aware of that." He took another right onto the main road.

"Where *are* we going?"

"Savernake Forest. Where my ex-wife has convinced herself Radd buried Tamsin. Where she often goes to mourn her, I believe."

"Why there?"

"No possibility of interruption, Umber. No prying eyes or ears. That's why. That and something else we'll come to later."

"You promised me the truth."

"So I did."

"When am I going to get it?"

"Soon enough. There are a few questions I want to ask you first."

"Such as?"

"Why did you choose to study the letters of Junius?"

"*What?*"

"I mean, was there any particular reason?"

"Why in God's name should you care?"

"Humour me on the point." Hall took the Salisbury road at the double-roundabout just beyond the bridge over the Kennet and headed towards the forest that was waiting ahead of them, still and silent in the moonless night. "There's a good fellow."

"I specialized in eighteenth-century British politics. Junius was an ideal case study."

"No other reason? Nothing more . . . personal?"

"I'd always been curious about him. There was an old copy of the letters in the bookcase at home. Something of an heirloom in my father's family."

"Was it, now?"

"But I can't believe you're dragging me out here to discuss Junius."

"He does have a bearing on what we need to discuss, Umber, take it from me. But that can wait."

The road curved as it climbed Postern Hill. At the top, Umber knew, Savernake began. The old Norman hunting forest had once stretched for many miles to east and west. What remained was a remnant, but a large remnant nonetheless. Several square miles of heavily wooded land in which bodies could plausibly be buried—and secrets likewise.

"Jane believes our three children are all dead now, Umber. Do you believe that?"

"Do *you*?"

They drove in silence, the unanswered cross-questions contending in the darkness between them. The car's headlamps arced across the screen of trees ahead of them as they crested the rise. Then Hall said, with quiet emphasis, "Of course not."

Umber was at first too dumbstruck to respond. Hall was as good as admitting that Tamsin was alive and that he had never once thought otherwise in all the twenty-three years since her supposed death. "You mean . . ."

"Tamsin is Cherie . . . is Chantelle. That's what I mean. You know it. And I've always known it."

"You've *known*? All along?"

"Oh yes."

"But—"

"Sometimes I've envied Jane her certainty. The simplicity of her grief. The finality of it. Tamsin dead rather than taken. Buried rather than hidden." Hall sighed. "But only sometimes."

"I don't understand. How—"

"Wait." Hall braked sharply and pulled in off the road. The cones of light from the headlamps tunnelled ahead of them along a track leading into the woods. Hall drove slowly, tyres crunching over the rough surface, suspension wallowing through the potholes. "Let's get clear of the road," he said.

Fifty yards or so sufficed. At that point Hall steered into the side of the track and stopped. He turned off the engine and, a second later, the lights. Darkness closed around them like a hood. Then Umber saw the glow of the dashboard lighter. Hall had taken a cigar out of his pocket. He lit it, replaced the lighter, then lowered the window. The damp night air drifted in, thinning the pungent smoke.

"What now?" Umber asked.

"I talk." Hall drew on the cigar. "And you listen."

C H A P T E R

THIRTY-FIVE

I've always done my best for my children, Umber. You may find
that assertion ironic in the light of what you know. And you
may find it even more ironic in the light of what you're about
to learn. But it's true. I've done everything in my power to protect
them. Everything.

"I'm going to tell you a story. In every important sense, it's the
story of my life. It begins—and I suppose it ends—with money.
The making of it. The multiplying of it. And the spending of it. I
don't do much of the last. No need, really, with Marilyn on hand.
And the first isn't strictly my line. But the second? I'm a past master
at that. One of the best. One of the very best. The keeping, the con-
cealing and the breeding of wealth. That's my speciality. My voca-
tion, if you like.

"You could call it a gift, this skill of mine. Many have. I have. I
don't any more, though. I understand all too clearly now how big a
curse it can be. Not because of the money itself, but because of the
sort of people it's brought me into contact with. My particular kind
of talent attracted a particular kind of client. The kind I should
never have trusted. Because they never trusted me. It's lack of trust
that does for you in the end, every time.

"My career in banking was entirely aboveboard until I met . . .
let's call him Smith. I suspect you may have met him recently yourself, in Jersey. You may also have seen his oversized yacht moored in
St. Helier Harbour. At the outset of our relationship, I believed Smith
was a *bona fide* businessman. Likewise the friends he recommended

me to. Later, I realized they were all criminals. I could have stopped acting for them at that point. I *should* have. But I didn't. The commission they paid was generous. And there was a thrill, I don't deny, to working for them. Plus a good many fringe benefits. They were difficult people to say no to. Though, to be honest, I never put that seriously to the test. They weren't the sort of criminals you ever read about, of course—the sort who get caught. They were the big fish.

"I referred to Smith's network as the consortium, though needless to say they never called themselves anything of the kind. They thrived on caution and anonymity. They were powerful, with interests and associates around the world. But they were also invisible. And they wanted to stay that way. They had money to invest. Lots of it. More than they could handle. Which is where I came in. I made their money work for them—discreetly.

"I also laundered it, of course. The profits they made through me left no trail that could be followed to their doors. That was easier to do then than it is now. But I don't have to involve myself much in that kind of activity any more. After a certain point, which we passed long ago, the process becomes self-replicating. The system takes over. And it's a good system. Foolproof. I should know. I designed it.

"Let's be under no illusions. The crimes these people made their lavish livings out of were as vile as you can imagine. They wore smart suits. They spoke softly. But that was merely the side of them they chose to show me. The other side . . . I didn't want to see.

"I persuaded myself I deserved the considerable rewards that working for the consortium brought me. I acquired responsibility for managing the greater part of their finances. I set up my own business and became wealthy in my own right. I maintained a notional presence in conventional banking, but it was only cover for my activities on behalf of the consortium. I was *their* banker, exclusively, piloting the proceeds of their crime through legitimate and lucrative investments around the world via respectable institutions and untraceable accounts. It was a great time. I loved my work.

"I don't any more. I haven't for many years. I still act for them, of course. I don't actually have any choice in the matter. It's not the sort of job you can resign from. But I would if could. Like a shot.

"What it boils down to is this. They decided they couldn't continue to rely on my discretion. I knew too many of their secrets.

I was their one potential weakness—an unacceptable risk, but also indispensable. They needed a way to bind me to them, to guarantee my loyalty absolutely. And they found such a way: the theft of my youngest child. That was their plan. Brutal, simple, effective. Such is the nature of men like Smith.

"Their calculation was that to ensure the safety of my other two children and in return for evidence of Tamsin's continued wellbeing, I would serve them unquestioningly. And so I did. Ironically, Miranda's death, which formed no part of their plan, rendered it even more effective. I only had Jeremy left then to fear for. And my fear was all the greater as a result.

"Carrying that secret dread around with me destroyed my marriage. But what could I do? Tamsin's life would have been forfeit—as well as Jeremy's—if I'd told anyone the truth. I had no choice but to do their bidding. Tamsin was lost to me. But she wasn't dead. She could lead a happy and fulfilled life under another name provided I never tried to find her and let the world believe what Jane believed: that *both* our daughters were dead.

"The flaw in any plan, of course, is the unpredictability of events. Griffin saw what happened and followed the van. He had to be disposed of. And he was. But then someone else had to be found to account for the car you saw driving past the pub. And Miranda's death raised the stakes. The planned abduction became a callous murder. Worse, it was an unsolved murder, which meant it didn't fade from the public mind. So then I was required to hire Wisby to give the impression I was doing everything in my power to crack the case. And eventually it was decided someone had to be found to admit he'd killed both girls. Step forward Brian Radd. As a sex offender, he needed the kind of protection in prison only someone like Smith could arrange for him. In return for that, he was willing to confess to anything. And he got his protection, didn't he? Until the day he died.

"Then there was Tamsin herself—Cherie, Chantelle—growing to rebellious adulthood. And Sally, driven by her certainty that Radd's confession was false, looking, always looking, for the girl she believed was still alive. And then finding her, by chance, in the pages of a magazine.

"So they killed Sally, dressing it up to look like suicide. The man you know as Walsh was good at that kind of thing. He wasn't so good at hide-and-seek, though. Cherie gave him the slip, became Chantelle and, eventually, last year, contacted Jeremy.

"Well, you know about that. So do I now. Flushing out Marilyn. Sending the letters. Stirring up all the secrets. And what you don't know you can guess. Someone must have tipped the consortium off about Sharp's intention to question Radd. Taking him out was an overdue precaution on their part. But they had to tread carefully. They probably considered killing you, Sharp *and* Wisby. But that would have risked splitting the official version of events wide open. So, they played it softly. Softly by their standards, anyway.

"It didn't work, did it? In the end, there were too many hatches to batten down. Jeremy's death has made them doubt my reliability. I just don't have enough to lose any more. But I'm untouchable. I've wrapped up their investments so tightly they know they can't un-ravel them without me. If I went without putting matters in order, most of their money would go with me. They had me where they wanted me. Now they're not so sure. I was a problem solved. Now I'm a problem all over again.

"I'm glad to be paying them back in some small measure for the hell they've forced me to live through these past twenty-three years. I didn't deserve to be treated as they've treated me. Recently, I've discovered that it was even worse than I thought. I never doubted Marilyn was a gold-digger. I was happy to overlook that for the fun she brought back into my life. But now I realize she was one of them all along, steered into my path after Jane and I split up to give them early warning of any backsliding on my part.

"How can I be sure of that, Umber? Her possession of the Junius letters proves it. That's how. She was there when they grabbed Griffin. They'd have wanted a woman on hand to look af-ter Tamsin. That must have been Marilyn's role. She took the books from Griffin's car and hid them. Why? As ammunition to use against the consortium if the need ever arose. That would be my guess. When Jeremy started pressurizing her, she panicked and tried to get rid of them. But she kept the fly-leaves. That was a big mistake. She should have destroyed them. She really should.

"I found them, you see. I don't think she realizes yet they're not where she hid them, but she soon will. I spoke to Tamsin on the telephone earlier today. Chantelle, I should say. But she'll always be Tamsin to me. She sounded desperate. Well, she must have been, mustn't she, to phone me of all people? We agreed to meet tomorrow morning. She told me the truth about the letters. And I agreed to tell her the truth about her life.

"I've had Sharp on to me as well. He hasn't worked everything out yet, but he's getting close. Enforced idleness in La Moye has given him time to think a lot through. He believes he might be in a position to squeeze the truth out of me, or at least some of it. He might be right. I fixed his release on bail, just to show Smith and his friends they couldn't always have things their own way. I didn't tell Sharp that, of course. Nor did I disabuse him of the notion he seems to have got into his head that you've been nobbled.

"I'm supposed to be meeting Sharp tomorrow as well as Tamsin. It promises to be a busy day. The burial of a son. The resurrection of a daughter. And then . . . the sky falls in.

"That's what it would mean, Umber. Be in no doubt. If Tamsin returns to life, twenty-three years' worth of lies collapses around her and the truth emerges. Then Smith would need a firebreak between the consortium and me. To create it, he'd have to kill me. And Tamsin too.

"Plus you, of course. I mention that in case you need an incentive to do what I'm going to ask you to do. It truly is a matter of life and death.

"I have the fly-leaves with me. Match them to the books Tamsin has and you've got evidence linking Marilyn with Griffin's murder. If anyone's been buried in this forest for twenty-three years, it's him. I want you to meet Tamsin tomorrow morning and tell her what's happened. I want you to persuade her to turn her back on all this. I want you to take her away. I have a letter for you to deliver to a man called Ives. He has an office in Zürich. Ives has access to funds held on my behalf and can arrange new identities for both of you. With his help, you can disappear. Go wherever you want, as long as it's far from here. It's an escape route I devised for my own use a long time ago. But now I realize escape is simply not possible for me. The consortium would come after me. They'd never stop looking, because they couldn't afford to. In the end, they'd hunt me down.

"Different considerations apply to you and Tamsin. They'll decide, however reluctantly, to let you go, because in the wake of all this they'll need to lie low. They'll have their money, after all. I've seen to that. Smith must already be worried that they've shown their hand once too often. Sharp's continued probing will force him to be careful. And the suspicion that I've passed the missing fly-leaves on to you will prompt Marilyn to urge caution. You'll be in the clear. My guess is that they'll arrange for the case against Sharp to be dropped. Maybe the case against Wisby as well, though that will be more difficult to pull off. They'll want everything dropped.

"This is the deal, Umber. Tamsin says she'll be at Pewsey railway station when the seven twenty-four for London leaves tomorrow morning. Does she mean she'll be on the train when it pulls in or waiting on the platform? I'm not sure. There'll be quite a few commuters at the station. Maybe she wants witnesses to our reunion. Maybe she doesn't trust me. I could hardly blame her if she didn't. I used to catch the first train up to London from Pewsey every weekday, you know. When we were one big happy uncomplicated family, in those halcyon days I can hardly remember now, before the twenty-seventh of July, 1981. She's hardly likely to know that, of course. But I think of it a lot.

"I've booked the pair of you on a noon flight from Heathrow to Zürich. Be sure you're on it. And be sure Tamsin understands why you have to be. If I met her tomorrow, I wouldn't have the strength of mind to go through with this. That's why I mustn't meet her. Because this is her only hope. And she's the only child I have left.

"Take this envelope. The tickets to Zürich are inside. It also contains the letter to Ives and the Junius fly-leaves. You'll find the inscriptions on them very interesting. It's small wonder Griffin wanted to show them to you. I imagine you might have made quite a splash in the historical world with such information twenty-three years ago. Not now, though. It'll have to be your secret.

"This is the only way out, Umber. The only certain way. I have a gun under my seat. When you've gone, I'll put it to my head and pull the trigger. Suicide, the night before my son's funeral, in the forest where Radd's thought to have buried Tamsin's body. I've got a note in my pocket to leave on the dashboard. It'll make the coroner's job very easy, very straightforward. 'Took his own life while the balance of his mind,' et cetera, et cetera. You follow? Smith and his friends won't have to worry about me any more. And that means they won't have to worry about Tamsin. Or you. Provided you're never heard of again.

"I'm giving you a fresh start. Tamsin too. For her sake, naturally, not yours. But take advantage of it, there's a good fellow. I don't know what she's planning tomorrow. A graveside confrontation with her mother, perhaps? It mustn't happen. Talk her out of it. Talk her onto that plane. She trusts you. She'll go with you when you tell her why she has to.

"What does the future hold? For me, nothing. For you and Tamsin, who knows? She's young enough to be your daughter. And she is a kind of orphan. Take her in out of the storm, Umber. Do that for me. And for yourself. End this. Tomorrow.

"It's time you left. I've said enough. There's no need for you to say anything. Just take the envelope and go. It's the only assent I need from you. Wait along the track until you hear the shot. You won't have to wait long. I can promise you that."

C H A P T E R

THIRTY-SIX

There was a score or more of London-bound passengers waiting on the up platform at Pewsey railway station next
morning as the minutes ticked round till the arrival of the
7:24 to Paddington. It was on time, according to the information
screen. Some people were already glancing down the track for a
sight of it approaching. But as yet there was nothing to see beyond
the illusory convergence of the silvery-grey lines of rail in the
misty distance.

The person best placed to see the train first was standing on the
footbridge. He had been there longer than any of the passengers,
but showed no inclination to join them on the platform. The holdall
resting by his feet and his casual, weather-worn clothes marked
him out from the smarter-dressed commuters who had left their
four-wheel-drives and company saloons in the station car park and
were dividing their attention between chunky wristwatches and
broadsheet newspapers as the arrival of the 7:24 drew near.
Paddington was an hour away from them, the City an hour and a
half. These aimless minutes of waiting at Pewsey were a featureless
fragment of a hectic day. They meant nothing. They were forgotten
even as they passed.

They weighed slow and heavy in the mind of David Umber, however. He was here, as Oliver Hall had told him to be. He was here,
short of sleep and ragged of nerve. His thoughts were clear, but

taut, stretched thin by doubt and anxiety. He had resolved to do what Hall had beseeched him to do. But if Chantelle did not step off the London train, his resolution would count for nothing.

There had been no sign of her at the station when he had arrived by taxi from Marlborough three quarters of an hour before. He had not seriously expected there to be. The train was always the smarter bet. He wondered where she had been staying. Taunton, maybe? Exeter?

It occurred to him then that Taunton and Exeter were places he knew reasonably well. But they were places he could never return to. The escape route Hall had mapped out for him was a flight into semi-permanent exile. It was a fresh start with a heavy price. A long time would have to pass before he could risk contacting his parents. His friends, in Prague and elsewhere, would be lost to him. David Umber was standing at the edge of his world.

But he was still alive. And he would go on living, whatever name he used. Not so Oliver Hall. The sound of the gunshot that had ended his life—the exact, muffled note of it—still echoed in Umber's memory. The sound—and the long, vast silence of the forest that had engulfed it.

He tensed. There was the train, materializing in the distance as a dark, growing shape. He picked up his bag and headed for the steps leading down to the platform.

By the time he reached it, most of the waiting passengers had spotted the train themselves and were edging forwards, some hurrying towards the far end of the platform where the first-class carriages would be found, others bunching in the central stretch, near the gate in from the road. Umber threaded his way into the latter group and stood amongst them. The rumble of the approaching train grew.

Then the carriages were rolling past, slowing as they went. Umber shrank back, scanning the windows for a glimpse of Chantelle. But he could not see her. He heard himself muttering a prayer. "Please, God, let her be aboard."

The train came to a halt. The doors opened. The waiting passengers hurried forward. Looking towards the front of the train, Umber saw no-one get off except the guard. He turned to look the other way.

And there she was. Chantelle. He knew it was her at once by her dark, baggy clothes and pale, expectant face. He stepped out of her line of sight, into the gateway next to the station building, resisting the urge to run towards her for fear she would take fright and jump back onto the train. He could see her gazing nervously past him along the platform, her grip on the rucksack hoisted on her shoulder visibly tightening. She was braced for a first sight of her father and had no reason to think he might hide from her.

The last of the train doors slammed shut. The guard blew his whistle. Chantelle hesitated, as if wondering whether she should stay or go. There was a second blast on the whistle. The lights above the doors went out, signalling that they were locked. Chantelle glanced over her shoulder to check there was no-one waiting at the end of the platform behind her. The train began to move. She glanced back.

And Umber stepped into view.

She gaped at him, open-mouthed and wordless, as the train accelerated, the draught blowing her hair across her face. The rear turbine roared past them, exhaust fumes billowing and drifting in its wake.

Then the train was gone. And the station was empty. Save for two people, standing twenty yards apart, staring fixedly at each other.

"Shadow Man," was all Chantelle could find to say in the end.

"Your father isn't coming, Chantelle." Umber stepped cautiously towards her. "He sent me."

"You didn't come back to the car. I thought I'd lost you."

"So did I."

"You're all right?"

"I'm fine."

"Where's my father?"

"Come and sit down." He pointed to a bench a little way along the platform behind him. "There's a lot I have to tell you."

The next train to London was due in an hour. For most of that hour they would have the station to themselves. No-one came and no-one went as they sat on the bench and Umber told Chantelle all that had happened to him since their parting in Jersey.

She wept, shedding tears for a man she could not and now never would remember: her father, who had ruined her life and somehow contrived to offer her another to take its place. She was weeping for her mother as well of course, the mother who, though still alive, was yet as good as dead to her, as dead as the mother in turn believed her daughter to be. She was weeping for the unfairness of it all.

"I was giving in to all kinds of fantasies on the way here," Chantelle said when he had finished. "My father turning out to be a nice guy despite everything. Taking me to meet my mother and my stepsister and making everything all right again. Giving me back my family. I saw my mother on the flight from Jersey, would you believe? Of all the ironies. I saw her, but I couldn't speak to her. I could still speak to her today, though, couldn't I? At the church. Or the cemetery. She'll be there, in just a few hours, to say goodbye to Jem. And I could be there too. But if I am . . ." She thumbed the tears away from her eyes and gazed imploringly at Umber. "What my father planned for us, will it work? Will it really work?"

"I think so, yes."

"And nothing else can?"

"I don't see how."

"But Tamsin has to stay dead?"

"Yes."

"And they have to bury Jem without me?"

"Yes."

"We'll be on a plane to Zürich, while they're shovelling the earth in on top of his coffin?"

"Chantelle—"

"It's OK." She held his hand. "What will they say about you, Shadow Man?"

"I don't know. Nothing good, I suspect."

"I kept the Juniuses safe for you." She nodded to her rucksack on the bench beside her. "Never thought you'd get the fly-leaves, though."

"Neither did I."

"How long before we have to go?"

Umber glanced at his watch. "Half an hour. Till the London train gets in. It stops at Reading. We can take the coach from there to Heathrow."

"And fly away from everything?"

"That's the idea."

"When there was no answer from that number you gave me—
the psychotherapist's—I thought you must have . . ." She shook her
head. "It was weird to hear his voice on the phone. My father's, I
mean. I couldn't think of anything else to try. I just . . . hoped I
could shame him into telling me the truth."

"You did. But he told it to me instead. I don't think . . ."

"He could have faced me with it?"

"He's done his best for you, Chantelle. Strangely enough, he always has done."

"The two of us together. That was his idea?"

"Yes."

"You sure you want to go with me?"

"Would you rather go alone?"

She frowned. "'Course not."

"There you are, then."

"But—"

"I'm sure, Chantelle. OK?"

"OK." She took a long, slow breath. "Half an hour, you said?"

"About that."

"I think I'll take a stroll. Stretch my legs. I . . . need some space.
Y'know?"

"I know."

"Don't worry. I won't go far."

She rose and walked away, head alternately bowed and thrown
back. She passed the steps leading up to the footbridge and pressed
on along the platform, her arms folded pensively across her chest.
Umber wondered what she was thinking. They were, in many ways,
strangers to each other. That would change, though. It was bound
to, in the days and weeks—and months and years—that lay ahead
of them.

"What will they say about you?" she had asked. And there had
come no ready answer. Claire, Alice, George Sharp, the Questreds:
they would not understand. It was, ironically, essential they should
not. It was vital his conduct should be a mystery to them, vital he
should never explain himself, especially to those he most owed an
explanation.

"I guess that makes us even, Sal," he murmured. "Now we're
both destined to be misjudged."

The zip on Chantelle's rucksack was not fully closed. Through the gap Umber could see the pale vellum spines of the Juniuses, kept safe for him, just as she had said. The sudden need for certainty came over him. He tugged the zip another few inches open and lifted the volumes out. They were tied together with pink ribbon. Chantelle must have bought it specially. He smiled at the thought as he released the knot.

Placing the two volumes on the bench beside him, he leant forward, opened his holdall and pulled out the envelope Oliver Hall had given him. He tipped it up and a smaller envelope slid out into his lap. He raised its torn flap and delicately removed one of two flimsy pieces of paper—the missing fly-leaves. He opened the first volume of the Junius and matched the jagged left-hand edge of the fly-leaf he had chosen to the dog-tooth fragments held by the book's binding. The last scintilla of doubt vanished. The match was perfect. He gazed in wonderment at the inscription, still unable to imagine how different his life would have been if he had seen this twenty-three years ago. Both fly-leaves were inscribed *Frederick L. Griffin, Strand-under-Green, March 1773,* but only the one Marilyn had torn from the first volume bore the additional inscription, in the same hand, at which Umber stared fixedly as he closed the book and held the fly-leaf before him. Junius's "gentleman who transacts the conveyancing part of our correspondence" had been identified at last. Umber chuckled at the surpassing irony and glanced along the platform, hoping to catch Chantelle's eye, eager to show her this final confirmation of what he could still scarcely believe.

She was looking in his direction, but did not seem to notice his signal. Then he realized she was looking past him, squinting into the distance, focusing on something she could see down the line. He turned to see for himself.

It was an approaching train, speeding towards them. The rails had just begun to sing. It could not be the London train. It was far too early. And it was travelling too fast to stop anyway. It was probably a goods train. One had sped through earlier on the other line while they had been talking.

He looked back at Chantelle. In that instant, fear gripped him. She was standing at the very edge of the platform, well beyond the yellow danger line. She was holding her arms stiffly at her sides.

Her face was a mask of concentration, her mouth half-open, her eyes staring, her brain judging distance and speed and time in precise ratios.

Umber sprang up from the bench and started running towards her. The train's horn blared. Chantelle did not move. The noise of the train grew. The note of the rails' reverberation deepened. Umber's feet pounded the concrete as he ran, his lungs straining, his limbs stretching, his injured knee jarring. He had never run faster in his life.

But he was still too slow. The distance he had to cover was too great. *"Don't!"* he shouted. But Chantelle could not have heard him above the roar of the train even if she had wanted to. There was a second blast of the horn. The dark blur of the locomotive swept past Umber. In the shrinking instant before Chantelle jumped into its path, he closed his eyes.

Umber had stopped running, his final strides carrying him blindly to within a few yards of where Chantelle had been standing. The deafening clatter of the train filled his ears as the long line of cars surged past him. He leaned forward with his hands on his knees, gulping air, his heart thumping, his mind in chaos.

The train was gone. Noise and motion were spent. The present was a frozen moment. Umber opened his eyes and looked up.

Chantelle was crouching on the platform, her hands held over her mouth, looking straight at him. She had not moved from the spot where she had been standing. She had not jumped.

Umber stared disbelievingly at her. Then he felt his lips curling into a broad, spontaneous grin. "Chantelle," he said, shaking his head in relief. "Chantelle."

"I'm sorry," she said, lowering her hands. "Christ, I'm sorry."

"I thought you were going to jump."

"I know." Something between a sob and a gasp came over her. She squeezed her eyes shut. "So did I."

Umber stood upright and moved across to her. Clasping her beneath the arms, he pulled her gently to her feet, then led her back towards the bench.

"Are you OK?" he asked banally, when they were sitting down again.

"Reckon so." Chantelle pulled a tissue out of her pocket and dabbed her eyes. "Now I know I can't do it."

"What made you think you wanted to?"

"Jem. My father. The past. Everything, I suppose."

"And what stopped you?"

"I guess I'm just not the type. I thought I was." She forced a smile. "But I found out different. In the split-second when I so nearly went through with it. When the train was almost on me. Suddenly, I wanted to live. Like never before."

"Thank God for that."

"Looks like you're stuck with me now."

"That won't be a problem."

"Don't be too sure. I can be a real pain sometimes."

"That's all right. So can I."

"Not as big a one as me, I'll bet." She sighed and looked down. "What's that?" She pointed to a small piece of paper lying at their feet. Umber was half-surprised to recognize the few lines of antique writing visible on it. He leaned forward and picked it up. "Is it what I think it is?"

Umber nodded. "I was going to show it to you . . . just now. I'm not sure . . . it matters any more."

"What does it say?"

"You really want to know?"

"I may as well. Seeing all the fuss there's been about it."

"OK." Umber cleared his throat. "The initial inscription reads: *Frederick L. Griffin, Strand-under-Green, March 1773.* That's the same on both fly-leaves. But on this one, from the first volume, it continues underneath, in the same hand, though written many years later, I assume: *For my ward, John Griffin, in memory of those two of Junius's most trusted friends and assistants who predeceased him: Mrs. Solomon Dayrolles, his loyal amanuensis; and Mr. Robert Umber, his valiant courier.*"

"What does it mean?"

"It means Frederick Griffin came into possession of the book in March 1773, which we know is when it was sent to Junius. Then, towards the end of his life, Griffin passed the book on to his ward, dedicating it to the memory of two people who had helped Junius in his letter-writing campaign."

"So . . . Frederick Griffin was Junius?"

"Looks like it."

"And these two were his helpers?"

"Apparently."

"But one of them . . . has your surname."

"Yes." Umber smiled. "So he does."

"A relative?"

"An ancestor, I imagine."

"Did you know about him?"

"Not until last night."

"But . . . how can that be?"

How indeed? Umber truly had no answer to give. He was not sure he ever would have.

"David?"

It was, he realized with a shock, the first time Chantelle had ever addressed him by name. Something had changed between them. He was the Shadow Man no longer.

"*David?*"

EPILOGUE

It is a little after noon on the first Friday of April, 2004. Shower clouds are in chase of one another above the early spring landscape. Sunlight and shadow feint and dodge between the standing stones at Avebury. A short, tubby, middle-aged man dressed for hiking moves at a slow, reflective pace across the northern inner circle of the henge. He stares thoughtfully at the pair of stones known as Adam and Eve as he passes them, but he does not stop.

A few miles to the east, at Marlborough Cemetery, a burial is in progress. The mourners are gathered at the graveside, heads bowed, as the priest recites the prayer of committal. He is speaking softly, but in the prevailing silence his words carry across this other expanse of standing stones. "Forasmuch as it hath pleased Almighty God of his great mercy to take unto himself the soul of our dear brother here departed . . ."

Some miles to the south, a police cordon has been slung across the start of a track through Savernake Forest known as White Road. Two cars with Wiltshire Constabulary badges on their doors have pulled onto the grass verge of the main road next to a blue and white Volkswagen camper van. Three emergency vehicles have drawn up along the track itself behind a parked Bentley, which men in white overalls are inspecting with painstaking care.

Several miles to the east, at Ramsbury, a telephone is ringing in a picturesque cottage at the western end of the village. There is no-one at home to take the call. The answerphone cuts in. And the ringing stops.

Many miles to the south, off Jersey, a telephone is also ringing, in the master cabin of a vast, sleek-lined private cruiser as it noses out from St. Helier Harbour into the sea-lane. It is ringing. And soon it will be answered.

But not before British Airways Flight 714 to Zürich has lifted off the runway at Heathrow Airport and soared into the sky.

It began at Avebury. But it did not end there.

AUTHOR'S NOTE

The known facts about Junius, the pseudonymous eighteenth-century polemicist, are faithfully represented in this novel. All quotations from his letters are accurate and the production of a specially printed vellum-bound edition of them for Junius's personal use is well documented. The historical consensus is that the letters were the work of War Office clerk Philip Francis, but certainty on the issue is impossible. The question of how Francis was able to deploy a handwriting style for Junius in such elegant contrast to his own, entangled as it is with speculation about whether he employed an amanuensis, and, if so, who that amanuensis might have been, has never been satisfactorily resolved.

So it is with the controversy over whether George III, while still Prince of Wales, secretly married Hannah Lightfoot and fathered by her a son, George Rex. A certificate of their marriage at St. Anne's Church, Kew, on 17 April 1759, bearing the apparently authentic signatures of George, Hannah, Dr. James Wilmot and, as one of the witnesses, William Pitt, at that time Secretary of State for the Southern Department, can be inspected at the Public Record Office, located, ironically, in Kew.

The certificate was denounced as a "gross and rank" forgery by the Probate & Divorce Court in 1866 when considering a petition by Dr. Wilmot's great-granddaughter, Lavinia Ryves, for recognition of her related claim to be the legitimate granddaughter of George III's younger brother Henry, Duke of Cumberland. But the verdict, which flew in the face of the testimony of the leading handwriting expert of the day, can hardly be considered conclusive, given what the consequences would have been of pronouncing the certificate genuine. In strict legal logic, Victoria would have been required to vacate the throne. Some things are not meant to be. And some things are not allowed to be.

One of many strange events bearing on the mystery is the theft of the parish records from St. Anne's Church, Kew, during the night of 22/23 February 1845. The motive for the theft remains, as was presumably the intention of those who commissioned it, unknown.

As for the bizarre similarity between the topographies of Avebury and the Cydonia complex on Mars, all are free to make of that what they will.

ABOUT THE AUTHOR

ROBERT GODDARD is the author of sixteen bestselling novels, including *Borrowed Time, Into the Blue, Hand in Glove,* and *Play to the End,* all available from Delta, and the forthcoming *In Pale Battalions, Never Go Back,* and *Beyond Recall.* Goddard lives in England, where he is at work on his next novel.

If you enjoyed Robert Goddard's
SIGHT UNSEEN, you will want to read all of the
novels from an author whose "manipulation of
suspense and surprise rarely fails to dazzle."*
Look for them at your favorite bookseller.

And read on for an early look at

IN PALE BATTALIONS

BY
ROBERT GODDARD

coming soon from Delta Trade Paperbacks

New York Times Book Review

IN PALE BATTALIONS

Childhood memories fit their own, intricate pattern. They cannot be made to conform to the version of our past we try to impose upon them. Thus I could say that Lord and Lady Powerstock and the home they gave me at Meongate more than compensated for being an orphan, that a silver spoon easily took the place of my mother's smile. I could say it—but every recollection of my early years would deny it.

Meongate must once have been the crowded, bustling house of a cheerful family, as the Hallowses must once have been that family. Every favour of nature in its setting where the Hampshire downs met the pastures of the Meon valley, every effort of man in its spacious rooms and landscaped park, had been bestowed on the home of one small child.

Yet it was not enough. When I was growing up at Meongate in the early 1920s, most of its grandeur had long since departed. Many of the rooms were shut up and disused, much of the park turned over to farmland. And all the laughing, happy people I imagined filling its empty rooms and treading its neglected lawns had vanished into a past beyond my reach.

I grew up with the knowledge that my parents were both dead, my father killed on the Somme, my mother carried off by pneumonia a few days after my birth. It was not kept from me. Indeed, I was constantly reminded of it, constantly confronted with the implication that I must in some way bear the blame for the shadow of grief, or of something worse, that hung over their memory. That shadow, cast by the unknown, lay at the heart of the cold, dark certainty that also grew within me: I was not wanted at Meongate, not welcomed there, not loved.

It might have been different had my grandfather not been the grave, withdrawn, perpetually melancholic man that he was. I, who never knew him when he was young, cannot imagine him as anything other than the wheelchair-bound occupant of his ground-floor rooms, deprived by his own morbidity, as much as by the lingering effects of a stroke, of all warmth and fondness. When Nanny Hiles took me, as she regularly did, to kiss him goodnight, all I wanted to do was escape from the cold, fleeting touch of his flesh. When, playing on the lawn, I would look up and see him watching me from his window, all I wanted to do was run away from the mournful, questing sadness in his eyes. Later, I came to sense that he was waiting, waiting for me to be old enough to understand him, waiting in the hope that he would live to see that day.

Lady Powerstock, twenty years his junior, was not my real grandmother. She was buried in the village churchyard, another ghost whom I did not know and who could do nothing to help me. I imagined her as everything her successor was not—kind, loving and generous—but it did me no good. Olivia, the woman I was required to address as Grandmama in her place, had once been beautiful and, at fifty, her looks were still with her, her figure still fine, her dress sense impeccable. That we were not related by blood explained, to my satisfaction, why she did not love me. What I could not explain was why she went so far as to hate me, but hate me she undoubtedly did. She did not trouble to disguise the fact. She let it hover, menacing and unspoken, at the edge of all our exchanges, let it grow as an awareness between us, a secret confirmation that she too was only waiting, waiting for death to remove her husband and with him any lingering restraint on her conduct towards me. There was an air of practised vice about her that was to draw men all her life, an air of voluptuous pleasure at her own depravity that made her hatred of me seem merely instinctive. Yet there was always more to it than that. She had drawn some venom from whatever part she had played in the past of that house and had reserved it for me.

My only friend in those days, my only guide through Meongate's hidden perils, was Fergus, the taciturn and undemonstrative *major-domo*, "shifty" as Olivia described him and certainly not as deferential as he should have been, but none the less my sole confidant. Sally, the sullen maid, and humourless Nancy Hiles both went in awe of Olivia, but Fergus treated her with an assurance, bordering on disrespect, that made him my immediate ally. A cautious, solitary, pessimistic man who had expected little from life and consequently been spared many disappointments, perhaps he took pity on a lonely child whose plight he understood better than she did herself. He would take me on covert expeditions through the grounds, or down to the wooded reach of the Meon where he fished of a quiet afternoon, or into Droxford in the trap, when he would buy me a twist of sherbet and leave me sitting on the wall outside Wilsmer's saddlery whilst he went in to haggle over a new bridle for the pony. For such brief moments as those, kicking my heels on Mr Wilsmer's wall and eating my sherbet in the sunshine, I was happy. But such moments did not last.

It was Fergus who first showed me my father's name, recorded with the other war dead of the village, on a plaque at the church. Their Name Liveth for Everymore, the inscription said, and his name—Captain the Honourable John Hallows—is all that did live for me. I would stare at it for what seemed like hours trying to conjure up the real living and breathing father that he had never been to me, seeing only those stiff, expressionless, uniformed figures preserved by photographs in back copies of the *Illustrated London News*, glimpsing no part of his true self beyond the neatly carved letters of his name.

As for my mother, of her there was no record at all, no grave, no memorial of any kind. Fergus, when I questioned him, prevaricated. My mother's grave, if she had one, was far away—and he did not know where. There were, I was to understand, limits to what even he could tell me. Whether he suggested it or not I cannot remember, but, for some reason, I decided to ask Olivia. I cannot recall how old I was when it happened, but I had followed her into the library where she often went to look at a painting that hung there.

"Where is my mother's grave?" I said bluntly, partly intending the question to be a challenge. All hatred is, in time, reciprocated and I had come to hate Olivia as much as she hated me; I did not then appreciate how dangerous an enemy she could be.

She did not answer in words. She turned aside from that great, high, dark painting and hit me so hard across the face that I nearly fell over. I stood there, clutching the reddening bruise, too shocked by the pain of it to cry, and she stooped over me, her eyes blazing. "If you ever ask that question again," she said, "if you ever mention your mother again, I'll make you suffer."

The mystery of my mother thenceforth became the grand and secret obsession of my childhood. My father's death, after all, had a comforting simplicity about it. Every November there was an Armistice Parade in the village to commemorate the sacrifice of Captain the Honourable John Hallows and the many others like him. Though not permitted to join the Brownie troop that took part in the parade, I was allowed to go and watch and could imagine myself marching with all the little girls who, like me, had lost their fathers. But, at the end of the parade, they went home to their mothers; I could not even remember mine.

Sometimes, though, I thought I could remember her. It was impossible, of course, if what I had been told of her was true, but Olivia had succeeded in making me doubt everything I had not personally experienced, and there was one, dim, early memory, seemingly at the very dawn of my recollection, to sustain what I so wanted to believe.

I was standing on the platform at Droxford railway station. It was a hot summer's day: I could feel the heat of the gravel seeping up through my shoes. A train was standing at the platform, great billows of smoke rising as the engine gathered steam. The man standing beside me, who had been holding my hand, stooped and lifted me up, cradling me in his arms to watch the train pull out. He was stout and white-haired. I remember the rumble of his voice and the brim of his straw hat touching my head as he raised his free hand to wave. And I was waving too, at a woman aboard the train who had wound down the window and was leaning out, waving also and smiling and crying as she did so. She was dressed in blue and held a white hankerchief in her right hand. And the train carried her away. And then I cried too and the stout old man hugged me, the brass buttons on his coat, cold against my face.

I recounted the memory to Fergus one day, when we were returning from a mushrooming expedition. When I had finished, I asked him who he thought the old man was.

"Sounds like old Mr. Gladwin," he replied. "The first Lady

Powerstock's father. He lived here . . . till *she* sent him away." By *she* Fergus always meant Olivia.

"Why did she do that?"

"She'd have had her reasons, I don't doubt."

"When did he go?"

"The summer of 1920, when you were three. Back to Yorkshire, so they say. A proper caution, was Mr. Gladwin."

"Who was the pretty lady, Fergus?"

"That I don't know."

"Was she . . . my mother?"

He pulled up and looked down at me with a frown. "That she was not," he said with deliberate slowness. "Your mother passed away a few days after she had you. You know that. No amount of wanting is going to make you remember her."

"Then . . . who was the pretty lady?"

His frown became less kindly. "I told you: I don't know. That Mr. Gladwin, he was a close one. Now, look to that napkin or you'll pitch your breakfast into the lane—and mine with it."

If the pretty lady wasn't my mother, who was she? What was old Mr. Gladwin, my great-grandfather, to her? There were no answers within my reach, just the secret hope I went on harbouring that maybe my mother wasn't really dead at all, just . . . sent away, like old Mr. Gladwin.

I, too, was shortly to be sent away, to preparatory school in North Wales. It was the junior wing of Howell's, which some of the girls found austere and rigorous but where I felt at home from the very start. There were no shadows at school, no unspoken secrets from the past threatening to overtake me. It was the holidays I came to dread, the times when I knew I would have to return to Meongate to find Olivia waiting for me with her menacing smile, to find my grandfather even more frail and uncommunicative than when I'd left, to find Fergus a little less forthcoming each time with the priggish young lady he thought I was becoming.

Being sent away to boarding school at the age of eight meant I knew virtually nobody in Droxford—of my own age or any other. That, I suppose, is why I did not learn sooner about the murder of Meangate, why I was ignorant for so long of that fragment of our family's mystery.

I think it was the Cribbins boy who had first told me. He used to help with the gardening during the summer holidays and was one of the few village children I had anything to do with. One warm, overcast afternoon, Cook gave me a glass of lemonade to take out to him in the orchard where he'd been put to cutting back brambles. We stood talking while he drank it. He asked me what the house was like inside.

"Haven't you ever been inside." I retorted, a touch haughtily, for Howell's had trained me well.

"No fear," he said between gulps. "My dad's told me."

"Told you what?"

" 'Bout the murder."

"What murder?"

"Don't you know, Miss? There were a murder done at Meongate, years ago. My dad told me."

"Oh that?" I replied. "Of course I know about *that*." It wouldn't have done to let him see that it had been kept from me.

The obvious person to ask for information was Fergus. I found him polishing the silver in the pantry.

"Murder, you say? Well, maybe there was and maybe there wasn't. What would Cribbins know?"

"Stop teasing, Fergus."

He laid down the knives he had been cleaning and stooped close to my ear. "I'm not teasing," he whispered. "*She'd* skin me alive if she heard me talking about it. It's a subject best left alone."

He knew better than to think I would leave it alone. The following afternoon, I tracked him down on the riverbank, at his favourite spot for fishing, where I could be certain we would not be overheard.

"Well? You can tell me here."

"Tell you what?"

"About the murder."

He grunted and flicked his line. "They're not biting today."

"*Fergus!*"

"I can see I'll get no peace till I tell you. It was during the war. One of his lordship's guests. Shot in his bedroom."

"Which bedroom?"

"Don't worry. It wasn't yours. It was one of those that are shut up."

"Who was he?"

"I told you: a guest. I forget his name."

"Who killed him?"

"They never found out."

"Gosh. You mean it's never been solved?"

"Not to this day."

"How exciting."

"I wouldn't call it exciting."

"You wouldn't call anything exciting."

He smiled. "Well, take heed of this: don't mention it to *her*. She'd not thank you for it."

"Was the murdered man a friend of hers, then?"

Fergus chuckled. "*She* doesn't have friends. You should know that. Now, clear off before you frighten away all the fish in the river."

I taxed Fergus several more times on the subject but learned nothing. I dared not even ask anybody else. Cook and Sally had been handpicked, it seemed, for their avoidance of gossip. Perhaps, in Olivia's eyes, it compensated for their other deficiencies. They, I felt certain, would not help me. Besides, only to Fergus was I prepared to admit how little I truly knew of my family's history. Hints and snatches of hazy memory were all I had to go on.

I must have been a plague to Fergus with all my endless, unanswerable questions. Which room was the one where the murder was committed? Which room was my parents'? Why were there no pictures of them? Where was my mother buried? What did she look like? Why was Mr. Gladwin sent away? Who was the pretty lady? He would just tap his nose, say he couldn't remember or couldn't tell me, then distract me with one of his puzzles involving string and matchsticks.

Even the little he did give away would probably have ensured his dismissal had Olivia known of it. Returning from one of her trips to London, trips which grew ever more frequent as the years passed, she would first ignore me, then subject me to withering inquisitions. What had I been doing? Who had I been talking to? What books had I been reading? Occasionally, as I grew older, she would ask my opinion of a new dress she had bought, or of some sparkling addition to her jewellery. Sometimes, I would make the mistake of admiring the item.

"It looks well because I wear it well," she would reply. "On you it would be . . . wasted."

I never noticed Olivia take any interest in art, as distinct from adornment, with the exception of the picture that hung in the library. She often went there and since she read nothing beyond fashion catalogues it can only have to been to look at the picture. It was a dark, horrid, rather perverted piece depicting a man in chain mail entering a castle bedchamber to find a naked woman awaiting him, draped across the bed. Looking at it used to make me shiver.

I could never quite explain my aversion to it to my own satisfaction until one day when Olivia was away and Sally had the afternoon off. I crept up to her bedroom in secret, just for the pleasure of defying her by trespassing there.

I remember the blue velvet curtains were drawn against the sun but were stirring slightly in the breeze from the half-open window behind them. Their heavy movement moved blocks of sunlight across the wide bed and the dressing table, on which stood a vast array of perfume bottles and cream jars, tortoiseshell-backed brushes and silver-framed mirrors: all the paraphernalia of Olivia's preserved appearance. I wished only, in that moment, to be standing in my mother's bedroom knowing she would shortly return, the lipsticks and combs belonging to her, not to this woman I hated. But it could not be. Olivia was the only mistress Meongate knew and I was her enemy. I looked at the layer of dust and powder Sally had left on the mirror—and smiled grimly.

As I turned away from the dressing table, my eye was taken by a painting hanging on the opposite wall. I caught my breath. It was nearly a copy of the one in the library. But no. When I inspected it more closely, I saw that, though the scene and characters were the same, they were differently arranged. The man was now also lying on the bed, caressing the woman, kissing one of her breasts while fondling the other. The woman was looking slightly to one side and her face . . . I jumped back, startled. The woman's face was Olivia's when younger. Olivia's when her beauty did not need the props it now relied on. In the painting, she lay naked, as I had never seen her, but her expression was one she often wore. It was her very own patented blend of boredom and hatred.

For what must have been several minutes, I stared at the picture, transfixed, struggling to fathom the meaning of what I saw, repelled yet drawn by all that was blatant both in its placement—there, in a lady's bedroom—and in what it depicted—the writhing, coupled limbs, the man's mouth pressed to the woman's yielding breast; above all by the sneering indifference of that face I felt sure I knew.

For days afterwards, I could not rid my mind of the painted image of Olivia. When she sat opposite me over dinner, passing disingenuous remarks to Lord Powerstock between mouthfuls, all I could see was her naked, pillaged form. When I walked into a room and found her there and and she looked up to note my presence with a cool, reproving glance, all I could see was the averted, cynical gaze of the woman in the painting. And when I looked again at the picture in the library, I saw it in a new light.

Who was the artist, I wondered. Why did he choose Olivia as a model? I could not ask even Fergus to tell me that. I could only add it to the list of unanswered questions held in my mind.

Soon, besides, my curiosity found another target. I had felt no interest in the hexagonal gazebo that stood above the wing of the house—the door to which, reached by a flight of spiral stairs, had always been kept locked—until Fergus let slip one day that my father had used it as an observatory and that his telescope, so far as he knew, was still set up there. I at once became determined to see it. I badgered Fergus to give me the key and, at length, he yielded, on condition that I breathed not a word of it to anyone. I agreed: it would be our secret.

The observatory itself, when I crept up there, proved to be a disappointment. Just a few pieces of dusty furniture and an old brass telescope mounted on a pedestal. But what the telescope enabled me to do was quite a different matter. It let me escape from Meongate. When I'd learned to train and focus it, I could watch the squirrels as they climbed the trees in the park or the rabbits as they hopped warily across the paddock. I could study a shepherd moving his flock on the slope of the downs or, after dark, gaze endlessly at a sky dense with stars. I could sit there, safely hidden, imagining my father noting down the arrangement of distant constellations, wondering if he had been the one to leave the half-empty box of matches on the shelf. crying softly sometimes when all the doubts and sadnesses weighed me down and I wished for nothing but to be able to look through the telescope and see him, hand in hand with my mother, patrolling the lawns of his rightful home.

Wishing and dreaming was all I could do to bring them back.

To my schoolfriends, I claimed that my father had been posthumously awarded the DSO and that my mother had died of a broken heart. I described her as the most beautiful woman I had ever seen. As far as I could tell, they believed me. Sometimes, I almost believed it myself. After all, at Howell's I could pretend whatever I liked. Only when I returned to Meongate did the pretending have to stop.